Arion reach  **across a small bla** **aming plastic.**

There were no markings on the card. It could have been one of those if-you-had-to-apply-for-it-you-couldn't-afford-it credit cards reserved for multibillionaires. She'd read about them in a magazine once. Or it might have been a loyalty card for die-hard coffee addicts. Perla had no way of telling.

She looked from the card to Arion's face. 'What's that for?' she asked suspiciously.

'That card lets you into that lift. The lift will take you straight to my penthouse. You'll wait for me there—'

'No.' Perla stopped what was coming before he could finish.

His nostrils flared. 'Excuse me?'

'I won't do…whatever it is you have in mind. I know what you think of me, but you're wrong. What happened between us that night wasn't cheap and it wasn't tawdry. Not for me at least. And I despise you for thinking I'd stoop that low to get you to help me—'

'Be quiet for one second and listen.'

The rough command in his voice dried her words.

'You have nowhere to stay. I have a meeting in… exactly eight minutes—which will last for five hours. Minimum. Unless you intend to wander the streets in the rain until I'm finished, my offer is the best you're going to get.'

Surprise stamped through her. 'Oh, you mean you want me to go up and just…wait for you?' she asked.

'Why, Mrs Lowell, you sound disappointed...'

THE UNTAMEABLE GREEKS

Rich, powerful and impossible to resist

Sakis, Arion and Theo Pantelides—three formidable
brothers who have risen up from the darkness of their pasts
to conquer the world. Powerful, gorgeous and fabulously
wealthy, these deliciously arrogant Greeks can have any
woman they want—but none will ever tame them.

Until now?

WHAT THE GREEK'S MONEY CAN'T BUY
April 2014

Sakis is hungry to give in to the forbidden temptation
of his buttoned-up PA—but will the cynical Greek
pay the price for breaking his golden rule?

WHAT THE GREEK CAN'T RESIST
June 2014

Perla Lowell is the last woman Arion
should want yet he can't deny himself one night
with this irresistible temptress—but what will happen
when the dark-hearted Greek discovers the consequences
of succumbing to his desire?

Don't miss Theo's story, coming soon!

WHAT THE GREEK CAN'T RESIST

BY
MAYA BLAKE

Published in Great Britain 2014
by Mills & Boon, an imprint of Harlequin (UK) Limited,
Eton House, 18-24 Paradise Road, Richmond, Surrey, TW9 1SR

© 2014 Maya Blake

ISBN: 978 0 263 24648 3

Harlequin (UK) Limited's policy is to use papers that are natural,
renewable and recyclable products and made from wood grown in
sustainable forests. The logging and manufacturing processes conform
to the legal environmental regulations of the country of origin.

Printed and bound in Spain
by Blackprint CPI, Barcelona

Maya Blake fell in love with the world of the alpha male and the strong, aspirational heroine when she borrowed her sister's Mills & Boon® at age thirteen. Shortly thereafter the dream to plot a happy ending for her own characters was born. Writing for Harlequin Mills & Boon® is a dream come true. Maya lives in South East England with her husband and two kids. Reading is an absolute passion, but when she isn't lost in a book she likes to swim, cycle, travel and Tweet!

You can get in touch with her
via e-mail at mayablake@ymail.com,
or on Twitter: www.twitter.com/mayablake

Recent titles by the same author:

WHAT THE GREEK'S MONEY CAN'T BUY
  (The Untamable Greeks)
HIS ULTIMATE PRIZE
MARRIAGE MADE OF SECRETS
THE SINFUL ART OF REVENGE

Did you know these are also available as eBooks?
Visit www.millsandboon.co.uk

CHAPTER ONE

THE CAR PARK was as quiet as she'd hoped it would be. Inside her trusted Mini's soothing cocoon, Perla Lowell bit the tip of her pen and searched fruitlessly for the right words.

Four lines. Four paltry lines in two hours were all she'd managed to come up with. She swallowed her despair. Three short days from now she'd have to stand up in front of friends and family and make a speech…

And she had no words.

No, scratch that. She had words. But none rang true. Because the truth… No, she couldn't…*wouldn't* subject anyone to the truth. Her whole life for the past three years had been a colossal lie. Was it any wonder her hands shook every time she tried to write? That her heart pounded with self-loathing for the lies she had to perpetuate for the sake of appearances?

But how could she do anything else? How could she repay kindness with humiliation? Because doing or saying anything else other than what was expected would bring devastation that she couldn't live with.

Anger mingled with despair. With a vicious twist she ripped the paper in two. The cathartic sound echoed through the car and spilled out into the night air. As if loosening the stranglehold she'd exercised on her emotions for longer than she cared to remember, the tears she'd been unable to shed so far now pierced through her tightened chest into her throat.

Her fingers gained a life of their own. Two halves of paper became four, then eight. She ripped again and again, until the sheet spilled through her hands in little wisps of illegible confetti. She upended her hands and watched the mess strewn all over the passenger seat. With a jagged groan, she buried her face in her hands, expecting finally, *finally,* to shed a tear.

The tears never came. They remained locked inside, as they had been for the last two weeks, taunting her, punishing her for daring to wish for them when deep down she knew to cry would be shamefully, deeply disingenuous.

Because, deep inside, she felt…relieved. At a time when she should've been devastated, she felt a shameful lightening of being!

Slowly, she dropped her hands and stared through the windscreen. Her vision cleared and she focused on the palatial Georgian structure in front of her.

Despite its recent multi-million-pound revamp, Macdonald Hall had retained its quintessential old English charm, along with its exclusive membership-by-invitation-only Macdonald Club, and the extensive gold standard golf course that lay beyond the imposing façade.

The centuries-old establishment's only nod to the common man was the cocktail bar, which was open to the public from seven until midnight.

Perla sucked in a deep breath and glanced down at the ripped paper. Guilt bit deep as she acknowledged how good it'd felt to let go. Just this once, to not hold herself back, to not watch her every word or smile when she felt like cursing her fate. To be normal…

The feeling wouldn't last, of course. There was still tomorrow to get through and the next day, and the next.

Dark anguish had her reaching for her bag.

She was far enough away from home not to be recognised here. It was, after all, why she'd driven for over an hour to find a quiet spot to compose the hard-to-find words.

Granted, her journey had been futile so far. But she wasn't ready to return home yet; wasn't ready to face the cloying compassionate gestures and well-meaning, concerned but probing looks.

Her gaze refocused on Macdonald Hall.

One drink. Then she'd drive back home and start again tomorrow.

Opening her bag, she searched for the small brush to run it through her hair in an attempt to tame the unruly curls. When her fingers touched the tube of lipstick, she nearly dismissed it.

Scarlet wasn't really her colour, and normally she wouldn't even glance at one that described itself as *Do Me Red*; she only had the sample lipstick because it'd come free with a book purchase. She would never dare to wear anything so bold. So daring. Even on other women, she found the colour too sensual, too *look-at-my-mouth*.

Fingers trembling, she uncapped the tube, angled the rear-view mirror and carefully applied the lipstick. The unexpected result—the wanton, blatantly sultry image that stared back at her—had her rummaging through her bag for a tissue to reverse the damage. When she came up empty, she paused. Her gaze slowly slid back to the mirror.

Her heart hammered.

Was it so bad? Just for tonight, would it be so bad to look, to *feel* like someone else other than Perla Lowell, *complete fraud*? To forget the pain and unrelenting humiliation she'd suffered for the last three years, if only for a few minutes?

Before she could change her mind, she fumbled for the door handle and stepped out of her car into the cool night air. Her party days might be long behind her but even she knew her simple black sleeveless dress and low black pumps were appropriate for a cocktail bar on a quiet Tuesday night.

And if it wasn't, the worst that could happen was she would be asked to leave. And right now, being thrown out of an exclusive cocktail bar where no one knew who she was would be a walk in the park compared to the monumental farce she had to go through.

A smartly dressed concierge greeted her and directed her through a parquet-floored, oak-panelled hallway to a set of old-fashioned double doors with the words *Bar* fashioned in burnished gold plate above them.

Another similarly dressed man opened the door and tipped his cap to her.

Feeling seriously out of her depth, Perla took fleeting note of the discreetly expensive wood and brocade décor before her eyes zeroed in on the long, low-slung bar. Seriously intimidating rows of drinks were displayed on a revolving carousel and, behind the bar, a bartender twirled a sterling silver set of cocktail shakers while chatting to a young couple.

For a split second, Perla considered turning on her heel and marching straight back out. She forced herself to take a step and another until she reached the unoccupied end of the bar. She'd come this far… Sucking in another sustaining breath, she slid onto the stool and placed her handbag on the counter.

Now what?

'What's a fine girl like you doing in a place like this?'

The cheese-tastic line startled a strained laugh out of her as she turned towards the voice.

'That's better. For a second there, I thought someone had died in here and I hadn't been told,' the bartender's white smile, no doubt tailor-made to drive hormonal girls wild, widened as his gaze traced her face in blatant appraisal. 'You're the second person to walk in here tonight looking like you're a fully paid-up member of the doom-and-gloom brigade.'

In another lifetime, Perla would've found his boyish, perfectly groomed looks charming. Unfortunately, she existed in *this* lifetime, and she'd learnt to her cost that the outside rarely matched the inside.

She willed her smile in place and folded her hands on top of her purse. 'I…I'd like a drink, please.'

'Sure thing.' He leaned in closer and his eyes dropped to her mouth. 'What's your poison?'

Her gaze darted to the cocktails on display. She had no clue what any of them were. The last time she'd been in a bar like this, the drink in fashion had been Amaretto Sour. She wanted to ask for a Cosmopolitan but wasn't even sure if that was still in vogue these days.

She gritted her teeth again and contemplated walking out. Sheer stubbornness made her stay on the stool. She'd been pushed around enough; endured enough. For far too long she'd allowed someone else to call the shots, to dictate the way she lived her life.

No more. Granted, the scarlet lipstick had been a bad idea—it was clear it drew far too much unwanted attention to her mouth—but Perla refused to let that stand in the way of this one small bolstering move.

Squaring her shoulders, she indicated a dark red drink with lots of sunny umbrellas sticking out of it. 'I'll have that one.'

He followed her gaze and frowned. 'The Pomegranate Martini?'

'Yes. What's wrong with it?' she asked when he continued to frown.

'It's a bit…well, lame.'

Her lips firmed. 'I'll take it anyway.'

'Come on, let me—'

'Give the lady what she wants,' a low, dark drawl sounded behind her right shoulder. The smooth but unmistakable cadence in the masculine voice spelled a foreign accent, possibly Mediterranean, that caused a shiver to dance down Perla's spine.

She froze in her seat, her back stiffening as sensation skittered over her skin.

The bartender visibly paled before nodding quickly and sidling off to prepare her cocktail.

Perla felt his silent presence behind her, a palpable force field that bore down and surrounded her with unmistakable power. Her mind shrieked with danger, but for the life of her she couldn't move. Her hand tightened over the strap of her handbag, her fingers plucking frantically at the beads that decorated the dark satin exterior.

'Turn around,' came the low command.

Her back stiffened some more. Another man who wanted to push her buttons. 'Look, I just want to be left alone—'

'Turn around, if you please,' he instructed again in that low, growly voice.

Not *please* but *if you please*. The slightly old-fashioned turn of phrase piqued her curiosity. Coupled with the dark rumble of his voice, Perla was seriously tempted to do as he asked.

But not enough to give in. She remained facing forward.

'I just saved you from becoming the potential target of a chancer with delusions of swagger. The least you can do is turn around and talk to me.'

Despite her stomach flipping again at the impact of his voice, Perla's lips tightened. 'I didn't want nor need your help…and I don't really want to talk to anyone so…'

She glanced towards the bartender with the intention of cancelling her order. The long drive here…the inspired words she'd hoped to write…the idea of a quick drink… the courage-lending scarlet lipstick—probably *that* most of all—had all been an unmitigated disaster. Again she felt pain tighten her chest and fought to keep her emotions under strict control.

Behind her, the man who thought he was her saviour stood in imposing, stifling silence. She knew he was there because his scent lingered in her nostrils—intriguingly spicy, masculine and raw—and she could hear his firm, steady breathing. Again an alien sensation skittered over her skin. The urge to look over her shoulder scythed through her but she refused the urge. She'd failed herself in so many things. Perla refused to fail at this one thing.

Lifting her hand, she tried to catch the bartender's attention but his gaze was focused behind her...on the man whose presence, even without her knowing who he was or her having seen him, spelled power with a capital *P*.

She watched in stunned silence as the bartender nodded in answer to a silent command, rounded the counter with her drink and headed towards a dark corner of the bar.

Outraged, Perla finally turned to find the man—tall, dark-haired and incredibly broad-shouldered—retreating to the table where her drink had been placed along with another, presumably his.

Pure anger spiked through her. Her heels landed on the polished wood floor and she was marching over to him before she fully registered her intention. 'What the hell do you think you're—?'

He turned to face her and the words dried in Perla's throat.

Gorgeous. Astoundingly. Gorgeous. The description lit up like a neon sign in her head—bright, bold, insistent. And so unbelievably real, Perla could only stare in astonishment. Even as she took in the sheer vitality of his olive skin, the lethal bone structure that made up his striking features and the tinge of grey in his hair and designer stubble—her personal, stupidly debilitating weakness—she knew she should never have turned around; never have followed him.

She should've heeded her instinct and walked straight out.

Dear Lord, hadn't she learned from her mistake? She gave a slight shake of her head and tried to step back. She had no business being here; no business staring at a man the way she was staring at this stranger. If anyone found out…

Move!

Her feet wouldn't comply.

Deep hazel eyes bored into hers, then slowly traced her body from head to toe and back again. Perla found herself holding her breath, her fingers once again working frantically over the beads on her handbag.

The breathtaking stranger's gaze paused at her hair. 'Is that colour real?' he rasped in that knee-weakening, pulse-stroking voice.

'Excuse me?'

'That shade of red. Is it real?' he demanded.

A little bit of her entrancement receded. 'Of course it's real. Why would I dye—?' She stopped as it occurred to her then that he didn't know her and therefore wouldn't know that the last thing she concerned herself with was vanity in the form of artificial hair colour. There was no one to please or pander to and she was too busy surviving to think about frivolous things such as what colour to dye her hair. 'It's real, okay? Now will you explain what you're playing at? That's my drink you've just commandeered.'

'Your manners seemed to have deserted you. I'm merely redressing the situation.' He pulled out a chair. 'Please sit down.'

Lifting an eyebrow, she remained standing.

With a shrug, he remained standing too.

She blew out an irritated breath. 'My manners haven't deserted me. You stepped in and took over a situation I had under control. What did you think, that the bartender would've vaulted over the counter and assaulted me in plain sight of the other customers?' she snapped.

He broke his fascination with her hair and dropped his gaze to capture hers. 'What other customers?' he asked.

'The couple over there—' She broke off as she looked around. The young couple were gone. Aside from a waiter who was clearing a few other tables, only the tall stranger and bartender remained in the bar. As she watched, the waiter walked through a set of swinging doors and disappeared.

She swallowed. 'This is a reputable place. Things like that don't happen here.'

'And what exactly do you base that statistic on? Are you a frequent visitor?'

She flushed. 'No, of course not. And I'm not naïve. I just…I just think—'

'That predators in Savile Row suits are less vicious than those in hoodies?' His smile didn't reach his eyes.

'No, that's not what I meant. I came here for a quiet drink.' Her gaze dropped to the bold and garish-looking cocktail standing next to his dark-coloured spirit.

This was fast getting out of hand, and she needed to think about getting back. Or she would have more explaining to do.

He indicated the chair one more time. 'You can still have it. And you needn't worry about making conversation. We can sit here and not…talk.'

His words piqued her curiosity. Or maybe she just wanted a distraction from the pain and chaos that awaited her the moment she left this place.

She forced herself to look at him—really look past the surface hurt-your-eyes gorgeousness of the man—past the powerful shoulders underneath the impeccable suit and loosened silk tie. His hair was slightly ruffled, as if he'd shoved a hand through it once or twice.

The brackets around his mouth were deeply grooved and when she chanced another look into his eyes, what Perla glimpsed made her heart hammer.

In that instant she knew he wasn't here to prey on unsuspecting or vulnerable women. That wasn't to say women would be safe from the sensual aura and sheer charisma that oozed from him. Far from it.

But for tonight, in this very moment, whoever this man was, the emotions lurking in his eyes weren't of a predatory nature. The pain she saw resonated with her on so deep a level, she found it hard to breathe through it.

His eyes narrowed, as if sensing the direction of her thoughts. He stiffened and his mouth firmed. For a moment she thought he was going to change his mind about his earlier invitation.

Abruptly he moved a step forward, touched the back of the chair. 'Sit down. Please,' he repeated.

Perla sat. In silence, he pushed her drink towards her.

'Thank you,' she murmured.

He inclined his head and raised his glass towards her. 'To not talking.'

She touched her glass to his; a surreal feeling overtook her as she stared at him over the rim of her glass and took a sip of her cocktail. The potent alcohol hit the back of her throat, warming and cooling at the same time. The tartness of the pomegranate burst on her tongue, making her close her eyes in a single moment of pleasure before the strength of his scrutiny propelled her eyelids back open.

Once again, he seemed fascinated with her hair. It took every ounce of self-control she possessed not to fiddle with it. She sucked harder on her straw, partly to finish the drink quicker so she could leave and partly because it gave her something to do other than stare at this hauntingly beautiful man.

They sipped their drinks in silence.

With a very unsettling amount of regret, Perla set her empty glass down.

The stranger followed suit. 'Thank you.'

'For what?'

'For controlling the urge to indulge in idle chit-chat.'

'I told you, that's not what I came here for. If it was, I'd have brought a friend. Or come earlier when I knew there would be more people here. I presume you chose this time for the same reason.'

A shaft of pain flitted over his features but was gone in the next instant. 'You presume correct.'

She shrugged. 'Then there's no need to thank me.'

He stilled, the only movement his gaze as it flew once again to her hair. When it traced down to her mouth, Perla became very much aware of the scarlet lipstick. Before she could stop herself, she licked her tingling lower lip.

His low hiss was an alien sound that sent a fresh wave of goose bumps over her skin. She'd never elicited such a reaction in a man before. Perla wasn't sure whether to be pleased or terrified.

'Are you staying here, at Macdonald Hall?' she asked, in the hope of deflecting the unsettling feeling his hiss had elicited.

The stranger's hand tightened slowly into a fist on the table. 'For tonight and the next few nights, yes.'

She looked from his hand to his face. 'Why do I get the feeling that you don't want to be here?' she asked.

'Because we don't always get to decide our own fate. But I'm obliged to be here for the next few days. It doesn't mean I'm pleased about it.'

She glanced at his empty glass. 'Then I suppose you'll be upgrading to a bottle instead of a glass shortly?'

He shrugged. 'Drinking is one way of making the time pass faster, I suppose.'

Danger crawled across her skin, sparking a flame in her belly, but Perla couldn't move. 'When you're alone in a bar at almost midnight, I don't really see much else to entertain you.' Her voice emerged huskier than she'd ever heard it.

He raised a dark eyebrow. 'But I'm not alone. Not any more. I've saved you, a damsel in distress, and my reward is your company for now.'

'I'm not a damsel in distress. Besides, you don't know me from a blade of grass. I could be one of those predators you described, for all you know, Mr...?'

Her blatant demand for his name went unanswered as he nodded to the bartender and indicated their empty glasses.

'I don't think I should have another drink—'

Hooded hazel eyes trapped hers. 'But we're just getting to know one another. You were telling me about being a ruthless predator.'

'And you wanted to be alone less than ten minutes ago, remember? Besides, what makes you think I want to get to know you?'

His small smile was both self-assured and self-pitying, a curious, intriguing combination. 'I don't. Forgive me for the assumption. If you wish you leave, you may do so.'

Again the courteous words laced with arrogance set her teeth on edge. But Perla found she couldn't look away from the fascinating man, whose extremely powerful aura held a wealth of pain and sadness that drew her...made her hesitate.

She licked her lips and immediately regretted it when his gaze latched onto the movement. 'I don't need your permission but I...I'll stay for another drink.'

He nodded solemnly. '*Efharisto*.' The way his voice and sensual lips formed the word made her stomach perform an annoying little flip.

'What does that mean?'

'Greek, for *thank you.*'

'Oh, you're Greek? I love Greece. I visited Santorini a long time ago for the wedding of a client. I remember thinking at the time it's where I'd like to get married one day. That has got to rank up there as one of the most beautiful places on earth—' Perla drew to a sharp halt as his face tightened suddenly. 'I'm sorry. Mindless chit-chat?'

One corner of his mouth lifted. 'It's not as mindless as I thought it would be. So you love Greece. What else do you love?'

Her gaze dropped to the table, then immediately rose to meet his, almost against her will. 'Is this the part where I say long walks in the rain with that special someone?'

'Only if it's true. Personally, I detest the rain. I prefer wall-to-wall sunshine. And the sea.'

'And the special someone is optional?'

That look she'd caught on his face earlier returned— the cross between ragged pain and guilt—and this time it stayed for several moments before he shrugged.

'If you're lucky enough to have the choice, and to hang onto your good fortune.'

She bit her lip but was stopped from answering as the bartender delivered their order. Again silence ensued as they sipped their drinks. Only this time, when his gaze travelled over her, she boldly watched him back.

The silvery strands that blended into his temples coupled with the designer stubble gave him a seriously gorgeous but distinctly imposing look that sent her heart thudding faster. He looked vaguely familiar. Mentally shrugging, Perla concluded she must have seen him in the newspaper or on TV. His air of importance and easy way he commanded power lent itself to that theory. And, of course, he was here, at Macdonald Hall, one of the most exclusive private sport clubs in the country.

His fingers curled around his glass and she watched him lift his drink to his lips, his gaze staying on hers. Heat rushed through her, filling her up in places she'd begun to think were frozen forever. Perla tried to tell herself it was the alcohol but in an angry rush of rejection she forced herself to face the truth. She was done lying to herself, to glossing over the bare truth in order to lessen her pain.

No more!

She was attracted to this man. To his gorgeous, pain-etched face, the haunted hazel eyes, the strong stubbled jaw she wanted to run her fingers over just to see if it felt as rough as his manly, callused fingers. The mental pictures reeling through her head should've shocked and shamed her. But, for tonight, Perla was determined to suspend shame. And really, when had looking been a crime? And he was as exquisite a specimen as any.

'Be careful, little one. This big, bad wolf has vicious, merciless teeth.'

The softly voiced caution ripped her from her thoughts.

What was she doing?

In a rush, she put down her barely touched drink, stood up and snatched her handbag. 'I...you're right. Caution is usually my middle name so, um...thanks for the drink.' Her tongue felt thick with the lack of knowledge of the proper etiquette. 'And for the company.'

Her breath caught when he stood to tower over her. 'Did you drive here?' he demanded.

'Yes, but I barely touched my second drink and—'

'My driver will deliver you home.'

A mixture of fear and anxiety roiled through her. Imagine the gossip if she returned home in a strange man's car! Granted it was almost midnight but it would only take one sighting for the rumour mill to spin into overdrive. She had enough on her plate to deal with as it was.

'No. That's very kind of you but it's not necessary.'

His striking, very hypnotic eyes narrowed. In that moment, all Perla noticed were his insanely thick eyelashes and the way his mouth turned down when he was displeased. The urge to take that look from his face shocked her into stepping back. When she took another step back, he followed.

'Let me at least walk you to your car.'

'I'm perfectly capable—'

'That wasn't a suggestion.'

'Didn't you warn me about Savile-Row-dressed predators a short while ago?'

That sad, almost haunted smile made another appearance. Those endlessly fascinating fingers delved into his bespoke jacket and emerged with his smartphone. He tapped the three-digit emergency number into it and extended it to her, pointing to the dial button. 'Hit that button if I so much as exhale the wrong way between here and your car. But make no mistake, I'm walking you out of here and seeing you into your car.'

With a shaky hand, she took his phone. His fingers brushed then stilled against hers. Warmth infused her. Without thinking, she rubbed her fingers against his and heard his sharp intake of breath as he fell into step beside her.

The walk to her car took minutes but it felt like the longest walk of her life. Beside her, the tall, dark and dangerous stranger lessened his significantly long stride to match hers. Over and over again, Perla felt the heat of his gaze travel over her. She forced herself not to glance at him. To do so would've wavered her intent, made her give in to the intensely mortifying need that had taken root inside her.

But, with each dreaded step to her car, Perla felt as if she was fighting a losing battle. What had she achieved by coming here? So far, a big fat *nothing*. She hadn't even broached the task she would give everything not to have to deal with. A task she would've given everything not to return to.

Surely it wasn't wrong to make this moment with this perfect stranger last a little longer? She gave an inward sigh.

Who was she kidding? Fate had stuck two fingers up to her over and over. Why should tonight be any different?

She stopped beside her car and turned towards him. With a deep breath, she held out his phone. 'I told you this wasn't necessary. But again, thanks.'

He barely glanced at the gadget. 'You're not out of danger yet.'

She looked up into his face. 'What do you mean?' she asked, her voice a touch too breathless.

He stepped closer, his body heat slamming into her, making her head spin. 'Hang onto it for a little while longer. I don't want to end our conversation, not just yet.'

Perla's pulse rate shot up even higher. 'Why?'

'Because…' He seemed to catch himself just then. A frown creased his brow and he shook his head.

When he stepped back, a spasm of fear that she was losing him made her lean towards him. 'Because…?'

He focused on her. Hazel eyes pinned her to the spot, then rushed to her hair, over her face, her neck, down to her toes before coming back to her face. He muttered something under his breath, something in his native tongue that held no meaning for her.

'Tell me your name.'

Her mouth dried. 'It's…Pearl.' She cringed inwardly at the small fib but, growing up, her unusual name had often been mistaken for the more common *Pearl*. Besides, the anonymity made her feel less exposed.

His hooded gaze dropped to her lips, its message so blatantly sexual, her breath stalled in her chest. 'I have an irresistible urge to kiss you, Pearl. Does that make you want to run?'

The rawness behind the words rocked her to her soul, resonated beside her own turmoil. She watched his eyes slowly grow darker, more tormented. Before she could consciously stop herself, she reached up and cupped his taut cheek.

'No. But it makes me want to know what's wrong,' she said softly.

He made a rough sound under his breath, like a proud but wounded animal. 'Nothing I wish to bore you with tonight.'

'What makes you think I'll be bored? Perhaps I need the distraction as much as you do,' she said in a rush of confession. She swayed closer and stopped herself a mere whisper from him. 'Perhaps I want to give you what you want because it's what I want too?' It felt a little absurd, having this conversation with him. But it also felt…oddly right.

'Be very careful what you wish for, little one,' he breathed.

'Oh, but I have been. Very careful. Too careful at times. I'm tired of being careful.'

His hand reached up to cover hers, pressed her hand harder into his jaw. Underneath her fingers, his stubble bristled against her palm, sparking an electric current that transmitted up her arm and suffused her whole body.

'Don't offer temptation you won't be able to deliver on,' he warned.

'Are you challenging me?'

'I'm offering a word of caution. I don't wish to frighten you so perhaps you should leave now,' he grated out. 'Or stay, if you're brave enough. I accept that the choice is yours. But decide quickly.'

Contrary to his words, his fingers caught and imprisoned a thick strand of her hair, his movement almost reflexive as he passed the tresses through his fingers repeatedly.

Caught in a sensation so alien and yet so right, Perla closed that last tiny gap between them. Strong hands immediately caught her to him. She collided with over six feet of lean muscle that knocked the air out of her lungs.

Before she could draw breath, his lips settled over hers. Every thought flew out of her head as she became lost in pure, electric sensation. He kissed her as if she was life-giving oxygen, as if he needed her to survive. That knowledge more than anything caught a fragile spot inside her; shook it free and allowed her to enjoy this, to become a part of this small healing process that they both needed.

With a groan, she pressed herself closer until she could feel his heartbeat against her breasts, the ridged chest muscles crushing her softer ones. Both his hands encompassed her waist and lifted her up onto the bonnet of her car. Then he plunged both fingers into her hair, angled her face up to his and proceeded to dive deeper into their kiss.

Only the need for air finally separated them.

Perla's breaths puffed out into the cool night and threatened to cease altogether when she saw the smear of scarlet on his lips.

Reaching up, she touched his mouth. He made a sound of mingled pain and pleasure and she almost lost her mind.

'I…I…' She wasn't sure exactly what she wanted to say. Only that she needed to make sense of what was happening to her. 'Is that enough?' From the depths of her soul came a yearning for him to say no.

When he shook his head, her heart soared.

'No, it's not. The taste of you is intoxicating. I want to drown in you.' He captured her face in his hands and kissed her some more, murmuring phrases in Greek she had no hope of understanding. When he released her, he was breathing hard. Pulling her close, he rested his forehead against hers. '*Theos*…this is madness, but I can't let you go. Not yet.' He pulled back and tilted her face to his, his hazel eyes swirling with the same potent need that twisted inside her. 'Stay with me tonight, Pearl.'

Her decision was instant; so frighteningly committed that she forced herself to remain silent when she wanted to blurt it out. Her fingers moved again over his soft, sensual lips. He captured them and kissed her knuckle. It occurred to her that she held his phone in her other hand. One small movement of her thumb and this would be over—decision made.

Or she could give the answer she wanted, no, *needed* to give. Take back a small piece of herself before she had to face the world again.

'I don't even know your name,' she ventured.

'My name is Arion. If it pleases you, you can call me Ari.'

She shook her head. 'It pleases me to call you Arion.'

She loved the way her lips curled around his name. So much so, she said it again. 'Arion…'

His eyes darkened. 'You like my name?' he rasped.

'I *love* your name. I've never heard it before… Arion.' She couldn't resist the temptation to try it out one more time.

He caught her up to him and banded one arm around her waist. His laser-like gaze scoured her face as if he was trying to read her innermost thoughts. 'The way you say my name… You are dangerous, Pearl *mou*.'

Laughter, long suppressed under the pain of just *existing*, scratched from her throat. 'Wow…I'm *dangerous*? That's a first.'

'What have other men called you?'

The question sobered her up. Familiar humiliation threatened to crawl over her but she determinedly pushed it away. Tonight was *her* night, *her* choice. She refused to let thoughts of past failures intrude.

'What do you think they've called me?'

'Breathtaking. Stunning. A beauty Aphrodite herself would be jealous of,' he breathed against her neck as his lips caressed her skin. 'Your hair is incredible, the colour of a Greek sunset.'

Perla's breath hitched in her lungs. Unbidden, tears sprang into her eyes. Blinking wildly before he spotted them, she forced herself not to be drawn in by the seductive words.

'Am I close?' He lifted his head and rubbed his stubble—as rough as she'd imagined it would be—against her cheek.

Liquid heat melted her insides.

'Not even a little. But don't let that stop you.'

'Beautiful Pearl, I want to see your hair spread over my pillow. I want to bury myself in it, strangle myself with it.' The hoarse litany made her draw back and stare at him. Once again, his face was stamped in pain. But, alongside it, desire, strong and unmistakable, burned right into her soul. 'Does that frighten you?'

'I want to say no, but I am a little frightened, yes. I've never done this before but I want to. Very much.' So badly she couldn't think straight. The need to forget, just for a short while, what faced her in the next few days, was so strong she couldn't breathe for the need of it. 'Right now, I'm so desperate for you I don't know how long I can stand it.'

'Then stay. I will give you everything you desire.' About to kiss her again, he suddenly froze. 'Unless you're not free to be with me?'

'What do you mean?'

'Is there a lover or a husband?' came the tight, throaty demand.

The arrow of guilt that lanced through her made her freeze too.

This is your night. Yours! Tomorrow will come soon enough.

'I'm free to be with you, Arion. I'll stay with you tonight if you want me to.'

His suite was *probably* the last word in luxury; the fixtures and fittings ones she'd *probably* have ogled if she'd had a chance to take even a single note.

But with Arion's mouth on hers, his fingers in her hair and his body pressed close and hot against hers, Perla didn't notice one single thing about the third-floor suite, except that the *RS* button he'd pressed in the lift stood for Royal Suite.

She did notice the large red velvet sofa he laid her down on the minute they entered his suite's pitch-sized living room. Although the memory of it disappeared once he'd shrugged off his jacket and tie and freed his shirt from his trousers.

His chest once he unbuttoned his shirt instantly made her mouth dry, then flood with longing as she stared at hard contours and smooth bronzed muscles. Hairless and divine, his stunning beauty made need she'd never known pulse through her.

But that was a fraction of what she felt when he dropped his trousers and stepped out of his cotton boxers. His erection stood strong and proud...and big.

Just then, the enormity of what she was doing hit her between the eyes.

She was about to lose her virginity to a complete stranger.

CHAPTER TWO

A DEEP SHUDDER ripped through Perla and she barely stopped her teeth from chattering like a wooden marionette in a child's hand.

The sound she made as Arion, the man she had no knowledge of a mere hour ago, came towards her made him pause and frown.

'Are you cold?' he asked.

She was anything but. She shook her head, forcing a laugh. 'No. I'm a little nervous. I haven't—' She stopped. What was the use of telling him of her inexperience? Whether she pleased or disappointed him, she'd never set eyes on this gorgeous man again. They were using each other to forget their pain, to hold the darkness at bay. This wasn't the time to spill innermost secrets. It was the time to forget they existed. 'It's nothing.'

He nodded as if he understood. Then he took a single step forward, and angled himself over her. 'I'll make it good. I promise,' he vowed, and she forgot everything else.

The kiss was hotter, deeper than the one he'd delivered at the car. This time his tongue probed her mouth with a sensual force that spoke of his need. Fists clamped in her hair, he went even deeper, his groan of satisfaction echoing her own as her fingers sought and found firm, heated, *naked* shoulders.

His skin felt like pure heaven. Velvety smooth and oh

so gloriously luxuriant, she explored him from shoulder to back, then lower. When she moulded her hands over his bare bottom, then dug her nails into his taut flesh, he wrenched his lips from hers with a tortured groan. His breath came out in pants as he stared down at her, eyes dark with lust.

'Promise me you'll do that when I'm deep inside you.'

Heat drenched her from head to toe. From somewhere she summoned the strength to speak. 'I promise.'

He licked the corner of her mouth in a move so simple and yet so powerfully erotic, she felt as if her insides would combust. She gave a heartfelt groan when he pushed himself off her. 'For that to happen, *glikia mou*, you need to be as naked as I am.'

Perla stared down at herself, stunned that the power of his lust hadn't melted the clothes off her. When he grabbed her arms and pulled her up, she went willingly. The slide of her zip was loud and intrusive in the silent room. Unwanted thoughts once again threatened to ruin the moment. *What the hell are you doing? Leave. Leave now!*

As if he could tell, he quickened his movements. Within seconds, he was bending over her once more, his mouth trailing down her neck, washing away her doubt, re-igniting the flames that had merely been banked.

'Tell me how you like it, Pearl *mou*,' he rasped against the valley between her breasts. 'Tell me your favourite position and I'll do it to you.'

Panic momentarily seized her. She searched her mind for terms she'd heard of. 'Doggie style,' she blurted, then cringed as her face flamed.

Thank God he didn't notice. For some strange reason, he seemed as fascinated with her breasts as he'd been with her hair. Moulding them in his hands, he licked first one hardened nipple, then the other, then pulled them simultaneously into his mouth. At her deep groan, he smiled.

'That is one of my favourite positions too,' he said. His teeth grazed over her nipples, then he trailed kisses lower… lower, until she realised his destination.

He ignored the staying hand she put on his shoulder.

'No…'

'*Yes!*' With a hot look from darkened eyes, he parted her thighs.

She held her breath but, at the first sweep of his tongue, she exhaled as pleasure she'd never known rushed over her. Before she could react to that first wave, he began a series of flicks that made stars dance before her eyes. Expertly, he pleasured her, relentless in his need to make her lose control. Buffeted by sensations she'd never experienced, Perla fought both the urge to withdraw from that wicked tongue and press her hips closer. Her head thrashed on the cushion as an unfamiliar sensation pushed her towards a blissful peak.

'Arion! Oh, God… Oh!' She let out a scream as her climax broke over her. Jerking uncontrollably, she sobbed as pleasure washed over her and sucked her under. When he gathered her in his arms and pulled her into his body, Perla sobbed harder.

Through it all he murmured soft words of praise and comfort, a balm her soul desperately needed. An eternity later, he started to pull away. Her protesting mutter was met with another kiss.

'Patience, *pethi mou*, now the real fun begins,' he said with dark promise.

Slowly, Perla rubbed the tears from her eyes.

Opening her eyes, she found him kneeling on the sofa, sliding on a condom. The sight of him, large and powerful and ready, sent another pulse of lust through her.

When he probed her entrance, Perla felt a moment's twinge, a shaky feeling of disconnect. It faded away the moment he pressed himself deeper. At her body's further resistance, he paused with a groan.

'You're not ready. I'm sorry, I was a little impatient.'

She slid her hands through his hair and barely resisted raising her head to kiss him. 'I want you.'

He gave another groan and kissed her. 'You're not ready and I don't want to hurt you.'

Mistaking his meaning, Perla spread her thighs wider and ventured her hips closer. 'I'm ready now.'

Arion raised his head, a slightly puzzled look crossing his face. 'Pearl—'

'Please, don't keep us waiting.' Emboldened by his groan, she pressed even closer. He slid in another delicious inch.

The discomfort grew as he pushed in but the rush, the pleasure that followed behind it was so much worth the momentary pain. Perla's breath fractured as she sighed in bliss. Arion's grip tightened in her hair with the full surge of his body.

'*Theos!* You're so tight. So gorgeous.' The warmth of his breath washed over her neck a second before his lips found and captured hers. His tongue slid into her mouth, its movement as bold and as raw as his full, relentless thrusts.

Bliss washed over her so completely, Perla had no idea where sensation started and ended. Clamping her legs around his waist, she took him fully into her body. Pleasure crested in giant waves over her. But, just as she prepared to give herself over to it, he pulled out of her. Rising to his feet, he tugged her off the sofa and onto the floor.

'On your knees,' he commanded. 'It's time to give you what you want.'

Her heart hammering with excitement, Perla complied.

He came up behind her, bent her over the seat and entered her from behind.

'Oh, my God!' The cry was ripped from her soul, pleasure so profound radiating from inside her she thought she'd pass out.

Arion's fingers slid through her hair over and over as he thrust inside her. Perla had never thought of her hair as an erogenous area. In fact, up till that moment, she'd never thought pleasure like this was possible.

Dear heaven, how wrong she'd been. She screamed as he pounded into her, his hoarse voice reciting her name over and over. Once again the precipice approached, the stars beckoning with a radiance she knew would touch her for ever. Behind her, Arion slid back and rested on his knees. Firm hands urged her back, all the while continuing the relentless pace that stalled her breath.

'Ride me,' he encouraged, his deep voice raw and urgent.

Spreading her legs wider, Perla eased herself back, the change in pace escalating her pleasure even higher. Hands gripping the sofa to steady herself, she rode herself to ecstasy. Her breath choked on a scream as her orgasm hit her. One hand clamped around her middle, Arion eased another hand over her belly to tease her clitoris, prolonging her climax. The wave seemed endless; he continued to thrust inside her despite her pleas for mercy. Just when she thought she'd expire from pleasure, she heard his deep groan. He buried his face in her hair, his thrusts growing uneven as pleasure spasms gripped him.

Several minutes later, he planted kisses on her neck and shoulder, one hand still gripped on her waist. 'I can't decide whether you're an angel or a witch, sent to torment me or bring me heaven.'

Her breath caught on a soft blissful sigh. 'Can I be both?'

'With hair like that, you can be anything you want.'

She managed to lift her head to glance over her shoulder at him. 'You have a freaky fascination with my hair.'

'A fascination which includes seeing it spread over my pillow.' He pulled out of her with a dark groan, scooped her into his arms and headed down a short hallway.

Once again she barely registered her surroundings. But, even while he secured another condom, Arion's gaze held her captive, the look he sent her exciting her in ways she'd never have dreamt was possible. When he took command of her body once more, Perla gave herself over into his arms, a willing slave for the pleasures in store...

She woke with a start, then fought to regulate her breathing so as not to wake the sleeping man beside her.

A sneak peek at the bedside clock showed it was half past two in the morning.

Perla glanced at Arion—goodness, she didn't even know his surname. Well, he didn't know her real name, which was a blessing in disguise, she supposed. Not that their paths would cross again in a million years.

Her gaze devoured his sleeping form. God, he was truly spectacular, and the pleasures he'd shown her would remain unforgettable. Watching the steady rise and fall of his massive chest, she felt her nipples peak again as excitement crawled over her.

She bit her lip and forced herself to get up. She dressed in silence, holding her breath every time he moved. The small part of her that hoped he would wake and stop her leaving was ruthlessly squashed.

They could never be more than ships passing in the night. She carried too much baggage and, from what she'd glimpsed in his eyes, he carried a shipload of his own baggage. All the same, her fingers slowed on her zip. Maybe it didn't have to be this way, maybe she could...

Stay? Dear Lord, what was she thinking?

Doing anything of that sort was totally out of the question. She had *no* choice but to leave.

If for no other reason than the fact that between now and Friday morning when she had to stand before a congregation and speak, she had her dead husband's eulogy to write.

CHAPTER THREE

THE SMALL CHAPEL was packed to the rafters. Outside, a clutch of news vans and reporters were stationed, poised and ready for the opportunity to snap any picture that would feed the media frenzy of the notoriety behind this funeral.

So far, Perla hadn't found the courage to turn around to see just how many people had wedged themselves into the tiny chapel. The one glance as people had filed in had been enough to terrify her. But she hadn't missed the trio of limousines that had crawled past and parked ominously on the chapel lawn.

Morgan's bosses. Probably Sakis Pantelides and various executives from Pantelides Shipping Inc. The letter announcing their attendance had arrived yesterday.

She supposed she should be thankful they were bothering to attend, considering the nefarious circumstances leading to Morgan's death. A small, bitter part of her wished they hadn't bothered. Their presence here would, no doubt, keep up the media frenzy, and she also couldn't dismiss the fact that she'd had to keep demanding information from Pantelides Inc. before she'd been given very brief details of what had happened to her husband.

Granted, Sakis Pantelides had been gentle and infinitely considerate when he'd broken the horrific news to her but the fact remained that Morgan Lowell, the man she'd married, and whose secret she'd kept—*still kept*—had died under suspicious circumstances in a foreign country after trying to get away with defrauding his employer. Pantelides Inc. had kept a lid on the fact to protect itself from adverse publicity.

What no one realised was that *this* was yet another morsel of unwanted truth she had to keep to herself; another detail she couldn't share with Morgan's parents, who had idolised their son and remained devastated by his death. She'd been forced to gloss over the truth for their sake. Again…

She clenched her hands and forced herself to focus. She had more important things to think about now, like how she could stand up and speak of her husband when another man's face, the fevered recollection of another man's hands and the thrust of his hard body repeatedly flashed through her brain.

Dear God, what had she done? What had she been thinking?

Although guilt clawed through her belly, the shame she expected to feel remained way below an acceptable level. In fact she barely felt anything except the forceful presence of her one-night lover, deep inside her, surrounding her, pulsing around her like a live electric current with every breath she took.

She'd taken three showers this morning, all in the vain hope of washing herself free of his scent. But it was as if he'd invaded her thoughts as well as her pores. Behind her, whispered voices surged higher and she heard shuffling as the congregation made way for new arrivals.

Perla's breath stalled as she caught the familiar scent again. She bit her lip and closed her eyes. *God, please give me strength because I'm seriously losing it here.*

When her elderly neighbour and only friend Mrs Clinton's hand covered hers, she gratefully clutched it. The discerning woman had wisely put herself between Perla and

Morgan's parents but she felt their heartbreak with every fibre of her being.

For their sake, for the kindness and open warmth they'd shown her, she had to keep it together. They were the reason she'd borne this humiliation for so long. Morgan had known that. Had banked on it, in fact, and used it as the perfect blackmail tool when she'd threatened to leave him—

'Not long before it starts. Don't worry, dear; in less than an hour, it'll be over. I went through the same thing with my Harry,' she whispered. 'Everyone means well, but they don't know the best they can do in times like these is to leave you alone, do they?'

Perla attempted a response and only managed a garbled croak. Mrs Clinton patted her hand again reassuringly. With relief, she heard the organ starting up. As she stood, Perla caught the scent again, and quickly locked her knees as she swayed.

She glanced to the side and saw a tall, imposing man with a thin scar above his right eye standing next to a striking blonde.

Sakis Pantelides, the man who'd phoned two weeks ago with news of her husband's death. His condolences had been genuine enough but after her discovery of just what Morgan had done to his company, Perla wasn't so sure his attendance here was an offer of support.

Her gaze shifted to the proprietorial arm he kept around the woman, his fiancée, Brianna Moneypenny, and she felt a twinge of shame-laced jealousy.

He caught her gaze and he gave a short nod in greeting before returning his attention to the front.

She faced forward again, but the unsettling feeling that had gripped her nape escalated. The feeling grew as the ceremony progressed. By the time the priest announced the eulogy reading, Perla's stomach churned with sick nerves. She pushed it away. Whatever emotional turmoil she was experiencing had nothing to do with the Pantelides family and everything to do with what she'd done on Tuesday night. And those memories had no place here in this chapel, today.

No matter what Morgan had put her through, she had to do this without breaking down. She had to endure this for his parents' sake.

They'd offered her the only home she'd ever known, and the warmth she'd only ever dreamed about as a child.

Another pat from Mrs Clinton gave her the strength to keep upright. She thought she heard a sharp intake of breath behind her but Perla didn't turn around. She needed every ounce of focus to stride past the coffin holding her dead husband…the husband who, while he'd been alive, had taken great pleasure in humiliating her; the husband who even in death…seemed to be mocking her.

She got to the lectern and unfolded the piece of paper. Nerves gripped her and, although she knew it was rude, she couldn't look up from the sheet. She had a feeling she would lose her nerve if her gaze strayed from the paper in her hand.

Clearing her throat, she moved closer to the microphone.

'I met Morgan at the uni bar on my first day on campus. I was the wide-eyed, clueless outsider who had no clue what went into a half-fat, double-shot pumpkin spice latte—except maybe the pumpkin—and he was the second-year city dude every girl wanted to date. Even though he didn't ask me out until I was in my last year, I think I fell in love with him at first sight…'

Perla carried on reading, refusing to dwell on how overwhelmingly wrong she'd been about the man she'd married; how utterly gullible she must have been to have had the wool pulled over her eyes so effectively until it was too late.

But now was not the time to think of past mistakes. She read on, saying the *right* thing, *honouring* the man who right from the very beginning of their marriage had had no intention of honouring *her*.

'...I'll always remember Morgan with a pint in his hand and a twinkle in his eye, telling rude jokes in the uni bar. *That* was the man I fell in love with and he'll always remain in my heart.'

Unshed tears clogged her throat again. Swallowing, she folded the sheet and finally gathered the courage to look up.

'Thank you all for coming—'

She choked to a halt as her gaze clashed with a pair of sinful, painfully familiar hazel eyes.

No.

Oh, God, no...

Her knees gave way. Frantically, she clutched at the lectern. She felt her hand begin to slip. Someone shouted and moved towards her. Unable to breathe or halt her crumpling legs, she cried out. Several people rushed towards her. Hands grabbed her before she fell, righted her, helped her down from the dais.

And, through it all, Arion Pantelides stared at her from where he stood next to the man she'd guessed was Sakis Pantelides, icy condemnation blazing from his eyes and washing over her until her whole body went numb.

Ari tried to breathe past the vice squeezing his chest, past the thick anger and acrid bitterness lashing his insides. The pain that rose alongside it, he refused to acknowledge.

Why would he feel pain? He had no one to blame but himself. After all life had thrown at him, he'd dared to believe he could reach out and seek goodness when there was none to be had. Only disappointment. Only heartache. Only disgust.

But still the anger came, thick and fast and strong, as he stared at Pearl...no, *Perla* Lowell, the woman who'd lied about her name and slithered into his bed while her husband's body was barely cold.

Disgust roiled through him. Even now, the memory of what they'd done to each other made fiery desire pool in his groin. Gritting his teeth, he forced his fists to unclench as he stamped down on the emotion.

He'd let himself down, spectacularly and utterly. On the most sacred of days, when he should've been honouring his past, he'd allowed himself to succumb to temptation.

Temptation with absolutely the wrong woman.

One who'd turned out to be as duplicitous and as sullied as the husband she was burying.

'Do you know what's going on with her?' His younger brother, Sakis, slid a glance at him.

Ari kept his gaze fixed ahead, jaw clenched tight. 'It's her husband's funeral. I'd have thought it was obvious she's *drowning in grief.*' How bitter those words tasted in his mouth. Because he knew they were the last emotion Perla Lowell was feeling. A woman who could do what she'd done with him forty-eight hours before putting her dead husband in the ground?

No, grief didn't even get a look-in.

Whereas he... *Theos.*

His gut clenched hard at the merciless lash of memories. He'd gorged himself on her, greedy in his need to forget, to blank the pain that had eviscerated him with each heartbeat.

Turning away from the spectacle playing out on the altar, he followed the trickle of guests who'd started to leave the chapel.

'Are you sure that's all?' Sakis demanded. 'I could've sworn she totally freaked out only when she saw you.'

Ari rounded on him as they exited into dappled sunshine. 'What the hell are you talking about?'

'I don't know, brother, but she seemed to be fixated on you. I thought maybe you knew her.'

'I've never been to this backwater until today, and I only came because *you* insisted you couldn't make it. What are you doing here, anyway?'

'It was my fault. I insisted.' Brianna, his beautiful soon-to-be sister-in-law spoke up. 'I thought, as Lowell's former employer, Sakis should be here. We tried to call you to let you know but your phone was off and the staff at Macdonald Hall said you'd checked out yesterday.'

His jaw clenched harder at the reminder.

He'd been running a fool's errand, desperately trying to track down the woman who'd run out on him in the middle of the night. A day and a half, he'd driven up and down the damned countryside, searching for the Mini whose red paint was a poor match for the vibrant hair colour of the woman who'd made him lose his mind and forget his pain for a few blissful hours.

Theos! How could he not have seen that it was all an illusion? They said sex made fools of men. They'd said nothing about the deadly blade of memory and the consequences of a desperate search for oblivion.

Bringing his mind into focus, he lowered his gaze away from his brother's blatant curiosity.

'We've paid our respects, now can we get the hell out of here?' he rasped.

Sakis nodded at a few guests before he answered him. 'Why, what's the hurry?'

'I have a seven o'clock meeting first thing in the morning, then I fly out to Miami.'

Sakis frowned. 'It's only two o'clock in the afternoon, Ari.'

His body didn't know that because he'd been up all day and all night, searching…chasing a dream that didn't exist.

He was losing it. He needed to get out of there before he marched back into that tiny chapel and roared his fury at that red-headed witch inside.

'I *know* what time it is. If you want to stay, feel free. I'll send the chopper back to Macdonald Hall for you two.' He couldn't get out of here fast enough, although every single bone in his body wanted to confront the duplicitous widow and give her a hefty piece of his mind.

With a nod at his brother and Brianna, he cut his way through the gawping crowd, uncaring that his face was set in a formidable scowl.

From the corner of his eye, he saw a flash of red hair heading his way. Although anger rose up within him, it took a monumental effort not to turn his head and see if it was Perla.

Clenching his fist, he stalked faster towards his limo, the need to be gone a fierce, urgent demand.

'Arion, wait!' Her husky voice was almost lost in the cacophony of the funeral spectacle. And it *was* a spectacle. Morgan Lowell's starring role in his own death via a drug overdose had ensured the media would make a meal of his funeral, even with the scant facts they knew.

Ari froze with one hand on the car door. Slowly, he sucked in a deep breath and turned to face her.

The widow in black. How very apt.

The widow whose bright, fiery red hair shone in the daylight with an unholy, tempting light, the same way it had gleamed temptingly across his pillow three nights ago.

Against his will, his body stirred. Blood pounded through his veins, momentarily deafening him with the roar of arousal. Before he could stop himself, his gaze raked over her.

Although her dress was funeral black, demure, almost plain to the point of drab, he wasn't fooled. He knew what lay beneath, the hot curves and the treacherous thighs, the delight he would uncover should he…

No. Never in a thousand years would he bring himself to touch her. They'd come together in a moment he'd thought was sacred, monumentally divine. Instead, it'd turned out to be a tawdry roll in the hay for her.

'Hello…Arion. I'm guessing your surname is Pantelides.' Green eyes searched his with wariness.

'And I now know your full name is *Perla* Lowell. So tell me, what role are you playing here now? Because we both know the grieving widow routine is just a front, don't we? Perhaps you're silently amused because you have saucy underwear underneath that staid black?'

She gasped, an expression that looked shockingly like deep hurt flashing across her face.

Theos, how utterly convincing she was. But not convincing enough to make him forget he'd nearly lost his mind hanging on for dear life as she rode him with merciless enthusiasm a little over forty-eight hours ago.

'How dare you?' She finally found her voice, even though it shook with her words.

'Very easily. I was the guy you were screwing when you should've been home mourning your husband. Now what the hell do you want?'

Her complexion had paled but then her skin was translucent thanks to her colouring. And yes, his words had been cruel, deliberately so. But she'd sullied his own memory of what the date had meant to him for ever.

And *that* he found hard to forgive.

'I was going to apologise for the…um…small deception. And to thank you for your discretion. But I see I needn't have bothered. You're nothing but a vile, bitter man, one who sees nothing wrong in bringing further pain and anguish on an already difficult day. So if you were truly on your way out of here, I guess the only thing I have to say is *good riddance.*'

Ari hardened his heart against the words. She was in the wrong here, not him. She was clearly deluded if she thought he had something to be ashamed of. Turning, he yanked the back door open.

Before he slid in, he glanced at her one last time. 'Have fun revelling in your role of grieving widow. But when the crowd is gone and you think of reprising your *other* role, be sure to stay away from Macdonald Hall. Before the hour's out, I intend to supply the management with your name and ensure you're never allowed to set foot in there again.'

Fugue state.

Perla was sure that perfectly described her condition as she drifted through the wake, shaking hands, accepting condolences and agreeing that yes, Morgan had been a lovely man and a generous husband. On occasion, she even smiled at a distant uncle or great-aunt's fond anecdote.

The part of her that had reeled at Ari Pantelides's scathing condemnation an hour ago had long been suppressed under a blanket of fierce denial with Do Not Disturb signs hammered all over it.

At the time, she'd barely been able to contain the belief that he thought her some kind of scarlet woman or a trollop who frequented bars in the hope of landing a hot body for the night.

She audibly choked at the thought.

Mrs Clinton, who'd faithfully stuck by her side once they'd returned to the house she'd shared with Morgan and now shared with his parents, gave her a firm rub on the back. 'You're almost there, dear girl. Give it another half hour and I'll start dropping heavy hints that you should be left alone. Enough is enough.'

She glanced at the old dear's face. Perla had never confided the true state of her marriage with Mrs Clinton, or anyone for that matter. The very thought of it made humiliation rise like a tide inside her.

But she'd long suspected that the older woman somehow

knew. Seeing the sympathy in her old rheumy eyes, Perla felt tears well up in hers.

Suddenly, as if the bough had broken, she couldn't stop the tide of hot, gulping tears that rose from deep inside.

'Oh, my dear.' Warm arms hugged her, providing the solace she'd been so cruelly denied throughout her marriage. The solace she'd imagined she'd found in a luxury penthouse suite three days ago, but had turned out to be another cruel illusion.

'I'm sorry, I shouldn't...I didn't mean to...'

'Nonsense! You have every right to do whatever you want on a day like this. Propriety be damned.'

Hysterical laughter bubbled up from her throat but she quickly smothered it. When a glass containing a caramel-coloured liquid that smelled suspiciously like brandy appeared in front of her, she glanced up.

The exquisitely beautiful woman who'd introduced herself as Brianna Moneypenny, soon-to-be Brianna Pantelides, held out the drink, sympathy shining from her expertly made-up eyes.

Perla wiped her own eyes, acutely conscious that she was messing up the make-up she'd carefully applied to hide the shadows under her eyes.

'Thank you.'

'No need to thank me. I've helped myself to a shot too. This is the third funeral Sakis and I have attended in the last month. My emotions are beyond shredded.' She sat down next to Perla, gracefully crossed her legs and offered a kind smile. 'It's nothing compared to what you must be feeling, of course, and if there's anything we can do, please don't hesitate to ask.'

'I...thank you. And please extend my thanks to your fiancé and...and the other Mr Pantelides for taking the time to come...' Perla's voice drifted off, simply because she couldn't think straight when her mind churned with thoughts of Arion Pantelides and the accusations he'd thrown at her. And even though she'd seen him get into his car, she couldn't stop her gaze from scouring the room, almost afraid to find out if he'd returned to tear a few more strips off her.

'Arion has left but I'll let him know,' Brianna said. A quick glance at her showed a sharp intellect that made Perla hope against hope that the other woman wasn't putting two with two and coming up with the perfect answer.

As it was, Perla felt as if she had the dreaded letter *A* branded on her forehead.

'Of course. I appreciate that he must be busy.' She didn't add that, in the light of what Morgan had done, they were the last people she'd expected to attend his funeral. Instead, she took a hasty sip of the brandy for much needed fortitude, and nearly choked when liquid fire burned down her throat.

'Well, he is. But he volunteered to come down here when he thought Sakis couldn't make it. And yet he seemed to have a bee in his bonnet about something. To be honest, it's the first time I've seen him that ruffled.' The speculation in her voice made Perla wish she'd worn her hair down to hide the colour rising in her face. 'It was quite a sight to behold.'

'Um, well…whatever it is, I hope he resolves it soon.'

'Hmm, so do I—'

'Brianna.' Sakis Pantelides chose that moment to approach them and offer his own condolences. Perla fought to find the appropriate response despite the nerves tearing through her stomach.

Then she watched as he turned to his fiancée, his face transforming with a very visible devotion that made Perla's heart lurch with jealousy and pain.

She'd long ago harboured hopes that someone would look at her like that. She'd foolishly believed that someone would be Morgan. Instead, he'd married her and black-mailed her into deceit and humiliation.

As an orphan, tossed from foster home to foster home all her childhood, she'd learned to mask the raw pain and despair of being the odd child that nobody wanted. But the hollow feeling in her belly had never gone away.

Meeting Morgan and suddenly finding herself the sole focus of his charm and wit had tricked her naïve self into believing she'd finally found someone who loved and cared for her, not out of duty, or because the state was paying them to do so, but because she was worth loving.

He'd roughly pulled the wool from her eyes within days of their wedding. But, even then, she'd foolishly believed she could salvage something from the only steady relationship she'd ever known. But weeks had dragged into months and months into years and by the time she'd accepted that she'd once again been cast aside, like a broken toy no one wanted to play with, it'd been too late to leave.

Her shaky breath drew glances from Sakis and Brianna but she couldn't look them in the face. She'd revealed so much already. She feared opening her mouth would be cat-astrophic, especially as she could feel Sakis Pantelides's keen gaze boring into her.

God, please don't let him guess what I did with his brother.

'I think it's time we left Mrs Lowell in peace, Sakis,' Brianna murmured.

Sakis nodded. 'My lawyers will be in touch with the paperwork regarding your husband's employment entitle-ments. But if you need anything in the meantime, please do not hesitate to get in touch.'

She glanced at him and immediately glanced away when his gaze narrowed.

He can't know!

Panic clawed at her. Surely Arion hadn't told him?

From the corner of her eye she saw Morgan's parents heading towards them. Clearing her throat, she fought the panic and pasted a suitable smile on her face.

No matter what had gone on between Morgan and her, Terry and Sarah Lowell had welcomed her into their hearts. She couldn't repay them with betrayal.

'I appreciate it, Mr Pantelides. Have a safe journey back to London.'

She turned away, grateful for the distraction that Morgan's wheelchair-bound mother brought to stop her wondering just what Sakis Pantelides knew about her carnal activities with his brother.

And she certainly couldn't think about Arion Pantelides and the heat that rushed under her skin every time she re-lived what had happened in his hotel room three days ago.

What had happened between them was now firmly in the past. Never to be repeated. What she needed to concentrate on now was picking up the shattered pieces and commencing the uphill battle that was the rest of her life.

CHAPTER FOUR

Three months later.

PERLA LOOKED UP for the umpteenth time as the Pantelides Inc. reception phone rang. The superbly groomed receptionist answered in dulcet tones and sliced another cool look at Perla before turning away.

Her teeth gritted and for a second she fought the urge to march over to the desk and demand she call upstairs again and get her the meeting she'd come here for.

Instead, she smoothed her hand down the black pencil skirt she'd spent her dwindling funds on and forced herself to remain seated. She'd turned up with no prior appointment, but only because her phone calls and emails had gone unanswered. And, truth be told, she'd only been waiting an hour and a half.

But being in the architecturally imposing building that bore the Pantelides name made her nerves jangle with each heartbeat, despite chastising herself that the likelihood that Arion Pantelides was in residence was negligible.

As the head of Pantelides Luxe, the branch of the conglomerate that ran its luxury hotels and casinos around the world—yes, she'd researched him in a moment of madness—Arion Pantelides spent very little time in England. And even if he were here, she'd asked for an appointment with the head of HR in Sakis's absence, not his brother.

So, really, there was no need for her to feel as if she were playing dare in an electric lightning storm.

Nevertheless, when the phone rang again, she held her breath. Expertly waxed eyebrows arched her way and a manicured hand motioned her forward.

Sighing her relief, Perla approached the desk as the receptionist hung up.

With another glance, which was now tinged with heavy speculation, the receptionist slid a visitor's badge along with a short silver key across the sleek glass counter.

'Please wear this at all times. Take the last lift on the right. Turn the key and press the button.'

Perla wanted to ask which floor she needed but she didn't want to look a fool, so she nodded her thanks and walked on shaky feet to the lift.

As it turned out, there was only one button to press. After inserting the key, she stabbed the green button that simply read *AP* and held her breath as the doors slid smoothly shut.

Her trepidation rose along with her meagre breakfast as she was whisked up at warp speed.

She barely had time to swallow the sudden nausea that assailed her before the lift doors were sliding open again. She started to step out, then froze as ice washed over her.

Arion Pantelides stood before her, tall, breathtaking, imposing…and as granite-faced as he'd been on the day she'd buried Morgan.

Perla swallowed. And swallowed again before she could speak. 'I think there's been some sort of misunderstanding. I'm not here to see you. I came to see your brother, my late husband's employer. Or, in his absence, I asked for the head of HR.'

'Sakis isn't here.' He confirmed what she already knew. 'He's on an extended honeymoon.' That voice, deep, husky, tinged with a haunting quality that she'd found intriguing since their first meeting, feathered along her nerves, sending her insides quaking with emotion so strong she wanted to take a step back from it.

Perla bit her lip. 'Yes, I know he got married last month but I didn't know he was still away… I was hoping he was back…' She drifted to a stop, her gaze trying desperately not to stray over his hauntingly beautiful face. A face that had featured in her dreams more times than she cared to acknowledge even to herself.

'He would've got married sooner. He delayed it because your husband's involvement in the Pantelides oil tanker crash was still under investigation. It would've been in bad taste to celebrate what is supposed to be the happiest day of any man's life with events like that hanging over everyone's head.'

The veiled mockery in his tone made her hackles rise, but it was the memory of his blistering anger the last time they'd met that made her insides quake.

She sucked in a deep breath. 'I apologise for the inconvenience—'

A slashing gesture with his hand stopped her words. 'He'll be back in two weeks. Feel free to come back then.'

The lift doors started to shut. Galvanised into action, she threw out a hand to stop it just as he did the same. Warm fingers grazed hers, sending electricity zapping through her. Perla jumped back and felt her heart thunder as she caught the look he levelled at her.

'I'm…I'm afraid this can't wait. Just point me in the direction of HR and I'll be out of your hair…'

As if reminded of that part of her, he stepped back and his lazy gaze trailed upward to rest on the hair she'd pulled back into a tight bun. Once he'd looked his fill, those hazel eyes, whose mesmerising flecks she recalled so vividly, recaptured hers. 'The whole HR team is on a day's training in Paris.'

Her stomach plummeted with despair. 'You're kidding, right? The *whole* team?'

He raised a brow at her.

'This really is an emergency. I came here specially. I need to talk to someone.'

Just like that, he shrugged, turned and walked away.

With every fibre of her being she wanted to let the doors shut once more and be plunged back to the ground floor, back to safety. But too much depended on her trip here today. Much too much.

So she took one step into Arion Pantelides's vast, opulent domain.

The architecture of the Pantelides Tower had looked formidable and stunning from the outside. Inside his office, the glass, chrome and steel structure blended with earthy tones made the place simply magnificent.

A wide roll-top desk, obviously an expensive antique, took up one corner of the glass-walled room, offering a breathtaking view of the river and the iconic buildings across the water. Under her feet, a deep gold carpet muffled her tentative footsteps.

She managed to take that all in in the handful of seconds before Arion folded his leanly muscled frame behind his desk.

Fighting her rising irritation, she glanced back at him. 'Did you hear what I said? I need to talk to someone. It's important.'

'By all means, if this can't wait, tell me what the problem is and I'll see if I can accommodate you.'

He was toying with her, like a jungle animal toying with his prey. But she would not give him the satisfaction of thinking he could pounce and annihilate her again without consequences.

Even though the need to turn tail and flee stalked through her, she held her ground. Because what other choice did she have? She couldn't exactly flounce out of here. Her situation was too dire. They needed a solution now or Morgan's parents would lose the house in which they'd brought up their son. After what they'd been through, Perla couldn't stand by and do nothing whilst they suffered another blow in addition to the one they'd already been dealt by losing their only child.

Pursing her lips, she reached into her bag and brought out the file she'd compiled. Stepping forward, she slapped it on the table in front of him.

'According to these letters, neither Morgan's parents nor I are entitled to his death-while-employed insurance pay out. That can't be right. I know he signed on for that benefit.'

Arion steepled his fingers and watched her dispassionately over them. 'Ah, so you're here to collect on your husband's death.'

She couldn't stop herself from flinching at his tone. And he saw it because his eyes gleamed with something akin to satisfaction.

She straightened her spine. 'I'm only asking what is rightly due to me as the spouse of a man who died while employed by your brother's company. I've read the small print. I know my rights, so I'd thank you not to make me sound like a vulture, Mr Pantelides.' She kept her voice firm because she sensed that any weakness would be met with scalpel-sharp ruthlessness.

Abruptly, he sat forward. Even across his desk, his imposing figure dominated, enclosing her in his powerful aura and making her pulse race.

Steady breaths. Just breathe.

'Trust me, *glikia mou*. No red-blooded man would look at you and liken you to a vulture. There are other, more exotic creatures perfectly apt to describe you.'

Really? Perla nearly groaned in relief when she realised she hadn't asked the question out loud.

'I'd prefer not to be thought of in terms of creatures great or small. Are you able to help me with this or am I wasting my time here?' she snapped.

Arion shrugged and glanced at his watch. 'Unfortunately, I have a lunch meeting in fifteen minutes.' He reached across and grabbed the papers from the table. 'Are you staying in town?'

She frowned at the unexpected question. 'No, I'm returning to Bath this evening.'

'Then don't let me stop you. Someone will be in touch soon.'

Something in the way he said that made suspicion rise higher. 'And just how soon is *soon?*'

Another careless shrug. 'I can get my brother to email his head of HR and get them to look into it but he's somewhere in the South Pacific. In a state of wedded bliss, who knows how often he checks his emails.' A shadow crossed his face, a tiny hint of what she'd glimpsed that night in the Macdonald Hall car park. Despite the need for self-preservation, her heart twisted.

'Arion…' He immediately stiffened and she bit her lip. *Wrong move, Perla! Keep on point.* 'Mr Pantelides, I don't have the sort of time you're offering. Could you…would you be willing to look into this yourself for me? Please?' she added when he remained frozen.

His eyes hardened. 'Is this where you trot out the for *old time's sake?*'

A heated flush crawled up her neck. 'No, I wouldn't be so crass as to refer to an occasion we'd both prefer to forget…but of course you won't believe that about me so I don't even know why I'm bothering. Look, I'm not sure whether you know about my circumstances, but Morgan and I lived with his parents after we got married. We were always going to move out and get a place of our own but that never happened. Two years ago, his mother was in a bad accident. Terry, Morgan's father, had to give up his job to look after her. Times have been hard for them. Without Morgan's insurance payment, they could lose their house. I know I'm nothing but a piece of trash in your eyes but they don't deserve to lose their home so soon after losing their son.'

She sucked in a breath and risked a glance at him. His expression remained stone-cold. For several minutes he didn't speak. Then he reached into his desk and slid across a small black triangular piece of gleaming plastic.

There were no markings on it. It could've been one of those if-you-had-to-apply-for-it-you-couldn't-afford-it credit cards reserved for multi-billionaires she'd read about in a magazine once. Or it could've been a loyalty card for die-hard coffee addicts. Perla had no way of telling. She looked from the card to Arion's face.

'What's that for?' she asked suspiciously.

'That card lets you into that lift.' He nodded towards the small lift to one side of his office, across from the one she'd come up in. 'The lift will take you straight to my penthouse. You'll wait for me there—'

'No way.' Perla stopped what was coming before he could finish.

His nostrils flared. 'Excuse me?'

'I won't do…whatever it is you have in mind. I know you think I'm nothing but some common whore but you're wrong. What happened between us that night wasn't cheap and it wasn't tawdry. Not for me at least. And I despise you for thinking I'd stoop that low to get you to help me—'

'Shut the hell up for one second and listen.' His rough command dried her words.

Her fist clenched. 'How dare you speak to me like—?'

'You said you have nowhere to stay. I have a meeting

in…exactly eight minutes which will last for five hours. Minimum. Unless you intend to wander the streets in the rain until I'm finished, my offer is the best you're going to get.'

Surprise stamped through her. 'Oh, you mean you want me to go up and just…wait for you?' she asked.

'Why, Mrs Lowell, you sound disappointed.'

Severely taken aback, it took her a minute to regroup. 'I assure you, I'm not.'

He held out the card. 'Good.'

With a hand she cursed for trembling, she took it and headed slowly for the lift, trepidation in her every step.

'Oh, and Perla?' he murmured mockingly.

She stopped and turned back to him. 'What?'

'Don't look so frightened. You're not going up to a den of iniquity. There's more to my apartment than a bed and a pole for you to perform on.'

Her hand tightened on the card. 'Wow, I'm shocked you even have those. The way you've been acting, I'd imagine a torture rack and thumb screws would be more accurate furnishings for the women you send up there.'

His eyes darkened and the hand lying on the table clenched into a fist. She'd scored a point in their battle of wills. Finally. But the victory felt hollow. With every word and every gesture, Arion tainted their one night together, letting bitterness fill the space where she'd known a few hours of joy. If only she could forget. But forgetting was impossible. Not when he sat there, so vital, so impossibly gorgeous.

So infuriatingly captivating.

'I've never invited a woman to my penthouse. Ever.'

'Oh, then I'll consider myself one lucky woman. Don't worry, I'll try not to skip with joy and ruin your priceless floors.' She quickened her steps towards the lift, eager to be out of his sight and escape that merciless tongue. The plastic key slid soundlessly into the designated slot and the lift whispered open. She turned and faced the office, not in the least bit surprised to find Arion's gaze fixed squarely on her.

She wriggled her fingers in a careless wave. 'See you in a few hours, charmer.'

He didn't take his eyes off her, nor did he respond to her mockery as the lift door shut. But the look in his eyes sent a shiver of unease through her.

And with every hour that passed, despite having been whisked up into what felt like the lap of luxury—Ari's personal chef had served her the most delicious three-course meal, after which she'd had a call from the concierge to find out whether she wanted a facial or pedicure while she waited—her tension escalated.

So much so that when she heard the lift whisper open she stopped breathing. She jerked up from the suede sofa and her feet hit the floor with a thud. The magazine she'd been reading—one of many supplied by the concierge—spilled onto the floor. She bent to pick it up and straightened to find him a foot away, those piercing hazel eyes pinned on her.

'You...uh, do you have news for me?' she blurted, more to stem the overwhelming force of his presence than a need for immediate answers.

But then she didn't see the need for pleasantries. They weren't friends. Hell, they weren't even lovers. They were two strangers who'd given in to a mad moment that had returned to haunt them with merciless cruelty.

'Is that how you greeted your husband when he returned from work?' he rasped.

Her shocked gasp made him freeze. She watched a contrite grimace cross his face.

'Forgive me, that was beyond tasteless,' he rasped.

'Not to mention extremely disrespectful. You know

nothing about my life with Morgan.' And she intended it to remain that way.

He clawed a hand through his hair. 'No, I didn't. I'm sorry.'

With jerky movements, he loosened then yanked his tie off and flung it on the sofa where she'd been sitting.

Not expecting his immediate apology, Perla was left floundering. 'Apology accepted,' she murmured, a little absently because suddenly she found herself wondering what it would be like to have a real husband come home to her.

A husband like…Arion?

Hell, no. They would drive each other homicidal within weeks.

But during that time too they would have hot, exquisite, mind-melting sex.

The heat that rushed over her made her take a step back and give herself a mental slap. She wasn't here to reminisce over dreams that wouldn't come true in a million years. She was here to save Terry and Sarah's home—*her home*—before the bank made good on their threat of repossession.

Focus.

But then how could she, when Arion, having discarded his tie, was now in the process of undoing his top buttons, revealing the gloriously sleek muscled chest she'd explored without shame or inhibition a little over three months ago?

He caught her stare and a look passed through his eyes. One she didn't want to interpret. One that made her rush to speech.

'I'm sorry if I seem to be rushing you but I'm hoping to catch the last train back to Bath tonight.'

He sauntered over to the drinks cabinet and poured a large whisky. She shook her head when he indicated the extensive array of drinks with a lifted brow.

She needed to keep her wits about her. The memory of

what had happened the last time she'd shared a drink with him was a reminder never to indulge around him. Ever.

'I had Sakis's people look into it.'

'And?'

He knocked back the drink without taking his eyes off her. 'You said he signed the part of his contract that allows you to receive spousal income on his death?'

'Yes.'

'So you're not aware he signed the Under-Forty waiver thereafter?' he asked.

Unease dredged through her stomach. 'What's an *Under-Forty waiver?*'

'All employees under forty can take the option of death insurance or a yearly double bonus in place of compensation to family on death. Once an employee turns forty the option is no longer available. Your husband was—'

'Morgan was a long way from forty when he died,' she supplied through numb lips.

Ari nodded. 'According to his line manager, he asked for that clause to be amended in favour of receiving the double bonus and he never reinstated the original clause. Therefore, you are not entitled to receive funds.'

Ari watched her expression go from shock to disbelief to anger, then back to disbelief. She opened then shut her mouth. Then her gaze narrowed suspiciously.

'Please tell me you're not toying with me or making this up because…because of…'

'For someone who seems intent on making me believe our incident is behind you, you seem to leap back to it at the slightest opportunity.'

'I wasn't… I just…I can't believe Morgan would do that to his parents.'

To his parents. Not to her. The curious statement set off alarm bells in his brain. He didn't like alarm bells. They reminded him that he'd refused to listen to them clanging long and hard in the years before his father's real character had been brought to light.

They reminded him that in the end he'd lived in false hope that the father he'd looked up to wouldn't attempt to throw him to the wolves to save himself.

'You think that the husband you were so happy to betray was less than honest with you? Need I point out the irony there?' he bit out more sharply than he wanted to, the memory of betrayal and devastation growing rawer by the minute.

'I didn't betray Morgan.' Again an expression a lot like pain crossed her face. He hardened himself against it. Much like he'd hardened himself against thinking about her all the way through his meeting. A meeting he had barely been able to control because he hadn't been able to tear his mind away from the fact that she was here, in his living space, touching his things, leaving the hypnotically seductive scent of her body all over the place.

Theos, what had he been thinking, offering her the use of his apartment when he could just as easily have sent her across the street to the luxury guest apartments they used for visiting executives? Because he hadn't wanted to risk her strutting into another bar, catching the eye of another hungry predatory male and offering them a taste of what she'd offered him.

Stasi!

The admonition did nothing to lift his mood. 'I have no interest in lying to you, nor do I take pleasure in prolonging this meeting. You came here seeking information. I've provided it. What you do with that information is now up to you. I suggest you come clean with your in-laws and find a way around it.'

Her eyes darkened further as she stared at him. '*Find a way around it*, just like that? You think it's that easy?'

He shrugged. 'I fail to see how any of this is my problem.'

She raised both hands and slid them through her long vibrant hair—hair she'd released from its tight bun at some point in the last few hours.

Ari found himself helplessly following the seductive ripple. Heat speared through him as he watched her pace to the window and back to where he stood, her agitated, breast-heaving breathing doing incredibly groin-hardening things to him.

She glared at him, the beginning of fire sparking those amazing green eyes. 'Surely I should've been informed of this change in his contract since I stood to lose from the amendment?' she railed at him.

The blatant statement of avarice made bitterness surge through him. Arion's father had torn their family apart, ripped it from its very foundations. All because of greed for money, carnal pleasure and power.

In the three months since his last encounter with Perla, he'd tried to blot the chaotic memories her actions had brought from his mind. He'd told himself that reacting to her the way he had at Macdonald Hall was because he'd been caught on the raw.

But, watching her now, he felt the same insidious desire creeping through him, damning him for being weak and helpless against his body's reaction to her.

When he'd finally been brought to justice, his father, although he hadn't shown an ounce of contrition, had confessed that he hadn't been able to help himself in the face of temptation.

A wave of despair washed over Ari now as he contemplated that perhaps he had a similar trait.

Hell, no!

But even that thought wasn't enough to stop his gaze from dropping to the hectic rise and fall of Perla's breasts as she paced his living room.

An image of her perfect rosy nipples and how they'd tasted in his mouth smashed through his mind.

Smothering the recollection, he took a few, much needed steps to his bar. 'It is what it is. Have you eaten?' he asked, then wondered why he was prolonging this meeting.

She dropped her hands, her expression incredulous. 'My life is in tatters and you're asking me if I want to eat?'

'Cut the melodrama. I was merely attempting to be courteous. I have nothing else to say to you on the matter of your husband's employment. Feel free to leave. Or stay and join me for dinner.' His hand tightened around the decanter as the invitation slipped out, almost without conscious thought.

'Why do you snarl every time you say the word *husband*? Morgan was your brother's tanker pilot, and I know things didn't end well…'

Ari raised a brow. 'You think things didn't *end well?*'

He knew Sakis had done a stellar job in saving the company's reputation and hidden the true extent of Morgan Lowell's sabotage from the press. But was she also oblivious to her husband's betrayal? Or had she merely blinded herself to her husband's true nature, the way she'd blithely hidden the fact that she was newly widowed when she'd climbed into his bed?

'I'm not trying to belittle what happened. I just don't understand why you look as if you have dog poo on your shoes whenever I use the word *husband!*'

'Perhaps I don't wish to be reminded of the dead.' Death had brought too much suffering, had left devastation in its path, wounds that could never be healed. Knowing it was death that had made their paths cross in the first place didn't ease the vice around his chest.

His answer seemed to sober her. 'No, neither do I,' she said.

Her steps were decidedly less agitated when she went to retrieve her large bag from the corner of his sofa.

She was leaving, walking out of his life again. That single thought sent a spark of fierce rebellion through his stomach. He didn't realise he'd placed himself between the lift and her until she stopped in front of him.

'Thank you for your help, Mr Pantelides.' Her words were polite enough and her eyes were determined enough but he didn't miss the slight wobble to her mouth.

Ari wanted to slide his thumb over that mouth, loosen it until its velvet plumpness slid smoothly against his skin.

'What are you going to do?' he asked.

Her eyes narrowed. 'I thought you didn't care?'

'People tend to get litigious in your circumstances. For your own sake and the in-laws you claim to care about, I would hate for you to take that route.'

She hitched her handbag up onto her shoulder, her eyes back to full glare. 'I detect a veiled threat in there. But, from where I'm standing, I have nothing to lose so I may or may not speak with a lawyer to weigh my options.'

'From where I'm standing, you have none. Do you have a job?'

Her gaze slid away and he got the distinct feeling she was about to be less than truthful. 'Kind of.'

'Kind of? Doing what?'

She carefully avoided his gaze. 'Oh, this and that. Not that it's any of your business.'

'And does *this and that* not provide you with enough to keep a roof over your head?'

Her eyes darted back to his, defiance burning in their depth. 'If you must know, I'm not working at the moment. But I had a job before I got married. Morgan encouraged me to take a leave of absence for a while so his mother wasn't left alone for long periods of time. Terry was a long-haul lorry driver.'

'Right, so your husband convinced you to abandon your career to play babysitter to his mother. And you agreed?'

'There's that tone again. Why the hell am I even bothering?' She tried to move past him. 'Goodbye, Mr Pantelides. I hope you don't get a nosebleed from that super lofty position on your high horse.'

He caught her by the waist. The slide of her cotton shirt over her skin reminded him of how it'd felt to undress her, to bare her softness to his touch. Ari's mouth watered with the fierce need to experience that act again.

Weak... Theos, he was weak, just like his father.

'Let me go.'

'No,' he said, feeling a thread of real fear in that word. He should let her go. Forget about her. Forget how she'd made him feel that night. Because everything that had come after that moment of bliss had brought him nothing but jagged pain.

'Yes! I refuse to talk to you when you act like I'm some lowlife who's wandered into your perfect little world.'

'The circumstances of our meeting—'

'Can be placed squarely at your feet. I told you to leave me alone in that bar. But you were too busy playing the alpha *me-big-man-you-little-woman* role to listen to me. If you'd left me alone to have my drink we wouldn't be in this position.'

He whirled and propelled her back against the wall next to the lift. He didn't like that description of him. Didn't like that he'd seen what he wanted and just gone for it. It struck too close to home, made him too similar to the man he'd desperately tried to forget all these years.

And yet, as if from another dimension, he heard his reply. 'You mean this position when all I can think about is tearing that prissy little skirt off you, yanking aside your panties and slamming inside you?'

Her gasp was hot on his face. He welcomed it. Welcomed the excuse to plunge his tongue between her lips and taste her the way he'd been longing to taste her since she'd walked into his office today.

She pushed frantically at his shoulders but Ari wasn't in the mood to be denied. Not until he'd taken a little bit of the edge off this insane, pulsating need. Besides, her lips had started to cling, to kiss him back.

He groaned as her tongue dashed out to meet his, tentatively at first, then with progressively daring thrusts that made his blood rush south with dizzying speed. He hitched her higher up on the wall, felt her moan vibrate through them as he palmed her breast.

God, she was hot. So damned hot. Her nipples were already hard nubs beneath his thumbs as he teased them. Her cries of pleasure made him thankful she was here with him, not in a bar somewhere being hit on by other men.

Her fingers scraped over his nape and up through his hair, then dropped back down to restlessly explore his shoulders.

Theos, she was as hungry for him as he was for her.

With impatient fingers he slid up her skirt. The scrap of lace he encountered made his blood boil some more. With a rough growl, he shredded them.

'Oh, God! I can't believe you just did that,' she gasped and stared down at the tattered lace in his hand.

'Believe it. My hunger for you is bordering on the insane, *glikia mou*. Be warned.' He took her lips in another kiss, bit down on the plump lower lip and felt her jerk with the sensation.

Without giving her time to think, he sank to his knees and parted her thighs.

Her eyes widened as she read his intention. 'Arion...'

He hadn't had time to explore her like this last time. But this time he fully intended to gorge on her.

'No,' she said, but he could read the excitement in her eyes.

He managed to drag his lips from the velvet temptation of her inner thigh and the seductive scent inches away. 'Why?'

'Because you'll hate yourself if we do this again. And you'll hate me. For whatever trivial reason, you think I soiled something for you by sleeping with you three months ago. Frankly, I don't want to have to deal with whatever that was again.'

The reminder sent a spear of ice and jagged pain through his heart. Before he could stop himself, he rose and his hand slid to her throat.

Her eyes widened, not with fear, but with wariness at the look he knew was on his face. Every condemning thought he was trying to keep at bay came flooding back.

'*Trivial?* You think my reason for blaming you for sullying that day is *trivial?*' Pain made his voice hoarse, his heart thud dully in his veins. He distantly registered the quickening pulse beneath his palm but he was too lost in his own turmoil to react to it.

'I don't know! You never told me why. You were only interested in shredding me for—'

'For sleeping with a soulless wanton and ruining my wife's memory for ever?'

CHAPTER FIVE

PERLA FELT THE blood drain from her face. From head to toe she went numb. So numb she couldn't move. Or speak. Or do anything apart from stare at the pain-racked face of the man who held her upright.

When the full meaning of his words sank in, she jerked from him, pushing him back with a strength that felt superhuman but only made him take one single step back.

'Your *wife?* You…you're *married?*' The word choked out of her throat.

His nostrils flared and the skin around his mouth whitened. 'Was. Same as you. Bereaved. Same as you. The night we met, I was mourning. *Unlike* you.'

The accusation slashed across her skin, waking her numbness. The tingle of pain came with a healthy dose of anger. 'What makes you think I wasn't in mourning too?'

'Let me see, you were discussing cocktails with the bartender and doing nothing to bat off his very clear interest in you.'

'And you think that automatically makes me less of a person? Because I wasn't snarling at a total stranger?'

'Your actions weren't those of a bereaved widow.'

'Everyone handles grief differently. Just because you chose to sit in a corner nursing your whisky and demanding silence doesn't mean you have the monopoly on heartache.'

She watched his face harden further. 'And what of the

events afterwards? Which step of the grieving process did you tick by sharing the bed of a stranger before your husband was even in the ground?'

Despite her reeling senses, she fought to keep her voice steady. 'That's what bothers you, isn't it? The fact that I committed some cardinal sin by seeking solace before I'd buried my husband.'

'Was that what you were doing? Seeking solace?' His gaze bored into her, almost as if he was willing her to answer in the affirmative.

Because that would make him see her in a better light?

She shook her head and started to straighten her clothes. 'Does it matter what I say? You've already judged and found me guilty. I slept with you three days before my husband was in the ground. Trust me, you don't detest me more than I detest myself. But tell me, what's your excuse? Why did you sleep with me, other than that I was a willing body with a fascinating hair colour you couldn't resist?'

Her question made him jerk backward. He frowned and slowly his hand fell away from her throat. Hazel eyes dropped to his hand, and she watched it slowly curl into a fist, then release.

'For some of us, the pain reaches a point when it becomes unbearable. You were there. You offered a willing distraction.'

For some of us...a willing distraction...

Perla wasn't sure which of the two statements hurt deeper. What she was sure of was that Arion believed both statements; believed she'd gone to the bar at Macdonald Hall for her own selfish reasons other than with grief in mind.

And, in a way, wasn't he half right? The actions that had propelled her out of her car had had more to do with her frustration and anger at what Morgan had done to her than with pure grief.

The grief had come later, of course. Because, despite everything else he'd put her through, his loss hurt the two people she'd come to see as surrogate parents.

Terry and Sarah had partly filled a void she'd longed for Morgan to complete. They'd treated her as their own, and for someone who'd known only the coldness of the state foster system for most of her life, it'd been a blessed feeling to finally be part of a loving family. To feel a degree of being wanted she'd never experienced before.

Of course, she couldn't tell Arion that; he wouldn't believe her. She'd all but thrown herself at him in that car park, just after prattling on about Santorini and weddings.

She knew her actions had fallen far short of that expected of a newly bereaved wife. But she refused to let him keep denouncing her as a whore.

'I went into that bar for a drink, nothing else. I've never picked up a man in my life. You were a mistake that shouldn't have happened. But you happened. We had a moment. You can choose to shame me over it for as long as you live if it makes you feel better. I prefer to put it behind me, forget it ever happened.'

Hazel eyes narrowed and her breath caught. She'd been trying to reason with him. Instead, she'd made him angrier.

'If you wanted to forget you shouldn't have come here today. You should've appointed a representative and made them deal with this situation on your behalf. Coming here and parking yourself in my lobby tells me forgetting was the last thing on your mind.'

'You're wrong! Besides, I live in the real world, Mr Pantelides. Representatives and lawyers cost money. Hiring one to do the job I was perfectly capable of doing myself is irrational. The only thing this trip's cost me is a train ticket.'

One smooth eyebrow rose. Then his hand glided back to her neck, then down to her shoulder to rest just beneath her breast. 'Are you sure?' His breathing had grown slightly ragged and his other hand was now flexing through her hair, toying with it.

'Mr Pantelides—'

'You once told me my given name pleases you,' he murmured in that deadly low voice.

Her breath hitched. 'How can I forget if you keep reminding me?'

'Perhaps I don't want you to forget. Perhaps I want you to relive the pain and devastation and the pleasure with me.' One thumb teased her nipple and she felt her knees give way. 'If I have to be like *him,* then maybe I deserve whatever I get.'

The rawness in his voice struck deep inside her. 'Like who?'

He shook his head. 'No one. We've already committed the crime, Perla *mou.* The guilt will never leave us.'

Sensation bombarded and it was all she could do to keep her thoughts straight. 'So your solution is to commit the crime again?'

'If you'd stayed away, that would've ended the matter. But you're here now, front and centre, and I find that I lack the willpower to let you walk away.'

Her shocked laughter scraped her throat. 'You speak as if I have some sort of power over you—'

'You enthralled me from the moment I saw you.' The words were spoken with no pleasure. None. There wasn't even a hint of a compliment in there.

'I'm sorry I affect you that way. Let go of me and I'll remove myself from your presence.'

His laugh was self-deprecatory. 'I've had you wedged against this door for the last twenty minutes. A gentleman would've offered you a drink, shown you the spectacular view from the tower deck, then offered to have you chauffeured home.'

'There's absolutely nothing stopping you from doing that.'

'But there is. Perla, I'm not a gentleman. Your panties are shredded at my feet and in the next sixty seconds I intend to be deep inside you.'

The words murmured, hot and urgent, against her neck made her close her eyes against the drugging inevitability that assailed her. Need, ten times more powerful than she'd experienced the first time with him, shot to her sex, leaving her drowning in liquid heat.

Perla barely managed a squeak when he swung her up in his arms and strode purposefully down a hallway. He stopped at the first door on his right and thrust it open to reveal a large white-carpeted bedroom. Black and chrome stood out in sharp contrast to each other, with no warmth or decorative aesthetics to lighten the mood.

He deposited her on the bed and pulled off her skirt, then froze. His mouth worked soundlessly for several seconds before the groan exploded from his chest.

'I thought I imagined how exquisite you were but I didn't.' Again the words were spoken with a starkness that caused a sliver of ice to pierce her pleasure.

'Arion...'

He rubbed the back of his knuckles across her sex, then stepped back and undressed with swift, jerky movements.

Pulling her thighs wide apart, he muttered something in his native language, his fingers biting into her thighs.

Sucking in a needy breath, she glanced up at him and almost wished she hadn't.

He looked tortured, his face a hard mask of desire as he surged inside her. He'd already damned himself by sleeping with her the first time.

They were caught in a spell neither seemed capable of breaking, and she watched that knowledge eat him alive as he penetrated deeper inside her.

'Ari...' It felt wrong, but it also felt so right, just like it had the first time.

The need to pull him back from his torment, if only for a moment, made her reach for him.

She touched his face and he refocused on her. Hazel eyes stared deep into hers as he increased the tempo of his thrusts. Almost possessed, he took her pleasure to another level. By the time her orgasm tore through her, she believed she'd touched something sacred. With a guttural cry, he followed her into ecstasy. Deep convulsions ripped through him as he collapsed on top of her. Her hand slid from his face to cradle his sweat-slicked neck. She shut her eyes as sensation drifted into calm. She knew it was elusive; that what they'd done was in no way calming or solace-giving.

They'd given in to their animal instincts. Had let that damning temptation run free. And yet...

Before she could complete the thought, he surged upright and swung himself off the bed. Keeping his back turned, he pulled on his boxers and trousers.

'The bathroom's through there. Get dressed and come and find me. We need to talk,' he threw over his shoulder before he left the room.

Dazed and confused, she lay there for several minutes, staring at the beautifully designed chrome ceiling lights. It took several deep breaths and a severe talking-to before she managed to pull herself together.

She returned to the living room to find him at the window, still shirtless and breathtakingly gorgeous.

He turned at her entrance and raked a hand through his hair. 'Are your in-laws expecting you back tonight?' he asked, his eyes exhibiting none of the tormented pleasure she'd witnessed minutes ago.

'Yes,' she responded warily, wondering where he was going with his enquiry.

He nodded. 'Then I'll make it fast. Pantelides Inc. has

been through a lot in the past few years. I don't wish to draw any more unwanted attention to the company.' He went to the desk and picked up a pad and pen.

'Write your account details on here. I'll have funds transferred to your account first thing in the morning.'

The pain she'd been holding in a tight ball since she got up from his bed burst into her chest. 'Excuse me?' she rasped.

'I'm not unsympathetic to the fact that your husband left you in dire straits. I'm trying to make some form of reparation,' he replied, his voice still devoid of emotion.

'By sleeping with me and immediately offering me money afterwards?' Her own voice was sickeningly shaky and pain-filled but she didn't shy away from it. She wanted Arion Pantelides to know exactly what she thought of him. 'Why don't you come right out and book me for a repeat performance next Tuesday?'

His jaw tightened. 'What happened tonight won't happen again.'

'*Hallelujah!* Finally, something we both agree on. I thought you were pretty vile to accuse me of the things you accused me of before. But this…this is a new low.'

His grip tightened around the pad until it buckled beneath his strength. His gaze lowered but the rigid determination in his face didn't abate. 'Okay, perhaps the timing is unfortunate—'

'*You think?*' she snapped.

'But the offer remains. It's your choice whether to accept it or decline.'

'You can shove your offer where the sun doesn't shine!' She stalked past him to where she'd dropped her bag what felt like a thousand years ago. Snatching it up, she marched to the lift and pressed the button. Nothing happened. She stabbed harder, feeling her chin wobble with impending tears.

Dear God, no! No way was she going to cry in front of him.

'You need this.'

She turned. He was holding up the triangular card he'd given her earlier. She went to snatch it from him but he pulled it back at the last second.

'Perla—'

'No, don't say my name. You lost the right to speak to me when you offered me money for sleeping with you, you disgusting bastard.'

'Stop and think for a moment. The two situations have nothing to do with one another. You're being melodramatic again.'

'And you're being a complete ass who is holding me here against my will.'

'Think rationally. It's almost midnight. You're putting yourself in danger by attempting to return home at this time of night.'

'After everything you've said to me, you expect me to believe my safety concerns you?' She gave a very unlady-like snort and glanced pointedly at the lift.

'Perla—'

'The only thing I want from you is to make the lift work, Ari. I want to leave. Right now.'

He sighed, and again she heard that weariness in his voice. 'I may not be a gentleman but I'm not averse to being schooled.'

She frowned when she realised he wasn't mocking her. He really meant it.

Turning, she faced him fully. 'First off, I wouldn't force a woman who wants to leave to stay against her will.'

He nodded, came forward and offered her the card. She took it.

'Second, don't ever, *ever* try to give a woman you've

just slept with money. No matter your intention, it comes off as super sleazy.'

Hazel eyes gleamed before his eyelids veiled his expression. 'But your situation still needs to be addressed.'

'It's my problem. I'll take care of it.'

He took a deep breath and she couldn't stop her eyes from devouring the sculpted chest that rose and fell. 'What were your skills before you gave up your career?'

The out-of-the-blue question threw her for a moment. Then she cleared her throat and tore her gaze away from the golden perfection of his skin. 'I was an events organiser for a global conglomerate.' She named her previous employer and his eyes widened a touch.

The fact that she'd managed to impress Arion Pantelides sent a fizz of pleasure through her.

'I'm leaving for LA in the morning but Pantelides Luxe has been on a recruitment drive for the last six weeks.' He scribbled a name and number on the mangled pad and passed it to her. 'If you're interested in interviewing for a job, call this number and speak to *my* head of HR.'

Unsure how to take the offer, she stared at him. 'Why are you doing this?' she finally blurted.

'I'm trying to find an alternative solution to your problem. Is this too not acceptable?' he asked, his face set in its usual world-weary lines.

'It's acceptable but I'm not sure it's the right solution for me.'

He shoved his hands into his trouser pockets. 'From where I'm standing, your options are slim to nil. Don't take too long in deciding or you'll find yourself back to square one.'

'Okay…thanks.' Her limbs felt heavy as she turned away. She told herself it was because she was drained from the head-on collision with Arion, and not the disconcerting realisation that she didn't want to leave. Because *that* would be ridiculous.

She slid the card through its slot and heard the smooth whirring of the lift.

'May I make another suggestion?' he asked. The sensation of his breath on her neck told her he'd moved close. Far closer than was good for her equilibrium.

She glanced over her shoulder. Up close, his sexy stubble made her want to run her hand over his jaw, feel its roughness just one more time. 'What?' She forced herself to speak.

'Allow my driver to get you back home?'

The thought of slogging through the rain to catch the last train to Bath made her waver dangerously. The sudden realisation that she could be doing so minus her panties made her stomach flip over.

She could stand on principle and endure a hugely uncomfortable journey, or she could give in this once. 'Okay.'

'I'll give him a half hour heads-up. It'll give us time to eat something on the tower deck before you leave.'

It took all of two minutes the next day to realise she had zero options. And really, had her head not been full of singeing memories of what she'd done with Ari the night before, she'd have come to that realisation a lot sooner.

But as much as she'd tried to push the shocking events that had stemmed from her complete lack of control from her mind, the more the vivid memories had tumbled forth.

She'd slept with Ari Pantelides for a second time, even after his blistering condemnation of her reasons for doing so the first time. Almost a day later, her internal muscles throbbed with the delicious friction of his possession.

But, even now, it was the vivid memory of his tortured face that haunted her.

Enough!

Perla glanced down at the piece of paper Ari had handed her. A quick call to a local lawyer this morning had reiterated Ari's warning. She had no recourse because Morgan had changed the terms of his contract.

Unless a miracle fell into her lap—and she was cynical enough to realise those were rarer than unicorn teeth—she and Morgan's parents were headed for the welfare office.

While her prior experience had been with only one large chain of hotels, she'd excelled at her job and enjoyed it enough to feel a tiny thrill at being given an opportunity to re-enter the business world again.

As for Ari…

According to her previous search, he was rarely in London and therefore the chances that they would meet again were minuscule.

Ignoring the stab of discontentment that realisation brought, she grabbed the phone and dialled the number before she lost her nerve.

The swiftness with which her previous job history was taken and the interview scheduled left her floundering. As did the realisation that the interview itself would be spread over two days.

Feelings of insecurity started to rush back, a legacy, she knew, from her dealings with Morgan. Although she hated herself, she couldn't stop the feeling from growing.

When she found her fingers hovering over the phone an hour later, contemplating calling back to cancel the interview, she pursed her lips and straightened her spine.

Morgan might have succeeded in whittling away her self-confidence, through threats and blackmail, but giving in now would see her in the far more precarious position of being without means to support herself and his parents.

Besides, she was getting ahead of herself. Maybe she wouldn't even get this job—

No!

She might not believe in unicorns but neither would she succumb to doom and gloom. Taking a deep breath, she stepped back from the phone and went to find her in-laws.

Explaining to them why she had to return to London again so soon was a little delicate, seeing as she'd told them the outcome of her previous visit. She didn't want to get their hopes up because she'd been out of the job market for far too long and knew realistically she could fall flat on her face the first time, positive thinking or not.

'Are you sure that's what you want to do? London is so far away,' Sarah said worriedly.

'Nonsense, it's only a short commute by train. And don't forget, we need all the help we can get right now. We wish you all the best, Perla. Don't we, Sarah?' Terry glanced at his wife.

Sarah smiled, her eyes brightening a little from the devastating sadness still lurking in their brown depths. 'Of course we do. It's just that…we don't know what we'd do without you now that Morgan is…' Tears filled her eyes and she dabbed at them with the hanky Terry slipped into her hand.

Perla felt her throat clog and quickly swallowed. *This* was the reason she'd stayed. The reason she'd kept Morgan's secret and given up her career.

Watching them console each other in their grief, the need to protect them surged higher. From the moment she'd been introduced to Terry and Sarah Lowell, they'd taken her into their hearts. After the devastation of Morgan's revelation, she'd known, just as he'd deviously surmised, that she couldn't turn her back on the only promise of a proper home she'd ever known.

Neither could she reveal the secret that would've destroyed his parents.

The familiar guilt for the secret she carried and could never share made her rise from her seat. 'I...I'd better go and brush up on my interview techniques.'

In the hallway, she paused for a second to steady her breathing. Then she straightened.

Morgan was gone. Terry and Sarah were her responsibility now.

Briskly, Perla entered her bedroom and busied herself sorting through her meagre clothes. Three interviews in two days meant she would have to be inventive with her wardrobe.

The black skirt and satin shirt she'd worn to London would have to make another appearance. As would the black dress she'd worn the night she'd met Ari.

Laying the garments on the bed, she couldn't help the treacherous bite of sensation that nipped at her. Both outfits held memories she'd rather forget, of Ari's hands on her body, undressing her, stripping her bare before taking her with masterful possession.

Heat flared high, making her fingers shake as she scraped back her hair and forced the memories away.

She had no business thinking about another man in this house; in this room. Even if that man was the only person in her life who'd made her feel special and wanted for a brief moment in time. Even if the memory of his face as he'd taken her forced feelings of protectiveness as well as desire to surge into her chest.

It was over and done with. Move on.

'Congratulations and welcome to the company.'

Perla heard the words from far off, still numbly disbelieving that she'd actually got through the gruelling interviews to secure a job on the Pantelides Luxe events management team.

'I...thank you.'

The two other candidates who'd also been offered similar jobs out of the twenty-five candidates wore similar expressions of pleased wonderment.

She'd got the job, with a salary and benefits that had left her mouth agape when she'd read them on her contract. Now she forced herself to focus as the head of HR continued to speak.

'For those who require the option, your first month's salary will be paid to you in advance of month's end. Just tick that option when you sign your contract. But remember if you should decide to leave the company before the first thirty days are up, you will be required to reimburse the company.' He looked directly at her as he said that.

Slowly anger and embarrassment replaced the stunned pleasure.

Had Ari Pantelides been so unprofessional as to share her private financial affairs with others? It was bad enough that she'd seen the morbidly curious looks on a few of the employees' faces as she'd been introduced. She was well aware that the widow of the man whose actions had caused a Pantelides oil tanker to crash and pollute a breathtaking African coast only a few short months ago was the last person they expected to seek employment in this company.

Knowing that her financial dire straits were being shared with others made her skin crawl with shame.

Forcing her head high, she returned the older man's stare, barely hearing the end of his welcome speech as she tried to grapple with her emotions. Fifteen minutes later, contract in hand, she started to leave the room.

The low hum of her mobile had her rooting through her handbag.

'Hello?'

'I understand congratulations are in order.' The voice, deep and gravel-rough, sent a pulse of heat through her belly.

'I...how did you get my phone number?' she blurted to cover her inner floundering.

'You're now my employee, Perla. Prepare yourself for the fact that some of your life is now an open book to me.'

A shiver went through her at the low, dark promise. As much as she tried to tell herself she wasn't affected, his voice did things to her that were indecent. Her hand tightened on the phone. 'So open that you decided to share some of it with your HR director?' she demanded.

'Excuse me?'

'Did you tell your HR director that I needed money?' The very thought of it made her flush with mortification.

'Why would I do that?' He sounded amused. Vaguely it occurred to her that he didn't sound as tormented and as bleak as he had a few days ago. Why that thought lifted her heart, she refused to contemplate as she reminded herself why she was annoyed with him.

'Because he offered a month's salary in advance. I may have been out of the general workforce a while but even I know that salaries don't get paid in advance.'

'Did he offer only you that option?' he asked.

'No, he offered it to the other new employees as well.'

He remained silent for several heartbeats. 'The reason for that perk is because most of the people I hire for the role you're filling are young, dynamic graduates. *Broke*, young, dynamic graduates who I expect to hit the ground running. The last thing I want them to be thinking about is how to pay their rent or feed themselves. If and when I headhunt other talent, I offer them signing-on bonuses too. Either way, everyone gets the same treatment.'

The bruised hurt eased a little. 'Oh, so I wasn't singled out for special treatment?'

'Now you sound disappointed,' he mocked in a low tone that was equally as lethal to her senses.

'I'm not.' And of course, now he'd explained the reason for the stipulation, it made total sense. How better to keep his employees happy and loyal than to ease the one thing certain to add to their anxiety in their first months of employment? Realising there was something else she needed to do, she cleared her throat. 'Thank you…for giving me this opportunity. I promise I won't let you down.'

Again a thoughtful silence greeted her words. 'I'm glad to hear it, Perla, because I'm giving you the chance to prove it sooner rather than later.'

Her heart jumped into her throat. 'What do you mean?'

'It means I'm throwing you in at the deep end. You fly out to join me in Miami after your accelerated orientation tomorrow. My assistant will provide you with the details.'

CHAPTER SIX

TEN VIP GUESTS.

Miami Fashion Week.

What could go wrong? It turned out to be plenty as Perla doused yet another metaphorical fire four days later, this time in the form of a wardrobe malfunction for one of the guests—a social media mogul's wife, minutes before she was due to head down to the Pantelides V3 Hotel & Casino.

She curbed the urge to blurt out that she was an events organiser not a stylist and placed a phone call to summon the harried stylist. Twenty minutes later, after the crisis had been averted, the young blonde cast a grateful glance at Perla as they rode the lift down to the lobby.

'I should've gone for something like what you're wearing instead of this…this thing.' She indicated the blue organza multi-layered dress that showed off more cleavage and bare back than Perla would ever be comfortable showing.

Her own knee-length silk dress, although slashed dramatically at the waist and side, was covered with thin mesh netting that made her feel not quite so…exposed. And the long fitted sleeves made of the softest leather offered further boosting confidence.

'That black totally rocks against the vivid colour of your hair. You must give me the name of your colourist. Everyone tells me red and curly is the new black this season.'

The blonde flicked her straight hair back and offered a brittle smile.

Again Perla bit her tongue, smiled back and discreetly checked her watch. The pre-runway show drinks would be served in exactly six minutes. Although she realised she was probably being rude by not responding and discussing her now extensive wardrobe that had come courtesy of her generous Pantelides clothes expense account, she couldn't think beyond the fact that in a few minutes she'd be coming face to face with Ari for the first time in almost a week.

By the time she'd arrived in Miami, he'd left for New York and she'd been given three days to prep for the arrival of the special guests, who ranged from a young senator to Hollywood royalty.

The earlier sailing trip around Biscayne Bay had been a success despite one guest almost ending up being launched overboard after one too many mojitos.

Keeping her fingers crossed for the same success tonight, she pasted a smile on her face as the lift doors opened onto the foyer that led to the cordoned-off VIP lounges where the runway shows were being held.

Ari Pantelides stood with a group of guests. Head and shoulders above most men, he was the first person she saw when she stepped forward.

The punch to her solar plexus winded her for an instant. Her mouth dried as she took in his imposing shoulders and breathtaking physique.

It really was a sin how one man could possess such a strikingly commanding presence. He turned to another guest and Perla caught a glimpse of that designer stubble. The memory of its roughness against her breasts and thighs sent a pulse of heat straight between her legs.

God, she really needed to get a grip. Like, right now!

Of course, he chose that moment to turn his head towards her.

Hooded eyes speared hers before they rose to rest on her hair. Recalling his fascination with her hair, she fought the foolish urge to touch the elaborate knot she'd worked the tresses into.

You're here to work!

The stern reminder focused her a little.

Turning to the blonde woman at her side, she said, 'I'll be around if you require anything else, Mrs Hamilton. Otherwise, I'll see you at the show in an hour.'

She left Selena Hamilton to find her husband and headed straight for the head waiter. After reassuring herself that everything was running smoothly, she found a quiet corner and activated her mini tablet. Double and triple-checking every detail was essential. The two designers whose shows they would be visiting were temperamental at the best of times and, with runway shows, seating arrangements could descend into chaos with little warning.

'*Kalispera,* Perla.'

Her hand trembled and she nearly lost her hold on her tablet as the deep voice washed over her. Her one visit to Santorini meant she understood the greeting.

Her head snapped up and her eyes collided with steady hazel eyes. 'Good evening, Ar…Mr Pantelides. How was your trip?'

His eyes narrowed slightly at the hasty correction but he didn't comment on it. 'Predictable. You seem to have settled in okay. I hear your boat trip today was interesting.'

It wasn't a question and she had very little doubt that he'd been checking up on her since her arrival.

'Yes, it hasn't been smooth sailing, pardon the pun, but the orientation was very useful. And your head of Events let me shadow him for a day to get the hang of things. That was useful too…' She stopped when she realised she was babbling. But, with him standing so close, she was dealt the full force of his powerful aura and the spicy scent of his aftershave. She'd smelled him up close and personal and knew continuing to breathe him in was not a very wise idea. 'Anyway, I need to get back to work.'

He stopped her with a brush of his fingers down her arm. Electricity shot through her body. 'How did your in-laws take your new status?' he asked.

She froze, looked at him to see if he was being sarcastic but his eyes only held mild interest. 'A lot better than some of the Pantelides employees.' She bit her lip at the slip. She'd meant to let the avidly curious looks and whispers behind her back slide right over her. But it'd been hard not to be affected.

Her stomach hollowed when his eyes narrowed. 'Who's been giving you a hard time?' he asked, his voice low and dangerous enough to send a shiver down her spine.

'Sorry, I didn't stop long enough to take names. Besides, can you really blame them? Morgan's actions nearly brought down your company.'

He stilled. 'So you know the full details of what he did?'

Perla frowned. 'Of course I know. Even though your brother tried to protect me from the whole truth, I got enough from the papers to put the pieces together. Frankly, I was surprised Morgan's benefits weren't stripped from him, all things considered.'

His jaw clenched for a moment before his face cleared. 'Those benefits weren't advantageous to you in the end, though, were they? It must have been upsetting to find out that the man you loved would betray you that way?' This time there was a definite question in his tone. His incisive gaze bored right into her. As if he was trying to understand her. And, more specifically, her actions on the night they'd met.

To admit that she hadn't been thinking straight when she'd slept with him—least of all of her dead husband—would only make things worse. 'It's not easy to find out, no.' But compared to the bombshell she'd received on the night of her wedding it was a walk in the park.

'I'm aware that betrayal has a way of messing with people's minds.' A hint of that torment she'd glimpsed made an appearance. As did the curiously strong need to alleviate it for him.

Brushing it away, she answered, 'Are we talking people generally or do you have personal knowledge of this?'

He stepped closer, blocking out the rest of the room and giving her no choice but to inhale his scent, to look into those unique gold-flecked hazel eyes. 'I've been dealt a few life lessons but I'm talking about you. Was that why you slept with me?' he breathed with a quiet intensity. 'To assuage your sense of betrayal?'

'Why are we going over this again?'

He murmured something pithy under his breath. 'Perhaps I'm trying to make sense of it all. Trying to square things in my mind so I can move on.'

Shame scythed through her as she admitted that she didn't want it squared away. She wanted to remember that night; to treasure it as the special moment in time it'd been for her. Of course, she knew she could never tell him that.

Straightening her spine, she returned his stare. 'Morgan's decisions and actions were his own. For my part, I married him for better or worse; he was the man I'd pledged to honour and cherish. And yes, before you remind me again, I broke that vow before he was even buried. Was I upset that things turned out the way they did? Of course I am.' A trill of laughter from a guest grounded her to where she was. 'I also think that this is the last place we should be discussing this. Frankly, I'd prefer it if we buried the subject once and for all. Can we do that, please?'

He stared down at her for several minutes before he inhaled deeply. He took a single step back and nodded. 'Consider the matter buried.'

She managed to nod before glancing over his shoulder. Several guests were looking their way, no doubt wondering why she'd commandeered Ari's attention. 'I need to get back to work, earn the generous salary you're paying me.'

His lips pursed but he gave her enough room to slide past. 'I look forward to seeing you in action.'

Perla wasn't sure if it was a threat or anticipation. And she couldn't dwell on it because her insides were churning from the exchange. Once again, it had seemed as if her reason for sleeping with him mattered to him.

Far from being a distraction as he'd claimed, it seemed he couldn't stop thinking about that night any more than she could.

Could she trust him not to bring it up again? Could she trust herself not to blurt out that it'd meant more than just a means to alleviate her pain?

She sucked in a deep breath and pinned a smile on her face. She'd survived Morgan and the debacle that had been her marriage.

She was a lot stronger now for it. She just needed to keep reminding herself of it.

Both runway shows went without a hitch. Watching from the back, Perla breathed a sigh of relief when the lights went up and her guests started to finish off their vintage champagne. Another few minutes and she could start herding them back to the limos to return to the Pantelides Casino for the gambling part of the evening. That was the most important part because it was why Ari had organised this event in the first place—

'Relax,' Ari said from beside her. How could a man so big, move so silently? 'You're off to a good start if Selena Hamilton is singing your praises. According to her, the two of you are BFFs now.' He picked up two glasses of pink champagne from a hovering waiter's tray and offered one to her.

'I wouldn't go that far but I'm glad she's pleased.' She took the champagne but didn't take a sip, much as she wanted to. The need for liquid courage was what had placed her in Ari Pantelides's crosshairs in the first place.

She was not going to make the mistake of drinking around him ever again.

'She isn't the only one who is impressed by your efficiency.'

Unable to help herself, she looked up at him. Hazel eyes captured hers and her breath snagged in her chest. 'Oh?'

'Her husband was equally effusive. Twice as much, in fact.' A hard bite had materialised in his tone.

She swallowed. 'What are you implying?'

He shrugged. 'He has wandering hands. Make sure you're not caught between them.'

On the surface, it seemed like a fair warning. Perhaps she was reading more into the situation than was necessary. They stared at each other for several heartbeats before she nodded. 'Thanks for the heads-up.'

His eyes flicked to her hair and again the punch of heat returned. Never in her wildest imagination would she have thought the colour of her hair would produce such a reaction. But every time Ari's gaze slid hungrily over her hair she felt hot, bothered and more than a little on edge. Before she could stop it, a small sound escaped her throat.

His gaze locked on hers once more. The air thickened around them, blocking the sounds of the party and locking them in their own sensual cocoon.

'Please, don't.' She was very much aware that she was begging. For as long as she could remember she'd wanted someone to notice her, give her a little bit of their time and attention. Although she'd found that to some extent with Terry and Sarah, it ultimately wasn't the right kind.

The attention Ari was giving her now *felt* like the right kind. Which was extremely frightening because it was the skull-and-crossbones kind, guaranteed to annihilate her with minimal effort.

'I'm as puzzled by my fascination as you are, *pethi mou*,' he murmured. 'Or perhaps my inner ten-year-old is still reeling from the discovery that his favourite TV actress's red hair came from a bottle,' he said dryly.

'How traumatic for you. Would it be better if I dyed my hair black or shaved it all off?' she half teased.

He sucked in a sharp breath and his grip tightened around his glass. 'I invite you to dare,' he breathed in a low, dangerous voice.

'You know, this would be the moment when I tell you that it's *my* hair, and I can do with it what I choose.'

'And I would in turn threaten to lock you up in a faraway dungeon until you came to your senses.'

Against her will, she felt a smile curve her lips. His mouth twitched too, as if sharing her amusement, but then his face turned serious again, and they went back to staring at each other.

Dirty, delicious thoughts of dungeons and shirtless heroes cascaded through her brain, sending spikes of desire darting through her body.

Realising just how pathetic she was being to take pleasure in the possessive tone in his voice, she cleared her throat. 'Can I make a suggestion?'

He took a sip of his drink without taking his eyes off her. She desperately wished she could follow suit but she needed to stay as clear-headed as possible. 'Go ahead.'

'Perhaps if we agree to stay out of each other's way, this…*thing* will eventually go away.'

'Haven't you heard the new saying? *Abstinence makes the heart grow fonder?*'

'I think we can both agree our hearts aren't the problem here.'

His face slowly froze until it was a hard, inscrutable mask. 'No. They're most definitely not.' The depth of feeling in his voice made something sharp catch in her chest. Again that torment stained his expression.

'You must miss her very much. Your wife,' she blurted before she could stop herself.

His fingers tightened so forcefully around the stem of his glass she feared it would snap. 'Sofia's death is a loss to the world. And to me.' The agony in his voice cut right into her heart.

Unable to look into his face, bleak with pain and guilt, she glanced away. Her own fingers were curled around the warming glass of champagne which trembled wildly, threatening to spill its contents. Hurriedly, she set it down on a nearby table.

'I never got the chance to say it before. I'm sorry...for your loss. Um, please excuse me. I think I'm needed now.'

She hurried away before she could do or say something rash, like ask him to define what that kind of love felt like. Or expose the emotion writhing through her that felt shamefully like jealousy.

She'd wanted a love like that for herself, had built all her hopes around Morgan, who had taken her desperate need and used it to blackmail her. Fate had kicked her in the teeth for daring to hold out her hand and ask.

She wasn't foolish enough to even contemplate asking a second time. The lesson had been well and truly delivered.

Ari watched Perla walk away, stunned by what he'd just revealed. He never spoke about Sofia. Never. Not to his brothers, not to his mother. And certainly not to traitorous strangers he'd made the colossal mistake of sleeping with.

And yet, with one simple sentence, he'd spilled his guts;

would've spilled some more if Perla hadn't rushed away. Because the admission of how Sofia—a warm-hearted, gentle innocent whom he'd ruthlessly clung onto and used to soothe his ravaged soul right after his father's betrayal—had come into his life and ultimately left it, had been right there on his tongue.

Absently nodding to a guest who'd approached and started talking to him, he tried to reel in his flailing senses.

It was unconscionable that he still felt this unrelenting pull towards Perla Lowell. What had happened between them—twice—should've been enough to curb whatever appetites he hadn't even realised were growing until he'd met her.

At first he'd thought his fascination with her was because she was the first woman he'd slept with after Sofia. That had been his excuse in the weeks following his discovery of her real identity.

And the second time?

He gritted his teeth. The second time, their emotions had been running high. So high, he hadn't had the common sense to use a condom. Hell, even that little nugget hadn't hit him until he was halfway across the Atlantic on his way to the US. A shudder raced under his skin at the sheer stupidity of his actions.

How many times, growing up, had he cautioned his brothers on the responsibility of taking care of their sexual health and those of the women they slept with, especially after finding out the bitter and humiliating legacy their father had left behind?

Granted, both Sakis and Theo were old enough now and no longer his responsibility. But for him to have fallen in the same trap, under the same spell that—

Enough. Beating himself up about it would achieve nothing. He smothered his thoughts and concentrated on the guest next to him, expertly hiding his distaste when he saw who it was trying to get his attention.

'She's something, your new organiser.' Roger Hamilton's gaze was fixed on Perla as she spoke to his guests, her smile open and friendly. The clear interest in his eyes sent a bolt of anger through Ari.

'She's also off-limits.' The snarl in his tone was unmistakable.

Hamilton's eyes widened, then his thin lips curved in a sly, knowing grin. 'Right, she's marked territory. Got it, buddy.'

Ari gritted his teeth and opened his mouth to deny the assertion. 'Very marked. And I'm very territorial. Are we clear?' *Theos*, where had that come from? He was losing his mind. There was no doubt about that.

Roger slapped him on the arm. 'As crystal, buddy. But tell me something; between you and I, is that hair colour real?'

Ari's fists clenched so hard his knuckles screamed in protest. From the first, he'd found an almost unholy fascination with Perla's hair. To hear that same fascination in another man's voice made the blackest fury roll through him.

'That, *buddy*,' he breathed, 'is something you'll never find out.'

From then on, he made sure he kept a room's width between himself and Perla at all times. Not that he actively needed to. She seemed just as determined to stay away from him.

A thought that should've pleased him, but only succeeded in darkening his mood further. On impulse, he pulled his phone out of his pocket and dialled.

Theo answered on the first ring. 'A call from the big man himself. I haven't been naughty, have I?'

'You tell me. And while you're at it, tell me what the

hell is so captivating about Rio that you can't seem to tear yourself from the place?'

His youngest brother laughed. 'Sun, sea and wall-to-wall gorgeous women. Need I say more?' Despite his tone, there was something cagey that set Ari's radar buzzing.

'Is everything okay, man?' The worry that never abated when it came to his brothers rose higher. Of all his family members, Theo had been the youngest and most vulnerable when their world had unravelled, thanks to his father. That worry had never gone away.

'Of course. How about you? Normally, you send me terse one-line emails asking me to report in.'

'Half of which you never answer. Thought I'd try another means to get your attention.'

Theo remained silent for a minute. 'You sure you're okay, bro?'

A flash of red caught his eye and he tensed further. 'I'm fine. But it would be good to row again, all three of us, some time soon.'

'Ah, you're nostalgic to get your ass whopped. I can oblige. But would this need to burn energy have anything to do with the headache you've created for yourself by hiring the Lowell woman?'

He gave an inward sigh. 'You've heard?'

Theo snorted. 'The whole company's wondering if you've lost your mind. Hell, *I'm* wondering if you've lost your mind. *Theos*, she's not blackmailing you in any way, is she?' he asked sharply.

The tense note in Theo's voice made Ari's hand clench over his phone as a wave of pain swept over him. Theo had been kidnapped as a teenager and their family held to ransom for a tense two weeks before he'd been released, which made the subject of blackmail a very volatile one.

'No, she needed a job, she proved to have the skill and I gave her one.'

'Did you run it past Sakis, because I'm pretty sure he'll blow a gasket once he crawls out of his love cocoon and returns to the real world.'

Ari's jaw tightened. 'I'll deal with Sakis. In the meantime, have your assistant check schedules with mine about our next rowing session. I want to get together sooner rather than later, and get to the bottom of exactly what you're doing in Rio.'

'Dammit, anyone would think I was still twelve instead of a grown man.'

'You'll always be a twelve-year-old to me, brother, simply because you can't help but act like one.' He noticed the gruffness in his voice but couldn't help it.

He hung up to Theo's pithy curse and realised he was smiling. Pocketing his phone, he looked up and found Perla's gaze on him. Wide green eyes held shock and wonder, which she quickly tried to bank. When he realised it was in reaction to his smile, he cursed under his breath.

Was it really so strange that he would smile? Was he such an ogre that he'd given the impression that smiling was beyond him?

Yes...

A lance of pain speared his heart. Smiling and laughter had become a thing of the past for him, ever since he'd lost the most precious thing in his life through hubris and carelessness. He'd believed he'd paid enough, sacrificed enough for his family and deserved happiness of his own. He'd believed he'd bled enough to owe fate nothing else.

He'd been careless with Sofia's health, given in to her penchant to always look on the bright side, when deep down he'd known the bright side rarely existed. Guilt rose to mingle with the pain, wiping away every last trace of mirth from his soul. He had no right to smile or laugh. Not when he had blood on his hands...

Realising Perla was still staring at him, he turned away abruptly. But the unsettled feeling wouldn't go away.

Perhaps Theo had been right. Had he lost his marbles by employing her, despite her obvious talent? He knew had he looked harder, he'd have found someone equally talented to employ who didn't rock the boat or make his male clients salivate just by the sight of her. He pursed his lips. Hell, she herself knew she was distracting enough to have made some of his employees talk, made her own life uncomfortable—

Frowning, he removed his phone from his pocket and dialled his assistant. 'Contact my head of HR—I want a conference call first thing tomorrow. Tell him I want to discuss Perla Lowell.'

CHAPTER SEVEN

'WHY DID YOUR HR director just call to check up on me?
And please don't tell me he does that with everyone else
because I asked David and Cynthia and he didn't call them
so I know I'm the only one he's called.'

Ari continued to admire the stunning penthouse view
from his latest hotel set in the heart of Washington DC and
forced himself not to react to the huskily voiced accusation or the unwanted intrusion. But it was difficult not to
turn around; not to tense against the electricity that zapped
through him at her presence.

It'd been three weeks since Miami, and the last time he'd
seen Perla. He'd left the day after Fashion Week and busied himself with his other casinos and hotels on the West
Coast. But he'd needed to return because Pantelides WDC
was by far his most successful hotel yet and he needed to
throw his every last waking moment into making it the
jewel in the Pantelides Luxe crown.

That he'd spent far too much time thinking about Perla
Lowell was something he preferred to view as simply making sure she wasn't causing any more ruffles in his company. Of course, he'd have preferred if word hadn't got out
that he was doing so but...

He sighed. 'Discretion really seems to be thin on the
ground these days.'

Her gasp sounded just behind his left shoulder. He tensed

further, bracing himself for the impact of the sight and scent of her.

'So you're not denying it? You do realise how you've made me look by doing that, don't you?'

'What exactly did my director say to you?' he asked.

'He asked me how I was getting on with work and with my colleagues.'

'And you immediately jumped to the conclusion that I was trying to undermine you somehow?'

'Did you or did you not ask him to call to check up on me?'

'Perla, you brought a potential workplace problem to my attention. And I took steps to rectify it. I think my director may have taken his directive a little too seriously given who you are. If you think it was an unnecessary step—'

'I do,' she flung at his back.

Ari gritted his teeth and tried to remain calm as she continued.

'Now you've said something—'

'Actually, *you* said something. Had you come to me instead of seeking verification from your colleagues, they would've been none the wiser.'

'So you're saying this is my fault?' Outrage filled her voice. 'And can you turn around when I'm talking to you, please?' she snapped.

With another sigh, he started to turn. 'I think you're blowing things out of proportion—' He stopped dead when he caught his first glimpse of her.

Her hair was a long, dark, *wet* ribbon curling over her naked shoulder. And she wore a black bikini with the thinnest strings that looked as if they were about to succumb to the laws of gravity. Heat punched into his gut so viciously, he had to lock his knees to keep from stumbling backward against the floor-to-ceiling window behind him. Around her waist, a carelessly knotted black sarong rested on her hipbones.

'I'm not blowing things out of proportion. The fact is you've severely undermined me in the eyes of my colleagues.'

'Did it occur to you that singling you out for attention could be for a beneficial reason rather than a detrimental one?'

He couldn't breathe. And he couldn't move. Even though words emerged from his mouth, his tongue felt thick and all his blood was rushing painfully south. In exactly one minute, she'd know the effect she had on him.

The intensely crazy, intensely electrifying effect he'd thought he had under control.

Her mouth dropped open and her eyes widened. 'I… no, I didn't.'

His smile felt a little tight around the edges. 'Perhaps you should've given it a little further thought then. As for David and Cynthia, don't rule them out completely. They may be receiving phone calls as well. You may simply have been lucky number one, this time.' His gaze slid over her once more and he wondered how many other people had seen her in that bikini, her exquisite body on full show? He forced himself not to think about it.

She frowned. 'I find it hard to believe that you check on every single employee…' She stopped and took a breath. 'Ari, why did you really do it?'

The sound of his name on her lips sent hot lust-filled darts to his groin. 'Why does it upset you so much?' he murmured.

Her eyebrows shot up. 'Are you serious? I have to work with these people!'

He shrugged. 'Then I'll leave it in your capable hands to smooth things over, assure your colleagues that my HR director was conducting a simple employee assessment and you jumped to a conclusion. Because that's what really happened.'

'God, you really expect me to believe that, do you?'

'I do.'

'You must think I'm really gullible.'

'If I did, you wouldn't be working for me. And you shouldn't take too much stock in what others think of you. Unless that's the problem here? Are you saying you don't trust your own judgement, Perla?'

She froze. Before his eyes, her face leached all colour. Her fingers twisted around each other in a clearly distressed way that made him curse inwardly. 'Yes,' she whispered raggedly. 'That's exactly what I'm saying. I'm…I'm not a very good judge of character.'

The visible distress made something catch in his chest. Before he could think better of it, he closed the distance between them and took her chin in his hand. This close, the scent of her warm body mingled with the chlorine from her swim hit him in the throat. His blood pounded harder, but Ari consoled himself with the fact that with her gaze on his, she wasn't witnessing what her proximity was doing to him below the waist.

'What makes you think that?'

'I got it spectacularly wrong with you, didn't I?' she asked.

His mouth firmed. 'But I wasn't who you were thinking of just now.' He knew it as certainly as he knew his name.

'What, you read minds now?'

'No. But, unlike you, I can read people. Who was it, Perla?' he asked, although he had a fair idea.

'Does it take a genius to figure out that I misjudged the man I married?' she said, confirming his theory. 'I thought he was someone I could depend on. Instead, he…he…' She closed her eyes and shook her head. The pain in her face and her words struck a dark chord within him. A chord he absolutely did not want struck.

But he couldn't help it as memory gathered speed through his brain.

He'd grown up depending on his father, looking up to him, hanging on his every word. For most of his early years, he'd wanted nothing more than to follow in his father's footsteps, only to find out that they were the shoes of a philanderer, an extortionist and a fraudster. A man who would take his son's idolisation and attempt to use it against him...to manipulate it for his own selfish needs.

His gut tightened against the ragged pain he'd thought long buried but that seemed to catch him on the raw much too often these days. It didn't help his disposition to know that Perla was always present when it happened. That perhaps they shared a connection with hurt and betrayal.

'If you're talking about your husband, he was just one man. Don't let him cloud your judgement about everyone else. Trust your instincts.'

'*Trust my instincts?* I don't think that's a very good idea. My instincts told me *you* were a good guy. But you turned on me like I was some sort of criminal when you found out who I was.'

'I no longer think that, or you wouldn't be here.'

She opened her mouth to speak, paused, then eyed him. 'But that's only half true, isn't it? If you'd thought I could really cope on my own you wouldn't have stepped in.'

He dropped his hand, then immediately flexed it at his side when it continued to tingle wildly. 'You told me how long you'd been out of the corporate world. That, coupled with your husband's activities, placed you in a vulnerable position.'

'And you were trying to *save* me? How unnecessarily noble of you.' The hand she'd placed on her hips drew attention to her pert breasts. Breasts he'd feasted on for a long time that first night. Breasts he wanted to touch, to caress again more than he wanted his next breath.

He whirled away and focused on the views of the GW Monument and Capitol Hill in the distance, lit up beacons of power, hoping his brain would find a different focus other than replaying the sight of her in that pulse-destroying bikini.

'So, are you done berating me?' he asked. He wanted her gone before he did something completely stupid. Like finding out just how robust the wraparound sofa behind him would be with both their weights pounding it.

'No. I don't need saving, Ari.'

'Fine, I won't interfere. Even though you've clearly exacerbated a simple assessment directive, perhaps I should've just let things play out. Let's move on, shall we?'

Behind him, she heard her soft sigh. 'Move on. That's easy for you to say.'

His chest tightened. 'No, actually, it's not,' he said, then froze. *Where the hell had that come from?* Pushing his hands into his pockets, he hoped she would let the careless slip slide.

Instead, she came closer until she stood next to him. 'What do you mean?' she asked with a soft murmur.

He clenched his jaw for several seconds, then felt the words spiral out of him. 'It means I know what it feels like to be under scrutiny. To know that people are looking at you and forming judgements you have no control over. That at best you were being judged with pity and at worst with scorn and malice.'

She sucked in a shocked breath. 'God, who…why…?'

He turned and glanced at her. Her wide eyes were drowning in sympathy and her mouth was parted with agitation. The realisation that she wore that look for him struck him in the gut. 'You don't know about Alexandrou Pantelides, my father?'

She shook her head.

Giddy relief poured through him. 'Then I prefer to keep you in the dark just a little while longer.'

'Was he…was he the one you meant when you said *him* that day in your office?'

Another time, another slip. When it came to this woman, it seemed he didn't know when to shut the hell up. 'Yes,' he confessed.

'And you don't want to be like him? What did he do to you?' she asked, sympathy making her voice even huskier.

'Nothing I wish to share with you.'

Although a tinge of hurt washed over her eyes, she kept her gaze on him. 'Okay. But you know there's nothing to stop me from searching the Web for information the moment I leave here.'

His insides tightened at the thought of Perla knowing just how mired in deceit and humiliation his past was. 'No, there isn't. But it'll be an extra few minutes when I know you're not forming an opinion about me the way you think others are doing about you.'

'But if you know how it feels then why did you contact HR?'

'I saw a potential problem. I stepped in to fix it. It's what I do.' After his father had slashed their lives into a million useless pieces, seventeen-year-old Ari had assumed the role of protector. Protecting his mother and his younger brothers from the press intrusion after Alexandrou Pantelides's sleazy dealings and philandering lifestyle had come to light had, overnight, become his number-one priority.

His brothers, after severely rocky years, had grown into stable, intensely successful individuals. And his mother had eventually found peace. He'd believed his family was safe…

Until fate had shown him otherwise…

Theos, this was too much! Resentment that he'd inadvertently taken a trip down memory lane yet again coiled through him.

Sucking in a deep breath, he faced Perla. 'You've aired your grievance. I've listened. Now don't you have work to be getting on with?'

The harshness of his voice stung. 'It's my day off, but Ari—'

He let his gaze slide down her body, ignoring the fire sizzling through his veins. 'And was this what you meant when you suggested staying away from each other? Because this plan—' he indicated her skimpily clad form '—is a poor attempt at removing temptation from both our paths.'

'I'm sorry. I wasn't thinking… I just reacted—'

'Well, make a better judgement call next time!'

She flinched as if he'd struck her. But he couldn't regret his tone because he was drowning in hell. He'd almost opened up about secrets he shared with no one. And the temptation to unburden had been great. But not to her. Not to the woman whose husband had caused the media to dredge up all the bitterness and humiliation only a few short months ago.

He tightened his jaw and watched, fascinated, as she pulled herself together with a grace and dignity he found curiously admirable.

Crossing her arms round her middle, she glared at him. 'We're weak when it comes to each other. Striking out at me for your weakness is cowardly and beneath you. Stop it. Believe me, I can bite back.'

He felt a wash of heat surge up his cheekbones. 'You need to leave. Now. Before I do something we'll both regret.'

'Ari—'

'A word to the wise. No man likes being told he's weak; it can be misconstrued as a challenge. Leave. Now, Perla, before I invite you to honour your promise of biting me.'

Eyes wide, she backed quickly towards the door. 'We'll need to find a way of working together eventually, Ari.'

'Let's discuss it further when you're not wearing a whisper-thin sarong and a clinging bikini that's just *begging* to be ripped off.'

Perla tried not to count the ways things had gone spectacularly wrong as she left Ari's penthouse. First her headlong flight from the swimming pool, bristling with intense irritation and hurt, had been ill-timed. She should've waited to cool down before confronting him.

And what, in goodness' name, had she been thinking, going into his presence wearing two tiny pieces of Lycra and an even flimsier sarong?

But of all the things slamming through her mind, it was the look on his face as he'd confessed that he'd walked in her shoes that struck deepest and made her kick herself for picking the wrong time to confront him.

His pain had been unmistakable. It was a different sort of pain from when he'd spoken about his wife but the dark torment had been present nonetheless.

Just how much had Arion Pantelides been through? And what the hell had his father done to him?

She reached her suite five floors below and immediately glanced at her laptop set atop the most exquisite console table. She dismissed the voice that whispered that knowledge was power. However foolish it might be, she couldn't forget the relieved look on Ari's face when she'd confessed to not knowing who his father was.

There'd been a point in time a few months ago when she would've given her right arm to remain oblivious to what Morgan had done.

If Ari craved privacy, she would grant him that.

As for his anger at the way she'd gone to him, dressed in only a bikini and a sarong… She glanced down and saw her body's visible reaction to him. Her nipples were sharp points of fierce need and the way her chest rose and fell in her agitation…

God, no wonder he'd been angry!

She sank onto her bed, overwhelmed by her body's turbulent response.

It was clear that staying away from each other the last three weeks had achieved none of the clarity and purpose they'd both sought. If anything, the attraction bit harder, the hunger sharper.

It was also clear that she'd overreacted to the HR director's call and possibly made her work situation worse.

But she was sure she hadn't imagined the cynical looks between her colleagues when all her suggestions on the various stages of the opening night for Pantelides WDC had been accepted without question. Pleased that she was being valued as a hard-working member, she'd put forward more suggestions.

It was why she'd begun questioning herself, and the call coming so close to that had made her storm from the rooftop pool with every intention of confronting Ari and taking him to task.

Of course it had nothing to do with the fact that she'd been unable to stop thinking about the man since Miami; she had found herself growing curiously bereft with his continued absence and the fact that her body seemed to have pulsed to life the moment she'd found out he was back.

She was here to do a job. She seriously needed to focus on that and nothing else.

Let's move on…

Pursing her lips, she pulled off her sarong. Ari was annoyingly right.

They had two weeks before this spectacular hotel set in the heart of America's political and cultural capital opened.

The hotel itself was a jaw-dropping architectural masterpiece, and fully expected to achieve six-star status within the next few weeks. They'd already hosted the industry critics, who'd since given glowing reviews.

With prime views of the Lincoln Memorial and Capitol Hill, the mid-twentieth-century building had been given a multi-million-dollar facelift that had seen it propelled to the realms of untold luxury and decadence.

Marble, slate and gleaming glass were softened by hues of eye-catching red-and-gold furniture and art that captured the imagination, and the five top-class restaurants were already booked well into the new year.

Regardless of her own shaky issues, Perla was hugely excited to be working on the hotel opening.

After showering and slipping on her bathrobe, she ordered room service and pulled open her laptop. Her research into the Washington scene had thrown up a few ideas for the opening. She'd already secured the jazz quartet said to be a favourite of the President to her list and confirmed the special tour of the Smithsonian and the White House for the VIP guests who would be staying overnight. Her idea of a midnight cruise on the Pantelides yacht had also been greeted with enthusiasm.

Feeling her confidence return, she pulled up the details of Oktoberfest on a whim, then immediately discarded it. Somehow she didn't think beer-drinking went well with Ari's vision for his hotel.

But there was nothing wrong with checking it out for herself while she was here. Something to do to take her mind off the fact that Ari was once again within seeing and touching distance...and the knowledge that her pulse skittered every time she admitted that fact.

Her doorbell ringing brought welcome relief from her thoughts. The scent of the grilled chicken and salad made her stomach growl and reminded her she hadn't eaten since a hastily snatched bagel and coffee first thing this morning.

Ravenous, she ate much faster than she should have, a fact she berated herself for when she bolted out of her chair, rushed to the bathroom and emptied the contents of her stomach a mere hour later.

'Are you all right? You look a bit peaky.'

Susan, the assistant concierge, peered at her as Perla waited for the list and notes she'd typed up last night to finish printing.

Perla nodded absently and smoothed her hand down her black skirt and matching silk shirt she'd worn for the meeting with Ari and the rest of the key hotel staff.

Glancing down at herself, she wondered if she'd made the right choice. The shirt hadn't felt this tight across the bust when she'd picked it as part of her work wardrobe a month ago. The gaping between the top buttons had forced her to leave the first and second buttons open and she questioned now whether she shouldn't have changed her outfit altogether.

But after waking up twice more to throw up, she'd eventually fallen into a deep sleep and missed her alarm.

Which was why she was hopelessly late—

'Do you intend to join us for this meeting, Perla?'

Ari stood behind her, tall, imposing, gorgeous beyond words. In the morning sun, the sprinkling of grey at his temples highlighted the sculpted perfection of his face. But it was his unique hazel eyes that made her belly spasm with heat and a whole load of lust.

'I…I was just coming.'

'Good to hear.' He turned on his heel and strode back into the conference room.

'Someone's got an armadillo in their bonnet,' Susan whispered, her eyes wide with speculation.

Perla grabbed the sheets, gave a non-committal smile to

Susan and hurried across the marble floor in her three-inch heels, only to freeze when she entered the room.

The only seat left at the small conference table was next to Ari. She'd have to sit beside him, breathe in his spicy cologne, feel the warmth of him and place herself within his powerful aura for however long the blasted meeting took. Her throat dried as her heart rate roared.

Ari glanced up and sent her another impatient look, one that made her stash her unease and walk to his side.

Ideas for the opening event were discussed and tossed or kept as Ari saw fit. Half an hour later, he turned to her. 'Do you have your list?'

She nodded and passed copies around. 'The top four are secured. The other three are yet to be finalised...'

'*Oktoberfest?*' Ari demanded.

Perla frowned and glanced down at the sheet in her hand. 'Sorry, that wasn't supposed to be on there. It was an idea I thought of floating but I don't think it's the right image for this hotel.'

'You're right. It's not.'

Several of her colleagues exchanged glances. Perla ignored them. Pursing her lips, she met Ari's direct stare. 'Like I said, it wasn't supposed to be on the list—'

'But it would be perfect for the San Francisco hotel.' He put the list down and caught up a pen, flicking it through long, elegant fingers. 'Contact their concierge, tell them to trial it and give us feedback on how it goes. And make sure you take credit for it. As for the rest of the suggestions, I'm on board with the jazz quartet and the White House tour. Add it to the other maybes and we'll discuss a shortlist at the next meeting.'

Warmth oozed through her but her veins turned icy when she spotted the repeated exchanged glances. From the corner of her eye she saw Ari's jaw tighten as he brought the meeting to a close.

In her haste to leave his disturbing presence, she dropped her file. She retrieved it and straightened to find him blocking her path to the door.

Her heart jumped into her throat. 'Did you need something?'

His gaze drifted over her and he frowned. 'Is everything in your wardrobe black?'

'Excuse me?'

'Black doesn't suit you. It makes your skin look too pale.' His eyes dropped lower, the opening of her shirt.

She forced herself not to reach up and button her shirt. Or touch her skin to test if it really was on fire since his gaze burned her from the inside out. 'You stopped me from leaving to disparage my clothes?' She casually leaned against the table and lifted an eyebrow, although casual was the last thing she felt.

He rocked back on his heels and shoved his hands into his pockets. For several seconds he didn't speak. 'I see that I've made things difficult for you here,' he finally said.

The hint of contrition in his tone made her breath catch. Nonchalantly, she tried to shrug it away. 'It's partly my fault. I overreacted. I'll deal with it. As you said, I need to trust my instincts and my talent, and not what other people think.'

He nodded. 'Bravo,' he said. Thinking he would move out of her way, she started to take a step and paused when his mouth opened again. 'And if it doesn't earn me a sexual harassment charge, may I suggest you find a better fitting shirt that doesn't display all your assets?'

Her gasp echoed around the room. 'It's not that bad! And stop talking about my assets or I'll have to point out that shoving your hands in your pockets like that pulls your trousers across your junk and displays *your* assets. Not that I'm paying a lot of attention, of course,' she added hurriedly and felt her face flame.

God, she needed her head examined!

One eyebrow slowly lifted. 'Of course.' He remained planted in front of her, as if he had nothing better to do than to rile her.

Unable to stand his intense gaze, she glanced down and saw just how much cleavage she was displaying. *God!*

'I just…seem to have put on a little weight, that's all. And I was running a little late this morning so there was no time to change…' She grew restive beneath his continued silent scrutiny. 'Seriously, it's not that bad.'

His nostrils flared and a look passed through his eyes that made her think he was toying with the idea of arguing the point. Instead, he opened the door. 'After you,' he said.

Walking in front of him across the large marble foyer felt like walking the plank on some doomed pirate's ship. She was aware of the intensity of his scrutiny on her back, her legs…her bottom. Electricity sparked along her nerves and spread throughout her body.

Slowly she noticed the sound of last-minute preparations in the vast space had gradually faded as people stopped to stare.

David and Cynthia, the two colleagues who'd been recruited the same time as her, stood at the solid wood-carved reception, watching with blatant curiosity. She didn't need to turn around after she passed them to know they were whispering behind her back.

Same as she didn't need to turn around to notice the moment Ari veered off towards his own office. Because her skin stopped tingling and her pulse began to slow.

By the time she shut herself away in the tiny office behind the concierge's station, she was shaking. Going to her coffee stand, she flicked the kettle on and practised her breathing as it boiled. She poured water onto the tea bag, then immediately gagged as the scent of camomile made her stomach roil violently.

Abandoning tea in favour of water, Perla waited for the sickness to subside and threw herself into her work.

She spent the rest of the day finalising catering requirements, confirming bookings and chasing RSVPs. The turkey sandwich she ordered for lunch stayed put and she breathed a sigh of relief. The last thing she needed was to get sick within the first month of starting a new job in which she already felt compromised.

But by six o'clock her feet ached, her head throbbed with a dull ache and the debilitating weakness that had dogged her all day was weighting her limbs. Shutting off her computer, she dug through her bag and located the painkillers she always kept to hand. Swallowing two, she took the lift to her suite, collapsed onto the bed, kicked off her shoes and pulled the covers over her head.

The buzzing of her phone woke her an hour later.

Dazed, she pushed the hair off her face and snagged the handset. 'Hello?'

'Perla.'

Excitement jack-knifed through her body.

God, the way he said her name should be banned. Or she needed to charge for it. Because she was sure she suffered a tiny nervous breakdown every time his voice grated out her name like that.

'Um…hi,' she mumbled, squinting in the darkened room.

'Did I wake you?' There was a frown in his voice.

'No, I was just…no.'

'I've been thinking about your predicament.'

'What predica…? No, I told you, I'll handle it.'

'You may not need to. Have you had dinner yet?' he asked.

She tried to make her brain work. 'No, I haven't.'

'Meet me at the Athena Restaurant in half an hour,'

he said, naming the five-star restaurant on the first floor of the Pantelides WDC, headed by a very sought after Michelin-starred chef.

Perla flicked the bedside lamp on and struggled to sit up. Thankfully, her headache seemed to have disappeared. 'Um…why?'

'I have a proposal to discuss with you. A new opportunity you might be interested in.'

The thought of meeting with Ari so openly again after this morning and being the cynosure of all eyes made her nape tighten. Exhaling, she faced up to the fact she had to deal with that sooner or later. She refused to let gossip rock the self-esteem she was trying hard to rebuild.

She cleared her throat. 'I'd love to hear your proposal but I think the Athena is fully booked tonight. And yes, I know you own the hotel and can chuck someone out but I'd feel bad. Do you think we can order room service instead?'

For a few seconds, silence greeted her suggestion. 'Given our track record, do you think being in a hotel room alone together is wise?' he rasped.

Liquid heat flooded her belly, followed closely by chagrin. 'Um, you're right, it's not. I'll…come to you.'

'Half an hour. Don't keep me waiting.'

She hung up and threw the covers off. Going to the bathroom, she took a quick shower, pleased that she felt a whole lot better now than she had all day.

The dress she chose was functional and stylishly respectable without being overtly sexy. Pulling on the slingbacks she'd discarded earlier, she caught up her black clutch and black wrap and left her room.

Despite telling herself this was just business, butterflies fluttered madly in her stomach as the lift rushed her downward.

She stepped out of the lift and was about to head towards the foyer when her phone pinged.

Come outside. A

Slowly, she swivelled on her heels and headed out into the cool October night. Beneath the elegantly columned portico of the hotel, Ari leaned, cross-legged and cross-armed against a gleaming black sports car.

The sight of him, magnificently imposing, arrestingly gorgeous, was incredibly dangerous to her well-being. He wore a dark blue cotton shirt with black trousers and a matching jacket that hugged his wide shoulders.

The intensity of his stare as it drifted over her made her body grow hot all over. And even though he didn't say anything, by the time his gaze returned to hers she had the distinct impression he was displeased.

But then what else was new? Ari alternated between finding her irritating and being incredibly considerate.

Given the choice, I'd settle for a little bit of peace.

'What did you say?' he asked, straightening from the car to open the passenger door for her.

Realising she'd muttered her thoughts, she blushed. 'Nothing. I thought we were meeting inside?'

He shook his head. 'Change of plan. I thought we could experience what Washington DC has to offer. You had a Greek restaurant on your list. Care to try it?' he asked.

Pleased that he'd remembered, she smiled. 'I'd love to.'

He straightened, waited for her to slide in and shut the door behind her.

Unable to stop herself, Perla watched him round the bonnet. God, even the way this man moved demanded attention. His lean, sinewy grace seemed innate.

The moment he shut the door all her senses flared to life. His scent was intoxicating, addictive in a way that made her want to throw herself across the console and slide her greedy hands all over him.

Expecting him to start the car and drive, she glanced at him and caught his rigid profile. When his fingers wrapped around the steering wheel and gripped tight, she knew he was fighting the same raw need.

She must have made a sound because a choked noise filled the tense space.

'Ari...'

He sucked in a jagged breath. 'We are not teenagers and we are not animals.' His voice was rough, darkly husky. 'We have enough self-control to be able to resist this...this *insanity* between us.'

Her hand tightened around her clutch. 'I agree.' Although fighting it felt like a losing battle right now.

'What happened between us can't happen again,' he continued gratingly. The mild self-loathing in his voice finally pierced the cocoon of sensual delirium.

Stung, she whipped her head to stare out of her window. 'I get the message loud and clear, Ari.'

'Do you?' he demanded, and she knew he was staring at her because she could feel the intensity of his gaze on her skin.

She bit her lip to stop another helpless moan from escaping. 'You hate me because I remind you of something in your past. I don't know what exactly. Maybe it's connected to this insane temptation we can't kill. I could find a reason to hate you too but what good would hate do either of us?'

'I don't hate you,' he growled. 'There are a lot of things I feel but, rest assured, *hate* isn't one of them.'

A little bit of the hurt eased but hearing that self-loathing still present in his voice made her heart lurch. 'That's good to hear.' She took a deep breath and immediately regretted it when his scent filled every atom of her being. 'I'd suggest handing in my notice and finding a new job if I could—' She jumped at the snarl that filled the car. 'But I've only been working a few weeks, and my chances of finding another job are—'

'You're not quitting this job. You're not going anywhere.' He pressed the button that started the ignition but he didn't drive away. 'You signed a contract so you're staying put.'

CHAPTER EIGHT

ARI MADE SURE his words left no room for doubt or ambiguity. Which was laughable, considering he was nowhere near as stalwart under the barrage of the emotions coursing through him.

He'd firmly believed he had regained some control after yesterday's incident. It was the reason he'd called to discuss business with her. He'd been so certain, after seeing her in that bikini and not jumping on her like some hormone-riddled teenager, he could see Perla, be within touching distance of her without experiencing that unbridled depth of yearning that seemed to claw up from his very soul.

A soul he'd believed withered and charred after Sofia... after his father...

But now, with her seductive, addictive warmth so close, her husky voice seeming to caress him whenever she spoke, he knew resisting this insanity wouldn't be as easy as he'd thought.

But resist he had to. The guilt that had ridden him from the very moment he'd slept with Perla still resided beneath his chest. It fought savagely with his intense attraction but it never went away...

I remind you of something in your past...

She had no idea how accurate that was.

'Okay, I'll honour my contract. But, um...do you think

we can get out of here? The valet attendants are beginning to get frantic at the backed-up traffic.'

A quick look in the rear-view mirror confirmed her words. With a twist of the wheel and a foot on the accelerator, he squealed out of his hotel's driveway and onto the freeway. The sound of the throaty engine drowned out his thoughts for the precious few seconds it took to regain a little bit of his control.

Masculine pleasure at the purr of the powerful engine beneath him soothed his turbulent pulse and he inhaled slowly.

Next to rowing, alone or with his brothers, powerful engines like these were his passion. Except he didn't get to indulge enough. It was probably why he'd succumbed to temptation—

Stasi! Enough with the excuses. Perla had hit the nail on the head. They'd been weak with temptation and he'd succumbed. Not once but twice. The only way to avoid being no better than his father would be to make sure it didn't happen again.

'Ari, could you slow down a little, please?'

A quick glance showed her death grip on the bucket seat. He cursed under his breath and eased off the pedal. 'My apologies.'

She nodded and her fingers relaxed. 'What did you want to talk to me about?' she asked as he signalled off Connecticut Avenue and slid to a stop in front of the Greek restaurant. Perla didn't know it but it was one of his favourite restaurants outside of his homeland.

As they were led in, he found himself following the line of her body again. The way her black dress hugged her tight behind, the way her black wrap caressed her shoulders and her black heels made her legs go on for ever.

His thoughts screeched to a halt. She was wearing black

again. And not just a touch here and there but black from head to toe…as if she was making a statement.

Was she?

'You're scowling again.'

They'd reached their table and she was already sitting down, while he stood beside it, arrested by his crazy thoughts. He gritted his teeth, pulled out his chair and sat down.

Business. Focus on business.

'You asked what I wanted to talk to you about.'

She nodded as he beckoned the *sommelier*. She ordered a white wine spritzer and he a full-bodied claret. Once they were alone again, he took out his mini tablet and set it on the table between them. A few swipes and he had the page he was looking for.

'My new resort and casino in Bermuda, set to open in two months.'

Her brow rose. 'Another one?' She leaned closer and swiped through the pictures. Slowly her mouth fell open. 'It's spectacular.'

He allowed himself a small smile. 'I worked closely with the architects to achieve the results I wanted—a private resort which caters to extreme water sports lovers without taking anything away from the signature luxury casino.'

'Water seems to be a major theme for you, doesn't it? Eighty per cent of your portfolio is built on or around water.'

He was impressed that she'd done her homework. 'I grew up around water and started rowing from a very early age.'

'You rowed?' she asked in surprise.

'Competitively for six years, four of those with Sakis and two with Theo.' It had been one of the few ways he and his brothers had coped with their shattered lives.

She played with the beads on her purse. 'Did you win?'

'Of course.'

She laughed, the sound so pure and delightful, his stomach clenched. '*Of course*. How many titles?'

'Five that are worth mentioning. My mother has all my trophies from when I was a child.'

Her head tilted to one side, traces of laughter lingering in her eyes. 'I can't quite picture you as a child. You look as if you were born looking like you do now.'

Against his will, his smile widened. 'For my mother's sake, I'm glad that wasn't the case.'

A sudden wave of anguish passed over her face, erasing the laughter. Then it was gone. Reaching out, she took a slice of bread from the basket the waiter had set between them and broke off a piece. 'Is your mother still around?'

He tried not to let his mixed feelings about his mother show. 'Yes. She lives at the family home in Athens.'

Curiosity built in her eyes. 'Do you see her often?'

He shrugged. 'When I'm in Greece. Which isn't often enough, she tells me.'

'Are you two close?' He detected the faint longing in her voice and wondered at it. It suddenly struck him that, beyond the intense sexual pull and the actions of her dead husband, he didn't know much about Perla Lowell.

'We used to be. There was a time when I shared everything with her. She was my best friend and she encouraged my every dream. Then…my father happened.'

Her breath caught slightly. 'He…*happened?*'

The usual fierce reluctance to revisit the past spiked through him, even though he'd been the one to open the door. Despite his reticence, he found himself nodding. 'A few months before I turned eighteen, a journalist uncovered my father's duplicitous life. Details of fraud, corruption, embezzlement all came to light.' His insides twisted with remembered agony that he hoped his face didn't reflect. 'Overnight, our lives were turned upside down. I was working in one of my father's companies and was in the office with my father when the fraud squad stormed the building.'

Her eyes widened. 'That must have been very difficult to witness.'

'It would've been if I hadn't realised quickly that I would be busy trying to save my own skin.'

'*What?* Why?'

For a moment, he considered not uttering the words. Considered hiding it from her the way he'd hidden this fact from his brothers, from his mother. Only a distant uncle knew what Ari had suffered, and Ari had made sure to enforce the attorney-client privilege that prevented his uncle from ever divulging the truth.

'My father tried to shift some of the blame of his fraudulent activities onto me. He implicated me in a few of his bribery scams and tried to get me to take the fall so his charges could be lessened.'

Her eyes darkened with shock. 'Oh, God! Why would he do that?'

'I was his firstborn son, and had taken a keen interest in the business since I turned sixteen. I had a good head for figures and the authorities knew he'd been grooming me to eventually take over from him. Because I was still under eighteen when he was arrested he figured I would get off easily. For a short while the authorities believed him.'

Her eyes grew dark with sympathy. 'That's horrible. How did your brothers take it? Where was your mother?'

Unable to stop, his lips twisted as old wounds were ripped open. 'Sakis and Theo didn't know… I never told them.'

Her mouth dropped open. 'You didn't?'

He shrugged. 'What good would it have done? By the time we were done with my father, enough devastation had been spread around. It was my duty to protect them from more hurt. Revealing that I possibly faced jail when they were counting on me was not an option.'

'But…you've been carrying it for all this time…'

'Human beings are predisposed to carrying a hell of a lot of baggage,' he answered. 'And I have very broad shoulders,' he added, in the hope of lightening a suddenly heavy atmosphere. But her eyes only grew more solemn, as if she shared his pain, sympathised with his blighted past.

'Broad shoulders or not, you shouldn't have had to bear that on your own. Your mother…'

'Retreated to our villa in Santorini and locked herself away. Her husband's betrayal was too much for her. She couldn't cope.' He'd needed her more than ever in the darkest time of his life. And she'd abandoned him. Just as she'd abandoned Sakis and Theo when they'd needed her the most.

It had taken a long time for Ari to forgive her, a long time to get past his anger and bitterness at her weakness. But he'd learned to smother it. Because he'd needed to get past his personal devastation in order to take care of his brothers. To salvage the charred remains of the family business his father had decimated with his greed and carelessness.

He jerked as Perla's hand touched his in gentle sympathy. 'I'm sorry that happened to you.'

Sincerity blazed from her clear green eyes. Sincerity he wanted to take and wrap around his damaged heart. Instead, he forced himself to nod.

Slowly, he pulled his hand away.

Because, even in the midst of excruciating reminiscing, he could feel that pull again, that potent hunger that lurked like the sweetest siren call, ready to tempt him.

'Why?'

Her fingers curled around her piece of bread. 'Because… because no one deserves to go through what you did.'

Their drinks arrived and he took a healthy gulp of wine,

exhaling in satisfaction as the fire in the alcohol temporarily replaced the fire of lust. 'But I survived. Some would say I triumphed.'

'But you're still affected by it, aren't you?'

He tensed. 'Excuse me?'

'Yesterday you didn't want me to find out what your father had done. Clearly you're still affected by what happened.'

'Are we not all shaped by our pasts to some extent? You're clearly steeped in the past and reacting to your own experiences.'

Her cheeks lost a bit of colour. 'What makes you say that?'

'Yesterday *you* admitted your lack of judgement when it comes to dealing with people. I don't need to be a genius to work out the root cause of it.'

Paling further, she shook her head. 'I…I'm not…'

'Tell me how you met Lowell?' he asked before he could stop himself. 'Of all the men you could've dated, why him?'

'Because I didn't have a crystal ball that could look into the future to see how things would turn out. And you say *of all the men* as if I had hundreds at my feet.'

He barely stopped himself from glancing up at her hair. The idea that no man had shown interest in her was laughable. 'So he was the first man to show his interest?' He tried to force a neutral tone and barely pulled it off.

'He was charming; he paid me the right sort of attention…at the beginning. I believed I was making the right choice, that we had the same goals and that my feelings were reciprocated.'

Anger roiled through his belly. 'Instead, he abandoned you shortly after you were married?'

Shocked eyes met his. 'How did you know that?'

'I'm a major shareholder in the company he tried to destroy. My brother dealt with the bulk of the investigation but I saw enough.'

Her gaze grew haunted, then it slid away and she reached for the glass of water. After a few sips she set the glass down. 'So you know a great deal about me.'

'Enough to know there are no mention of your parents anywhere on record. You take care of your in-laws but what about your own parents?' he asked, eager to get away from the subject of dead spouses.

The earlier anguish he'd glimpsed returned. 'I don't have… I was placed in the foster system when I was one month old. My birth mother left me in front of the social security office with my first name and my date of birth pinned to my blanket. My birth date could be wrong because there was no birth certificate, although the doctors are fairly sure I was born in the month I was left but there were no hospital records so I don't even know *where* I was born. So no, I have no record of who my parents are,' she murmured in a voice ravaged with pain. 'I'm the child no one wanted.'

His fingers tightened around his glass and he realised he was holding on tight so he wouldn't reach out for her like she'd reached out for him.

Only he wanted to take her face between his hands and kiss away her pain. He wanted to rewind time, take a different track of conversation that was so far off what he'd come here for it was ludicrous. He should've stuck to business, facts, figures.

Not their painful personal pasts. And he should certainly not be sitting here, hanging onto that connection that stemmed from opening up and sharing his desolate history with her.

He wasn't a *sharer*.

'Perla—'

She forced a laugh. 'How do we always end up on the personal when we vow never to again?'

'We're especially bad at pulling the forbidden out of each other.'

'Or exceptionally good?' she joked.

He stared at her. And just like that the madness descended again. He tried to shift away from it but it clawed into him, sank its merciless talons into his gut and held him down. Almost in slow motion, he watched her mouth part, her nostrils quiver delicately as she sucked in a desperate breath.

Theos!

She gave a distressed shake of her head and glanced down at the now powered down tablet. 'The resort. We were discussing the resort,' she said after clearing her throat.

He forced his mind on track. 'Yes. I wanted to float the idea of you handling the pre-opening VIP events for the Bermuda resort on your own. If you agree to take on the task, you'll have to work fast to organise it. The guests arrive at the resort at the end of next week.'

'The pre-opening event is so your A-list clients can experience the resort and spread the word to their other A-list friends by the time the resort opens properly, correct?'

He nodded. 'So it needs to be extra-special. Your input here in Washington has been invaluable and you can choose to stay here if you wish, but I think this is more along the lines of what you used to do in your previous position, only on a much larger scale?'

'Yes, but I've never worked in such an exotic location before.'

'This will be your chance to prove yourself then. I want to see how you fare spearheading a larger project.' He sipped his wine—absently acknowledging he would have to abandon his beloved sports car in favour of another means of transport to return to the hotel—and watched her digest the information.

Slowly her stunning green eyes widened. '*Spearheading?* Are you serious?'

'You can handpick your own team, hire and fire as you see fit. You'll be provided with the initial list of attending guests but you can extend the list if you think you can handle it.'

'You *are* serious!' Shocked happiness erased the last evidence of her bleak foray into the past and, watching her, enchantment eased through him.

Examining himself closer, he realised he felt lighter than he had in a long while. He refused to believe unburdening his past to Perla had succeeded in lightening the heavy load of bitterness and pain, but he had no other explanation for it.

When he found himself smiling in reaction to her still stunned expression, something tugged hard in his chest. 'Serious enough to promise a quick firing and slow roasting if you mess up my opening.'

She popped another piece of bread into her mouth. 'Which is really no better than a slow firing and a quick roasting since both sound horrific.'

He laughed and saw her gaze linger on his face and her eyes darken a fraction.

No, he wasn't going there. *They* were not going there.

He beckoned the hovering waiter and paused as Perla examined the menu. Slowly she pulled her lower lip into her mouth and pondered some more.

'Can I help?' he offered after several minutes.

She looked up in relief. 'Would you? I never know what to order when I go to a restaurant and I always end up hating what I choose and coveting what's on other people's plates.'

'I'll order a variety of dishes and you can decide which ones you like and which ones you don't.'

She smiled. 'That works for me. *Efharisto.*'

He froze, the sound of his mother tongue so erotically charged coming from her that he forgot to breathe. 'You're learning Greek?'

'I work for a Greek company. It seems wise to learn a few essential words like *thank you* and *where the hell is the coffee?* I find some of the pronunciations quite hard, though.'

'Let me know what you have difficulty with and I'll teach you.' Again the words slipped out before he could stop them.

What in heaven's name was wrong with him?

Mentally shaking his head, he recited the dishes he wanted prepared to the waiter and added a command for haste.

They discussed the Bermuda resort and her initial ideas. The passion she exhibited for business made him glad he'd offered her the chance. So much so, he slightly regretted it when their meal arrived and intruded on the atmosphere. Small platters of roasted vegetables, tenderly prepared meats served on a bed of traditional salad, hummus and oven-baked breads.

He watched her dig into the food with the same gusto she'd eaten that night at his apartment in London. Then, as now, he'd found her appetite refreshing.

Recalling her comment earlier about putting on weight, Ari's gaze slid to her breasts. They looked slightly heavier, plumper than they had in London, and her cleavage seemed deeper.

Warmth rushed into his mouth that had nothing to do with the sumptuous textures of the food and everything to do with recalling the exquisite taste of her hard nipples on his tongue. He forced his gaze away. Only to snap it back to her when she made a sound of distress.

Her eyes had widened and she was reaching for her water. 'Um...Ari...I don't feel so good.'

Ari frowned and he jerked to his feet. 'What's wrong? What is it?'

She dropped her glass and water splashed across the table. In one move, he was by her side, pushing her chair back so he could take her face in his hands.

'Perla?'

She jumped up and looked around wildly, drawing the attention of other diners. She must have spotted the signs for the lavatory because she grabbed her bag and lurched forward.

'Excuse me.' She clamped her hand over her mouth and fled.

CHAPTER NINE

THE DEBILITATING WEAKNESS was back again, weighting her limbs down and fanning a dull ache throughout her body.

But it was nothing compared to the crushing weight of suspicion anchoring her heart.

No matter how much she tried to push the thought away, it kept coming back, intruding, demanding to be heard, to be acknowledged.

Perla cast a furtive glance at the man who stood beside her in the hotel lift, his hand gripping her arm. He hadn't said a word since they left the restaurant. He'd been there when she emerged from the Ladies, pale, weak and shaky, barely able to meet his gaze when he'd enquired whether she wanted to leave.

The restaurant staff had been profusely apologetic but she hadn't had the courage to reassure them that what was going on was most likely not the fault of their food. She'd left the soothing of ruffled feathers to Ari, simply because she hadn't been able to think past the stark reality of what she could be facing.

They exited the lift and she followed him numbly. It wasn't until they were inside the suite that was easily three times the size of hers that she realised they hadn't returned to her suite but to his. He bypassed the living room, the study and the master bedroom and entered a second bedroom.

Before her stood what was easily an emperor-sized bed, complete with solid four-posters and cream silk muslin curtains. A bathroom and walk-in closet were visible through a golden-lit arch and beyond the windows Washington DC shone its powerful light over the city.

Her gaze returned from sweeping the room to find Ari standing with his hands on his hips, those mesmerising eyes fixed questioningly on hers.

'There's a new toothbrush through there if you need to use it?'

She nodded, dropped her clutch on the bed and darted into the bathroom. The need to escape was less to do with cleaning her mouth properly and more to do with delaying the inevitable.

Quickly, she brushed her teeth and rinsed her mouth. Then gripped the edge of the sink as a fresh wave of apprehension rolled through her.

Arion Pantelides wasn't stupid. The knowledge in his eyes told her his thoughts had taken the same path as hers.

'Perla.'

She jumped and whirled so fast, her vision blurred.

Callused hands steadied her, one curving around her waist and the other rising to cradle her cheek for a moment before he dropped his hand.

'Come.'

The gentle gesture threatened her equilibrium and she fought not to react as he led her back to the room and sank onto the bed beside her. He'd discarded his jacket and folded back the sleeves of his shirt.

The sight of the silky hairs on his forearm made sensation scythe through her but it was the look in his eyes that stopped her breath.

His fingers trembled as they caught her chin and an emotion moved through her heart she was almost too afraid to examine. 'How do you feel?' he asked in a low, deep voice.

Something in his tone made her glance at him. His face had lost a few shades of vibrancy and in his eyes dark, unfathomable shadows lurked.

Whatever was ahead of them, Perla knew it wouldn't be an easy road.

'I…I'm…' Her throat felt swollen and scratchy so she stopped.

'Here, have some water.' He passed her a glass and waited while she took a few sips. His gaze never left her and, feeling her hands begin to shake, she put the glass down.

Trepidation welled up inside her. 'Ari…'

More colour leached from his face. 'Before you say anything, Perla, I need you to be one hundred per cent sure.'

The depth of emotion in his voice made her heart flip over, then thunder with enough force to threaten her ribs. 'Why?' she asked before she could stop herself.

'Because the ramifications would mean more than you could ever imagine.' The roughness in his voice and the faint trembling of the hand still at her waist made her insides quake.

Incomprehensible emotions swirled around inside her. Unbidden, tears welled up in her eyes and slipped down her cheeks.

'*Theos*, do not cry. Please,' he ordered raggedly.

'Sorry, I'm not normally a crier,' she muttered, then cringed as more tears fell. 'I just can't seem to help myself.'

He gritted his teeth and brushed her cheeks with his thumbs, then stared down at her with dark eyes but said nothing as the tears continued to fall.

The knock on the door made him turn away but not before she caught another glimpse of jagged torment in his eyes. 'The doctor's here.'

'The *doctor?*' When had he even called him? 'Ari, I don't need a doctor. I feel fine.'

He stood and stared at her for a long moment before he shoved his hands into his pockets. 'I can send him away if that's what you want. But I think we need to make absolutely sure that you're not coming down with an illness. *That* is not negotiable. So we can do it now or we can do it tomorrow. Your choice.'

She gripped the covers, the feeling of hurtling towards the unknown growing by the second. But Ari was right. They needed to be sure nothing else was wrong before they went any further.

She nodded. 'Okay, we do it now.'

He left the room and returned moments later followed by a tall, lanky man with brown hair and serious brown eyes. He proceeded to look her over and fire questions at her that made her cringe. Ari stood, hand in his pocket next to the bed the whole time, his eyes never leaving her.

'The headache and fatigue worries me a bit, and your glands are slightly swollen,' the doctor finally said. 'My advice is to rest for a few days—'

'Yes, she'll do that—'

'No, she won't,' she countered sharply with a frown which he returned twice as hard and twice as dangerous. 'I'm not sick, Ari. Seriously, I'll be fine by morning.'

The doctor looked between them, clearly sensing the undercurrents. 'Or I can give you a flu shot just in case? Head it off at the pass?'

At her nod, he opened his bag and took out the needle. She tensed and tried to curb her nerves but Ari's narrowed gaze told her he'd seen her reaction.

Rounding the bed, he slid in beside her and pulled her close, his warm, hard body a solid comfort. 'You fear needles and yet you're refusing the simple alternative.'

'I'll take a small prick any day compared to days lazing about in bed.'

The small charged silence that followed gave her time

to hear her words echo in the room. Then a fierce blush washed over her face.

The doctor hid a smile as he focused on preparing the syringe. Ari's mocking laughter lightened the tense atmosphere a touch, although she could feel his tension. 'It's not gentlemanly to laugh at a harmless *double entendre*. Especially when it comes at the patient's expense.'

He blinked and his gaze dropped to her mouth.

This close, his designer stubble was within touching distance and the gold flecks in his eyes and the sensual curve of his mouth were even more mesmerising. The hand he'd slipped around her tightened, drawing her infinitesimally closer to his body. Heat oozed through her, breaking loose that wild yearning she seemed to be useless at keeping sealed up.

The doctor clearing his throat made her jump. The needle filled with liquid was poised against her skin. 'Stop! Will this harm a pregnancy?' she blurted.

Beside her, Ari tensed.

The doctor frowned. 'Are you pregnant, Miss Lowell?'

'It's Mrs...actually,' she murmured absently as her gaze swung and collided with Ari's. In that moment, she *knew*.

And so did he.

The doctor moved. With a swiftness that stunned the breath out of her, Ari grabbed the doctor's needle-holding hand and held it in a death grip. All without taking his eyes from hers.

'So you're sure?' he rasped.

She nodded.

Wordlessly he let go of the doctor's wrist. Lines of torment bracketed his mouth as he left the bed.

She was pregnant. With Ari's child. The two thoughts tumbled over one another in her brain, one seeking dominance over the other and neither coming out the victor. Because both thoughts were equally mind-boggling.

Vaguely, she heard him dismiss the doctor and leave the suite.

But all too soon he was back. Tall, imposing, bristling with emotions she was too cowardly to try and name.

For several minutes, he paced the room. Then he finally stopped at the foot of the bed. 'Did you know you were pregnant?' His voice was gritty with emotion.

'No, I didn't. I didn't even guess.'

'Not even when you were late? How late are you?'

The date flared like a beacon in her mind. 'Almost two weeks.'

He muttered a word she didn't need translation for. '*Theos!*' Running a hand through his hair, he resumed pacing. 'And it didn't raise any alarms?'

'No. My period has always been irregular.'

She thought back to that night and felt shame crawl over her skin when she remembered she'd been so into it, too far gone with delirium that she hadn't stopped to think about safe sex that second time.

And now she was pregnant.

Tiny waves of joy slowly spread through her stunned senses.

A child of her own. To cherish and love. And, if she was lucky, a child who would love her back.

She jerked upright, her hand rushing to cover her stomach. 'Oh, God, I took some painkillers this afternoon!'

His gaze sharpened on her. 'What did you take?'

She told him. 'W…would it have harmed the baby?'

He shook his head. 'The doctor told me which medicines are okay to take during pregnancy.'

Relief poured through her. 'You asked him?'

Ari stilled. 'Of course. This baby is mine too,' he grated out.

But it didn't take a genius to see that he wasn't thrilled

about it. Pain and hurt scythed through her joy. A second later a rush of protectiveness enveloped her.

'I realise this is unexpected. I don't want you to think that you need to be involved in any way...'

'Excuse me?' His voice was a rasp, his eyes dark with thunder as he stared at her.

Perla licked her lips, contemplated taking a sip of water and discarded the idea. She was too shaken not to pour it all over herself.

'I mean this wasn't planned or anything, so don't feel as if you have to participate in any decision-making. I'll take care of it.'

'You'll *take care of it?*'

The skin-flaying fury in his voice made her realise that once again she'd chosen the wrong words.

'No! I meant I'll take care of him or her after the birth.'

Dark implacable eyes bored into hers. 'So, just so we're clear, you intend to keep the baby?'

'Of course! I'd never, ever dream of...' She raised her chin. 'Yes, I intend to have this baby. What I meant was that I'll take sole responsibility so you don't have to worry.' Her eyes dropped to her stomach. This child was hers and she intended to protect him or her with her last breath.

'What gives you the right to assume sole responsibility for the child? Sexual responsibility is a two-way street.'

'I know, but I participated too without giving a thought to protection. Arion, all I'm trying to say is there's no need to get all macho and blame yourself for something that involved both of us.'

'Perla, look at me.' The order was soft, deadly.

She dragged her eyes from where she'd been staring at her stomach in silent wonder. The resolution and implacable determination in his eyes made her shiver.

'Do I look like the sort of man who would leave his child to be brought up by another man? And I assume you don't intend to remain single for the rest of your life? That you will seek another relationship at some point in the future?'

That thought was so unlikely she wanted to laugh. Except the look on his face told her he wouldn't find it funny. So she shrugged. 'I don't know. Maybe.'

'Let's try something else much simpler.' He drew closer to the bed. His hands hung loose at his sides and his open-legged stance was unthreatening. But she didn't fool herself for one second that Ari wasn't seething beneath that calm exterior. 'Do I look like I'm going anywhere?'

'Ari—'

'*Do I?*'

'No. You don't.' And she wasn't sure whether to be pleased or frightened by that admission.

If Ari wanted this child and, from his stance, she concluded he did…for now…it would mean she would have him in her life for the foreseeable future.

Her childhood in foster care had opened her eyes to the fact that not all children were wanted. No matter what the circumstances of conception, there came a point in time where some parents simply abandoned their children and walked away.

She had no intention of ever doing that to her child. But she couldn't speak for Ari. His childhood had created deep scars that rippled through his every decision. He'd been let down by the people who should've been there for him. In a way it was worse than never having felt the love of two devoted parents. She hadn't experienced that particular devastation because she hadn't had the fantasy in the first place. To know that he'd had parents who'd let him down, who'd let him shoulder the responsibility of caring for his brothers on his own was too distressing to bear.

A wave of despair swept over her. Would Ari let go of his pain long enough to let himself love a child?

'Good, I'm glad we've established that fact.' He stepped

back from the bed and turned towards the door. Without speaking another word, he left.

He returned less than ten minutes later with a tray of food which he set on her lap. The simple ham and cucumber sandwich made her stomach rumble and she remembered she'd barely eaten a few mouthfuls of dinner before her attack.

'I prepared it myself. Until I find you a personal chef who will be apprised of all your dietary requirements, I'll prepare all your meals myself.'

Her mouth dropped open for several seconds before she managed to snap it shut. 'Wait… What?'

He poured a glass of orange juice and handed it to her. 'Which part needs explanation?'

'The part…all of it. You don't have to do this, Ari.'

'Yes, I do. You're carrying my child. I absolutely have to do this.'

Again, the depth of emotion behind the words made her eyes widen. But when she looked at him, his eyes were veiled and his face inscrutable.

'Eat,' he instructed.

In silence she ate because as much as she wanted to argue with him, probe behind his words, she was starving. And she needed to do everything in her power to keep her baby healthy and safe.

She forced herself to eat slowly this time. She accepted a second glass of orange juice. Once she'd drained it, Ari set the tray aside.

'How do you feel?' Again there was that concern in his voice. But, coupled with that, there was a thin vein of anxiety that made her heart skitter.

'I'm fine. Right now I'm more interested in how *you* feel.'

He rose with the tray. 'My feelings are irrelevant. Get some sleep. We'll talk in the morning.'

She wanted to ask what exactly they would be talking about, but he was already leaving, his shoulders and back set in tense lines that made her nervousness rise higher.

Her hand slid down to rest on her abdomen.

Whatever it was, she could handle it. As long as it didn't interfere with the welfare of her baby.

He was having a child.

Ari barely managed to set the tray down before it slid out of his useless grip.

Shaking from head to toe, he gripped the edge of the granite counter in the suite's kitchen and tried to breathe. *He was having a child!*

The self-indulgent need to rail at fate was so strong the growl bubbled up through his chest before he managed to swallow it down. He stalked to the living room and contented himself with a fiery shot of single malt Scotch. Except he was no better equipped to handle the bone-crushing fear gripping him. It writhed like a poisonous snake inside him before sinking its merciless fangs into his heart.

Was he doomed to fail at this task too, the way he'd failed Sofia? He'd single-handedly taken care of his brothers and his mother, had ensured they were protected as much as possible from the fallout of his father's misdeeds.

And yet he hadn't been able to save his wife.

Or his unborn child.

Was fate taunting him again? Willing him to fail again? *No!*

His fist tightened around the glass and he set it aside before it shattered. This time things would be different. Because anything else was unthinkable.

He moved restlessly across the room, willing his pulse to slow, his insides to stop churning viciously with the acrid mix of guilt and fear.

He was going to be a father. His steps slowed and he

stopped in front of the view. Funny, he'd stood here just two days ago thinking he was in control of his world. It had been in the moments before Perla burst in and accused him of controlling her life.

Now he barely felt in control of his.

Whirling round, he walked out of the living room and entered his study. It might be the middle of the night in Washington, but it was still a working day in London and the rest of Europe.

His first call was to the Pantelides headquarters in London, where he gathered all the pertinent information he needed. Next he placed a call to his lawyers in Greece. His dealings with them so far had been purely business so he wasn't surprised at their thinly veiled shock as he outlined his wishes.

By the time he finished his calls, the horizon was lightening with the coming dawn.

Ari rubbed a hand across his jaw and rested his head against his seat.

He had no idea how Perla would take the conversation he intended to have with her come morning. There could potentially be many obstacles to getting his way but he intended to smash them all aside.

Because one thing had become clear in his mind from the second he'd found out Perla was carrying his child.

The welfare of his child was the most important thing in his life.

She was already up when he knocked on her door just after seven o'clock. Up, showered and dressed.

In black. Only the flame of her hair provided vivid colour in the harsh landscape. And she was in the process of coiling it into a tight bun when she followed him out to the dining room, where he'd set her breakfast tray.

Ari resisted the urge to pull her hands away from her

task. He also resisted the urge to command her to change her clothes.

She finished securing her hair and turned to him. Her gaze met his for a moment before travelling over his body.

Noting his attire, she looked back up. 'Have you slept at all?'

'No,' he replied, vaguely disturbed by his anger at her choice of clothes.

A look of concern crossed her eyes. He allowed it to touch him for a second, two seconds, before he looked away.

'Sit down. Drink your tea and have some of those dry crackers. They'll calm any nausea that triggers morning sickness.'

She looked at the tray and wrinkled her nose. 'Too late. I've already thrown up twice.'

He forced away the anxiety that tightened his nape. 'Drink it anyway.'

She sat and he poured her tea and passed it to her, noting the anxious glances she sent his way. Part of him wanted to reassure her. He curbed the feeling because he knew the road ahead wouldn't be easy.

'Aren't you having anything?'

'No. Until we find out which smells trigger your nausea, I'll eat my meals separately.'

'How come you know so much about morning sickness and nausea triggers?'

Ice formed in his belly, stealing his breath. But it was nothing compared to the pain that ripped through his heart as the guilt and fear returned twice as forcefully.

He looked up and saw the anxiety stamped on her face. 'Ari?'

'I know because my wife was four months pregnant with our first child when she died.'

Her cup clattered onto the saucer and her features

paled. 'Oh, my God. I'm… I don't know what to say. I'm sorry for—'

He slashed a hand through the air, unwilling to dwell on the past, unwilling to let her see the devastation that still had the power to shred his insides.

They had more important things to discuss than the subject of his hubris.

'Drink your tea, Perla. We have a lot to discuss.'

The shock of his revelation still clear in her eyes, she slowly picked up her cup and took another tiny sip. He waited until she'd eaten a cracker before he spoke.

'Do you have any health issues that I should know about?'

She placed her cup down. 'I'm allergic to shellfish but, aside from that, I've always been healthy and Morgan's health insurance provided me with annual check-ups. They always came back clean.'

The mention of her husband's name made his fists clench but he forced the feeling away. He needed to get over the fact that she'd been another man's wife only a short time ago.

'Good. Then we'll postpone a thorough health check until we return to London.'

Her eyes connected with his. 'We're returning to London?'

'Yes.'

'Why?'

'Because London is where we will be married.'

CHAPTER TEN

'No.'

'You've already said that. Twice.'

'I believe in making things crystal-clear so there's no misunderstanding. I won't marry you.'

Perla watched his nostrils pinch in that way that told her he was hanging onto his control by a thread. But the emotions coursing through her eroded any concern for his control or lack thereof.

Who would've believed that a proposal of marriage could bring so much pain? But devastating pain was exactly what ravaged her as they faced each other across his wide living room like two boxers about to engage in a fight.

'You've yet to give me a reason why not.'

'And you've yet to give me a valid reason why I should. Presumably it's because I'm pregnant. Regardless, the answer is still no.'

'Perla—'

'No is no, Ari.' Her hands shook as she thought back to what she'd been through the last three years. 'I got married under false pretences three years ago. I won't do it again, no matter the reason.'

His eyes sparked with curiosity. 'Explain.'

She paused. Could she reveal the final humiliation? 'I've already told you my marriage was…difficult. I also know how you feel about me and the circumstances under which we met. No matter how much you try to deny it, I know you despise what happened between us. Trust me, losing my virginity to a man who's mourning his dead wife on the anniversary of her death is bad enough. I refuse to become trapped in another sham of a marriage where I'm second best.'

She ground to a halt at his white-faced shock.

'Your *virginity?*' he rasped in a tone that could've flayed stone.

Perla flinched. Of course. Of all the things she'd said, that was the one he'd have picked up on. Turning around, she squeezed her eyes shut as the familiar shame dredged through her stomach.

'Perla.' He was right behind her, standing so close his breath washed over her exposed nape, making a shiver course through her. 'Did you just say you were a virgin when we slept together?' he asked, his voice spiked with emotions she couldn't name.

Clenching her hands into tight fists, she struggled to breathe. 'Yes.'

'Turn around.'

'No.'

'You really need to stop defying me so much. There are some things I will let slide. This isn't one of them. Turn around,' he demanded, more forcefully this time.

Heart in her throat, she opened her eyes and turned. The gold flecks in his eyes stood out with the intensity of his stare. 'You were married for three years. How were you still a virgin on your husband's death?'

She affected a shrug that felt far from casual. 'We never got round to it, I guess.'

He gripped her shoulders in an implacable hold. 'This is not the time to be facetious. Tell me how Lowell could have a woman such as you in his bed and walk away. Why a woman who could drive any red-blooded man to his knees with just one look could remain a virgin for so long within the bounds of marriage.'

'Because I did nothing for him!'

He frowned. 'You refused to sleep with him?'

She laughed, or rather she attempted to laugh. The sound scraped her throat and emerged a ragged croak. 'On the contrary, I threw myself at him. Hell, I even tried to seduce him *before* and after we were married. He suggested we wait. Stupid me, I thought it was the height of *romantic*; that he was being *noble!* But it turned out he didn't want me. You want to know why? Because my husband told me on our wedding night that he was gay!'

Hazel eyes widened. 'Lowell was gay?'

'I'm surprised you don't know, considering where he was when your investigators found him in Thailand.'

'We knew he'd taken residence in a disreputable part of Bangkok when he was found but I assumed...'

'He was whoring it up with women? No, Ari, the man I married was probably shacked up with a boyfriend when your men caught up with him. I didn't need to be a genius to read between the lines. And I don't need a crystal ball to know he changed the terms of his contract and plotted to crash the Pantelides tanker because he needed money to fund his secret life and the drug habit that killed him.' Raw humiliation threatened to consume her whole, especially when he let out a crude curse.

'Perla *mou...*'

'No, I don't want to talk about this any more. And I don't want to discuss marriage. You're proposing because I'm pregnant but nothing will ever convince me to get married again.'

'Not even the welfare of your child?'

She paled and he let out another curse. Swinging her into his arms, he walked to the sofa and sat down with her in his lap.

'This child means everything to me. I intend to give it everything it needs,' she whispered fiercely.

'Except a stable home and the unity of both parents.'

'That's a low blow, Ari. You had that for a while. But it didn't turn out great for you either, did it?' She regretted her answer but she had to fight back. She was no longer fighting for just herself. She had her baby to think of.

Ari's arms tightened around her. 'Our marriage will be different.'

'You cannot possibly know that.'

'I'm determined to win this fight, Perla.'

'Why does it have to be a fight?'

'Because you're resisting my every effort to make you see sense.'

'Just because I don't see things your way doesn't mean it's nonsense. If this hadn't happened, would *you* have ever remarried?'

The tightening of his jaw and the way his eyelids swept down gave her the answer she needed. 'So why does it have to be different for me?'

'Because this is no longer just about you.'

Simple words that made her breath catch. 'I know. But this is emotional blackmail.' And she refused to succumb to blackmail of any sort ever again.

'It's the truth. Tell me what your plan is for our child. Do you intend to return to your former in-laws after he or she is born, live with Lowell's parents with another man's child?'

A shiver went through her. 'Of course not. I'll find another place to live.'

'And when the child is older? What then?'

'I'll find adequate childcare and continue my career. Millions of women do it every day. Why should I be any different?'

'Because this child is not just any child. It is a Pantelides.

Whether you want to admit it or not, that makes it different from any other child.'

'I know you like to think you're special but—'

'No buts, Perla. I've lost one unborn child.' His gaze dropped to her flat stomach and he swallowed hard. 'If I'm lucky enough to become a father for a second time, nothing and no one will keep me from my child.'

A stalemate.

Despite knowing it was temporary, she hung onto the stalemate as Ari's private jet raced them towards Bermuda and the Pantelides resort project she'd undertaken what seemed like a thousand years ago.

It was hard to fathom that it'd been barely eighteen hours since she'd discovered she was carrying Ari's child.

Even harder to believe she'd agreed to give him an answer in the time the marriage licence would take to be ready.

But the look on his face when he'd made his vow had shaken her to the core. Shaken her into considering the fact that he meant it when he said he wanted a full-time role in their child's life.

After what she had been through, shoved from foster home to foster home and then eventually spat out at eighteen, did she not owe it to her child to give it the best care possible?

But then could she bear to tie herself to another man who clearly did not want her for herself? Morgan had used her to hide his true sexual orientation from those he believed would judge him.

With Ari, it was simply the fact that she carried his heir.

A wave of sadness washed over her and the tablet she was supposed to be using to jot down ideas for the resort opening blurred as tears welled in her eyes.

Tears. Another symptom of her pregnancy she couldn't

seem to stem. She brushed them away and looked up to find Ari watching her.

'What's wrong?'

'I seem to have discovered the pregnancy hormone that lets me cry at the drop of a hat. I should hire myself out to Hollywood.'

He stood from his wide leather seat and approached her with one hand outstretched. 'Come with me,' he commanded.

'Where are we going?' she asked, although she found herself putting her hand in his, allowing him to draw her up.

'We don't land for an hour and a half. You should take the time to rest.'

She stopped. 'I'm pregnant, not sick. I don't need to rest.'

'But you will. Or I'll turn this plane around and we can head to London.'

'I have work to do, Ari—'

'You were staring at a blank screen on your tablet.'

'I was *strategising*.'

'Yes, and it was so effective you were in tears.' He placed a firm hand on her waist and propelled her forward. He opened the cabin door and she entered a large, sumptuously appointed bedroom. The gold-and-blue décor screamed opulent sophistication but it was the bed that drew her attention. King-sized and high, it was piled with pillows and covered with a gold silk spread that begged to be touched.

Moving forward, she did just that, then went one better and sat on the edge of the bed. The firm mattress gave a little beneath her and, on a whim, she kicked off her shoes and scooted backwards just as a large yawn caught her unawares.

She looked up to find Ari regarding her with an amused expression. 'Fine. I can probably do with a little rest.'

He moved forward and started removing the cufflinks

from his shirt. As he folded the sleeves back, he toed off his shoes.

'What are you doing?'

'What does it look like?'

'But…' She stopped as she recalled that he'd been up all night. It suddenly struck her that he'd taken care of her all through the shocking discovery of her pregnancy and afterwards while he'd neglected his own needs.

She could insist he return to the cabin but that would be unnecessarily mean and, really, there was more than enough room on the bed for both of them. It wasn't as if he was about to tear her clothes off and make mad, passionate love to her.

They'd moved past that.

She pushed away the ache that lodged in her heart at the thought and lifted the cover.

The smile he gave her didn't quite reach his eyes and she noticed the tension lines around his mouth when he got into bed.

Expecting him to relax against the pillow, she held her breath when he turned sideways and propped his head on his curved arm. Hypnotic eyes travelled over her hair. 'You'll be much more comfortable if you take your hair down.'

'I don't think so. My hair has got me into too much trouble around you and your inner ten-year-old. It's staying up.'

Her hair had been an explosive subject between them. Far be it from her to tempt fate. Or, worse still, for her to tempt fate only to find fate couldn't care less.

His mouth twisted. 'Please yourself.' He relaxed against the pillows, crossed his hands over his chest and closed his eyes. Within minutes, his even breathing echoed softly through the room.

She stared because she couldn't help herself. And because, like the first time she'd watched him sleep, Ari's transformation in repose was breathtaking.

But now she knew the reason behind the constant torment that lurked in his eyes and the bone-deep weariness etched into his face, she was thankful he received peace in sleep.

For the first time since he'd told her, she let herself think of just what Ari had lost. Losing his wife was devastating enough, but his unborn child, too? Was it any wonder he'd been so desolate that day at Macdonald Hall?

Was it any wonder he'd wanted to find oblivion? Her heart ached and tears clouded her eyes all over again.

God, this needed to stop or she'd be a basket case long before this child was born. She couldn't afford to be a basket case. Couldn't afford anything other than her complete wits about her, her mind *and* her heart intact. She'd been through too much to put her emotions on the line again. Until she could find a way to guarantee that, there was no way she could consider Ari's proposal.

Because there were times when he showed her kindness that her foolish heart believed he could care for her.

And that was a slippery slope to heartache she had no intention of skidding down…

She woke to the sound of a steady heartbeat beneath her ear and a warm, familiar scent in her nostrils. But it was the fingers splayed over her stomach that made her eyes slowly drift open.

Ari was awake, his gaze fixed on her flat belly. She must have curled closer to his side of the bed in her sleep because he had one arm clamped around her while his other rested on her stomach.

As she watched him, a wave of despair washed over his face. The emotion was so strong her breath caught. He heard it and his eyes flew to hers. He started to withdraw, but she held his hand in place.

'What happened to her?' she asked softly.

He froze and his features shuttered. For several minutes she thought he wouldn't answer. 'She had a weak heart. The doctors were divided on whether she could carry a child to term without it causing a severe strain on her heart. I warned her it was too risky. She chose to side with the more optimistic doctors. Her heart gave out in her second trimester.'

The naked devastation in his voice slashed her insides. 'And you blame yourself.'

That was why the news of her pregnancy didn't bring joy. The look on his face had been one of deep, wretched torment.

His smile was grim as his eyes were bleak. 'Despite my fears, I let myself be convinced she would be all right. That our child would be all right. They both died.'

'Ari, you can't—'

He pulled away and got out of bed. 'We are not having this conversation now, Perla. It's time to leave the plane. We landed ten minutes ago.'

The Pantelides Bermuda was another architectural work of art. The blueprints and plans Ari had shown her at the restaurant were nowhere near as awe-inspiring as the real thing.

The long, palm-tree-lined drive along a private road gave way to six sprawling buildings linked together by curved wooden bridges.

Multi-roomed suites, each one containing a wide wooden deck, an infinity pool and a luxurious spa, faced a stunning private white-sanded beach. Four-poster beds built with local carved wood soared up to vaulted ceilings and crown mouldings that lent an air of old-world elegance, blending old and new in exquisite symmetry.

The exclusive three-storey casino made entirely of triple-paned glass was set away from the main resort on giant transparent stilts and accessed by private boats manned by discreet security guards. From the resort, the building seemed to be floating on water.

Once their luggage was loaded into an air-conditioned SUV, Ari turned to her. 'We'll take the full tour later. Right now I'll introduce you to your chef.'

'As long as it's not to another bed and a command to "rest", we're okay.'

His lips twisted but he said nothing as he climbed in beside her and drove them to their villa at the southernmost point of the resort.

The sight of the turquoise waters gave her another idea for the opening. 'I think I'll add scuba-diving to the activities.'

'Great. Consider rowing too.'

'Rowing?'

'Sakis and Brianna are joining us for a couple of days before the guests arrive. Sometimes the waters around here get a little choppy but I intend to row with Sakis. I'll let you know how I rate it.'

'That would be great, thanks.'

There was no sign of the ragged pain she'd seen on his face on the plane. He was back to Arion Pantelides, luxury hotel mogul and master of all he surveyed.

She held her breath when they reached the villa and the staff asked where to place their luggage.

'I'll take the smaller suite. You take the master suite,' Ari said.

Perla wasn't sure why her stomach fell with disappointment. Had she really thought he would insist on joint sleeping arrangements? Nothing had changed since yesterday aside from the fact that their indiscretions had resulted in a child. Sexually, they were done with each other.

Still she couldn't suppress her rising desolation as he

walked away. With two personal butlers seeing to the unpacking, Perla changed into the only bikini she owned and walked from room to room, acquainting herself with the layout of the villa. It was as she entered the solarium that she noticed the repeating item in each room.

She turned as Ari walked in. 'You've had an epi pen placed in each room?' she asked, her heart flipping over when she noticed he'd changed into khaki shorts and a white T-shirt.

'Yes,' he answered simply.

The thoughtfulness behind the gesture was so alien, she blurted, 'Why?'

He paused on the way to the French windows that led to the teak-floored deck, changed course and came to stand in front of her. This close, his proximity wreaked havoc with her pulse rate. Reaching out, he brushed his fingers down her cheek.

'I'm not taking any chances this time, Perla. Not with you, not with this baby.' His voice was a solid, solemn vow that struck deep into her heart.

Her eyes prickled and she sniffed hard. 'Are you determined to make me cry again?'

He grimaced and dropped his hand. 'Perhaps I need to learn to accept that tears are par for the course. Come and meet Peter, your chef.'

Slowly she followed him outside into the sunshine, desperately trying to get her wayward emotions under control. 'I really don't need a personal chef.'

'It is already done, *glikia mou*, so you have to live with it.'

She was trying to decipher the Greek endearment when a man dressed in chef whites stepped forward from behind the table where he'd been slicing fresh fruit.

'Your fruit platter is coming right up. And for lunch

I have some freshly grilled chicken kebabs with a green salad. If you need anything else, let me know.'

Ari steered her towards twin loungers by the pool. As they sat down, his phone pinged. The huge smile that split his face as he read the text made her breath catch.

'Theo is coming down too. He'll be here at the end of the week.'

A pang of envy spilled into her heart. 'You're very close, aren't you?'

He looked up and shrugged. 'They're my family. They mean everything to me.'

The simple statement made more tears prickle her eyes. He saw it and frowned. 'Perla?'

'You're so lucky. I mean…you've had tragedy, of course, but you've remained close with your family and that's… that's…'

He watched her with keen eyes. 'It's something you've never had.'

'No.'

He set his phone aside. 'Marry me and you can have it too.'

Her heart lurched and temptation shot hope into her heart. But still her instincts shrieked dire warning.

'It's not that simple. I can't…'

His face hardened. 'For the sake of this child we have to make sacrifices, Perla.'

'What do you mean?'

'I mean we both agree we're not an ideal match but we need to look beyond that to what's best for our child. Whatever lofty ideas you have of being an ideal single parent will always pale in comparison to what we can provide as a united family. That is the bottom line.'

'That may be your bottom line. It's not mine. I think it's more important that this child grows up in a loving environment.'

His face hardened further. 'And you don't think we can provide that?'

She held her breath until Peter had delivered the fruit platters and returned to the far side of the deck where he was preparing their lunch. 'Come on, Ari. After what you've been through, what we've both been through—'

'My past has nothing to do with this.'

Her heart sank. 'If you believe that then I'm going to need even more time to consider your proposal.'

'What the hell are you saying, Perla?'

'I'm saying you've been hurt and devastated. We've both been. We need to factor that into how much that will impact our child's welfare.'

'So you want me to spill my feelings to you before you consider marrying me.'

'No. But we need to get past the bitterness and deal with the pain before we can move on. That aside, we've barely spent more than forty-eight hours in each other's company.'

His eyes gleamed. 'And a good portion of that time we spent having sex. At least we know we're compatible in the bedroom.'

Heat crawled over her skin and burrowed inside to sting parts of her body she didn't want to think about right now. 'How does that help in bringing up a child?'

His gaze drifted over her flushed skin, and his smile held a great deal of mockery. 'You'd be surprised how compliant a well-sated man can be.'

She speared a piece of papaya with her fork as her face flamed. 'Well, I wouldn't know. I didn't succeed in that department during my marriage.'

He stiffened. 'You were wasting your passion on the wrong man. Our marriage will be different.'

'So…so you intend for us to…'

'Have sex? Yes, Perla. I have no intention of living like a monk.'

So she had an answer as to how the physical part of their marriage would be. But no clue as to the emotional. Could she contemplate a future with him, knowing he would never be emotionally available?

No. Sex, as she'd discovered, was great. But it would never be enough in the long run.

Despite losing her appetite, she forced herself to eat a few more chunks of fruit and summoned a smile when the staff cleared away their plates.

She looked up to find Ari staring at her, the question clear in his eyes. 'We agreed to a week, Ari.'

His lips compressed. 'What will be different in a week's time that we can't resolve today?'

Her hands shook and she took a sip of water. 'Maybe I can convince you to talk to me a little bit more.'

His eyes narrowed. 'And will this therapy session be a two-way thing?'

She'd already told him the most humiliating secret, but the deeper secret, the yearning for a connection, to belong... It was that deep yearning that had swayed her into Morgan's path in the first place. Could she share that with Ari?

She took a deep breath. 'I'm willing to try if you are. But we both have to be committed to try.'

'Perla...' His voice held mild disgruntlement.

'We agreed on a week. All I'm doing is adding a tiny addendum. You owe our child, at the very least.'

Ari felt his insides tighten and fought the need to demand an answer right there and then. With each minute that ticked past, he felt more and more on edge, as if some unforeseen wrecking ball hovered just beyond the horizon, ready to smash through the quiet joy bubbling beneath his skin.

Perla was right. He'd never intended to marry again, but waking up next to Perla on the plane to find her curled up so trustingly against him, he'd begun to dare to believe that he could have another chance to reclaim what he'd lost.

A part of him had died with Sofia and their unborn child. But he could forge a new family, be the father he'd always wanted to be, the one his own father had failed so comprehensively to be.

But in this he knew he had to be patient, no matter how much it killed him.

'I'm not a patient man.'

His chest tightened as her mouth curved in a tiny relieved smile. 'I'm learning that. Maybe I should also confess I'm a stubborn woman.'

His gaze flew to her hair and his groin tightened. He wryly admitted that his need to speed things up also stemmed from the fact that as a married man he wouldn't have to hold back on the need that clawed relentlessly through him day and night.

'Fine. I agree that we use this week to learn some more about each other.'

She smiled at Peter as he delivered their main course. Then her eyes returned to Ari. 'Does that mean I can ask you whatever I want?'

He'd opened that particular door. Attempting to slam it shut now would only make things worse. He gave a single curt nod and saw the speculative smile that curved her full mouth.

'Word of warning, though. I give as good as I get. And I don't always play fair.'

Her smile disappeared and Ari couldn't stop the laugh that rumbled out at her startled look.

He tore into his lunch and watched with satisfaction as she consumed hers. They were polishing off the last of the salad when she glanced furtively at him.

'Do your brothers know that I'm…pregnant?'

'No, I haven't told them yet. Ideally, I'd like to announce the pregnancy and our intended marriage at the same time.'

Her gaze slid from his and he forced himself not to react. 'Um…okay.'

Feeling the restlessness that had taken up residence in his body clamouring through him again, he got up. 'Time for the full tour, then I'll let you get to work.'

CHAPTER ELEVEN

THE DAYS PASSED in a blur of activity and by the time Sakis and Brianna arrived on Thursday afternoon, Perla had everything in place in anticipation for when the VIP guests arrived on Sunday.

Unlike their first meeting, Sakis Pantelides's smile was openly friendly if a lot speculative. She read the same keen interest in Brianna's stunning blue eyes.

'Ari tells me you're putting on a spectacular list of events for the opening.'

'He should know. He's been slave-driving me up the wall with his endless demands for perfection. Perhaps now you're here, you can get him out of my hair for an hour or two.'

Brianna laughed as she hugged her husband's arm. 'That seems to be a common trait amongst the Pantelides men. They never know when to leave well enough alone and trust us women to get on with it.'

Her husband sent her an indulgent smile so full of adoration Perla's heart snagged in her chest then dropped to her stomach in envy.

'Asking me to leave you alone is like asking the lark to stop singing first thing in the morning. It's simply impossible, *agapita.*'

A blush raced up her face and the powerful passion that arced between them made Perla look away.

Sakis turned to her. 'Where is my brother, anyway?'

'He's getting the scull ready for your rowing session this afternoon. I believe he wants to hit the water the moment Theo arrives,' she said.

What she didn't add was that Ari had been growing steadily more restless as the days had progressed this week. This morning they'd snapped at each other over breakfast, after which he'd disappeared with a curt instruction for her to take things easy. Or else…

God, why had she deluded herself into thinking they'd learn *nice* things about each other this week? So far she'd learned that even though he'd stated that he was happy for her to carry on working, he intended to keep a close eye on her at all times.

She only had to think of a need for it to materialise. Meals and snacks appeared minutes before cravings hit and there was always someone with a golf buggy, a wide-brimmed hat or a cool drink nearby.

That he also fully intended to extract a *yes* from her as soon as he could was also clear. As for the heated looks he'd sent her whenever she walked into his presence…

She shook her head and focused to find two pairs of eyes trained on her. 'Um…the concierge's assistant will escort you to your villa and I'll let Ari know you're here.'

With a smile she knew was a little strained, she walked away. After triple-checking everything on her list and clucking with impatience because she knew she was daw-dling, she jumped into her allotted SUV and drove down to their villa.

Ari was in the middle of a phone call when she walked into the cool, brightly lit living room. He advanced until he stood in front of her but carried on his conversation, one hand idly playing with her loose hair.

She'd started their stay by wearing it up but Ari had

found every opportunity to free it until she'd given up. There were some fights that just weren't worth the effort.

She didn't follow his conversation because it was conducted in rapid-fire Greek. But even if he'd spoken English, she wouldn't have followed it because of the feverish emotions coursing through her at his touch.

Each day since they arrived at the resort he'd laid assault to her senses like this, touching her whenever she was within a few feet, grazing his fingers over her stomach in a possessive move that sent her emotions into free fall every time. That had been when he wasn't snapping at her.

To say their time together so far had been a roller coaster would be an understatement.

She heard him end the call as his thumb traced over her mouth. Slowly he lowered the phone and his head began to descend.

'Were you looking for me?' he murmured.

'Yes. Your brother and Brianna are here.'

'I know. Sakis called me ten minutes ago.' His head moved closer. 'Theo is also on his way from the airport. He'll be here in less than ten minutes. He wants to row straight away so I've had the equipment sent down to the water.'

His lips flitted over hers and she tried to pull back. 'Ari...don't.'

He stiffened slightly. 'I've been a bear towards you all week. Let me apologise,' he coaxed in that deep, hypnotic voice.

Her breath gushed out of her as he sealed her lips with his. Their mingled groan echoed around the room, then faded away to be replaced with harsh breathing. They strained towards each other until she could feel the solid imprint of his body and the even more rigid outline of his arousal against her belly.

The need that tore through her made her spear her hands

through his hair. With a deep groan he picked her up and carried her to the sofa without breaking their kiss.

He was kissing his way down her neck when she finally came to her senses.

'No. Stop!'

He raised his head slowly, his eyes sizzling pools of need and frustration. 'Why the hell should I?' he growled.

'We can't...you can't use sex to apologise. Saying you're sorry is enough.'

A mirthless smile tilted one corner of his mouth. 'You really are naïve, aren't you?'

She blushed fiercely. 'Perhaps, but I also know that sex can confuse issues. You've been grumpy for days because you weren't getting your way. Sex will not achieve what you want.'

His eyes gleamed as he reared back. 'But it will make me feel a whole lot better. And you can deny it all you want but it will make you feel better too.'

She couldn't deny it but neither was she going to admit it. She sat up and straightened her clothes. The black sundress wasn't exactly appropriate for the tropics but it seemed black was all she'd packed. 'Anyway, we can't. We have guests who require our attention. But don't think I haven't noticed that every time I try to get you to talk to me like we agreed, you find something else for me to do!'

He stiffened and jerked to his feet. 'You're asking a man who has kept his innermost thoughts hidden most of his life to bare his soul, *glikia mou*. It's not as simple as hitting play on a machine,' he said, his voice charged with the echo of painful memory.

Her heart twisted for him, but she pressed on. Deep inside, she'd begun to hope that this would be the way to reach him, the way they could both move forward and begin the tentative steps to building a solid platform for their child.

'I know that. Of course I know that. But, as difficult as it is, we have to give it a shot, Ari.'

Slowly, he inhaled. Then he nodded and held out his hand to her. 'We will. Before we leave here. Now, you can come and watch me row my sexual frustration away. That will be your entertainment for the afternoon.'

She let herself be pulled up and felt some of her trepidation melt away. Immediately, thoughts that had hovered on the edge of her mind crowded in. Thoughts that involved whether she and Ari could make a marriage work despite all their baggage. That he seemed to believe it was possible had slowly eroded her own scepticism as the week had crept on.

The way Ari had taken care of her since her pregnancy came to light, she didn't doubt now that he would provide a parent's utter devotion and stability. And perhaps, over time, that devotion would spill onto her.

Her heart lurched painfully.

Morgan had shaken the foundation of her beliefs. But she'd discovered in the last few weeks that he hadn't totally annihilated her self-confidence. It was that renewed self-confidence that made her want even better for herself and her child.

At least, with Ari, she knew the lay of the land going in. The events of his past might mean he never cared deeply for her. So the only thing that she needed to be sure of was whether she could live without the love she'd been so desperate for the first time round.

Before we leave here...

She pushed away the lingering trepidation and concentrated on getting in the electric buggy that would take them down to the water, although it was hard not to keep glancing at Ari's bare thighs as he drove.

The youngest Pantelides was already on the waterfront with Sakis when they arrived.

Theo Pantelides was as tall as Ari but broader-shouldered with the same jet-black hair, although his bore no hint of the grey sprinkled at Ari's temples.

Equally as gorgeous, his eyes were several shades lighter than Ari's hazel and held the same speculation as Sakis's when they rested on her.

'So I finally meet the woman who's caused quite the stir at Pantelides HQ.'

'Theo…' Ari growled a mild warning.

Theo's smile was unrepentant as he held out a closed fist to her. A smile twitching at her lips, she touched her knuckles to his in a bemused fist bump.

'About time someone shook him out of his doldrums,' he added with a wink.

Sakis laughed and Brianna grinned but Ari's narrow-eyed stare held no mirth.

'Tell me you're ready to get your ass whipped and I'll happily oblige you,' he said through clenched teeth.

'Any time, old man.'

Ari's jaw clenched harder but the hand he clamped on his brother's shoulder to push him towards the boat was so affectionate it brought a lump to Perla's throat. He disappeared into the specially built boathouse and emerged minutes later dressed in a dark gold rowing suit that moulded to his body.

Perla tried not to stare at the perfect specimen of man that was Arion Pantelides but when he grabbed the end of the scull and hefted it over his shoulders, she struggled to get air past her restricted throat into her lungs.

Purely for self-preservation, she looked away. Then immediately looked back.

'God, don't even try to resist that. Don't get me wrong, I think Sakis is the best-looking of the bunch, but the three of them together like this, even I find it hard to breathe, never mind keep my eyes solely on my husband,' Brianna muttered.

She grinned at Perla's shocked laugh, fanned herself and moved closer to the edge of the viewing bench to watch the men set their scull on the water and climb in.

Sakis took the front seat, Theo the middle and Ari the last. They sank their oars into the water. Theo rolled his shoulders and laughed when Ari admonished him to be still.

Their chests rose and fell in rhythm, once, twice. Then they struck away from shore in flawless synchronicity.

'Wow.'

'I know, right? I've watched them row many times but I never get over how perfect they look together.'

Again Perla felt that tiny pang of jealousy. But she couldn't help but wonder if this could be her baby's life if she agreed to what Ari wanted. Her child, and by definition she, could be a part of this…togetherness. She didn't have to be on the outside looking in like she had her whole life. She could give her baby a ready-made family who would cherish him or her.

She watched the men row, her eyes continually drawn to Ari, who now had a grin on his face despite the determination in his eyes.

'Ari seems different.'

Perla jumped and turned to Brianna to find those incisive blue eyes on her. 'Um…is he?'

Brianna nodded. 'At the funeral he seemed ready to smash everyone's head in. Today he looks as if the only person whose head is in danger is Theo, which, considering that's par for the course, is worth mentioning.'

'And you think I have something to do with that?'

'Definitely. You and…that, I'm guessing.'

She followed Brianna's gaze to where her hand rested on her stomach. With a gasp, Perla snatched her hand away but not before Brianna gave her a sympathetic smile.

'I...no one knows,' she said hurriedly.

'Don't worry, your secret's safe with me.' Her hand rose to rest over her own stomach. 'I have a secret of my own. Although I have a feeling it won't remain a secret for long. Sakis has been bursting to tell the whole world. But I'm guessing he'll start with his brothers for now.'

'Congratulations,' Perla offered. Then curiosity made her blurt, 'How do you feel?'

'Frankly? Scared out of my mind. I didn't have the best of childhoods so I don't have a role model to fall back on. Sakis tells me I'll be a great mother but I think he's hopelessly biased.' Her smile was tinged with anxiety but full of love as her gaze swung back to the men. 'What about you?'

'Honestly, between Ari's determination to get me to marry him and the job I have to do here, I haven't had time to be scared, but—'

'Ari asked you to marry him?' Brianna's eyes were wide with surprise. 'That's huge! I presume he's told you what happened to his wife?'

Perla nodded.

'He wouldn't have made the decision easily.'

'He only wants to marry because of his child.'

Brianna frowned. 'I don't think so. I don't want to scare you but the reality is that every one in four pregnancies ends in miscarriage. If all he wanted was to give the baby respectability, he'd have waited until it was born to ask you to marry him.'

Perla shook her head, refusing to even begin to hope. 'Besides the baby, there's really nothing like that between us.'

'But there is *something*. There's incredible chemistry. Don't knock the power of great sex.'

She gasped. 'That's what he said,' she said then blushed as she realised what she'd let slip.

Brianna laughed. 'I knew there was an alpha horn dog

beneath all that suave Pantelides exterior. Now let's go and cheer our boys home before I give in to the urge to ask for details I have no business knowing.'

She jumped up and headed towards the waterfront. Perla followed at a slower pace and got there in time to see the brothers embrace at the news of Brianna's pregnancy.

Ari's gaze drifted to her as Sakis pulled his wife close and kissed her. His gaze dropped to her stomach but he said nothing, only helped his brothers stow the scull and oars in the boathouse before they all piled into the buggies to head back to their villas.

Dinner that evening turned into a family celebration, one that hammered home to Perla just what she could be missing out on if she refused Ari's proposal. All through the evening his eyes kept straying to her, the intent in their depths clear and determined.

By the time she excused herself and returned to her suite, her mind was in turmoil.

That turmoil continued for the next three days. Thankfully, she had no time to think.

From the moment the first luxury SUV rolled in with the guests her days turned manic. She barely saw Ari because he was equally busy entertaining guests in the plushly equipped casino while she dealt with organising the guests and directing the activities she'd planned for them.

She was busy sorting out the sky-diving group and pairing them with their instructors and guests on the last day when she heard a familiar voice.

She looked up to see Selena Hamilton heading towards her.

Perla's mouth dropped open before she could stop herself.

'So, what do you think?' Selena trilled, patting her new russet-coloured curls.

Perla forced a smile. 'You look great.'

Selena's smile slipped a fraction. 'I'm glad you think so. Roger thinks I look awful. What does he know, right?' She forced a laugh that didn't touch her curiously over-bright eyes.

Roger Hamilton strolled in at that moment. He completely ignored his wife and, grabbing Perla, kissed her on both cheeks.

'Sign me up for whatever you're organising, darling! I'm all yours.'

Behind him, Ari entered the room and froze to a halt. The thunderous look in his eyes made her stomach flip but she managed to keep the smile on her face as he walked to where she stood. Seeing the look he directed at Roger, she glared at him and shook her head once. His jaw clenched but he exchanged pleasantries until the instructor called for them to suit up.

Ari's hand slid over her nape and tilted her head up to meet his descending kiss. It was hard and quick. 'You take care of Hamilton, *glikia mou*. Or I will,' he muttered. Then he was gone.

Breathing a sigh of relief, she turned around just as Selena returned to her side. Before she could utter a word, Selena grabbed her arm. 'I think Roger is going to leave me,' she whispered fiercely.

'Are you sure?'

Her frenzied nodding made her curls bounce wildly. 'I think he's having an affair.' Her scarlet-painted lips wobbled and her eyes widened.

'You could be wrong...'

'What if I'm not? I can't live without him. He's everything I've ever wanted but I can see him slipping away from me.' Tears filled her green eyes.

'Selena, I don't think you should go sky-diving if you're feeling like that.'

She swiped her tears with perfectly manicured fingers.

'Nonsense. Roger wants to go sky-diving so I'm going with him.'

But a glance at Roger, who was busy flirting with a female instructor, suggested he had no interest in what his wife wanted. Perla glanced at Selena again and worry gnawed at her. Selena's glazed eyes suggested she was under the influence of something other than unhappiness. But there was no diplomatic way to ask without causing offence.

Gnawing at her bottom lip, she followed the guests out to the air-conditioned buses that would take them to the airstrip. Then climbed in with them.

'Where the hell is she?' Ari demanded for the fifth time. The concierge manager paled and reached for his phone again.

'I'm sorry, sir, but we think she may have joined one of the guest events.'

'You *think*? Try her phone again.'

The manager hurried to do his bidding. When he shook his head regretfully, Ari curbed the need to punch a hole in the desk.

'Giving your staff hell?' came a droll voice from behind him.

'Not now, Sakis.'

'Why? What's wrong?'

'I'm trying to find Perla. No one's seen her in the last hour.'

'And this is worrying because…?'

Ari pursed his lips. 'She's supposed to be at the villa, having lunch.'

He looked up as the assistant manager hurried forward. 'Mr Pantelides, I've just been told by one of the drivers that Mrs Lowell joined the sky-diving guests.'

For a moment, he couldn't compute the information. 'She *what?*'

The voices that responded were drowned out by the blood thundering in his ears. When his arm was grabbed in a firm hold and he was propelled down a hallway, he did not protest.

He heard a door shut behind him seconds before Sakis pushed him into a seat.

'Talk to me, Ari. What the hell is going on?'

He speared both hands into his hair and tried to stem the terror rushing through him. 'It's probably nothing. She can't possibly have gone *sky-diving*...'

'Yeah...that's what your man said.'

He tried to swallow. 'Well...she can't have.'

'Why not? If she's qualified—'

'Sakis. She's pregnant.'

His brother's mouth dropped open seconds before the colour leached from his face. They both leapt for the phone on his desk but Ari was quicker. 'I need your fastest driver out front in the next ten seconds.'

Sakis wrenched the door open. They passed Theo in the hallway and one dark look from Ari and his brother stemmed whatever wisecrack he'd been about to utter.

In silence, he fell into step beside them.

The journey to the airstrip was the longest of Ari's life.

Horrific scenarios he couldn't stem tumbled through his mind and the fingers that continually clawed through his hair shook uncontrollably.

Brightly coloured parachutes slowly loomed into view as their SUV roared down towards the designated area on the edge of the parachute landing site.

Theos, surely she hadn't...

Ari was out of the car before it'd come to a screeching halt. He heard the thunder of running feet behind him as his brothers followed him.

One by one he watched the eight parachutes drop lower, his heart hammering as he rushed from one to the other.

None of them were Perla.

'Ari?' He whirled round to find her stepping down from the air-conditioned bus, Selena Hamilton following behind her. Relief was followed closely by volcanic anger. This time, there were no feet thundering behind him as he sprinted to the bus.

He skidded to a halt in front of her. She started to speak. '*Not. One. Word.*'

Her mouth dropped open. Without giving her a chance to respond, he swung her up in his arms and marched her to the SUV parked a hundred yards away.

'Out,' he growled. The driver jumped out and held out the keys. He placed her in the passenger seat, secured her seat belt and ignored his brothers as he got in and slammed the door.

'I'm guessing we have to find our own ride back?' Theo quipped to Sakis.

Ari turned the ignition and peeled out of the airstrip, his heartbeat a deafening roar in his ears.

The journey to the villa took less than ten minutes. This time he didn't help her out. He headed straight into the villa and sought out the butler.

'I want you and your staff to take a break. Don't return until I tell you to.'

He returned to the living room to see the staff hurrying out and Perla standing in the hallway, her face pale and her teeth worrying her lower lip.

'Ari, please. You're scaring me.'

He threw the car keys across the room and watched them hit the wall and bounce on the marble floor.

'*I'm* scaring *you?*'

Her arched brows spiked upward. 'Can we try less snarling and more coherence?'

'You left the resort without telling anyone, without telling *me*. I thought you'd gone *sky-diving!*'

She started to laugh, then stopped. 'Wait, seriously? Why on earth would I? Anyway, I texted you to tell you that I didn't think Selena Hamilton should be on her own. I think she might have taken something. Luckily, I eventually managed to talk her out of sky-diving—'

'I didn't receive a text and you seem to be missing the point here.'

'Which is what, exactly? That I have to report my every move to you now? Well, you'll be happy to know that, aside from talking his wife down from a possibly fatal jump, I warned Roger Hamilton that if his eyes strayed to my cleavage one more time I'd gouge them out. I was very diplomatic about it, of course.' She smiled sweetly. 'Was there anything else you wanted to know?'

Ari couldn't believe his ears. He'd been scared out of his wits. And she was giving him sass. 'Are you serious?'

He watched her walk towards him until he could smell her. He raked a hand through his hair as she tilted her head and regarded him with steady eyes.

'Ari, you're seriously overreacting here. You can't mollycoddle me through this pregnancy. I know what this child means to you but I won't be wrapped up in cotton wool until the baby's born'

He whirled from her and paced to the window. 'You think I'm only concerned about the baby?'

'Come on, be honest—would you be this worked up if it was just me on that plane?'

The air drained out of him and he reeled from the accusation thrown at his feet. He opened his mouth but no words came out. Because the realisation that was dawning on him—had been dawning on him all week—felt too overwhelming to make sense of.

'Perla...'

'You know what I was thinking when I was on the bus?'

Slowly, he shook his head.

'I started off thinking perhaps I should count my blessings. My first husband was physically and emotionally unavailable but I *could* graduate to a physically available but emotionally unavailable one. And maybe, if this one doesn't work out, I might strike it lucky third time round—'

'There won't be a next time. If you marry me, you'll be stuck with me for this lifetime and the next.'

'Let's not get ahead of ourselves here. What I didn't say was that the thought of an emotionally unavailable husband would never work for me. Not now. I'm learning very fast that I'm an all-in kind of girl. So I'm not willing to risk my future happiness on a man who won't open up to me even a little.'

The emotion that slashed through him made his gut clench hard. He couldn't breathe. Could only remain still as she stared defiantly back at him, dared him to react to the gauntlet she'd thrown down.

He opened his mouth; no words came out.

He shook his head, damning himself for ten kinds of a fool when pain rolled over her face.

'Or you could just get lucky. Since you're so determined to hammer home just how incompetent I am at taking care of myself, maybe I'll just die and save you the trouble.'

Perla heard the words tumble from her lips and felt shock bolt through her.

Ari's face whitened and he actually stumbled back a few steps. Horror gripped her at how callous she'd been.

'Oh, God, I'm sorry.' She rushed to him but he flung out his hand to stave her off. 'Arion, I didn't mean it.'

His hand slowly lowered and he stared at her as if she was a monster. Perla's insides shredded as he took another step back.

'I'm sorry,' she repeated. Her stomach went into free fall when he remained silent. 'Please, say something.'

'Get out.'

'No, Ari. Please—'

He jerked forward and caught her to him. The kiss he delivered was harsh and pain-filled and devastatingly breathtaking. But it lasted less than ten seconds before he pushed her away and strode from the room.

She refused to shed another tear even though her throat thickened painfully with the need for release.

Going to her bedroom, she sank onto the bed, tried to make sense of what had just happened.

Pain had made her lash out in the worst possible way and strike Ari where it'd hurt the most. She'd gone too far. She had to fix it.

She rose, smoothed her hand down her dress and left her room.

He was in his study, his shoulders rigid, fists clenched as he stared at the ocean.

'Ari, we need to talk.'

He stiffened but didn't turn around. Grateful for not being thrown out, she stepped further into the room.

'We've both been through a lot. And our past is always going to be there. You were taking care of me the only way you knew how. I shouldn't have said what I said.'

He remained silent for a full minute. Then he turned. 'You want to know about my past? About Sofia?'

Heart in her throat, she nodded.

'My father fought for years to stay out of jail. He used lawyers and manipulated the system to try to escape justice. But the authorities were equally determined. The economy was in the toilet and he'd been lining his pockets with ill-gotten gains. They were slavering to make an example of him. Just when I thought it was ending, some other charge would be added to the list and the circus would begin all over again. The only people who mattered were my brothers and my mother. But even I couldn't protect them from the cruelty of the media and their so-called friends. Watching them suffer made me hate my father even more. Then he was convicted. Finally, I thought I could get some closure for my family. Before we could take a breath, he was gone.'

Perla frowned. 'What do you mean, gone?'

'He died in jail months into his thirty-year sentence.'

'How?'

'He caught pneumonia and refused treatment.' He gave a sharp laugh. 'After the chaos he'd caused, he went out with barely a whimper.'

'And you felt cheated?'

'I felt more than cheated. I wanted to hunt him down in the afterlife and strangle him all over again. I went on a month-long bender. I was on a very fast downward spiral when I met Sofia.' His eyelids descended, veiling his expression. But she saw his hands form fists. 'She…saved me.'

Perla's breath stopped. 'Oh…'

When he looked up again, his eyes were the darkest green, shadowed with pain. 'She brought me back from the brink of rage and despair. And I rewarded her by ignoring all the danger signs.'

'Surely, she must have known the risks of getting pregnant if she had a weak heart?'

'She knew. But she was convinced she would survive it. She was an eternal optimist.'

'Ari, you can't keep blaming yourself for what happened to Sofia. You got her the medical care she needed and she made a choice. The outcome was unfortunate but—'

'I could've insisted. I could've—'

'Ordered her about, just like you're trying to do to me?'

Colour slashed his cheeks and he looked away. 'You

can't control everything, Ari. Sometimes you have to let go and let things play out.'

'Is that what you're suggesting I do with you? Let you run around until something unforgivable happens?'

'You're assuming that you're the only one who cares for the welfare of this baby. But I want this baby more than anything else.' It wasn't strictly true. There was *one* thing she wanted equally as badly. 'But in order to give this baby what it needs, we need to put the past behind us and move on or it'll keep tripping us up, dictating our lives.'

'Move on. Just like that?' he asked through gritted teeth.

'No, not just like that. It's hard, I know, but I'm willing to give it a try.'

'You're willing to try when you're pregnant with my child but can't even move on from wearing funeral black every day?'

Shocked, she stared down at her clothes. The idea that her all-black wardrobe was sending a particular message hadn't even crossed her mind.

'Moving on isn't as easy as you think, is it, Perla?' he queried in a soft voice lined with steel. 'Come and talk to me about moving on when you change the colour of your wardrobe.'

'I'm talking to you now. And I didn't choose this wardrobe. You gave me a little more than a day to join you in Miami when I started this job. The stylist knew my history and she assumed I'd want to be decked out in black all the time because I was a widow, and frankly I didn't think it mattered in the grand scheme of things.'

His jaw tightened. 'It mattered.'

'They're just clothes, Ari. The fact of the matter is I want love. I wanted it when I married Morgan and I want it now.'

His gaze lasered on her. 'Why did you stay married to him after you found out he was gay?'

Ice welled through her veins. 'He told me on our wedding night that he'd married me because he didn't want anyone to find out. Especially not his parents.'

'The ones you continue to look after?'

She gave a slight nod. 'They worshipped him but he knew they wouldn't accept his sexual orientation. And... he knew how much I cared for them. I'd told him about my childhood and the foster system and he...he told me I could still have a family, provided...'

'You kept his secret?' he finished harshly.

'Yes. I begged him to come out. I even fooled myself into thinking I was getting through to him last Christmas.'

Ari's gaze sharpened. 'How?'

'He told me he was thinking about telling his parents. That he just needed time to sort out a few things first. Now, I realise he was probably planning something else.'

'Something like what?'

She gave a jagged laugh. 'Oh, I don't know, maybe he was planning to emigrate to Timbuktu? Or New Zealand? He took a bribe to crash Sakis's tanker so, whatever it was, it must have been worth the risk to him.'

He walked slowly towards her until he stood in front of her. His eyes were still shadowed but the agony had lessened. 'He took advantage of your kind heart and your unfortunate past to prey on you. The bastard didn't deserve you. You know that, don't you?'

'I know but it doesn't mean the need I have has abated. It's still there, Ari. The need to be loved. But I know you can't give me that. Am I right?'

Hazel eyes darkened and he looked away.

She tried to ignore the sharp stab of pain in her heart and forced herself to continue. 'I told you I'd make a decision once we talked.'

He tensed. 'And have you?'

She ignored all the self-preservation signs and blurted, 'Yes, I'll marry you.'

His head snapped back. 'You will?'

She nodded. 'I can choose to live in a fantasy where I get everything I want delivered to me on a silver platter. Or I can live in the real world where I get the baby and the family I've always yearned for. Two out of three will have to be enough.'

He caught her chin and raised her head so he could look into her eyes. 'You will marry me. You're sure?' His eyes blazed with an intensity that drilled to her soul.

Nervously, she swallowed. 'I'm sure.'

He gave a single nod. 'I'll put the arrangements in place.' He headed towards the door.

'Ari?'

He looked over his shoulder.

'About…what I said earlier…'

He shook his head. 'Forget it. We have more important things to deal with now.' He strode out of the room without another word.

Shaky legs carried her to the window as the tears she'd fought so hard against slid down her cheeks.

Against the stunning backdrop, the sun blazed down, uncaring that she'd given Ari the answer he'd been clamouring for, and yet she felt as if she was still slipping down a slope, destined for failure and heartache.

Her hand drifted over her stomach. For better or worse, she'd made the decision for her and her baby. She had to learn to live with it.

Three Pantelides jets flew out of Bermuda three days later, all headed for Greece and Ari's private island off the coast of Santorini.

Ari had announced that morning over breakfast that they were to be married in two days at his island home.

The news had been greeted with joy from Brianna but with more restraint from the two brothers. That neither of

them looked surprised told her they'd been fully aware of
the reason for Ari's mad dash to the sky-diving site yesterday.

Perla took the first opportunity to escape to the cabin
bedroom. Ari was busy on the phone, presumably putting
the arrangements he'd told her about in place.

The irony of it didn't escape her.

She was an events organiser who didn't even have a say
in her own wedding. At this moment she didn't even know
who would be attending; whether it would be a large ceremony or a hole in the wall with a priest and his brothers
as witnesses.

She fell into a deep, disturbed sleep and woke to find
Ari next to her. He was wide awake, staring down at her
with a look on his face that stopped her breath.

Before she could speak, he cupped her face in his hands
and slanted his mouth over hers. It was rough. It was deep.
And her soul sang with the feverish joy of it. She was completely unprepared when he wrenched his lips away seconds later.

'Arion?'

In silence, he climbed out of bed and began to undress.

Perla watched him, mesmerised by the dark beauty of
him and the stark need in his eyes that so echoed the one
in her heart.

She shook as he came back and stretched out next to her.
Naked, gloriously aroused, his eyes intent on hers.

'Do you really think we can move on from the past?' he
grated out, his voice little more than a whisper.

An egg-sized lump wedged in her throat. 'We can work
at it, give it everything we have. Brianna told me she didn't
have a smooth childhood either.'

'She didn't.'

'And I don't think Sakis escaped your family's devastation but they seem incredibly happy now.'

He continued to stare at her, his eyes glinting with a sheen that made her heart twist for him.

She didn't utter a word when he reached for her, slid down the zip of the light grey dress she'd bought from the resort shop that morning, and pushed the straps off her shoulders. Her panties and bra came next. Then he untied her hair from its loose knot and spread it over his pillow.

He kissed her mouth, her neck, her breasts, all the way to the heart of her, each touch, each kiss making her tremble and moan, and fight back scalding tears.

With just his mouth he brought her to a shuddering climax, then kissed his way back up her body.

Then he tilted her head up to meet his gaze.

'What you said…about dying…take it back. Take it back now, Perla,' he commanded, his eyes dark with torment, his voice gruff with pain.

Her hand settled on his chest, felt his heart thunder unevenly beneath her touch. 'I take it back. I never should've said that.'

He entered her with a guttural groan that filled the room. With each thrust her heart filled with emotions she dare not let out, emotions she'd always dreamed of voicing to that one special person. The knowledge that they wouldn't be well-received made her bite her lip.

He hooked his arms under her knees and surged deeper inside.

Ecstasy mushroomed through her. 'Arion!'

The sound of his name on her lips seemed to shatter him. Caught in the vicious web of passion, he climaxed with a tormented groan, brutally ripped from his soul.

It took several minutes for their heartbeats to slow, for total silence to return to the cabin. But just when she thought he'd drifted off to sleep, he turned towards her.

'We may not love each other but I promise to take care

of you, and to care for you. And I will guarantee you this. Every night. Every day. For the rest of our lives.'

Her heart lurched. Would that be enough?

It didn't matter. It was too late. Because she knew without a shadow of a doubt that she was in love with Arion Pantelides.

CHAPTER TWELVE

SANTORINI WAS JUST as magical as she remembered, even viewing it from onboard Ari's immense yacht moored half a mile away from the capital, Fira.

Far from thinking she would be spending the day before her wedding in Ari's villa, he'd brought her straight to his yacht once they'd landed.

Granted, the luxury that seemed an extension of the Pantelides name was everywhere her eyes touched.

But the feeling that she wasn't good enough to spend time in his family home refused to leave her. It didn't help that Brianna had been roped into keeping her company and was determined to cheer her up. It also didn't help that another stylist had turned up that morning with three full rails of brightly coloured designer clothes.

In a fit of anger and misery, Perla had sent the stylist away. She was perfectly well-equipped to choose her own clothes. Except now she refused to wear black or the grey dress she'd bought before they left Bermuda.

Leaving the suite that seemed to close in on her, she went along the wide galley and knocked on the door.

Brianna answered with a smile. 'I was just coming to find you. Oh, I thought you were getting dressed?' she said as she took in Perla's silk dressing gown.

'I was, but everything I have in my wardrobe is black.

I was wondering whether I could borrow something from you?'

Brianna's smile widened, and she stepped back. 'Of course. Help yourself.' She waved her towards the walk-in closet. 'And shoes too, if you want. I think we're the same size.'

Perla gaped at the sheer number of clothes, her eyes widening as she spotted some seriously expensive labels.

'Yeah, it's something you're going to have to get used to. I sent my stylist away a few times in the beginning too. Then I realised I was just delaying the inevitable. Our lives are too busy to accommodate spur of the moment shopping trips, and things will only get worse time-wise once the babies are born, especially if you want to continue working.'

Perla bit her lip. 'I don't know what will happen. I don't know where we'll live or even if we'll live together. Because Ari has chosen not to discuss it with me.' Tears surged in her throat and she whirled away from Brianna's concerned stare. Blindly, she reached for the first thing that came to hand and pulled out a burnished orange slip dress. 'This one?'

Brianna nodded. 'It's the perfect thing to go shopping in.'

Perla froze. 'Shopping?'

'You're getting married tomorrow. The least you can do is invest in some knock-out lingerie that'll blow Ari's mind. A woman can't have too many weapons in her arsenal.'

'That depends on what she's fighting for,' Perla murmured. Dropping her dressing gown, she slipped the dress over her head. The cotton felt cool against her skin and the colour lifted her spirits a fraction.

'Don't give up so easily, Perla. You've come too far to stop now. If you want Ari, make him stand up and take notice. Sometimes it's the only way to win against strong-willed men.' Her expression held a determination Perla couldn't help but admire. 'Are you ready?'

With a last look in the mirror, she pursed her lips. 'Almost.' She dashed back to her room and dug through her handbag until she found it. Uncapping the scarlet lipstick she'd worn the night she met Ari, she boldly smoothed it over her lips.

Brianna was waiting for her on the deck. Her eyes widened, then her smile grew. '*Now*, you're definitely ready. Let's go.'

The shops weren't as sophisticated as those on the mainland but they provided an eclectic mix that satisfied her immediate needs.

Perla bought two sundresses, one yellow, one green, and a pair of low-heeled sandals. Against her protests, Brianna dragged her to a wedding shop with every intention of forcing her to buy lingerie.

But Perla froze as she spotted a dress on the hanger. The simple cream Greek goddess-style dress could pass for evening-wear or wedding dress. The front was plain and sleeveless and its halter neck design would keep her cool in the Santorini heat. But it was the back that took her breath away.

The lace pattern travelled down the middle of the back and held the skirt that hugged the hips and flared to the floor in a tiny train.

'Wow. With your hair caught up, that dress would look gorgeous on you. Provided, of course, you want to look fabulous for your wedding day,' Brianna teased.

Curbing her indecision, Perla bought the dress. 'Can we go now?'

'Just one more stop.' They went two doors away and entered the most unique shop Perla had ever seen. Scent candles in all shapes and colours stood on pedestals while incense burned from assorted sticks. 'Sakis calls this my *juju* shop. I tend to get my way a lot when I burn a few candles on certain nights.' She laughed.

Forcing a smile, Perla felt herself sinking deeper into misery.

Leaving Brianna to make her selection, she browsed the shop. As she made her way to the front, she met a woman in her early thirties. The hostile look she sent her stopped Perla in her tracks.

A torrent of Greek followed, to which Perla shook her head and shrugged.

Brianna turned sharply and frowned. The woman continued to speak, her voice growing louder.

'I'm sorry, I don't understand.'

Brianna rushed forward and grasped her hand. 'Come on, let's go.'

'What's she saying?'

Brianna shook her head. 'It doesn't matter.' She hurried out of the shop.

'Yes, it does. You know what she was saying.'

'My Greek isn't that great,' she said, but Perla caught her guilty look.

She came to a dead stop on the pavement. 'But you understood enough. Tell me, please.'

Brianna's lips pursed and a look of unease crossed her face. 'The whole island knows that Ari is getting married again. His wife, Sofia, was from a large family here in Santorini. I think that woman was her cousin. They know he's marrying a redhead and I guess she thought it was you.'

'Well, she was right. What exactly did she say?'

Brianna grimaced. 'I think she said… God, if I get this wrong and Ari finds out, not even Sakis can save me.'

Ice trailed up Perla's spine. 'What did she say?' she demanded.

'She said Ari and Sofia's love was a match made in heaven; the love of the century. She said…'

'What?'

'She said Ari will never love you the way he loved her.'

The sob that rose from her soul shattered her heart on its way up. She saw Brianna pale and reach for her hand but Perla shook her away. 'If I'd understood that was what she was saying, I could've saved her the trouble. I already know Ari doesn't love me. He never will.'

'You need to get over here, fast.'

Fear spiked through Ari at Sakis's tone. 'What's wrong? Is Perla okay?'

'Yes, she's fine physically but something happened when she went out with Brianna... Look, just get yourself over here, pronto, *ne?*'

Ari ended the call and glanced at the chaos all around him. Carpenters and decorators rushed to do his bidding, to set up the place for what most couples would deem the most important day of their lives.

But, deep down inside, he knew the most important day of his life had come and gone. The most important day of his life had happened when he'd thought he was too mired in guilt and grief to ever function properly.

Even when he'd looked up from his drink at Macdonald Hall and his world had shifted he'd refused to acknowledge the importance of it.

She's fine physically...

His breath shuddered out of him as he grabbed his jacket and ran for the door of his villa. Every day since he'd met Perla Lowell had been important but he'd been too damned afraid to admit it to himself.

Well, it was time to stop hiding and dare to be as brave as Perla had been. It was time to take care of the single most precious thing in his life *emotionally*.

He reached his yacht in record time. Sweat poured off his temples as he flew down the stairs, barely acknowledging Brianna's anxious look or Sakis ushering her away as he headed down the galley towards his suite.

He turned the doorknob and found it unyielding. He bit back a curse and swallowed down the fear climbing into his throat.

'Perla, open the door.'

'No.' Even through the closed door he heard the pain in her voice and his chest tightened.

'*Glikia mou*, open the door now. I'm not going anywhere until you do.'

'Go back to the island where you belong. There's nothing for you here.'

'You're wrong. Everything I want is right here. This is where I belong.'

The silence that greeted him tore at his insides. He leaned his forehead against the door and fought the urge to smash it in. 'Open the door, Perla. *Please.*'

Another minute went by, then he heard the scrape of the lock.

The moment it opened a crack, he slipped inside. The sight of her tear-ravaged face eviscerated him. He started to reach for her but she pulled away sharply. He clenched his fist to stop from grabbing for her. He didn't like the hollowness filling his soul.

'Tell me what happened today.' He'd already heard the gist of it from Sakis when he'd called from the car after leaving the villa.

'It doesn't matter what happened. I thought I could do it, Ari, but I can't.'

His heart plunged to the bottom of his feet. 'You can't do what?'

'Marry you. I thought I could but I can't.'

'Not even for the sake of our child?' He hated to play that card, but he was desperate.

The misery when she glanced up at him made his heart bleed.

'I thought I could but I will not come second best for anyone.'

He frowned. 'Second best? Who told you you were second best?'

'No one needed to. I have eyes and a brain. You brought me here and you stashed me on your boat. Out of sight, out of mind. The moment I ventured off the boat I was reminded why I'll never be good enough for you.'

'What the hell are you talking about?'

'Sofia, your wife, will always be the love of your life. The woman at the shop called it the love story of the century. I thought I could live with that, but I can't…'

He ventured forward and exhaled in relief when she didn't cringe away from him. More than anything he wanted to reach for her but he stopped himself. She could bolt, and that would destroy him.

'I loved her, I won't deny that. She saved me from a dark, bleak place and brought me back from the brink. But I wasn't the best husband to her that I could be. I failed to save her the way she'd saved me. I should've been stronger for her sake.'

'Every time you talk about her, I hear the pain in your voice.'

'Because, despite knowing that she had the best medical care, a part of me still feels I let her down by not insisting she take the right advice.'

'So it's guilt that's been eating at you?'

'It was before, but not so much any more. As much as I regret what happened, I can't undo the past. You've taught me that I need to look to the future, to let go of things I can't change. And I have to believe that Sofia would want that for me too.'

'Then why did you stash me on the boat?' Her hurt was unmistakable.

'I'm sorry. I wanted to spare Sofia's relatives unnecessary pain, yes, but I also wanted to make sure the villa was ready for you. For our wedding. I haven't lived here for three years, and it was nowhere near as ready as I wanted it to be.'

Her fingers twisted round the tissue in her hand and his heart twisted along with it. 'But why here? We could've married anywhere else in Greece.'

He frowned. 'You don't remember what you said to me when we met?'

Confusion marred her forehead. 'What I said?'

'At Macdonald Hall, you said your first trip to Greece was to Santorini. That you'd always dreamed you'd get married here.'

Realisation dawned and her eyes grew wide.

'Yes, *glikia mou*, I wanted to give you that wish.'

'Why?'

'Because your happiness means the world to me.'

She sucked in a breath. 'Please don't say that. Please don't make me hope.'

'Why not?'

'Because you'll make me want the impossible.'

'What do you want, Perla? Tell me what you want and you might be surprised by how motivated I am to give it to you.'

When she said nothing, he ventured closer. The orange sundress she wore made her golden-hued skin glow. Unable to resist, he reached out and took her hand in his.

The shiver that coursed through her echoed through him.

'Please tell me what you want, *agape mou*.'

Green eyes rose to his. In their depths he saw courage, determination, naked longing and another emotion he hoped to God was what he imagined it to be.

'I want you. To love me.'

'Only if you love me half as much as I love you, Perla *mou*.'

She gasped. 'What?'

He kissed her knuckles and closed his eyes for a second when her fingers trembled against his lips.

'I love you. I knew from the first that what I felt for you went beyond mere desire, but I fought it because…well, you know why.'

'But on the plane you said—'

'Something stupid about us not loving each other? That was pure self-protection speaking. I thought I could have what I wanted while protecting my heart.' He shook his head. 'The truth is, I don't need to protect my heart; not from you. Yes, what I feel scared the life out of me but what you and I have also fills me with joy even while making me a little crazy. Every time I look at you, I crave you. Every time I make love to you, I want to do it all over again, immediately. It makes me insane but it also makes me feel more alive than I have in the longest time. I never want to lose you because I intend to drive myself insane for a lifetime. If what I had with Sofia is being described as the love of the century then ours will be the love story of the millennia.'

Her eyes filled with tears he didn't hesitate to kiss away. 'Oh, Arion. I thought you were doing all this for the baby.'

'When I wasn't sure you'd take me as I was I admit I tried to use our baby to sway you.'

'And I let myself be swayed because I didn't see any other way to be with you. Now I can tell you that I love you too, without being scared it'll push you away. Tell me you love me again, Arion.' Her eyes shone with a brilliance that stopped his heart.

Happiness rushed into his chest and he had no problem uttering the words. 'I love you. I wish I'd admitted that to us both sooner. But I intend to make up for lost time. You have my promise on that.'

He kissed her for a long time, only raising his head when they ran out of air.

'The house is almost ready. But you have a free hand to change anything you want before the wedding tomorrow.'

She licked lips swollen from his kisses, making him groan. 'Um, can I practise a woman's right to change her mind? Blame it on all the pregnancy hormones rushing through my body right now.'

'What do you want to change?'

She touched his face, leaned forward until their foreheads touched. Ari knew he wouldn't like what was coming but he didn't care. 'The wedding date. The venue. The guest list. *Everything?*'

She stopped his groan of protest with her mouth. And he let her.

EPILOGUE

'IS THIS BETTER?'

Perla placed her hand over her swollen stomach and sighed with happiness. 'Much better. I don't even miss the fact that I can't have champagne at my own wedding.' She glanced down at her hand and watched her new platinum wedding ring gleam in the setting Bermudan sun. The flash of her heart-shaped ruby engagement ring also caught the rays as Ari lifted her hand and kissed the back of it.

'You delayed us getting married for four months then refused to wait another two until the baby was here.'

'I thought I could hold out but the thought of calling you my own got too overwhelming.'

The look that crossed his face was one she'd seen on his brother's face as he gazed at Brianna. At that time she'd envied it. Right now, she basked in it and sent a prayer of thanks for her very own fantasy coming true.

'You've owned me since the moment I saw you, wearing that lipstick you're henceforth banned from ever wearing in public again. I just didn't know it yet.'

'Better late than never, I guess.'

He laughed and they both turned when Sakis and Brianna entered with their three-week-old baby. Dimitri Pantelides was fast asleep in his father's arms, one fist curled around Sakis's forefinger.

Brianna arranged his blanket more snugly around him,

then looked up with a cheeky smile. 'Did you guys see the woman Theo came with? She's stunning!'

'But she also looks as if this is the last place she wants to be,' Sakis added, his tone displaying a keen speculation that made Ari shake his head.

'And Theo the last person she wants to be seated next to. The spark between them could've rivalled last night's pre-wedding firework display.'

'Anyone know who she is?' Brianna asked.

Perla shook her head and looked at Ari, who shrugged. 'He introduced her as Inez da Costa, a business associate from Rio.'

'If she's a business associate, then I'm Santa's Little Helper!' Sakis said.

Ari grinned. 'Think we should go jerk his chain a little?'

'You stay here with your new wife. I'll go put my son to bed and then I'll get right on it. I owe him big for the ribbing he gave me during the Pantelides Oil party on my island.' Sakis grinned with unabashed relish. He walked off and Brianna rolled her eyes and followed him.

Ari leaned down and kissed the side of Perla's neck. 'Before you think of leaving me because of my crazy brothers,' he said gruffly, 'let me tell you again how much I love you. How much I'm honoured to have you in my life and how much I adore you for giving me a chance at true happiness.'

Her heart soared, and she gasped as their baby kicked in approval.

'I love you too, Arion. You've given me the same chance too and there's nowhere else I'd rather be.'

* * * * *

"I'm sorry we won't be working together any longer, Jaya."

"Thank you." She swallowed and wondered if she would turn into a complete fool and start to cry. Standing, she put her hand in his and tried for one firm shake.

Theo kept her hand. His thumb grazed over the backs of her knuckles.

Her skin tingled and her stomach took a rollercoaster dip and swoop.

She looked at his eyes, but he was looking at their hands. Her fingers quivered in his grip as he turned her palm up. She almost thought he was going to raise it to his lips.

It was Theo's eyes, Theo's expression that was always so aloof, but now it glowed with something that was aggressive and hungry.

He was going to kiss her!

She stiffened with apprehension and he straightened. Her hand wound up hanging in the air ungrasped as he pulled in a strained breath.

"This is not appropriate. I apologize."

"No, I—" *Please* let her dark skin disguise some of these fervent blushes. "You surprised me. I came in here reminding myself not to call you Theo. I didn't think you thought about me like that. I would—"

Was she really going to risk this? She had to. She'd never get another chance.

"I'd like it if you kissed me."

Dani Collins discovered romance novels in high school and immediately wondered how a person trained and qualified for *that* amazing job. She married her high school sweetheart, which was a start, then spent two decades trying to find her fit in the wide world of romance writing—always coming back to Harlequin Mills & Boon® Modern™ Romance.

Two children later, and with the first entering high school, she placed in Harlequin's *Instant Seduction* contest. It was the beginning of a fabulous journey towards finally getting that dream job.

When she's not in her Fortress of Literature, as her family calls her writing office, she works, chauffeurs children to extra-curricular activities, and gardens with more optimism than skill.

Dani can be reached through her website at www.danicollins.com

Recent titles by the same author:

A DEBT PAID IN PASSION
MORE THAN A CONVENIENT MARRIAGE
PROOF OF THEIR SIN
NO LONGER FORBIDDEN?

Did you know these are also available as eBooks?
Visit www.millsandboon.co.uk

AN HEIR
TO BIND THEM

BY
DANI COLLINS

Published in Great Britain 2014
by Mills & Boon, an imprint of Harlequin (UK) Limited,
Eton House, 18-24 Paradise Road, Richmond, Surrey, TW9 1SR

© 2014 Dani Collins

ISBN: 978 0 263 24648 3

Harlequin (UK) Limited's policy is to use papers that are natural,
renewable and recyclable products and made from wood grown in
sustainable forests. The logging and manufacturing processes conform
to the legal environmental regulations of the country of origin.

Printed and bound in Spain
by Blackprint CPI, Barcelona

AN HEIR
TO BIND THEM

This one's for my kids,
who managed to turn out amazing despite having a
writer for a mom. Or should I say not having a mom?

I often joke that our daughter
has done a marvelous job raising our son.
For that, and all the times Delainey made lunch
for Sam (and me) so I could write, I am deeply grateful.

I also owe a very special thanks to Sam
for his suggestion when I had ten thousand words to go
on this manuscript and I was stuck. He said, "Dude..."
(Yes, he calls me Dude, but this dude looks like a lady.)
"Dude, have the brother tell her something she doesn't
know about the hero." Post-secondary tuition saved!

PROLOGUE

THEO MAKRICOSTA BLINKED sweat out of his eyes as he glanced between his helicopter's fuel gauge and the approaching shoreline. He was a numbers man so he didn't worry at times like this; he calculated. His habit was to carry twice the fuel needed for any flight. He'd barely touched down on the yacht before he'd been airborne for his return trip. A to B equaled B to A, so he should have enough.

Except in this case *B* stood for *boat,* which was a moving point.

And he'd made a split-second decision as he lifted off the *Makricosta Enchantment* to go to Marseille rather than back to Barcelona. It had been an instinct, the type of impulse that wasn't like him at all, but uncharacteristic panic had snared him in those first few seconds as he took flight. He had wheeled the bird toward what felt like salvation.

It had been a ludicrous urge, but he was committed now.

And soaked in perspiration.

Not that he was worried for his own life. He wouldn't be missed if he dropped out of the sky. But his cargo would. The pressure to safeguard his passengers had him so tense he was liable to snap his stick.

It didn't help that despite the thump of the rotors and his earmuffs plugged into the radio, he could hear both babies screaming their lungs out. He already sucked at being a brother. Now he might literally go down in flames as an uncle. Good thing he'd never tried fatherhood.

Swiping his wet palm on his thigh, he pulled his phone from his pocket. Texting and flying was about as smart as texting while driving, but if he managed to land safely, he would have a fresh host of problems to contend with. His instincts in heading north instead of west weren't *that* far off. The perfect person to help him was in Marseille.

If she'd help him.

He called up the message he should have deleted a long time ago.

This is my new number, in case that's the reason you never called me back. Jaya.

Ignoring the twist of shame the words still wrung out of his conscience, he silently hoped her heart was as soft as he remembered it.

CHAPTER ONE

Eighteen months ago...

JAYA POWERS HEARD the helicopter midmorning, but Theo Makricosta still hadn't called her by five, when she was technically off the clock. Off the payroll in fact, and leaving in twelve hours.

Ignoring the war between giddiness and heartache going on in her middle, she reminded herself that normal hours of work didn't confine Mr. Makricosta. He traveled so much that sometimes he couldn't sleep, so he worked instead. If he wanted files or records or reports, he called despite the time and politely asked her for them. Then he reminded her to put in for lieu or overtime and thanked her for her trouble. He was an exceptionally good man to work for and she was going to miss him way beyond what was appropriate.

Staring at herself in the mirror, packed bags organized behind her, she wondered why she was still dressed in her Makricosta Resort uniform. She gave herself a pitying headshake. Her hair was brushed and restored to its heavy bun, her makeup refreshed, her teeth clean. All in readiness for his call.

After everything that had sent her running from her home in India, she never would have seen herself turning into this: a girl with a monumental crush on her boss.

Did he know she was leaving and didn't care? He'd never

overstepped into personal, ever. If he had any awareness
that she was a woman, she'd be shocked.

That thought prompted her to give a mild snort. If she
hadn't seen him buy dinner for the occasional single, va-
cationing woman, always accompanying her back to her
room then subsequently writing off her stay against his
personal expense account, she'd have surmised he wasn't
aware of women at all.

But he hooked up when it suited him and it made her
feel…odd. Aware and dismayed and kind of jealous.

Which was odd because *she* didn't want to sleep with
him. Did she?

A flutter of anxious tension crept from her middle toward her heart. It wasn't terror and nausea, though. It wasn't
the way she typically felt when she thought of sex.

It wasn't fireworks and shooting stars, either, so why did
she care that she might not have a chance to say goodbye?

Her entire being deflated. She had to say goodbye. It
wasn't logical to feel so attached to someone who'd been
nothing but professional and *de*tached, but she did. The
promotions and career challenges alone had made him a
huge part of her life, whether his encouragement had been
personal or not. More importantly, the way he respected her
as useful and competent had nurtured her back to feeling
safe in her workplace again. He made her feel like maybe,
just maybe, she could be a whole woman, rather than one
who had severed herself from all but the most basic of her
female attributes.

Did she want to tell him that? *No.* So forget it. She would
leave for France without seeing him.

But rather than unknotting her red-and-white scarf, her
hand scooped up her security card. She pivoted to the door.
Stupid, she told herself as she walked to the elevator. What
if he was with someone?

A few minutes later she swiped her damp palms on her

skirt before knocking on his door. Technically this fortieth floor villa belonged to the Makricosta family, but the youngest brother, Demitri, wasn't as devoted to duty as Theo, flitting through on a whim and only very seldom. Their sister, Adara, the figurehead of the operation, timed her visits to catch a break from New York winters, not wasting better July weather elsewhere when it was its coolest here in Bali.

Theo—Mr. Makricosta, she reminded herself, even though she thought of him as Theo—was very methodical, inspecting the books of each hotel in the chain at least once a quarter. He was reliable and predictable. She liked that about him.

Licking her lips, she knocked briefly.

The murmur inside might have been "Come in." She couldn't be sure and she had come this far, so she used her card and—

"I said, *Not now*," he stated from a reclined position on the sofa, shirt sleeves rolled up and one bare forearm over his eyes. In the other hand he held a drink. His jaw was stubbled, his clothes wrinkled. Papers and file folders were strewn messily across the coffee table and fanned in a wide scatter across the floor, as though he'd thrust them away in an uncharacteristic fit. His precious laptop was cocked on its side next to the table, open but dark. Broken?

Blinking at the mess, Jaya told herself to back out. Men in a temper could be dangerous. She knew that.

But there was something so distraught in his body language, in the air even. She immediately hurt for him and she didn't know why.

"Did something happen?" she queried with subdued shock.

"Jaya?" His feet rose in surprise. At the same time he lifted his arm off his eyes. "Did I call you?" Spinning his feet to the floor in a startling snap to attention, he picked

up his phone and thumbed across the screen. "I was trying not to."

The apology sounded odd, but sometimes English phras-
ing sounded funny to her, with its foreign syntax and slang.
How could you *try not* to call someone?

"I don't mind finding whatever paperwork you need,"
she murmured, compelled to rescue the laptop and hearing
the door pull itself closed behind her. "Especially if you're
dismayed about the way something was handled."

"*Dismayed.* Yeah, that's what I am." He pressed his
mouth flat for a moment, elbows braced on his wide-spread
thighs. His focus moved through her to a place far in the
distance. With a little shudder, he skimmed his hands up
to ruffle his hair before staring at her with heartrending
bleakness. "You've caught me at a bad time."

For some reason her mouth went dry. She didn't react to
men, especially the dark, powerfully built, good-looking
ones. Theo was all of those things, his complexion not as
dark as her countrymen, but he had Greek swarthiness and
dark brown hair and brows. With his short hair on end, he
looked younger than his near thirty. For a second, he reminded her of the poorest children in India, the ones old
enough to have lost hope.

Her hand twitched to smooth his disheveled hair, in-
stinctively aware he wouldn't like anyone seeing him at
less than his most buttoned-down.

He was still incredible. His stubbled jaw was just wide
enough to evenly frame his gravely drawn mouth while his
cheekbones stood out in a way that hollowed his cheeks.
His brows were winged, not too thick, lending a striking
intelligence to his keen brown eyes.

They seemed to expand as she looked into them. The
world around her receded....

"We'll do this tomorrow. Now's not a good time." The

quiet words carried a husky edge that caused a shiver of something visceral to brush over her.

She didn't understand her reaction, certainly didn't know why she was unable to stop staring into his eyes even when a flush of heat washed through her.

"I can't take advantage of your work ethic," he added. "It could undermine our employer-employee relationship."

Appalled, she jerked her gaze to the floor, blushing anew as she processed that she'd been in the throes of a moment and hadn't even properly recognized it as one until her mooning became so obvious he had to shut her down.

How? In the past few years, any sort of sexual aggression on a man's part had stopped her heart. Terror was her reaction and escape her primary instinct. Wistful thoughts like, *I wonder how his stubble would feel against my lips,* had never happened to her, but for a few seconds she'd gone completely dreamy.

Her body flamed like it was on fire, but not only from mortification. There was something else, a curiosity she barely remembered from a million years ago when she'd been a girl talking to a nice boy at school.

If she had the smarts she always claimed to, she'd let his remark stand. She'd excuse herself to Marseille and never be seen again.

At the same time, as discomfited as she was, her ability to have a moment was so heartening she couldn't help standing in place like someone testing cold waters, trying to decide whether to wade farther in.

Not that she'd come here for that. No, she wanted to say goodbye and he'd given her an opening.

"Actually, we don't have that kind of relationship anymore." With jerky movements she set his laptop on the coffee table and pressed the lid closed. "Today was my last day. I should have changed, but I'm having trouble letting go."

He sat back, hands on his knees, taken aback. "Why

wasn't I informed? If you're moving to the competition, we'll match whatever they're offering."

"That's not it." She sank onto the seat opposite him and grasped her hands together so she could portray more composure than she actually possessed. Emotions rose as she realized this was it, no more uniform, no more career with the Makricosta hotel chain, no more Theo. Her voice grew husky. "You—I—I mean the company—have been so good with training me and offering certifications. I would never throw that in your face and run to the competition."

"We believe in investing in our employees."

"I know, but I never dreamed I could go from chambermaid to the front desk in that kind of time, let alone manage the department." She remembered how frightened she'd been of getting in trouble for leaving her cleaning duties when she'd brought a lost little boy to the office, hovering to translate until his parents were located. Theo happened to be conducting one of his audits and was impressed by her mastery of four languages and ability to keep a little one calm.

"My confidence was at a low when I began working here," she confessed with a tough smile. "If you hadn't asked me if I planned to apply for the night clerk job I wouldn't have thought I'd even be considered. I'm really grateful you did that."

There. She'd said what she had wanted to say.

"My sister would disown me if I turned into a sexist," he dismissed, but his gaze went to his phone. His despondency returned to hover in the room like a cloud off dry ice. She sensed that whatever news was affecting him, Adara Makricosta had delivered it.

"Where are you going, if not two doors down?" he asked abruptly.

She lifted her gaze off the strong hands massaging his knees. He wasn't as collected as he was trying to appear.

For some reason, she wanted to take those hands and hold them still and say, *It'll be okay. You'd be surprised what a person can endure.*

"France," she replied, not wanting to talk about her situation, especially when it appeared he was only looking for distraction from his own troubles. "Marseille. It's a family thing. Very sudden. I'm sorry." She wasn't sure why she tacked on the apology. Habits of a woman, she supposed, but she *was* sorry. Sorry that she had to leave this job, sorry she was inconveniencing him, sorry that her cousin was dying.

She felt her mouth pulling down at the corners and ducked her head.

"You're not getting married, are you? This isn't one of those arranged things?" He sounded so aghast she had to smile. Westerners could be so judgmental, like all *his* relationships were love matches rather than practical arrangements.

"No." She lifted her head and he snagged her into another moment.

It occurred to her why she didn't feel threatened by this. They'd had a million of these brief engagements, all very short-lived. For over four years, she'd been glancing up to catch him watching her and he had been looking back to his work so smoothly she had put the charged seconds down to her imagination, convincing herself he didn't even know she was alive.

Our employer-employee relationship...

Was that what had kept him from showing interest before? It wouldn't surprise her. He held himself to very high standards, never making a false move.

But if that was what had held him back, what did it mean for her right now, when she was alone with him in this suite and he knew she was no longer off limits?

Ingrained caution had her measuring the distance to the door, then flicking a reading glance at him.

The air of masculine interest surrounding him fell away and her boss returned. "This is a blow to the company. I'll provide you a reference, of course, but would a leave of absence be more appropriate? Should we keep your job open for you?"

His sudden switch gave her tense nerves a twang, leaving her unsettled. Men never seemed to get her messages to back off. Having Theo read her so clearly was disturbing.

"I—No." She shook her head, trying to stay on topic, tempted to say she'd return, but Saranya's cancer made it very unlikely. She hated to even think about it, but she'd been through it with Human Resources and had to get used to reality. "I'm moving in with my cousin and her husband. She's very ill, won't survive. I'm close with their daughter and she'll need me."

"I'm sorry. That's rough."

She absorbed the quiet platitude with a nod.

"I don't mean to sound crass, but would money help?" he added.

"Thank you, but that's not the issue. My cousin's husband is very well-off. They were extremely good to me when I left India, taking me in until I was able to support myself. I couldn't live with myself if I wasn't with them through this."

"I understand."

Did he? His family seemed so odd. Estranged almost. His remark about his sister a few minutes ago was as personal as she'd ever heard him speak of her. The few occasions when she'd seen any of them together, none had shown warmth or connection.

Who was she to judge, she thought with a jagged pain? She'd been disowned by her family.

He seemed to have equally dismal thoughts. His gaze

dropped to the papers still scattered across the floor. He picked up his drink, but only let it hang in his loose fingers.

"Do you want to talk about…whatever is troubling you?" she asked.

"I'd rather drink myself unconscious." He sipped and scowled, "But I only have watered down soda, so…" He set it aside and stood, giving her the signal that heart-to-heart confessions were off the table.

She tried not to take it as a slight. He was a private man. This was the most revealing she'd ever seen him.

"I'm sorry we won't be working together any longer, Jaya. Our loss is the hoteliers in Marseille's gain. Please contact me if you're interested in working for Makricosta's again. We have three in France."

"I know. Thank you, I will." She swallowed and wondered if she would turn into a complete fool and start to cry. Standing, she put her hand in his and tried for one firm pump with a clean release.

He kept her hand in his warm one. His thumb grazed over the backs of her knuckles.

Her skin tingled and her stomach took a roller coaster dip and swoop.

She looked at his eyes, but he was looking at their hands. Her fingers quivered in his grip as he turned her palm up. She almost thought he was going to raise it to his lips. He looked up and the swooning dip hit harder. That was a *sex* look.

But it was Theo's eyes, Theo's expression that was always so aloof but now glowed with admiration and something else that was aggressive and hungry. He skimmed his gaze down her cheek to her mouth and sensations like fireworks burst through her. Zinging streaks of heat shot down her limbs and detonated her heart into expansive pumps.

She was experiencing sexual excitement, she interpreted

dazedly, and the sensations grew as he stepped closer and lowered his head. He was going to kiss her!

She stiffened with apprehension and he straightened. Her hand wound up hanging in the air ungrasped as he pulled in a strained breath from the ceiling. "You're right. It's not appropriate." Weary despair returned like a cloak to weigh down his shoulders. "I apologize."

"No, I—" *Please* let her dark skin disguise some of these fervent blushes. "You surprised me. I came in here reminding myself not to call you Theo. I didn't think you thought about me like that. I would—" Was she really going to risk this? She had to. She'd never get another chance. "I'd like it if you kissed me."

CHAPTER TWO

"JAYA—"

The gentle let-down in his tone made her cringe. She'd lost him to her habitual rejection of male closeness, but wanting a man to touch her was so *new*. She couldn't help that it scared her.

He searched her face with his gaze. "You have to know how pretty you are. Of course I've noticed you. I've also noticed you don't party like the rest of your age group. You're not the one-night stand type."

"I said a kiss, not that I wanted to sleep with you."

Her swift disdain amused him. He quirked his mouth and tilted back his head. "So you did. You can see what a philanderer I am, it didn't occur to me you weren't offering to stay the night." He made a noise of disparagement that seemed self-directed. His wide shoulders sank another notch.

He appeared so tired and in need of comfort. Conflict held her there another minute. She wanted him to see her as available, yet wanted to self-protect. It was frustrating.

"What age group?" she challenged, pushing herself as much as him. "I'm twenty-five. What are you? Thirty?"

"Are you? You look younger." His mouth twitched again as he reassessed her in a way that incited more contradictory feelings all through her.

Just go, her timid self said. *It's safer.* Her more deeply

buried self, the girl who had grown up determined to make
something of herself, believing in things like equal rights
and reaching her own potential, stood there and tried to
make him see her as someone who shouldn't be dismissed.
Someone with value and values.

"Having a career is important to me. Makricosta's has
been a second chance to build one and I haven't wanted to
do anything to jeopardize it. You won't be surprised to hear
I send money to my parents. I can't afford to drop shifts
because I'm hung-over."

"I'm not surprised at all. You've always struck me as
very loyal. And sweet. Virginal even." It was almost a question.

The backs of her eyes stung and she lowered her gaze
to her clenched hands. "I'm not," she admitted in a small
voice, not wanting those memories to intrude when she felt
so safe with him.

"And you've been judged for that? Men and their double
standards. I hate my sex. Judge *me*. I sleep with women and
never talk to them again. I really do that, Jaya," he confessed with dark self-disgust.

She heard the warning behind his odd attempt to reassure. She appreciated the effort—even though he had it
all wrong. Yes, she had been judged, but for a man's crime
against her, not any she'd committed.

"I hate men, too," she admitted. *But not you,* she silently added.

"Ah, some bastard broke your heart. I excel at being
the rebound guy, you know." Here was the generous ty-
coon with the hospitable expression who asked a guest if
she was enjoying her stay and wound up sharing her table
along with further amenities.

"Is that why you pick up those tourists?" she couldn't
help teasing, amused by this side of him in spite of her exasperation. "You're offering first aid?"

"I'm a regular paramedic. 'He cheated? He's a fool.'" He shook his head in self-deprecation. "I should be shot."

"Are you really that shallow?" She didn't believe it. The women were always relaxed and euphoric, never morose, when they checked out. She was envious of that. Curious.

"I'm not very deep." He rubbed his face. "But I don't lie. They know what they're getting."

"One night," she clarified, wondering why he thought he had nothing to offer a woman beyond that.

"One night," he agreed with an impactful look. His hands went into his pockets and he rocked back on his heels, saying, "And apparently you restrict to one kiss. But I'll take it if you're still offering."

The craving in his gaze was so naked, she blushed hard enough her cheeks stung. Covering them, she laughed at herself and couldn't meet his eyes. "I'm not a certified attendant."

"There's not a woman in the world with enough training to fix me. Don't try." Another warning, his tone a little cooler.

She shook her head. This was about fixing herself, not him. "I just keep thinking that if I leave without kissing you, I'll always wonder what it would have been like."

That sounded too ingenuous, too needy, but his quietly loaded, "Yeah," seemed to put them on the same page, which was remarkable. He stared at her mouth and hot tingles made her lips feel plump. She tried to lick the sensation away.

His breath rushed out in a ragged exhale. He loomed closer, so tall and broad, blocking out her vision, nearly overwhelming her. But when his fingers lightly caressed her jaw and his mouth came down, she was paralyzed with anticipation.

There'd been a few kisses in her life, none very memorable, but when his mouth settled on hers, unhurried and hot, she knew she'd remember this for the rest of her life.

The smooth texture of his lips sealed to hers. He didn't force her mouth open. She softened and welcomed his confident possession, weakening despite the nervous flutters accosting her. He rocked the fit, deepening the kiss so she opened her mouth wider, bathed in delicious waves of heat. Their lips dampened and slid erotically. His tongue was almost there, then not, then—

He licked into her mouth and she moaned, lashed with exquisite delight. This was the kind of kiss she'd only read about and now she knew there was a reason they called it a soul kiss. Her hand went to his shoulder for balance. She lifted on her toes, wanting more pressure, more of him settling into her inner being.

With a groan, he slid his arm around her and pulled her tight against him, softly crushing her mouth while digging his fingers into her bound hair. It was good, so good. She reached her arms around his neck, loving how it felt to be kissed and held so tightly against his hard chest and—

He was hard *everywhere*.

Like hitting a wall, she pushed back, perturbed by how intensely she had been responding and the dicey situation she'd put herself in.

He didn't let her go right away, kind of steadied her first while staggering one step himself, then he ran a hand through his hair and swore under his breath. "Hellfire, Jaya. I suspected it'd be good, but I didn't know it'd be *that* good. Are you sure you don't want to spend the night?"

"I—" Say no. *Go.* But what if he was the one? The man who would get her past the hurdle of burying her sexuality out of fear? "I really wasn't expecting this." *Liar,* an inner vixen accused. "You're right that I don't have affairs. I don't know if that's what I want right now, but…" She found herself wringing her hands like the virgin he'd accused her of being. "I really liked kissing you."

"Are you trying to let me down gently? Because it's not necessary."

"No! I'm genuinely confused about what I want." It was almost a wail of agony she was so frustrated with herself.

His mouth pulled up on one side in a half grin that might have been patronizing if he hadn't softened it by saying, "You're not the one-night stand type, but your life has been derailed and sex would take your mind off things. Believe me, I sympathize."

She cocked her head, intrigued by these glimpses into the man behind the aloof mask. "Is that why you're asking me to stay?"

"That obvious, am I?"

"You're making me worry for my friends. Is there a problem with Makricosta's?" she probed.

"No," he assured promptly, then sighed and scratched at his hair like he could erase whatever was going on inside his skull. "Mine is a personal derailment. A family thing, not an illness like yours. I've been angry with someone for a very long time and learned today that I have no reason to be. I'm running out of people to hate and blame. I don't know what to do about that."

Kiss me, she thought. She couldn't believe he was opening up to her like this and way in the back of her mind, she suspected he would regret it, but right now it softened her into wanting to heal him. Madness. She was more broken than he was.

"You told me not to try fixing you," she reminded gently. "It's good advice. I honestly don't know if I can be what you're looking for tonight." She wanted to be, but the thought of that kind of intimacy opened such a gaping vulnerability in her, she could hardly breathe. "I keep telling myself to leave." She gestured toward the door.

"But you're still here."

She lifted a shoulder. "It sends the wrong message, I know."

Their gazes tangled and all she could think about was the heart-racing kiss they'd just shared. He claimed he was the opposite of a gentleman, but she sensed that despite his rock-hard physical power and authoritative command, he was capable of gentleness.

"Give up on me at any point. It won't bother me a bit," he coaxed with surface nonchalance, but she sensed a tighter intensity beneath. Because he wanted her that badly? Or the mental escape?

"Really?" She folded her arms, highly skeptical.

"It's a lady's prerogative to change her mind," he said with a fatalistic shrug, then grinned with surprising wickedness. "But I'll do my best to keep it interesting."

Her equilibrium rolled and dipped again, making her unsteady on her feet.

"I can't believe I'm having this conversation," she said, shaking her head at her own waffling forwardness and his sexual arrogance. "With *you*."

"I've trained myself not to fantasize about women wearing that uniform. It's pretty surreal for me, too."

She chuckled, then sobered as she met his avid look. He was holding himself under tight control and she suspected she'd always been aware of his ruthless self-discipline, that it was one of his qualities she was most attracted to.

"I really can't decide, Theo."

His expression eased a little. "You don't have to." He snagged her hand and led her to the sofa, his manner laconic. "We'll take it one kiss at a time. See how it goes."

"You *really* want to take your mind off things."

"I really do," he admitted, dropping onto the sofa and bringing her down beside him. "Will you take your hair down for me?"

After a tiny hesitation, she did, feeling incredibly vulnerable, like she was removing her clothing. Her severe appearance was a shield. Freeing her hair invited him to stroke his fingers through it. He fanned it out from her ear, creating tickling sensations in her scalp as he marveled at the length.

"It's so silky," he murmured.

No product or bleach to make it brittle, she almost said, then decided this would go better if she didn't compare herself to other women whose hair he had petted.

His patience surprised her. She didn't know why, seeing as he was the most unflappable man she'd ever met, but his contentment to take his time combing her hair with his fingers when he seemed so intent on getting physical almost made her worry he was changing his mind. Just when she grew restless, however, he flicked the tie at her throat.

"Can we take this off?" He tugged to loosen the bow.

"Are you going to tie me up with it?" she asked, trying to sound light, but filled with trepidation.

"Do you want me to?" His gaze skimmed over her as though he was reassessing all his preconceptions about her.

"No." Firm. Prudish even.

His lips twitched, but when his gaze came up from watching the scarf trail down her lapel, his lids were heavy and his voice laconic. "Good, because I want to feel your hands on me."

The scarf floated away and he moved in, settling a lazy, drawn-out kiss on her mouth that was reassuringly tender and sweet.

And, after a while, a tiny bit frustrating. She wanted more than this slow pace. She wanted the hand climbing her waist to quit stopping at the underside of her breast. *Touch me,* she willed, breasts feeling swollen and achy. She wanted the space where they leaned into each other to close so she could press herself to his wide chest. He'd come out

of the private lap pool here once, when she'd arrived with
a file. Even though he'd shrugged on a shirt immediately,
his washboard abs had been full-on. He was gorgeous and
she wanted to see his naked chest again.

She plucked at the buttons on his shirt, not quite nervy
enough to tug them open.

He broke away to look down at where her indecisive fingers lifted away from his breastbone. Without a word, he
one-handedly yanked, disregarding the exceptional quality
by tearing its holes, pulling it free of his waistband at the
same time so it hung loose on his shoulders.

Gasping at his near savagery, she touched her fingertips
to her sensitized lips.

He caught her hand and bit softly against the plump pad
at the base of her thumb. "I'm dying for you to touch me.
Don't worry, I won't rip your uniform. We'd have to account for the loss."

His husky comment made her laugh. Half of her dry
chuckle was mild terror because he was taking her hand to
his chest. She caught her breath as her fingerprints made
contact with the heat of his skin, taut over his hard muscles.

He shivered under her touch.

"You're so hot," she murmured.

"Thank you. I've always thought the same about you."

Smiling, she did something she hadn't imagined she
could. She leaned in and kissed his mouth while both her
hands skimmed over the intriguing ripples of his upper
chest, exploring the texture of a light sprinkle of hair and
satin skin over muscles that flexed under her caress.

He groaned, but rather than gather her into a tight crush,
she felt a tickling graze of fingers between her breasts. A
second later, she was the one to draw back and watch as
he finished opening her white-and-red Makricosta blouse.

Her ivory bra beneath was practical and almost adoles-
cent. She didn't have much to support and had never seen

the point in spending money on something only she would see. An urge to apologize rose to the back of her throat, but the way he traced the top of one small cup, caressing the upper slope of her breast, had her holding her breath.

"I have a wicked addiction to cocoa," he told her as he took his time spreading the shirt wide on her shoulders, patiently tugging it free of her skirt. His returning touch was whisper-soft as he grazed her ribs and found his way to the clasp in the middle of her back.

Her back arched from his caress and her bra loosened. She drew in a breath, hesitant, but his hand came around and cupped her breast. The sensation blanked her mind, holding her in thrall. So much heat. He was like an inferno, and so masculine, but reverent. There was aggression, she could feel the possessiveness in the way he enclosed her like he had every right, his touch firm, but he was gentle at the same time. Softly crushing, as if he knew she would enjoy the sensation of pressure increasing by degrees. He massaged flesh that felt heavy and achy and prickling in one tight spot.

His touch shifted as he leaned in to capture her mouth. Muscle flexed under her hands as she met his searching kiss with welcome. Sensations overwhelmed her, but a particularly sharp one pierced through her psyche. He thumbed her nipple, making it feel knotted and tighter and more sensitive. And so vulnerable, yet excited.

She whimpered, distressed by the rocketing spikes of pleasure going straight through her abdomen into a place that had retreated to hibernation a long time ago.

"God, Jaya, let me taste you."

He pressed her onto her back on the cushions, covering her so smoothly she didn't realize how she'd wound up under him, her bra pushed up and his weight pinning her hips, one leg between his, the other dangling off the edge of the cushions.

A gasp of shock scraped her throat as she pulled in air, trying to catch up to this new circumstance, trying to decide if she was okay with it.

"So gorgeous."

Damp heat closed over the pulsing tip of her breast. Knifing spears of delight pulled upward from her flesh.

Be scared, she told herself, but the scariest thing was how devastating this pleasure was. Her hands couldn't get enough of roaming his back. His bunched shirt kept getting in the way, irritating her. His weight on her should have terrified her, but when she bucked, it was slowly, because she couldn't help herself. Her leg couldn't find purchase alongside his so she let her ankle curl behind his thigh.

And she moaned. Aloud. Even though a distant voice said, *Don't. Don't be sexual, don't encourage him, don't embarrass yourself.* She couldn't help it. He had both her breasts cupped into mounds that he sipped and licked and tortured. It was incredible.

"Theo, I can't stand it."

He lifted to kiss her, swooping like a predator to ravage her mouth as he shifted their position and was fully between her legs. The layers of her wrinkled skirt had climbed so his fly came into firm contact with the cotton of her underpants.

Panic began to edge out her arousal.

She pressed his shoulders and he broke their kiss to set his damp forehead against hers. "I know, I'm pushing it, but this is as far as we're going. I've just realized I don't have any condoms." He smoothed her hair back from what must have been a stunned expression and kissed her once, quite hard. "You have no idea how sorry I am."

She did. Her hips wriggled involuntarily and he shuddered, pressing that most assertive part of himself to her vulnerable softness, pinning her motionless as he released a dry laugh.

"Okay, maybe you do." Kissing her with regret, he grazed his lips over her cheekbones and eyebrow. "You feel so good. You're so pretty. I don't want to stop touching you." His hand skimmed the outside of her thigh, making her trembling muscles contract to tighten her leg against him. "Will you let me make it good for you, at least? Can I know what it feels like to touch you?"

He set a sweet kiss on her chin while his hand climbed under her gathered skirt and learned the style and texture of her mood-killing matronly underpants.

She opened her mouth, thoughts scattering in a dozen directions by arousal and conflicting misgivings. Her mind refused to fix on anything let alone a clear yes or no.

Before she could form words, he shifted enough to cover her mound with a compelling rock of his hand. Stars shot behind the backs of her eyes.

"Like that?" he murmured, licking her neck and easing his touch to a lighter caress through the layer of cotton. Just a soft trace against a very intimate place that made her pulse with need. "Softer? Tell me what you like."

"I didn't come here for this," she managed to whisper, aware that she was becoming completely abandoned, letting her legs fall open to his incredible facility with a woman's body. Wanting whatever he'd give her. "But it feels so good."

"I know. Hate me later, but right now can I keep doing this? You're so incredible…"

He kissed her neck and sidled his touch beneath the cotton, knowing exactly what he was doing in a way that should have alarmed her, but she didn't care. At this moment, she really didn't care about anything except that he keep his attention on that exquisite bunch of nerves tangled into a signal that sent ripples outward through her abdomen. He wasn't in any hurry, seeming to luxuriate in circling and stroking, driving her crazy.

She bit at his lips, dying, wild, loving his touch and him for giving her this amazing build of pleasure, this incessant desire for physical contact with a man.

He said sinful things about what he wanted to do to her, sucked her nipple and said, "Let me kiss you here. I want to lick you. It'll be so good, Jaya—"

"No," she gasped. Her horror was pure, latent shyness, but the idea of him doing that was so wickedly intriguing her arousal spiked to something she couldn't contain. Convulsively trying to close her legs, she could only squeeze his wide, masculine hips, unable to stop what he was doing. She couldn't catch back her uninhibited response. Her only choice was complete surrender to him and her body's sharp need.

Her reward was a deep throb of sheer joy expanding through her in shuddering waves. Her throat filled with a cry of release that was more than just physical. It was emotional triumph. Freedom from the past. Joy at a man's touch.

CHAPTER THREE

INCREDIBLE TENDERNESS MADE her slither in sweet lassitude beneath him, loving the hard strength of him, the disheveled intensity holding him tense as she ran her fingers into his hair. She made him lift his head so she could look at him.

It was painfully intimate to let him look into her eyes when she had just shattered so completely. His hand stilled where he still had it tucked against her mons and an internal ache made her long to beg him to continue stroking her.

"Thank you," she whispered, hoping he put down her shiny eyes to arousal.

A slow, wicked grin spread across his face. "Stick around. There's more where that came from." He punctuated with a gentle, deliberate caress that slid low and penetrated her pulsing channel.

She tightened, part of her reaction instinctual resistance, but the sensation of clasping his thick finger was so delicious she moaned and lifted her hips a little, encouraging more.

"Ah, Jaya…" His hot mouth opened in a wet kiss against her neck and he deepened his possession of her.

"Wait," she gasped, still clasping his head and this time clutching him close with her arms hard on his shoulders while she stared at the back of the sofa. Was she really going to do this? Her body was on fire while her mind was cleaving in all directions.

He removed his hand from her underpants and she moaned in loss.

"It's okay," he murmured, skimming his lips against her jaw before he lifted his head and removed her hand from his hair. "You don't have to rip my hair out. This has gone further than you wanted to, I get it."

"No, I—" Disconcerted, she dropped her twitching fingers to his shoulders, sorry she'd hurt him, sorry she'd lost his exquisite caresses. She didn't want this to end, not yet. This was her chance to get over her past. "I have a pill in my room. One that, um, prevents a pregnancy after, um, unprotected sex." *Please don't ask me why I have it.*

Her voice faded toward the end. She was grossly unsure of herself and given how he'd pulled away, maybe he wasn't all that invested. He became very grave as he pondered what she'd said, making her hold her breath.

"I always wear a condom."

Disappointment sliced surprisingly deep. She swallowed and nodded. "I understand. It's okay. Like you said, this isn't something we intended, so—"

"No, I mean I'm clean. I've never gone bareback so you don't have to worry I'd give you anything."

"I…" *Had tests.* Again, she didn't want to think about Saranya taking her to the doctor once she'd got her out of India. That dark time was being overcome, here, tonight, with this man. "I'm clean, too."

He searched her face. She recognized the glaze of concentration in his eyes as a passionate force. It nearly squeezed the air right out of her.

"Swear to me you'll take that pill." His lips barely moved.

"My family would take out a contract on me if I had a baby outside of marriage."

He held himself in steely control and she could almost hear the computations of risk against desire. "I don't want to be a father. Ever. If you're thinking this might lead to something—"

"No!" she insisted, casting for the right words. "It's like you said about not wanting to think about certain things. I want something different in my mind." *A new memory. A good one.* "A baby would be a disaster. But I want to feel… you," she ended in a whisper.

His nostrils flared as he drew a deep breath, his nod brief and sharp before he pulled away, gathering her up as he found his feet. The strength in him as he lifted her and held her cradled to his chest made bells ring in her ears, but she found herself curling her arm around his neck and burying her face into the masculine scent in the crook near his shoulder.

What she had said was broad enough to be true in many ways. She wanted to think of men differently, but there was a part of her deeply enthralled in the now. She could barely form a thought beyond her need for physical contact with this man.

He set her on the bed and straightened, not turning on the light. Only the faint glimmer from the pool deck through the windows penetrated.

She hugged her knees as she watched him slide his belt free and toss it away, toeing off his shoes at the same time.

"Are we taking turns? Because I'm dying to see you," he said with enough ragged edge on his voice to make her shiver.

She looked down at her crumpled uniform, her shirt open, her bra still loose across her chest. Shyness was the only thing holding her back from undressing, she realized with a glistening lilt of joy. Not fear, just natural self-consciousness about undressing in front of a man.

As she hesitantly drew her shirt off her shoulders she confessed, "You've seen a lot of women. I don't know how I'll compare."

Down to his briefs as he peeled away his socks, he said, "I'm not very sure of my ability to hang on until I've given you everything I want you to have. I do *not* want to be the selfish bastard you compare every future lover to."

He wouldn't be, not by a long shot. And even though a quick coupling was probably better for her, given her hang-ups, she doubted it was a good thing to say. Besides, he stole the shirt she was trying to fold and lifted her bra away, dropping both to the floor. The air-conditioned room made her curl her toes, incredibly self-conscious of her naked breasts and beaded nipples as she forced her hands to remain beside her hips.

Sitting there in the half-light, staring at his muscled frame, she was accosted by a pull in her abdomen, but it wasn't fear or misgivings. It was longing. She wanted his hot, muscled body on hers. She wanted to feel those hard thighs between her own without cloth between them.

He started to remove her sandals and she kicked them off herself, letting him ease her onto her back in a sprawl under him as he loomed over her. The brush of his skin against hers was brand-hot, making her quiver with disconcertion. But the reassuring stroke of his hand up her waist to cup her breast calmed her nerves even as his expert touch sensitized her.

"Did I mention my addiction to cocoa?" he asked huskily. "I could sip these chocolate nipples of yours all night."

He bent to enclose her in wet heat and the return of excitement was like a blow, bringing up one of her knees. Sweet delight flashed through her, rippling waves of pleasure that didn't fade, only increased.

"I want to kiss you," she admitted as he shifted to tease her other breast. A coiled knot of tension pulled in her abdomen. It made her bold, impatient for the build and release of orgasm.

As he lifted his head to look at her, he skimmed a hand

down, silently asking her to lift her hips so he could push her skirt off. When had he lowered the zipper?

She complied and he reared up onto his knees, stealing the last of her clothes. Her thighs twitched, locking closed in nervous tension while she stared at the black briefs hugged tight to his hips and thighs. His erection was a thick, unapologetic ridge behind the stretchy fabric.

He sat back on his heels, knees splayed, hands in loose fists against his thighs. He let out a harsh breath, like he was under strain. "God, you're pretty."

He says it to all of them, she warned herself, but she couldn't help smiling. The way he studied her with the intensity he usually reserved for spreadsheets, but had that light of excitement and wolfish half smile on his face, seemed like genuine admiration. It affected her, relaxing her and making her want to writhe invitingly—if only she knew how.

"Will you kiss me again? Please?" She lifted a hand and he let out a gruff laugh as he stretched out beside her, leaning over her.

"I'll kiss every inch of you." He gathered her up to his muscled body and she felt bruised by the hardness of him. He was so hot, so strong beneath his taut, satiny skin. She couldn't resist stroking his back and shoulders as he kissed her. Their tongues flicked and delved and it felt totally natural. Better than natural. Necessary.

She did writhe then, moved by instinct, body involuntarily lifting into the stroke of his hands, arching to push her breast into his cupped palm, rolling her face into his caressing fingertips when he dragged his mouth to her neck. Then he was laving her nipple again, bringing the ferocious need into her loins. Mother Nature had a plan, quite obviously. She ached for attention between her thighs.

If only she knew how to make love as well as he did. He massaged her belly and grazed fingertips along the seam of her thighs, inciting her to relax them open. Then, finally, he was tracing into her wet heat, penetrating easily into the dampness that welcomed him. His caress was so stunningly *good*. As his thumb rolled over the taut peak of her clitoris, tiny sparks shimmered through her, gathering toward the implosion. She gasped, awed that she could feel this way again, from this deeply intimate touch.

He shifted, licked under her breast and kissed a trail down her abdomen.

"Theo," she panted.

"Every inch, Jaya." He left off caressing her and used his damp hand to crook her knee open, pressing a firm kiss to her inner thigh.

"No, Theo, please don't."

"Don't be shy." He came back onto his elbow beside her, his expression so feral and aroused she ought to have been terrified, but his voice was calm and controlled, his hand on her navel soothing. "I am seriously worried about not being able to last once I get my skivvies off. Let me make it good for you."

While a nervous giggle bubbled in her at his blunt remark, she knew her limits.

"This *is* good for me." Her voice hitched with deep emotion and she glanced up through stinging eyes, hoping he couldn't see in the shadowed light how out of sorts she was—enthralled and uneasy, but resolved. "I want to feel you inside me."

He muttered a curse, closing his eyes and averting his face.

Pressing into the mattress, she asked warily, "Are you angry?"

"What? No. But you're not helping my control with talk like that. Do you have any idea how long I've wanted to be inside you? Years. Since the first time I saw you."

He jackknifed off the bed, giving her space as he contin-ued his grumbling tirade while stripping his briefs.

"You said earlier that you didn't know I thought about you this way. Well, you've never once hinted you did, ei-ther. Do you know how sexy it is to hear you want me?"

As he straightened, she thought, *"want" is debatable.* She wanted to feel normal. She wanted to feel close to Theo. But that aggressive thrust of masculine power made her apprehensive.

He came back to cover her, a practiced knee pressing her legs open as he settled on her. She stiffened, waiting for the breach, but he only cupped her face and set a soft kiss on her upper lip.

"Did I kill the mood? I didn't mean to. This is the most bizarre night of my life."

"That sort of flattery restores it," she teased, because this was the considerate Theo she recognized. Even so, she was hyperaware of the hard, thick muscle pressed so close to her vulnerable folds.

Rather than laugh, he released a sigh that was hot and damp against her cheek. "I'm grateful you're here, Jaya. All the crap outside these walls…It can't touch us right now. I hope you feel like that, too. I don't want to be the only one finding escape."

"You're not," she assured him, shivering in nervousness, but certain this was what she wanted: escape from her past. "I'm using you, too."

"Good." He kissed her, the familiar press and pull draw-ing her back toward the arousal that had been simmering under her last-minute nerves. When he rocked his hips he furrowed open the softness of her, finding and reawakening her to pleasure, she jerked, surprised by the spike of desire.

His big body overwhelmed hers, but there was a sense of safety here, too. His chest rubbed hers, stimulating her nipples. His thighs were tense and abrasive, but she couldn't help stroking his legs with hers, oddly entranced by the sensation, inadvertently parting her legs and opening herself with the movement.

Her undulations brought him to her entrance. A whimper of mixed emotion escaped her, but she cradled his head and stroked the back of his neck and lifted her hips into the pressure, making this happen.

She braced for pain, but there was only a tremendous sense of fullness as he slid into her. Her muscles tightened instinctually, but that only heightened the friction—the sweet, delicious friction—of his burying himself deep into her body.

A shudder of reaction took her.

He squeezed her in constrictor arms, rocking himself deep and tight against her body, sending glittering sensations through her as he whispered, "Already? That's okay, I'm really close, too. Come for me. Let me feel it."

She caught back a sob, not hurt, not ready to orgasm, but shattered emotionally by how complete she felt. Pride in herself almost burst her apart, making her cling to him, wanting this moment of perfection to imprint in her mind forever.

After a few seconds, when she only stayed very still beneath him, he murmured, "Together then?" against her temple. His hard arms caged her as he withdrew and returned. "Tell me when."

Pure white light seemed to expand in her as he fit himself to her depths.

"Oh, Theo."

"Yeah." He thrust again, deeper. Like he wanted to lock himself into her forever.

It was fantastic. Sweet and primal and delicious.

And not enough.

"Don't stop," she gasped.

"Never." He kept moving, his hips meeting hers with more force.

Sensations danced with giddy promise through her. She couldn't speak, could only brace for another pulse as he returned again, his muscled tension a gathered force over and around her. Like a storm building.

She panted, greeting each thrust with an arching welcome of her hips. Thought receded and she embraced pure womanhood, primitive and earthy and natural as they mated. His scent was perfume, his groans behind his gritted teeth music. She smiled at her power over him and herself, reveling in the dance. Cries built in her throat as the silver threads of crisis gathered. Her hand went to his buttock, nails digging in as she tried to push him deeper, needing just a little more. She was so close.

Sweat adhered them and they struggled in ecstatic perfection, almost there, almost there...

Orgasm ripped through her and her ragged cry was pure liberation. Absolute completion as her body shuddered and clasped at his.

He let out a fierce shout of his own. In her trembling sheathe, his thick shaft pulsed, filling her with volcanic heat. She closed her arms and legs around him and willed this union to last forever.

CHAPTER FOUR

Present day...

AS HE SETTLED onto the tarmac Theo eyed the waiting limo. Jaya was smart enough to wait for the blades to slow before leaving the car, but he was anxious to see her. He told himself it was the babies he was worried about, and whether he'd have the help he needed in caring for them. It had nothing to do with the gnawing ache that had stayed with him during the eighteen months since he'd made love to her for hours before she'd hurriedly dressed so she wouldn't miss her flight.

His gut knotted. She'd seen him with his defenses blown apart by the family strife he'd been trying all his life to wall off. He'd never been as unguarded with a woman as he'd been that night, usually focusing strictly on the physical pleasure of his encounters and saying as little as possible.

With her, he'd reveled in the cessation of emotional pain. When she'd left him to the silence of the suite, he'd blamed his plummet back into misery on the return of his dark memories from childhood, but there was more to it. He used to look forward to Bali; he hated it there now. He missed her.

And he couldn't imagine how she'd react to this. He glanced back to the passenger cabin, able to see through the open door that his nephew had fallen asleep. His niece stared wide-eyed from a tear-stained face, startled into silence by the return to solid ground and the new noises of shutting down the chopper.

"I'll be right back," he told her, not sure if his words had any impact. He dropped outside to tether the machine. He'd fueled here in the past, so the hangar wasn't unknown. He still didn't like leaving his machine without prior arrangements. Choice, however, had been pitched into the Med when he'd flown out to the new Makricosta cruise ship only to see a gunner boat approaching from the horizon.

His brother-in-law, Gideon, had been all smiles on his arrival, bringing the babies to have a look at uncle's helicopter. The second Theo had delivered the news he hadn't wanted to share over the radio, Gideon's hand had bit into his arm. "You have to get them off this ship."

Not only did Theo have no idea what would happen to his sister and older brother, or their spouses, but what in *hell* would he do with two babies? Especially if this turned into a permanent situation?

Forget the worst-case scenarios, he reminded himself. Deal with the moment at hand. By his estimation, he had to perform triage for twelve to twenty-four hours before he'd receive new information that would allow him to make a fresh decision.

The limo driver came around to open the back door. Jaya emerged.

Until he saw her and his tension bled away, he hadn't realized how fearful he'd been that she wouldn't come.

The rotors had slowed to listless circles, but he was still struck by a sensation of wind gusting him off his feet. She was wearing her hair shorter, just long enough to touch her shoulders and it had a wave in it he'd never seen before. He liked it better than the tight, sleek bun. She looked younger and more carefree.

Sexy.

Not to say she wasn't looking professional and confident at the same time. Her suit was tailored and chic, the scarf at her throat familiar. A deliberately distancing touch, he wondered, since it was *not* Makricosta colors?

Are you going to tie me up with it?

Do you want me to?

She'd run her fingers through his hair and he'd almost died. Hell, he'd been so needy it was demoralizing.

She smoothed her hands down her jacket, the navy and ice-yellow smart and flattering on her slender figure. Her big, round sunglasses stayed firmly in place as she waited by the open door of the car, not approaching.

He motioned her to come into the interior of the helicopter. After a brief hesitation, she walked forward.

"Mr. Makricosta—"

He paused with one foot on the step and looked back at her, his ghostly reflection in her lenses a picture of one shielded face confronting another.

"Theo," he corrected, tempted to stand here until she said it, which was inane. If he'd had one plan when—*if* he ever saw her again, it was that he'd pretend they'd never slept together. Unfortunately, he kept hearing her whispery gasps of his name, lightly accented, in his dreams and wanted to know if he remembered it right.

"Would you please tell me what is going on?" A hitch of panic entered her tone as he let her question launch him up the steps and into the helicopter. She followed, protesting, "I can't go anywhere. I have commitments. Work and…."

She didn't finish, making him wonder what other commitments, but he didn't press her. "You got my text. You know I need a room. Somewhere no one will expect me to hole up. When I said this was an emergency—"

He indicated the two babies. He'd had the white leather seats outfitted with child harnesses so he could transport his siblings and their children, but the babies looked ridiculously tiny in the first-class armchairs.

"*You have kids?*" she screeched, standing taller in the low-ceilinged inner lounge of the Eurocopter.

Androu jerked awake and began to wail. Evie broke down into renewed tears.

"Nice going," he shot at Jaya.

She stared at Androu, seeming to go yellow beneath her natural mocha tone. "How old is he?" she hissed.

"They're not mine," he ground out, resisting a weird guilt attack even though he'd taken pains—and it had been painful—to ignore her messages and reinforce to her that she didn't have any claim on him. "Help me get them into the car." He handed her Androu and turned to unstrap Evie.

She took the boy into her arms like a natural, which he'd known she would be, even though her lips were so pale and frozen he wondered if she'd ever smile again.

It wasn't in her to take out her feelings on a child, though. The first time he'd seen her, a blond German boy's pale hand clutched in hers, he'd recognized her strong maternal instinct and liked her for it. Today she soothed Androu as she carried him outside where the change of scenery calmed him.

Evie remained stiff in his arms, inconsolable. They slid into the limo like bank robbers after a heist and the driver pulled away.

"You might have told me so I could have had proper car seats installed. This is dangerous, Theo."

Damn. His name sounded better than he remembered and made him hunger to hear it against his ear.

"So?" she prompted. "Who are they?"

"Can he be trusted?" he asked in a murmur, nodding at the driver. "Because I couldn't risk a phone call that might have been heard over the radio. I was texting one-handed—" He was interrupted by Jaya's sudden query to Evie.

"*Pyaari beti,* do you have to use the potty?"

Evie's distressed face nodded vigorously.

For the second time today, Theo's mind blanked with panic. She was on his knee!

"Oscar—" Jaya turned to say, but the driver was ahead of her, already slowing outside the terminal building.

"Wait—" Theo said as Jaya plunked Androu onto the cushion beside her and scooped up Evie.

"There's no waiting at her age. What is she, two?" She was out the door as the limo halted, the little girl wrapped onto her hip like a monkey.

Theo clenched his teeth and did the math on discoverability. He didn't dare let himself calculate the odds on Jaya stealing the toddler. He made himself believe he knew her better, even though he didn't. Not really. Not when he'd treated her the way he had.

Sleeping with Jaya had been wrong.

He wasn't a man who got anything wrong. Mistakes were a luxury he had never been able to afford.

Something about Jaya eroded his discipline, however. Two years ago, he'd started allowing himself to fantasize about an employee. Then he'd begun finding reasons to stay an extra day in Bali, to review reports he could generate himself. He'd rationalized a one-night affair and taken her to bed knowing it was not just unwise and bordering on unethical, it was downright stupid. She was sweet and generous, not the worldly, here-for-a-good-time kind of woman who would forget him as quickly as he forgot her.

God, he wished he could forget her.

The best he'd managed was not to return her tentative few calls. It had been a cruel-to-be-kind favor in her best interest. Not that he expected her to see it that way, but he had warned her they had no future. Surely she wouldn't hold a grudge when he'd been honest about that much?

Skipping his gaze between Androu, who was turning himself and scooting backward off the opposite seat, and the terminal doors that remained closed and reflected the black windows of the limo, he evaluated how much of a chance he was taking letting Jaya whisk Evie into public.

This airstrip catered to private aircraft belonging to celebrities and Europe's high society, which meant most people would have very little interest in anyone but themselves. It was a tempting place for paparazzi to hang around looking for the shot of their career, though. Evie's parents were scrupulous about keeping her out of the limelight. Dressed in her hotel uniform, Jaya would be dismissed as a flight attendant or a nanny. Since Evie's almond eyes and black pigtails didn't match either her adoptive father's blond hair or her mother's green eyes, the chances of anyone recognizing her were narrow.

It was still an interminable wait as Androu rocked his still learning feet across the short expanse to clutch at Theo's knee. "Mama," he said.

Oh, hell. Theo stared into innocent eyes that could have belonged to his little brother, Demitri, at that age. "I know, buddy," he said, even though he didn't know a damned thing except that Adara had done this surrogate parenting at a far younger age than he was, so he had to man up and make this work.

Adara had had Jaya's instincts, though. Somehow she'd hung on to them through the war ground that was their childhood and look what she'd made: Androu was a happy little cub who'd eaten fistfuls of his first birthday cake a few months ago.

"Papa," Androu said, making his request in that polite yet firm way his father had.

"Not here, either, sport." Theo eyed the driver who was

circumspectly keeping his eyes forward. *Discreet,* he'd said in his text to Jaya. *Emergency. I need discreet transport and accommodation.* He'd told her where and when to pick him up and she'd come through for him. Surely that meant she'd bring back his niece.

Androu picked at the seam on Theo's jeans, absorbed, allowing Theo to train his X-ray vision on the terminal doors, willing them to open.

What in hell was taking so long? A tiny thing like Evie couldn't have much liquid in her, especially when she'd cried most of it out. Thank goodness he'd had the sense to call Jaya. Putting a little girl on a potty was not something he would think to do, let alone know how to make happen. He was completely unprepared for this situation, like he'd been dropped on a deserted island with two little gremlins.

And Jaya.

God, she looked more incredible than ever. He still dreamed of that mouth, wide and full and feminine. Her body was better than ever. If he wasn't mistaken, she was holding onto a few more pounds, filling out her slender figure to voluptuous perfection. Her breast would probably overflow his hand when—

If.

Hell, *never.*

It couldn't happen. Best to cut those thoughts short now. Seriously, what was she *doing?*

He couldn't go after her, no matter how much he was tempted. He wasn't a movie star, but the Makricosta siblings had been featured in upscale magazines recently, promoting the cruise ship currently being taken over by pirates. Was it targeted? Were high seas criminals after a hefty ransom by kidnapping some of the richest people in the world? The inaugural cruise had drawn a very elite crowd.

One thing at a time, he ordered himself. Gideon would protect Adara at all costs and he, Theo, had removed the only distraction Gideon might have had. Once the tots were safely stationed, he'd check in with Gideon and the authorities Gideon had raced off to advise.

A sharp pain in his thigh had him jerking his knee from the source, jostling the boy who'd bent to taste denim with his newly cut teeth. Startled by his near fall, the corners of Androu's mouth went down and his eyes filled again.

"Wait. It's fine. Go ahead and use me as a chew toy. You just startled me."

Outside, the terminal doors slid open and Jaya appeared with Evie still on her hip. She clutched an overstuffed bag in her free hand and wore a harried look.

Theo moved faster than the driver, pushing open the door as she reached the car.

"Seriously? Shopping?" He took the bag and steadied her under an elbow as she crawled in, catching a full inhale of her exotic sandalwood and almond scent. It hit him like a drug that weakened his muscles and teased him with euphoria.

Unless he was very careful, coming to her would turn into another mistake. He couldn't let it happen. He released her to pull the door shut behind her.

"Funny," Jaya said tartly, then, "Thank you, Oscar. Directly to the hotel now, please. The underground entrance." She pressed a button to close the privacy window and steadied Evie beside her on the seat as the car began to glide forward.

Theo picked up Androu and settled him on his thigh, catching a look on Jaya's face that might have been stunned hurt, but she looked away. Better that she was hurt and hated him. It would be easier for both of them.

Turning a gentle smile to Evie, she said, "You've been very patient. Would you like your drink now?" She brought a bottle of water out of the bag and opened it, helping Evie to sip.

Androu put out a hand and made a noise of imperative.

"I bought one for him, too. Do you know if they have any allergies?"

"I don't think so." Not Androu anyway. Adara was always prattling on about every little thing Androu ate, touched or said. Theo only listened with half an ear, but he would remember if she was worried about something like that.

There were bananas in the bag with yoghurt cups and a bag of vanilla cookies. Food. Right.

"Good call," he told her as he spilled water all over himself trying to keep the greedy Androu from drowning. The kid didn't have the first clue about the physics of tipping a water bottle and ended up coughing it all down his chin. "I think he uses a special cup for this."

"Really? Perhaps you should have stolen it when you kidnapped him." She brought out a banana and broke off pieces, making everyone sticky but quiet and happy.

"This is Androu, my nephew, Adara and Gideon's boy."

"Oh, of course." Everything in Jaya changed, softening as her gaze hooked onto Androu's little face with as much fixation as her first stare, but with a touch of wistfulness now. "I'd heard gossip about a miscarriage when I was in Bali. I'm happy for them. He's beautiful."

Her tone was sincere, moved almost. Or maybe he was reading into it. His emotions had been stripped to their rawest form the last time he'd been with her. Today wasn't much better. He hadn't planned ever to see her again and when he had indulged in imagining he might, he'd pulled himself together.

"It's been an eventful couple of years," he couched, trying to gloss over all the inner tearing down and rebuilding he'd been forced to do without betraying how brutal it had been. "Look, Jaya. I came to you because I figured I could trust you. We've kept some family business out of the papers for my mother's sake and even though she's gone now, we prefer not to air our dirty laundry, but…" He shrugged. "Are you aware that Nic Marcussen is my older brother?"

"No, I didn't even know your mother had died. I'm so sor— Wait. Marcussen Media? *That* Nic Marcussen?"

"Yes."

"Married to Rowan Davidson, the actress? Who adopted a baby from—" She looked at Evie who tilted her almond-shaped eyes up curiously.

"Where's Mama?"

"She's coming to get you soon," Jaya reassured her, handing Evie another piece of banana. "Isn't she?" she prompted Theo.

"I sincerely hope so, but from what I saw from the air, they have to evade pirates first."

"Where? On the Med? You can't be serious!"

"I know what I saw and the authorities have been notified, but there's every chance we'll be looking at ransom negotiations. The last thing we need is a media circus, especially around the babies. Hell, they're kidnap targets. You were the closest person I could think of who could provide me a place to stay that was off the radar."

Completely practical, exactly as it was supposed to be, he assured himself.

"You knew where I was working?" Her clipped challenge held dual notes of hurt and ire, suggesting that if he had known, he should have called.

He bit back a sigh. "I was contacted as a reference," he lied, adding politely, "Congratulations."

"Oh, um, thanks," she dismissed with a self-conscious shrug. "It's a boutique hotel, very well respected even before the upgrades. They're looking to bring in a higher clientele and hired me because of my experience with Makricosta's. I guess I'm indebted to you…again." Her voice trailed off. The way she bit her lips together suggested she would rather be run over by this limo than face him after referencing their night together.

He pretended they'd left it at the point where she'd thanked him, as if the rest hadn't happened. "As I said then, the hoteliers here got lucky."

Her eyelashes flinched in a way that seemed to say, *Did you really just say that?*

He had. It was unkind, but he wasn't about to acknowledge how lucky he'd been that night. If his insensitivity toward her made his gut knot with sick self-hatred, so be it. He was here for only one reason.

Jaya visibly pulled herself together. "I've arranged the Presidential Suite. It's yours as long as you need it. I'll talk to the staff, keep housekeeping out of there, tell them you're antisocial." Her tight smile said, *It's not even a lie,* and the churning rolled in his stomach again. "My new boss isn't nearly as hands-on as you were. You'll be long gone before he asks who was in there."

Hands-on?

Her cool delivery let him know that two could play this game.

Androu curled his banana-coated fingers into Theo's shirtfront and tried to wriggle down to his feet, forcing Theo to break their stare.

"I need more than a safe place to hide," Theo said, tentative in his struggle with Androu, afraid of hurting his tiny body, but not wanting him hurting himself by trying to walk around in a moving vehicle. Androu grew frustrated and started arching with temper. "I don't know what to do with babies. I need your help."

"Like a nanny? I can call an agen—"

He shook his head, impatient that she was being obtuse. "I can't trust strangers. That chauffeur hearing my name is bad enough. I need complete discretion, at least until I know the situation on the ship. Twenty-four hours, maybe forty-eight, then we can reassess."

"We? You're suggesting me? No." She shook her head. "Definitely not. I can't." Her eyes grew big, panicked maybe, but she shielded them with a downward sweep of her lashes. "I really can't. It's impossible. No. Sorry."

Because of their history. Because he'd just been a bastard about it. *Damn it.* There was a reason he didn't make promises to women: he couldn't keep them, not the emotional kind. He didn't have it in him to fulfill and make happy. Not in a romantic way. In other ways…

He thought fast. "Look at what you gain. This is the son of the Makricosta chain of hotels and resorts. Do you recognize how much favor will be bestowed on the person who keeps him from harm? How do you feel about working cruise lines? Gideon has another ship launching next fall. You're climbing ladders so I assume your career is still very important to you. You'll be able to write your own ticket, Jaya. Anything you can't do, Adara will pay for you to learn. Hell, name your price and I'll pay it to know that I've got someone I can trust for the next few days."

"To babysit." Her mouth stayed in a flat, grim line of disgust.

"They're the toughest guests to please. Free dinner goes nowhere with them."

"Am I supposed to be laughing? Because I don't find this funny."

"Look, I know it sounds sexist. That's not why I'm asking. You're good with kids. Or does it bother you that I'd offer you money to help me?"

"Your being here bothers me, Theo," she snapped, turning her face away. "This is…" Her brow flinched into anguish.

Her anxiety was a kick in the chest, especially as he sensed that her refusal wasn't coming entirely from being scorned. There was a fear component. Something more emotional. It occurred to him there might be a man in her life making her hold back.

His insides shrunk to knotted pieces of rawhide. He couldn't bring himself to ask if that was the problem. He didn't want to know.

"It's a big favor, I realize that," he managed.

She choked out a laugh. "Is that what this is? A favor? A professional courtesy?"

"It's an appeal to your better nature. Think of the children."

"Are you serious right now?" She pursed her mouth in a furious white line.

"Jaya, I can't afford mistakes. Letting a stranger look after these kids would be wrong. I need *you*. Tell me what it will cost. I'll pay it."

CHAPTER FIVE

JAYA'S EMOTIONS ROSE and fell on his words along with her temper. *Think of the children.* Really. *Really?*

As for mistakes, he obviously thought they'd made one. The truth was the complete opposite.

Her eyes kept gravitating to Androu. The resemblance was startling. Her family was supposed to be the one with the cookie-cutter genetics that stamped out cousins who could ride each other's passports. To see so much of Theo in his nephew threw her for a loop and she was already in a tailspin at seeing the man himself.

One glimpse of the sky pilot with his broody expression behind mirrored aviators and she'd turned into a lovestruck schoolgirl again. Never mind that she'd spent the past year and a half taking on responsibilities she'd never dreamed herself capable of shouldering. Men had been completely off her radar, given her being needed so much at home. She'd shut down thoughts of a future with Theo when he had neglected to return her few calls. She hadn't felt sexy and romantic anyway. She'd been tired and grief-stricken and determined to continue her career for the sake of her pride.

Finally, in the past few months, things had begun to settle into a routine. She'd felt good, if wistful, at the way things had turned out. She was empowered and in control: the independent, worldly, modern woman she'd always longed to be.

And yet she'd leaped to respond to Theo's text and had grown breathless watching his athletic frame tether his helicopter. Her eyes kept stealing glances at his leather bomber jacket and black jeans that were old enough to be scuffed gray in all the right places, accenting the muscles of his thighs. He was tough and aloof and as quietly commanding as always, framing his demands with that polite, *I need. I need a file, I need lunch at one, I need you, Jaya. I need you to care for my babies.*

Her heart lurched.

"I need to think," she mumbled, even though this situation was beyond comprehension. Her mind was going a mile a minute, trying to figure out what to do. Where was Saranya when she needed her cousin's sensible advice? *Why did life have to keep throwing such hard curves in front of her?*

No time for a pity party, she reminded herself as Oscar turned into the underground parking garage and stopped next to the elevators.

They'd arrived at Theo's *discreet* accommodation. She hadn't known what to think of that text, but she hadn't been able to ignore it. You didn't slam doors in this business no matter how badly you wanted to. He was right about her interest in her professional development. She had plans and one affair eighteen months ago wouldn't derail them—no matter how life-altering the consequences had turned out to be.

Besides, she had told herself when the text had popped up, *he was probably making the request on behalf of a favored guest.* When she'd climbed into the limo, she'd told herself not to expect Theo at the private airstrip. She'd braced herself for a mistress.

Talk about special guests who needed personal attention!

As they rode up the elevator, she sent him yet another glance of exasperation. They each carried a child. He had the bag of minimal groceries in his hand and was looking at her. His narrowed brown eyes sent a prickle of heat into her center.

No. They weren't starting that again. She'd learned her lesson, thanks. Looking away was like ripping off a bandage, but she mentally scoffed, *Think of the children.*

Although, when it came to advancing your career through favors for influential guests, he was right that they didn't come bigger than this. Managing this gorgeous hotel on the Mediterranean coast was fun and fulfilling, but if she pulled off keeping both the Marcussen Media and Makricosta Resort heirs off the paparazzi radar, she'd have it made in the shade. Paris, London, New York… She could name her price.

As they entered her hotel's best suite, she automatically searched for flaws that needed correction, but the eclectic mix of 1960s reproduction furniture, pop art, and ultramodern amenities awaited judgment with quiet perfection. Where many of France's oldest hotels were rabbit warrens of tiny rooms with even tinier beds, this one had been upgraded into chic suites of fewer rooms that catered to a very affluent clientele. An open space in the middle of the sitting room would be perfect for the babies to play. Since a curved breakfast bar was the only partition to divide the kitchenette from the adjoining dining area, they'd be in sight while their meals were made.

She couldn't have planned it better, she decided, glancing at the impossible-to-scale glass fencing around the pool deck. There were even child safety locks on the glass doors that led to the pool's edge.

If only she didn't have the sense she was approaching one of those crossroads she and Theo had talked about that night in Bali.

Don't think about it, she warned herself. He obviously didn't reminisce about what they'd shared. The memories twinkling through her like fairy dust needed to be blown off, swept up and dumped in the bin.

"This kid stinks," Theo said, pulling her back to the present and brutal reality.

"I'll order some diapers and show you how to change him," she said, refusing to be moved by the kicked puppy look he sent her.

He tried to put Androu down, but the tyke clung on, demanding to be held.

"Seriously kid, you stink."

"He's scared," Jaya provided. "Almost as scared as you."

His head went back and a mask of aloof dismissal fell over his features.

Oh, had that penetrated his thick shell? Rather than bask in satisfaction, she suffered a twinge of conscience. Deliberately insulting people wasn't her thing. She'd been on the end of too many bullying tactics herself.

And Theo's discomfort with having care of these two babies wasn't funny. It broke her heart. He really wasn't keen on children.

Still, she couldn't help noticing with a pang, "He trusts you. Do you spend a lot of time with him?"

"Whenever I'm in New York," he shrugged. "Adara's always inviting me to dinner and handing him off to me. I copy what Gideon does and we get along okay. Airplane rides, right, sport?"

Androu grinned, put out his arms and tipped forward into space, trusting he'd be caught with a firm hand under his chest. He made a raspberry noise with his mouth as Theo did a slow circle and dive with him.

Jaya took it like a punch in the stomach. Turning away from the heart-wrenching sight of Theo playing with the boy, she carried Evie to the sofa and started an animated movie on the television for her.

"Think you can handle them while I make a few calls?"

"You'll stay then," he said as though it was a done deal, but she read the underlying tension in his intense stare.

She wavered, still annoyed that he was only here because he wanted a favor, not because he wanted to see her, but a little voice inside her said, *Quit pretending you have a choice.* All the safe, secure blocks and fences and supports she'd put under and around herself trembled in warning of a bigger shake-up, but it had been destined to happen sometime. Today was as good an opportunity as any.

It was so hard to be near him, though. He still got to her, so handsome despite being stubbled and rumpled and smelling faintly of leather and fuel and sweat. Maybe because he looked so nonplussed and human. Like he genuinely needed her. Again.

He wasn't interested in her, she reminded herself, hurt even though she shouldn't be. He'd warned her not to expect more than their one night. She hadn't. It wasn't like she'd been in love with him. Not deeply, anyway. Just tentatively.

No, it was the fact he hadn't called when she'd had a serious reason to reach out to him. He shouldn't have dismissed her like some ditzy woman who didn't understand the rules. When he had texted her today with his cryptic message, she had responded. She expected that same consideration from him. He should have called her back.

He should know that he had his own baby who liked airplane rides.

Theo spoke to Gideon while Jaya chattered in French, ordering supplies to be delivered to their suite. When she began speaking Punjabi, she lost him, which irritated him further than he already was.

Forcing himself to pay attention to his own call, he heard

Gideon say, "It's a stunt. The son of an African prince. He's chasing down his runaway wife, although the guns are real and so are the consequences. We're stationary while the French and Spanish navies draw straws on whose jurisdiction we're in. Of course the FBI wants a say because we have so many Americans on board. Meanwhile, our pirate is threatening to draw all of North Africa into the fight if we don't turn over his wife, but if she's stowing away, we haven't found her. The ladies are having kittens that I sent the babies off the ship. Are they all right?"

"Safe," Theo replied, eyeing Jaya as she toed off her shoes and shrunk by a couple of inches. Something in her expression seemed disturbingly vulnerable as she spoke with a lilt of persuasion into her phone. Her tone riled up oddly protective instincts in him when, on the surface, she looked more self-assured than ever.

Again he wondered if there was a man in her life, then cut off his speculation. The thought of her with a lover made him nauseous.

"Can you keep them out of sight?" Gideon continued. "Nic's planning a broadcast from his cabin—man can't stand to be scooped—but we want to leave the impression they're still here, otherwise..."

"Understood. We're off the grid."

"Excellent. We're a day from shore once we can move again and may have to wait for a slip in Marseilles. I'll be in touch with an arrival time."

Theo ended the call, mind eased that his siblings and spouses weren't in immediate danger. Now he just had to—

A knock sounded and Jaya lowered her phone to motion at Theo. "That will be the bellman with the things I asked him to bring up. Take Androu to the bedroom while he brings everything in."

Evie was rapt with her princess movie, dark head below the sofa back. He stepped out of the main room and continued to watch her as he listened to Jaya direct a pair of young men to leave everything inside the door. She continued her call as they left.

After hanging up a moment later, she walked him through his first diaper change, then briskly began moving objects to higher ground and double checking that doors were locked, particularly the one to the pool deck.

"We could swim with them later. They'd like that," she murmured, sounding distracted, her nervous tension palpable. Maybe because he was hovering, but he couldn't help himself. He told himself it was the new experience of child-minding. Androu still clung with determined little fists and tight legs which was a disturbing feeling that reinforced to him how inadequate he was with the task of reassurance. All Theo could do was hold him and follow Jaya around.

He wasn't used to her taking an avoidance tack, though. In Bali, she had looked him in the eye and smiled every time he caught her eye, then blushed and shied maybe, but she'd never refused to meet his gaze. Her brisk movements around the flat were as much about putting distance between them as securing the space for the children.

Aware he was seeking his own sort of reassurance, he made himself halt in one spot and quit tagging after her like a lost puppy, but he couldn't stop himself from watching her slender limbs and smooth efficiency. He couldn't help remembering that her skin had smelled like cloves and almonds and her hair had been a cool weight of silk that had warmed against his bare chest.

She paused to scan the equipment littering the entrance.

"That seems like a lot of stuff. Two highchairs and a booster?" It looked like there were three portable cots, not that he was an expert on baby furniture.

"We can deal with this later. What did your brother-in-law say?"

He brought her up to speed and she nodded jerkily. "So

a couple of days. You're really sure you want me here? I'll have to spend the night. That means—"

"It's an imposition, I realize. Do you—" He swore under his breath, unable to put off asking. He didn't even want to know, but it might help control his still thriving attraction. "Is there someone in your life this will affect?" he forced himself to ask.

She stilled, not looking at him. After a long second, she nodded. Then she lifted an expression that was frozen between tortured and fretful.

He swallowed, surprised how deeply the knife thrust and twisted even though he'd braced for it. Even though she had every right to get on with her life. He certainly had no right to possessiveness. This situation was going to be unbearable.

Let her call an agency.

Before he could work up the will to make the concession, soft, pitiful whimpers rose over a lullaby being sung on screen. Evie's sobs turned into a heart-wrenching wail that made Jaya's eyes pop. She rushed toward the girl.

"Baby, what happened? Did you hurt yourself?"

Theo lowered his lids in a wince. "I didn't realize what you'd put on. That's Rowan's voice as the fairy godmother."

Jaya gathered up the toddler in a cuddle and murmured words of comfort. Her swift loving care to a child she barely knew struck into his toughened heart like an axe, leaving a wound that gaped and ached. He'd just realized how perfect Jaya was on the heels of learning she belonged to another man. She *should* be with someone. She deserved to be happy.

He still hated himself for never calling her back. He'd never felt so alone and lonely—and he knew loneliness like other people knew the lyrics to a favorite song.

With his breath burning his lungs, he asked, "What should we do?"

He meant, *Should we call in someone else?* But she only rocked Evie and said, "There's nothing we can do. Little ones need their mamas." Her brow flinched before she tried to distract Evie with a cheerful, "But we could go swimming. Do you like to swim?"

The bait and switch worked and after waiting for swimsuits and special diapers, they all climbed into the pool. Again Jaya was a natural, showing him how to hold Androu and coach him to kick while Evie proved to be part mermaid, pushing herself free of Jaya's grip and swimming to the edge where she came up to grin proudly.

It was a surprisingly conflict-free hour as he shifted his focus onto the moment and the safety of the children. Okay, he was also pretty damned aware of Jaya's nipples poking against the wet cups of her modest one-piece black swimsuit, but thankfully the cool water kept his libido from responding too wildly. She was *way* off-limits, even further than when she'd worked for him, so he suppressed his interest as best he could.

They were back to their Bali roles, polite and capable of basic camaraderie as they discussed neutral topics like the children, the weather, and Marseilles.

Until she said, "Theo," with surprising gravity behind him.

"Yes?" he prompted, keeping his back to her as he boosted Evie toward the edge.

Ah, hell, he had his back to her. Inner tension came on so fast he felt like he solidified and fractured in the same breath.

The scars should have become less of an issue for him in the last year. His whole family had started coming to terms with their childhood, but he'd spent so many years clenching his teeth against it all that he couldn't bring himself to open up to any of his siblings about what was plain as the stripes on his back. There didn't seem any point and they were still so awkward with each other. He wanted to be friends with his older brother, but making that happen was easier if they both pretended the ugliness in their early lives hadn't happened. Maybe it was counterproductive, but all of them had been raised to be polite and ignore. They very easily fell back on that coping strategy.

Jaya was private and quiet, but she was soft. Anything that moved her started at heart level. If she asked him about this, it would be because she was concerned.

Knowing that made the cracks in him extend to even deeper places, touching into areas that were raw and sensitive. Thank God he had a baby to keep an eye on and didn't have to turn and face her pointed silence. He waited with ears that felt stretched and hollow, not ready for this conversation, not imagining he could ever be ready, but he didn't know how to avoid it.

After a long interminable moment, she asked, "What happened to your back?"

Ensuring Evie was out of the water and sitting safely on the edge, he kept a hand on her tiny frame and glanced at Jaya, dreading her pity.

Her anxious frown was so kind it made him want to shudder, like he'd had too big a taste of sugar. He swallowed back a thickness in his throat and was left with the bitter residue of a bleak time when he'd been insignificant and helpless.

"Exactly what you imagine happened," he answered in as controlled a tone as he could manage. Maybe he should have seen a counselor by now, but why? The emotional scars were as permanent as the physical ones. All he could do was accept them and try not to feel ashamed. He was smart enough to know it wasn't his fault, even if he'd grown up believing he must have done something to deserve all that abuse.

"Who—? When…? *Why?*" she choked.

"My father." A shadow of chagrin touched him. Shame that he had been so reviled by his own flesh and blood. Surely that meant there was something wrong with him.

Swallowing, he tried to find his equilibrium. He stepped back and nodded at Evie, inviting her to jump and swim toward him. Once he'd caught her up safe against his chest, he forced himself to look into Jaya's appalled face again.

"He was drunk." He tried to say it matter-of-factly, but a taut line inside him vibrated, making him unsteady. "I didn't keep my brother in his room as I'd been told."

"That's…" She shook her head and he could imagine someone as tenderhearted toward children as she was couldn't comprehend such cruelty. "How old were you?"

He reached for his well-practiced technique of shutting down, wanting to shrug off the details, but he couldn't seem to make it happen. No one had ever invited him to talk about this.

His body shivered as though the water he stood in was full of ice. "Eight. That's why I don't drink. That's why…"

He didn't want to apologize for Bali. They'd been using each other, she'd said so, but she had wound up expecting more after all. He'd let her down. He hated failure, but he didn't have anything else to offer. Maybe if she understood that, she wouldn't hate him so much.

Squinting into the sunlight reflected off the water, he spoke in a graveled voice. "That night in Bali…Adara had called me earlier that day to tell me she'd contacted Nic. We hadn't seen him in years, not since we were kids. Before he left home, our lives were pretty normal and decent. After Nic was gone, both our parents drank. Our father became violent. I blamed Nic because I never paused to think about how we were all kids when it happened. He hadn't had a choice, either. I hadn't considered that he might have suffered in his own way. When Adara told me he had…"

He shook his head, remembering how everything had

skewed in his mind, falling in a jumble he couldn't make sense of. Then Jaya had arrived, sweet Jaya, soothing and earnest and warm, wanting to say goodbye. He hadn't been able to bear the idea of her leaving. All he'd wanted was to keep her close.

"It was a lot to process," he said, hoping his strong dose of self-deprecation hid the impact her sharing herself had had on him.

"I understand."

"Do you?" he asked gruffly.

He wasn't a talkative man. He didn't have drinking buddies or squash partners. Men didn't typically share their personal garbage anyway. Not with each other, but he'd entrusted Jaya with his emotional safety that night. Maybe he hadn't shared his inner dialogue, but when she'd lain against him, naked and soft, her breath caressing his neck and her hair tickling his arm, he'd wanted to.

He wanted that emotional safety net again. Craved it like air.

Bending her dark head over Androu, she said, "I'm lying. I don't understand how anyone can be cruel to someone smaller than they are. It upsets me."

She looked up and the unprecedented connection he'd felt with her in Bali manifested like a beam between them, pulling them toward each other. The urge to move close and cover her mouth with his own was almost irresistible. He could practically taste her papaya flavor, could almost feel the cool mango smoothness of her lips against his.

A buzzer broke the spell.

Jaya's expression fell to one that was appalled and startled before she buckled her shoulders in a cringe. She wasn't given to swearing as far as he knew, but she muttered something in Punjabi that might have been a curse.

"Who is it?" he asked, worried they'd suffered a leak to the press.

"Quentin. I asked him to bring…" Her look of remorseful appeal made all the sharp edges in him abrade against each other.

"Your things?" he guessed. "Understandable."

A ripping sensation went through him nonetheless, tearing away the paper walls he used to disguise the fact his childhood still affected him. He thought, *Lucky, lucky man,* and hated his rival for being smart enough to win her heart and keep it. The bastard had better be good to her.

He waved her to climb the stairs before him then had to avert his gaze from her ass and the backs of her long slender thighs. "Is he staying?" *There'll be a murder-suicide in tomorrow's papers.*

"I thought we'd have more time to talk before he arrived," she said, handing him a towel before wrapping Androu like a Mexican burrito.

"What else is there to say?"

Her flashing glance was loaded as a hot pistol, but she only carried Androu inside. He followed on heavy feet, reluctant to meet her…what was the beau's label? She wasn't wearing a ring so they weren't married or engaged. Maybe they were only dating.

"We'll swim more later," he promised Evie as she protested leaving the pool to come inside. He paused to reach up and lock the door behind him as he entered, then forced himself into the foyer where more bags had landed among the flotsam there.

A stocky blond man chopped his German tirade short as he spied Theo over Jaya's shoulder. His blue eyes were sharp, his manner too damned proprietary.

Every male instinct came alive in Theo, despite having no claim on Jaya. He looked right into the man's eyes with challenge, mentally aware it was wrong, but he couldn't help himself. If the guy wanted her, he could damn well fight for her.

"So. You finally turn up," the German gruffed.

"Quentin, please." Jaya murmured as she turned to look at Theo. Her imploring eyes filled with compunction while she kept a hand in the middle of her paramour's chest. No, not on his chest. As she shifted, Theo saw the baby trustingly clutched in the man's curved arm.

Don't drop Evie, Theo reminded himself, but the sight of that mite with black hair, dusky skin and curious brown eyes was a kick in the gut. He was Jaya's. There was no mistaking the maternal protectiveness in her hand on the baby boy's tiny blue T-shirt.

Time stood still as he processed all of them standing there with babies in their arms, Quentin with his rumpled suit and grim expression, he and Jaya practically naked with towels around their waists. Yes, this was good and humiliating to meet the father of her child with his pants proverbially around his ankles and his ineptness with children on full display.

"Quentin is my cousin's husband. I told you about Saranya when I was leaving Bali. Do you remember?" Jaya asked.

"Of course." Not the father then. His mind cycloned as he attempted to process this new information. If Quentin wasn't the father, who was? To hide his inner chaos, he fell back on the scrupulous manners drilled into him as a child. "How is she?"

"Dead," Quentin said flatly.

Nice. Theo surprised himself by thinking he might understand Quentin's bitterness a little, given how agonized he was at the mere thought of Jaya not being available to him. He couldn't imagine how he'd react if she were beyond his reach in a grave.

"I'm sorry," he offered, aware how useless the words were, but it's what you said.

"You should be," the German growled.

I didn't kill her, Theo bit back, able to curb the desire to be cruel because Quentin wasn't involved with Jaya, but if he wasn't the man in her life, who was?

His gaze returned to the bright brown eyes that were almost familiar, yet not like Jaya's nearly black irises. A hit of déjà vu accosted him because he could have sworn he'd looked into those eyes earlier today...

The air dried up around him. His heart began to pound with thick hammer blows inside his chest. The kicked feeling in his gut tightened around a serrated blade that turned low and without mercy. If he had bones, they'd vaporized.

Don't. Drop. Evie. He rather desperately tried to recollect if Demitri had been to Bali or had business in Marseille last year.

"Will you please let me handle this?" Jaya's voice seemed to come from far away. She tried to take the baby from Quentin, but she already held Androu.

For the life of him, Theo couldn't approach and take his nephew, even though he knew he should.

"Let you play house?" the German grumbled. "For how long? There's a reason you and Saranya were always railroaded by the men in your family. You *let* them."

"So if I tell you to butt out and leave, you will?"

Quentin gave her a stern look, but followed it with a resigned sigh that ended in a kiss on her cheek. He transferred the baby into her arms and straightened to throw another bitter glare at Theo.

The animosity in that look told Theo who the father was. Not Demitri. Hell, he didn't know if he should be relieved or not. How he stayed on his feet, he'd never know.

"Call me if you need me," Quentin said to Jaya and walked out.

Jaya took a shaken breath as the door closed, then turned to face him. The two boys she held weren't far apart in age and despite the slightly darker skin tone on the smaller one, and the black hair where Androu's was brown, their eyes and mouth were mirror images.

The sensation of dissolving from the inside out continued to assault Theo. He couldn't form a proper thought. He tried, but this was more than he could grasp. More than he wanted to believe.

"This is Zephyr," Jaya said, voice strained, but firm and a trifle defiant. "My...*our*...son."

CHAPTER SIX

THEO STARED AT her like she was a stranger. His wide tanned chest didn't seem to rise and fall at all where he clutched Evie in a towel against it. His lips were white and severe, his stillness frightening.

Accusation sharpened his level glare.

"I tried to tell you," she began, then thought, *No*. No remorse. He hadn't returned her calls. That's why this was a shock to him. If she hadn't found the right time to bring it up in the past hour, well, he'd had plenty of opportunities in the past year.

Nevertheless, a vision of the striped scars on his back flashed into her mind's eye. Her indignation deflated and their situation became a tangle again. How had they even got here, staring like a pair of cowboys waiting for the other to draw?

Her arms ached worse than her head, but not as bad as her heart.

"They're heavy," she said. "Can we move into the lounge?"

"Of course." He stepped forward and lifted Androu from her, averting his gaze from Zephyr's shy smile.

Zephyr was an engaging little chap, happy as anything, and Theo's turning away from him struck at the very core of her, setting her blood to boil.

Hugging her baby's tiny frame into her wet swimsuit,

she told herself to turn around and walk out, leave Theo to his "real" family.

Zephyr's connection to the other children stopped her. Without her own cousin's love and support, her life would be very different right now. Those sorts of ties were sacred to her and Zephyr wasn't likely to enjoy many of them with her side of the family. Her parents and siblings were even less inclined to speak to her now that she had a bastard soiling the family name.

Was Theo really as narrow-minded as they were, capable of rejecting a boy who hadn't done anything except have the gall to come to life inside her?

"Did you seriously just wet through this towel onto my arm?" Theo asked Androu in an aggrieved tone. "This kid hates me."

"He's a baby. They don't know how to be malicious." *So don't blame Zephyr if you're angry at me,* she added in a silent bite.

A tense twenty minutes passed as she took Evie and Zephyr into her bedroom to dress the girl and herself, leaving Theo charged with Androu. When she emerged, Theo wore a more truculent expression than any toddler. He held a naked Androu and a disposable diaper that looked worse for wear.

"This is why I'm not cut out to be a father," he charged. "I can't even manage the basics."

"Well, you are a father, so I guess you'll have to learn, won't you?" she shot back, heart wobbling in her chest at her own audacity. But this was one thing she wouldn't let the implacable Theo Makricosta block out. It was too important, and not just to Zephyr.

"I wasn't supposed to be. You *promised.* You said it would be a disaster—"

"Zephyr is not a disaster. Do *not*—" She cut herself off from raising her voice, looking away for a second to gather herself, afraid she'd frighten the children if she gave in to the press of emotions strangling her. Tears were right behind the anger so she swallowed hard, trying to keep it all from releasing.

"We're all frazzled and hungry," she managed in a croaking voice. "I called room service while we were changing. I'll dress Androu and once we feed the little ones and they're settled, I'll explain. All right?"

He glared, but didn't argue. An hour later, as she scrubbed faces and hands, he washed his own hands and grumbled, "I'm wearing more than they ate."

"It's better than wearing *what* they ate," she countered, not sure how they'd managed to be such a well-coordinated team when they were barely speaking. He'd let her lead, which surprised her, copying her actions with great care and concentration, as if there was a perfect system for feeding a baby.

It was such a contradictory vision of him and did funny things to her heart. He was so gloriously inept, but so determined to master these little child-care tasks. Like he'd suffer terribly if he failed to do it right.

Get smacked, maybe. With a belt.

Oh, Theo. Her throat filled with words she couldn't voice.

"That's gross," he replied after taking a moment to get her meaning about what the kids ate.

"It's reality," she murmured, lifting Zephyr from his chair and adding, "Do you want to watch them in the other room or finish cleaning up in here?"

As the older pair toddled off in two directions, he gave her a boggled look. "Maybe we should call an agency."

She tensed. So much for their tentative accord. "You don't want me and Zephyr here after all then." It was all she could do to pretend his rejection of their son didn't shatter her.

"No, I mean we need more help. This is a lot of work! Has either of us sat down since we walked in here four hours ago?" He skimmed a hand over his dry but uncombed hair and stabbed a look at Zephyr. "But now we've got this development to manage, too. Discretion is more important than ever, so I guess that leaves us stuck doing it ourselves."

"Development?" she repeated, hysterical laughter competing with outrage. *Stuck?*

"Who else besides your cousin's husband knows I'm— That you and I—"

"Made a baby?" she provided tartly. She tried to remember that he wasn't the most verbal person alive and this was all quite a shock for him, but honestly, why was it so hard for him to acknowledge his son? "Are you ashamed of Zephyr?" she guessed in a tone that thinned to outrage as the possibility sank in. It was the worst thing he could throw at her, striking directly into her Achilles heel. Into her soul.

"I'm shocked! You had to know I would be." He'd changed into a basic white T-shirt that strained across his chest as he gestured toward the view of the sea. "I can't have my family finding out through some cheap sensationalism on the internet. We've suffered enough secrets and lies as it is." He pinched the bridge of his nose.

Unwillingly, she felt sorry for him, which was crazy. He didn't deserve it, but, "I did try to call you when I first realized I was pregnant," she reminded.

He sighed, brows coming together in a pensive frown. "I debated calling you back, I did, but Adara turned up pregnant and given her previous miscarriages Demitri and I had to take over her workload. Then our mother died. By the time the dust settled, there didn't seem any point in contacting you."

They'd both been going through a lot. She supposed she couldn't fault him too much for not returning her calls under those circumstances.

"But I trusted you to take that pill, Jaya. What happened?"

The blame in his tone stabbed her, even though she'd tried to prepare herself for it every time she'd mentally walked through this conversation. Yes, she'd failed to protect both of them from the consequences of their night together and she was willing to own that, but his anger and disappointment filled her with umbrage. She didn't want to feel defensive and solely responsible. He knew what could happen from unprotected sex. It didn't matter that she had a better understanding of what had driven him that night. He had still chosen to sleep with her to satisfy his own selfish needs.

Just as, when it came down to it, she'd kept their baby for her own selfish reasons.

"The pill was expired," she explained with as much dignity as she could scrape together. "I thought I'd be able to get a fresh one once I landed in France, but with the time change and Saranya being so ill, it was days before I came up for air. By then I'd missed the window. Then I thought I'd wait to see if I had anything to worry about."

She flinched from the intensity of his judgmental stare, sinking bleakly back into that time of despair, feeling again the torn sensation of having said goodbye to her life in Bali, and Theo, then facing an even more brutal goodbye with her cousin.

Lifting her chin, she finished without apology, "When it turned out I was pregnant, I couldn't take steps to end it. I just couldn't, not with Saranya dying in front of me. I needed something to look forward to. The promise of life and love."

Scanning the lounge to ensure the older kids were staying out of trouble, she tried to hide that she'd also needed her connection to Theo to continue. Her conscience had tortured her over not keeping her word, but she wasn't sorry. Not one bit.

"I tried to tell you because you deserved to know." She cleared her throat. "I didn't, and don't, expect anything from you. Not money. Not marriage. He was my decision. He's my responsibility."

There. That's all she'd ever wanted to say, even though she had ached every day to share her pregnancy and baby with Theo. Zephyr was such a little miracle. She wanted Theo to love him as much as she did.

"Oh, sweetie, don't eat that—" she blurted, realizing Androu had picked lint out of the carpet.

Rushing forward was a much-needed break from the weight of Theo's gaze. She couldn't face him after what she'd just said and didn't want to see his relief at being absolved of any duty or involvement with his son.

Theo tried to find comfort in her letting him off the hook. God knew he didn't want to explore the miasma of primordial goo that bubbled inside him as he considered what it meant to be a father.

Inexplicably he was hurt, however. Stinging with rejection at her wanting nothing to do with him.

Fortunately, he was too busy to dwell on whether he should feel sorry for himself or not. Once the kitchenette was tidied, there were beds to set up and pajamas to be ordered, then everyone had to be threaded into them—which was like pushing a rope up a staircase.

"I'm thinking we need bedtime stories and some stuffies. Do they have special blankets or sleeping toys? This could be a rough night," Jaya warned as she placed a call to a nearby shop before it closed.

"Unlike the day it's been?" he drawled, waving agreement to whatever she wanted to charge to the room.

He wasn't trying to fuel a fight. It struck him how painfully familiar this tension was, like a typical Makricosta gathering. They had a full-grown elephant between them in the shape of a dark-haired baby boy, but they remained civil, only speaking about the logistics of what needed to be done as they ran their mini-hotel. It should have been a relief, but he found the circumventing and pretending frustrating.

Was this his punishment for the mistake of not wearing a condom? Because he was feeling castigated, chastised and rebuked. Slapped around, knocked down and kicked to the curb.

Why? he found himself wanting to demand. *Why don't you want anything from me? Because you're afraid I'll screw up?*

He'd never been able to challenge his father, not without suffering worse for it, and he wasn't sure how to act around Jaya when he felt this abused. His primary instinct when his emotions were churned up was to isolate himself, but no luck on that score. It was all hands on deck and he was about as frayed and tired as the toddlers, barely keeping it together as he counted down the minutes to their bedtime.

If only Jaya would offer the same quiet reassurance she kept giving to the homesick tykes. He watched her adeptly keep them from shedding more than a few sniffles, relieved to know he'd made the right choice in tracking her down, but he was damned jealous of each cuddle and kiss she offered.

His gaze fell on Zephyr and he experienced the crack between the eyes that was his own egocentric vulnerability eighteen months ago. If only he could go back to the ignorance that had been bliss yesterday.

Not all the way back to Bali, though. He didn't regret making love to her.

Disturbed, he shifted his gaze to Jaya, worried she could read his betraying thoughts.

He wanted to resent her for letting him down, but after what she'd told him about her cousin, he couldn't find it in him to hate her for failing to take the pill. Maybe the promise of love and life hadn't been uppermost in his mind when his mother had been dying, but he had an inkling how helpless and hopeless she must have felt.

He couldn't judge her for using procreation as a coping strategy, either, could he? Not when he'd employed it with her—in a rather shortsighted manner—when he'd been under the duress of Adara's confession about Nic.

And where was the point in being angry about what she should have done? It couldn't be undone. The child was here.

Still, he couldn't face this, couldn't face fatherhood. What kind of an example had been set for him? Look at his back.

Not that the children had any idea how useless he was. Once they'd scattered their new toys across the blanket Jaya had spread on the floor of the lounge, Evie brought him a book.

"Jaya's the reader. I'm the sentry," he said, motioning to his sprawled body acting as a fence between the corner of a chair and the length of the sofa to keep them corralled.

"Peas," she implored with a heart-stealing smile, reeling him in an inch. Until today he hadn't spent much time with her, but she was the most gentle, tender thing he'd ever seen, enchanted with Baby Zepper, chattering like old friends to Androu, missing her parents and thus taking to Jaya with impulsive hugs and embraces.

"Sure, I'll read," Jaya said breezily. "If Uncle takes the next dirty bottom."

"Never mind. I got this." Theo sat up so his back was against the edge of the sofa.

Evie wormed herself into his side, making him lift his

elbow in surprise. The weight of her head felt surprisingly endearing as she let it droop against his rib cage.

He imagined she was just getting sleepy, but it still felt like a very trusting gesture, one that gave him a funny sensation of fullness around his heart.

As he started to read, Androu toddled over with a car clutched in his fist, drool glossing his chin. As he plopped down on Theo's other side, a drip fell to slide down Theo's wrist.

"Seriously, dude, I'm going to talk to your parents about your manners."

"He can't help teething," Jaya scolded, coming across with a tissue to dry the boy's face.

As she bent, Theo raised his hand so she could wipe the spit off his arm. Zephyr, balanced on her hip, read some kind of invitation from their body language and tilted out of her grip, reaching out with his short arms for Theo.

Jaya gasped, so caught by surprise she almost dropped the boy.

Theo had no choice but to catch him one-handed, guiding the boy into a safe landing against his chest. The tot flipped and slid into his lap like an otter down a log.

Distant base instincts cautioned him about the tiny feet kicking near his jewels, but a stronger, less easy to define reaction took over. He was shaken by the natural way Zephyr relaxed into him. It was passive aggression at its best, clashing into his protective inner walls with unseen yet gong-like reverberations. He'd been avoiding touching the boy, thinking he'd decide later whether he'd take an active part in the boy's life, after he'd figured out what to make of the situation and how many options he had.

He didn't want this puppy warmth sitting in his center, thawing the tight frozen pillars he used to brace himself against the world.

But when he looked up at Jaya, thinking to ask her to

take him, her expression was so vulnerable, so fearful of rejection on the boy's behalf, he couldn't do that to her. Hell, he couldn't do it to a child. To his *son*.

This situation was the most perplexing, dumbfounding circumstance of his life, but these little creatures were incredibly defenseless. Like her, he couldn't understand how anyone could hurt a child. He certainly couldn't do it himself.

Which didn't make him father material, he reminded himself, ignoring the clenched sensation around his heart. Kids needed a lot more than the basics of food and shelter and a soft place to sit. Nascent things like love were beyond him so she was setting him up for failure with Zephyr. That was not something he could easily forgive, but he couldn't hurt the boy out of anger with her.

Aware of Jaya standing over him, arms hugged across her middle, he refused to look up to see how she reacted to his playing human recliner.

"There was a farm up the road from my mother's house in Chatham," he said, trying for dismissive when he could hear the rattled edge in his tone. "I saw a sow there once, knocked over by her own piglets because they wanted to nurse. Now I know how she felt." He wasn't doing this because he wanted to, he implied. He had no choice.

He began to read aloud, silently willing her to go away. It was one thing to have his emotions hanging by a thread while children listened to him struggle through a story. They wouldn't know the difference, but Jaya was perceptive. He hated knowing she could tell how confused and defenseless this made him.

After a few seconds, she drew a hitched breath.

"Do you know if Androu has a bottle before bed? I'm going to make one for Zeph." Her voice was blessedly lacking in inflection.

"Text Adara and ask."

"Okay, but—" She started across to her phone. "What have you told her? Does she know I'm here?"

"I told Gideon I'd recruited you, but that was when we first got here. They don't know about…" He looked down at the dark head turning against his breastbone, more interested in the older babies and chewing his fist than the picture book.

Jaya didn't answer. He thought she was texting until he heard the familiar shutter-click of the camera app. He glanced up in dismay.

She shrugged. "This might never happen again." Her trim figure, encased in three-quarter length jeans and a lime-green shirt, disappeared toward the kitchenette.

He drew in a breath that burned his lungs, suddenly wondering whether he had any choice when it came to involvement in his son's life. Jaya might have made up her mind that *this might never happen again*.

CHAPTER SEVEN

"I CAN HONESTLY say this has been the most grueling day of my life," Theo said, flopping onto the sofa when he and Jaya came back to the lounge after settling all the babies.

"Try nineteen hours of labor," she chirped, picking up toys rather than sitting.

Guilt assailed him. He'd put his sister's pregnancy ahead of Jaya's. Unknowingly, sure, but at the time he'd convinced himself he was putting both women's best interests ahead of his own. Somehow he didn't think saying so would be an easy sell to the woman who'd struggled through childbirth alone.

"Was it bad?" he asked, bracing inwardly while leaning to gather the toys within reach.

"It wasn't a picnic, but it was fairly typical. He was worth it."

"That's what my sister says. I don't know how women do it." He searched her expression, awed that she wasn't berating him.

"You just do. There's no time to figure out how." Clenching a stuffed panda between her tense brown hands, she said, "Kind of like the way I sprang him on you. There wasn't any opportunity to prepare you, but you still seem furious so let's have it. Don't keep giving me the robot mode of being terribly polite. If you want to yell, yell. Except, don't wake the babies, but—" She sighed sharply. "I know you feel lied to, but I swear I didn't do it for money or to take advantage of you."

His heart turned over in his chest. He wished he could dismiss her as conniving. It would be so much easier to keep his own emotions out of it if she had none, but one of her main attractions for him beyond the physical had always been her earnest sincerity.

"I believe that money was the last thing on your mind."

Her smile of relief made him wish they could leave it there, but she needed to fully comprehend the rest. Leaning his elbows on his knees, he rubbed his face, trying to erase any sign of the turmoil still blowing like a hurricane inside him.

"But whether you want money or not, it's the only thing you'll ever get from me."

Her lips slacked in surprise, then pursed. Her brows drew together and she shifted her gaze to the darkened windows. "I don't want any."

"No, you want me to be a father, I can tell. But Jaya, that stuff I told you earlier about my lousy childhood. That's why I never wanted to be one." He looked past her knees, jaw clenching, seeing nothing but a blur of his past. "It's not just fear that I'll turn out like the old man and raise my hand—"

"You wouldn't," she said.

He lifted his gaze to focus on her face, trying to read her meaning. Was it a challenging, *You wouldn't dare?* Or an expression of confidence in him?

He mentally stepped away from trying to decipher her words, disturbed by how badly he wanted her to believe in him when he didn't know if he could believe in himself.

"I'd like to think I wouldn't, but if my life fell apart the way my dad's did and I tried to cope by drinking…" He rubbed the hard tension from his jaw, needing her to understand that whether she wanted something from him or not, there was nothing here. "Beyond that, though, is the lack of substance in me. I told you what kind of man I was that night in Bali. I'd make a terrible father. I don't make strong connections, ever. Kids need something better than what I'm capable of offering."

It was the hard truth, but he still searched her expression, wanting her to argue.

"Aren't you underestimating yourself?" Hope wound through her question like a strand of gold, catching at him, filling him with bittersweet satisfaction at how predictable she was. He wished he could live up to her view of him, he really did.

He shook his head. "The closest connection I have is with my sister and we don't talk about personal things." Well, he didn't. Adara had opened up about her marriage when it had almost fallen apart, but he'd only had to listen and stand by her. No reciprocation required.

"What about your brother? You said you talked to Adara about Nic that night we—I mean in Bali."

Inexplicably, he found himself rising, finding himself verging on retreat because her question stood on his toes and leaned into his space, but he couldn't walk out. He owed her some kind of explanation.

He tried to pace off his discomfort. "Adara talked, I listened. Since then I've told you more about how that has impacted me than I've ever admitted to anyone else."

"Really?" She cocked her head in surprise.

"This is what I'm saying, Jaya. I don't connect on a meaningful level. To be honest, I wish I *could* take a page from Nic's book. He grew up isolated and neglected and he's made a really good life for himself. A nice family with Ro and Evie. So has Adara with Gideon. I look at the way they dote on their kids and I'm envious, but I don't even know what words describe those things they demonstrate so how could I become like they are?"

She pressed her drawn lips together and swallowed like she was fighting back deep feelings. Her unblinking eyes glittered before she dropped her lashes to hide them.

"Not every man falls in love at first sight with his child," she allowed in a voice that made his heart shrivel. "It's different for a woman, especially when she carries the baby for nine months. The attachment is there from the minute she holds the baby."

"What if the attachment never arrives?" His worst nightmare was producing that same feeling of being unwanted and unloved that he'd grown up with. "What would that do to Zephyr if he expects it and it isn't there? Don't bother trying to answer that because I know how it feels. I thought I had an attachment to my father and he wound up attacking me with his belt."

She flinched like he'd struck her and he wanted to kick himself.

"I shouldn't talk to you about it." He paced away across the room. This was why he didn't talk about his personal life. "It upsets you to hear it and it doesn't do a damned thing to resolve it for me, but that's what I'm trying to get across. He broke that part of me. I don't know how to be what a child would need. I only know what not to be."

"That's a start."

"A very pitiful one. Zephyr deserves better. Be the mother I know you are and admit that. You wouldn't settle for anything less than the best for him."

She didn't say anything, only pressed her knuckles to her mouth and kept her head bent. She might even have nodded.

That hurt. It hurt so bad he couldn't breathe, even though—maybe especially because—it was the honesty he'd demanded.

"So let's talk about money," he said.

Her gaze came up, dagger sharp with disbelief. "I was

dead serious when I said the last thing I'd ever do is use him to extort anything from you."

"That doesn't mean you'll never struggle. He's the only progeny I'll have." He certainly wouldn't take any woman's word and play roulette with his sperm again. He should look into a vasectomy, he supposed, filing that thought for later because right now he couldn't imagine sleeping with anyone but the woman in this room.

Weird how he could be having this incredibly uncomfortable conversation and still be aroused by the way her breasts moved in the confines of her bra or her pants clung to her backside as she bent.

Forcing himself to set down thoughts too hot to entertain, he said, "Whether you want it or not, I'll set up a portfolio for both of you. You might as well have a say in it."

"Oh, Theo! I was going to leave Zephyr with Quentin tonight." She sprang into action again, tossing soft bears and cloth books into a box that groceries had been delivered in. "Then I saw how much poor Evie and Androu were missing their mamas and I couldn't deprive Zephyr of a night with his own. And I was mad at you! I was mad that you ignored my calls because I never wanted your stupid money or a relationship or anything for *me*. I only wanted to be decent and let you know you have a son. And now what are you doing? Offering me money and trying to pretend your child doesn't exist."

"I didn't say that," he growled, pushing angry fists into his pockets, slouching as he turned his back on her. "That's not what I said."

"Then take part in his life!"

"How? I've just explained that I don't want to hurt him, physically or mentally, but I very likely would!"

"But that's it, that's the vital piece you think you don't have. You already care about him. Don't you? A little?" *Don't beg,* she warned herself. He might be right. It might be better to buffer Zephyr against indifference if that's all Theo was capable of.

She really didn't want to believe that, though. She didn't want her son growing up feeling as she had, dismissed and unimportant. For heaven's sake, didn't he realize what a gift she'd given him? A *son*. That was supposed to elevate *her* value in his eyes.

Congratulations, Jaya. Modern women raise their children alone and *nobody* regards her as special. The clash of cultural mores made her furious.

"Don't write Zephyr off without even trying to get to know him. That's callous. It's cowardly. You be a better man than that," she demanded with a point of her finger. "I never would have slept with you if I believed you lacked compassion and the ability to respect someone for their worth."

"Really." He spun to confront her, head thrown back in challenge as he stared down his nose at her. "I thought we were using each other for escape that night."

And he was getting his back up because he thought she'd been after a deeper relationship after all. Maybe, yes, way down she had feelings for him that longed to be requited, but she shook her head vehemently.

"No. I mean yes, I was using you. But I wouldn't have used a man less decent than you are."

He barked out a disbelieving laugh. "Nice."

"That didn't come out right. I'm saying that I didn't expect to have sex with you, but it happened because I respect you. And I'm not sorry. I'm happy we made Zephyr. I was resigned to not having children so..." She was saying too much. With a pleat stressing her brow, she clammed her mouth and decided they'd talked enough for one night.

"Really?" He tucked in his chin. "You're the most natural person I've ever seen with kids. Was there something wrong that made you think you couldn't have any?"

They'd definitely talked enough.

"I told you my career was important to me," she mumbled, casting about for the last of the toys, but they'd tidied up all of them.

"And you still have a career despite being a single parent. Not always an ideal situation, I'm sure, but I can't believe you didn't see before Zephyr that kids and career can coexist. You must have considered it an option. You didn't say you weren't *planning* to have kids, but that you resigned yourself not to, like you didn't think it was possible. Are you okay, Jaya? Because my sister may not have confided all the trauma of her miscarriages, but I'm aware there can be complications with any pregnancy. It makes me a real bastard for not protecting you that night if I put your life at risk."

"Have you listened at all? I was textbook normal. I'm made to have babies and I'm not sorry I had him. Not one bit. That's all I meant. Now we should get some rest. Even if they sleep through the night—which they won't—they'll be up early." She tried to scoot past him.

He caught her arm.

She caught her breath.

Silly, silly Jaya. Still flushing like a preteen at this man's touch. Shyness kept her face averted. She didn't want him to see how much he still affected her.

His thumb brushed her bare skin, hot palm leaving an imprint of his firm but gentle grip. *Those hands.* Knowledge burned in a trail from the light caress of his thumb to the pit of her stomach and lower, flooding her inner thighs with tingling warmth. Her face stung with the pressure of a hard blush.

He cleared his throat and pulled his touch away like he felt the scald. When he spoke, he didn't pursue the other topic, but floored her with something else.

"When I asked if there was someone in your life, I meant

a man. Is Zephyr it, or is there someone else I should be worried about?"

"Would you be?" she asked, snapping her head up then regretting it. He must be able to read the flush of awareness savaging her, but he looked his old, contained self.

"This is complicated enough without navigating some other man's sense of claim." So aloof. So hands-off. She was back in Bali, heart tattooing her breastbone like a moth against a window, trying to reach the light.

She looked away and rubbed the feel of his touch from her arm. "No, there's not. What about you?" The question escaped as the horrifying thought occurred.

"Are you kidding? No."

"Still playing concierge for the Lonely Hearts Club?" she sniped, annoyed.

"Open to new members. Always."

Ouch. She set her jaw, trying not to let his flippancy bother her. He was only trying to prove his shallowness. *Maybe he is that shallow, Jaya. There's not a woman in the world with enough training to fix me. Don't try.*

She needed to believe he was better than what he was pretending though, she needed it like oxygen. It was how she had let down her guard with him that night. Yes, his rakish ability to give her pleasure had made the memories he'd given her particularly delicious, but her trust in him had been the groundwork. She had believed him to be a good, honorable man, which had allowed her to put herself in his care.

"Don't be less than you are, Theo."

"Don't imagine I'm more."

"I'm only expecting you to be you, the man who saw potential in me and gave me a chance to develop it. You're fair. You're kind. Sometimes you're funny. This isn't a test. You don't have to pass it right now. We have a few days. Apparently," she added with a jerky shrug. "Can't we use this time to figure out how to proceed? Do we have to spit out a settlement contract this evening so you can run out the door tomorrow? Maybe the reason you don't have close relationships is because you don't stick around to nurture them."

He rocked back on his heels. "Touché."

"Was that harsh?" she asked, not as repentant as she could have been.

"No, it's true. I'm as much of a moving target as I can make myself."

The reasons behind that coping strategy put a lump in her throat. She tried to swallow it back with little success.

"Well, this is a safe place," she reminded in a strained tone. "You made sure. No one can hurt you here."

For a few seconds she thought she might have gone too far, appealing to the frightened child in him.

His dry chuckle had a coarse edge. "Okay, sure. I suppose we're stuck here," he said without inflection. "No need to rush to act."

Stuck again. Reacting to that awful word, she said, "There are worse things than taking a day off to play with children, you know."

"I know." His shoulders slumped heavily.

Now she really did feel sorry, but he walked away before the apologetic hand she reached out could touch him.

It was a sleepless night and not just because he had to walk Androu twice. Theo's mind wouldn't stop so he was grateful to have a reason to pace. The boy's warm weight on his arm was oddly comforting as he patted his little back to soothe him.

Jaya had to show him how, of course, demonstrating on Zephyr. "He might be with me, but it's still a strange place," she whispered in explanation of the boy's restlessness. She settled him with expert swiftness and disappeared into her room.

He dragged his eyes off the way her hotel-issued robe draped the curve of her hips and showcased her slender calves. No man in her life and whose fault was that? His. He'd taken a chance with unprotected sex because he'd been anxious to lose himself and his problems in an orgasm.

Which wasn't entirely true. As he stared across the twinkling lights of Marseille to the dark expanse of the Med, he allowed that Jaya had never been like the other women he pursued. She was special. His need that night had been as much about a desire to be with her as it had been to escape his emotional turmoil. Her announcement she was leaving Bali had lit a torch of panic in him. He'd needed, quite literally, to hold onto her.

Maybe some primitive part of him had even been seeking the permanent connection of a blood tie. As much as he'd like to dismiss his failing to protect her as a state of crisis and thoughtlessness, he'd never neglected a condom in his life. He *always* thought ahead to consequences. Fear of a beating had predisposed him to it.

So he couldn't pretend he'd simply been carried away. He'd made a conscious decision to take a risk.

Creating a child without due care and attention seemed like the kind of enormous mistake he ought to be punished severely for. His body was reacting with the same tense anticipation of hell he'd grown up trying to ignore. The clogged chest, clogged throat and anxiety ought to be far behind him, but he could hardly breathe. Sleep had never been a safe escape. Voices could rise in the next room, furniture could topple. Babies could wake and nightmares became real.

The troubling memories kept him tossing and turning even after Androu settled. Then Evie woke like a five alarm fire, jarring him and making his heart pound.

No male voice shouted, though. No impossible demands were made of children barely old enough to reach a toaster.

Jaya worked her magic and scooped up the sad little girl, murmuring reassurances.

Androu wasn't happy about being woken from a sound sleep, but Jaya distracted him with a bottle then cuddled the pair into a nest of pillows and blankets on the floor in the lounge, a cartoon of sleepy baby animals flickering at low volume on the television.

"Maybe they'll fall back asleep. Listen for Zephyr while I have a quick shower?"

He was used to starting his day shortchanged on sleep because of a time zone shift, but he'd barely slept and it wasn't even six o'clock yet. No wonder new parents were so irritable.

A few minutes later, as he searched out the coffee in the kitchen, he heard a cry. It wasn't from either of the toddlers. As he moved into the hall, the unhappy sounds grew louder. Pushing into Jaya's room, he found Zephyr sitting up in his cot with big tears on his cheeks, eyes wide and lost.

It's not a test, Jaya had said, but it was. Not just of his fatherly instincts, of which he had none, but of his ability to keep his emotional blocks from damaging this baby.

Therefore, inadequate as he felt, he couldn't leave the tyke wet and scared to wait for his mother just because she knew how to reassure with affection and he didn't.

At least a diaper change was his first priority. Funny how that seemed like a reprieve from more demanding tasks. Surprisingly, he nailed it in one go. Even got the kid back into his jammies without misaligning any snaps.

Zephyr seemed to want to keep his blanket with him, so Theo wrapped it around the boy's tiny body and snugged him closer to the warmth of his own chest, concerned that the air conditioning was set too low in the lounge.

Whether it was the warmth of his body or he was still sleepy, he seemed content enough to be carried into the lounge.

The older babies had both dropped off and Theo found himself standing over them, Zephyr's silky hair under his chin smelling familiar even though it wasn't anything he really knew.

Babies were unwieldy responsibilities that were so great, they were to be run from, far and fast. That's what he'd believed and it was true, if you were five.

He was an adult, though, perfectly capable of things like changing a diaper and making a proper meal and laundering clothes. Fearing the responsibilities of fatherhood was irrational. Millions did it every day and no one would hold him accountable with a beating if he missed getting a bit of food out of a kid's hair during a bath.

Nevertheless, after his talk with Jaya last night, his terror at taking on the role of a father was worse, not better. He knew why, too. He still feared failing, but not because of the threat of violence. He couldn't stand the idea of disappointing Jaya.

Jaya came out of her bathroom to find Zephyr's cot empty and rushed out to the main room where she found Theo cradling their son like he'd been doing it all his life.

Her blood thickened to such sweet molasses, she couldn't move. Her limbs ached and felt weak.

She must have gasped because he glanced up and touched a finger to his lips, then tilted his head to see into Zephyr's tranquil face. In slow motion, like he was handling a chemical bomb, he tucked Zephyr next to his sleeping cousins on the floor and drew their blanket over him.

She was done. Finished. Melted into a puddle on the floor that housekeeping would have to mop up and wring out of the strings.

He added a final blow by fetching his phone off the dining table and snapping a picture of the children piled together like a litter of kittens.

Removing the hand she'd pressed to her mouth, she accused in a whisper, "You're sentimental."

He shrugged, striding toward the kitchenette where he set his phone on the table and began making coffee. "We're not likely to catch them all together like that again, are we? Not all asleep."

The breath she took was coated in powdered glass. "I thought about sending the photo from last night to your sister, but you haven't told her, have you? Will you?"

He slowed his movements. "Since she's my boss and it starts with explaining that I slept with an employee—"

"Not technically."

He kicked up a brow, unimpressed with the fine line. "Still not the best example." He pushed the button that started the espresso maker. "And I'm still wrapping my head around it. I'd rather keep things simple until I know how we're going to proceed."

She tried to hide her disappointment, then thought, *Why should I?*

"That's not really fair to Zephyr, is it? I mean, they're his cousins." She waved at the bumps under the blanket. "My relationship with Saranya was the most important of my life." Not an understatement. "We grew up together and when I needed her, she was there. You don't just call a cousin out of the blue when your life implodes. Not unless you've been close all along."

She braced against his asking her how her life had imploded, but he only folded his arms and hitched a hip against the counter.

"I didn't think of it like that. I keep thinking how much they're like us. The age mix is different, of course. I'm barely a year younger than Adara and Demitri is almost four years younger than me, but we were only a few years older than Evie and practically left to raise ourselves. Adara was all I had for a mother figure and she was looking after

Demitri. I guess some part of me thought it was too much to ask of Evie and Androu to take on Zephyr, but they have functioning parents."

"So does he," she reminded, wishing she could be amused by his almost naïve misreading of the situation, but it was so tragic. "Is that why Adara always seems so…" She searched for the right word to describe her former boss that wouldn't insult the whole family. "I always thought you and she seemed very introspective."

He snorted. "You mean aloof? Distant? Cold? I've been called worse and yeah, we're not the most demonstrative family, but Adara did the best she could. I can't fault her. I'd do anything for her."

Ignoring the pang of jealousy that struck, she listened deeper, hearing exactly how far he was willing to go on his sister's behalf.

"Did you step in to protect her from your father?" Part of her knew she shouldn't ask. She didn't want to open up her own wounds and show them off so she couldn't expect him to, but her heart ached for the boy he'd been.

He flinched and turned away to set a tiny cup on a silver saucer. "Not that it did much good. She still caught her share. Demitri was the one we worried about. He was so little."

"Oh, Theo. And you think you're not cut out to be a father?"

"Have you seen how Demitri turned out? If that's my work, I'd be scared. The man's a menace." He offered her the first coffee.

"You have that one. I like mine with steamed milk." She stepped into place before the machine and filled the receptacles. "And yes, I have met your brother. Thank goodness for the repellant that is the Makricosta uniform because we all would have been pregnant. He's very adept with the ladies."

"Were you attracted to him?" His sharp gaze made her very aware of her nakedness under the robe she'd pulled on when she'd realized Zephyr had been stolen from his cot.

"I can't deny he's good-looking, but no, not really attracted." *Not the same way I'm attracted to you.* She pretended that the spurt of coffee and steamed milk required close attention, using it to hide the betraying longing she shouldn't be feeling toward him.

"A year and a half ago you weren't dating because your career was too important. Now Zephyr's in the way, isn't he?"

"I wouldn't put it like that, but he's definitely a factor. I'm not about to introduce a string of men into his life. So yes, between him and what's been going on at home and starting my new job I haven't had time to date. But dating has never been a priority so I don't miss it." There, that glossed nicely over her reasons for still avoiding men.

Yet here she stood, vulnerable in a thin robe held closed by a slippery tie, in the presence of a virile man who could overwhelm her without even trying.

Would he try? She sidled her gaze over his broad chest. He was wearing yesterday's shirt that still had some of his nephew's supper on it. That made him seem very human and normal. If he crushed her against that stained cotton, her heart would sing.

When she glanced up, she found him staring into the part of her lapels where her upper chest was exposed. Behind the light satin of the robe, her nipples tightened. Why him, she wondered, but didn't actually care. It was just such a delightfully good sensation to react to a man.

With a harsh inhale, he visibly pulled himself together and looked away. "Are you still sending money home?"

Her sensual curiosity drained away.

"Yes." She didn't elaborate and deliberately put space between them, taking her coffee to the breakfast bar and positioning herself so she could see the kids if they moved. Partly it was decent child minding, but at a deeper level, she was confused and trying to figure out why she longed for Theo to make a move on her when she was still stinging from his dropping her from his life.

"Have you told *your* family about Zephyr?" he asked.

A spike of grief pierced her as fresh as the day her family had first shunned her, hanging up on her because she had dared to run away to live with Saranya, rather than stay in the ruin they all considered her life had become. "Put it this way. If you don't acknowledge him, my cousin's daughter and Quentin are his only support after me."

Silence. When she glanced back, he was scowling toward the lounge, arms folded in frustration. "There are plenty of people with old-fashioned views in America, but it still surprises me they'd ostracize you for having a baby out of wedlock."

She sipped her coffee, ignoring the opening to tell him it was more than that. She shouldn't feel ashamed, but there was also the bit where she'd have to explain that the steps she'd taken to leave India weren't entirely legal.

"Would—"

He didn't continue so she dragged her gaze to his again, finding him looking something like he had that night in Bali: slightly defensive, rumpled but gorgeous in spite of it. His jaw was stubbled, his hair disheveled, but his proud bearing and those hollow cheeks above a strong jawline made him one of those men who would get better looking with age.

There was no sign of uncertainty in his tall, solid stillness. His expression was impassive, as if he was asking after her plans for the day.

"Would it mend fences with your family if we married?"

He couldn't have hurt her more if he'd walked right by her yesterday at the hangar and pretended he didn't see her.

She wasn't a romantic. After being sexually assaulted, she had quit dreaming of the perfect man sweeping her off her feet with a proposal that made her cry happy tears—except possibly if it came from him.

Seriously, Jaya, you have to let this infatuation die.

But one thing she knew she wanted in any marriage proposal was for love to form the underpinning of it.

"Probably," she answered, forcing herself to reply honestly, but the word choked her. She had to sip at her coffee to clear her voice into working order. Eyes on the sleeping cherubs, she added, "But my country is full of women who married because they felt they had no other choice. I do have a choice and I'm not interested."

Another thick silence.

He had to be relieved, but she didn't glance over to interpret what he might be thinking. Her insides ached too much, especially near her heart. If he saw it, he'd know how much she longed for something deeper from him and that could send him running again, making Zephyr suffer for her foolishness.

For such a powerful, confident man, he was awfully gun-shy about being close to people. Given what she'd learned about him, she could see how he'd fear betrayal of the worst kind lurked behind the slightest show of warmth. His warnings against trying to fix him burned bright in her mind. It added up to a hopeless basis for a marriage so she felt compelled to douse any spark of that talk.

"I should answer some emails while I have the chance," she murmured, pushing herself into motion. "I won't have much chance to work through the rest of the day."

Theo watched her walk away, his tired body stirred by the graceful way she moved while the rest of him throbbed with rejection. Funny how he'd got used to women at least wanting to marry him for his money.

Not that he'd asked Jaya to marry him. He'd been careful

to phrase his question as a broad request for information, not sure why he'd brought it up when she'd said last night that she wasn't looking for money or a ring.

Still, the fact she wasn't even nibbling at the possibility of sharing her life with him was quite a slap.

But why would she want to tie herself to him? What did he offer besides money? He circled the globe every quarter, could barely change a diaper and was incapable of love. She was right to dismiss the mention of marriage.

It still left him hollow and empty.

Which was probably exaggerated by the fact he hadn't slept. As Jaya disappeared into her room, he moved to stand over the sleeping babies. They looked pretty zonked, but he couldn't take the chance of lying down on the sofa and failing to wake if they stirred. Androu was sprawled like a starfish, but Zephyr had rolled himself close to Evie.

Stealing a cushion from the sofa as a pillow, Theo settled on his side behind Zephyr then gently rested his arm across Evie's legs and settled one hand on Androu's knee. Reassured he'd hear and feel them if they woke, he let himself doze.

CHAPTER EIGHT

FEED, PLAY, CHANGE, swim, nap, change, read, play, change...
The day was eaten up quickly with the wash, rinse, spin
cycle of baby-wrangling.

"How do parents of twins manage?" he asked when Jaya
returned from taking a phone call in her room. Technically
he was on vacation, although his boss would definitely get
an earful over how relaxing this particular one had been,
but Jaya was putting out fires from downstairs at the rate
of two or three an hour while minding children at the same
time. "What if they have triplets? Or more? How do *you*
manage?"

He'd given so many horsey-rides on his ankle, he would
need a knee replacement, but Zephyr showed no sign of
tiring.

Jaya smiled. "I wasn't working when I first left Bali.
Saranya needed me and so did her daughter. Saranya tried
to hang on until I delivered, but..."

She ducked her head, taking a moment. Obviously talking about it was difficult and he had an unexpected urge to
physically reach out to her. It hurt him to see her hurting,
but he had his hands full and had never been one to act on
impulses, especially touchy-feely ones.

Still, he was sorry he couldn't somehow comfort her
when he saw how she struggled to lift a brave face.

"By the time she passed, I was so pregnant there was

no point in applying for a job. I landed this one about six months ago, but I still live with Quentin. He and I pay a neighbor to watch Bina and Zeph and spell each other off if she's not available. Quentin's been home for most of the year, doing research, so his schedule has been flexible. He'll be starting a new film soon, though. He makes documentaries and the next one will take him to South America. Bina is pressing me to go with them. Saranya and Bina always lived on location with him. I'm pleased with my life here, though, and Quentin doesn't need the money. I wish he'd stay, but he keeps saying work will take his mind off his grief." She shrugged and added in a pained tone, "They loved each other very much."

Theo had never wanted to fall in love and she'd just showcased another reason why it was a bad idea. Quentin's barely suppressed rage came back to him and he felt damned sorry for the bastard.

Nevertheless, he couldn't quit thinking about marriage.

"I'm surprised you're not plugged into the mother ship," Jaya teased, obviously trying to deflect from her own pain and lighten the mood. "I've never seen you go so long without at least one electronic device in hand."

"Haven't you?" he asked, taking a less than subtle stab at testing their shared memory. He was still raw from her rejection and wanted to remind her there had been something really good between them once. He wanted to know if this attraction was still burning as brightly on her side as it was on his.

She stalled in swiping across her tablet. Her cheeks, tanned to semi-sweet chocolate by their hour in the pool, seemed to darken. Her tongue flicked along her bottom lip in a betrayal of discomfiture that otherwise remained hidden behind her impassive expression and lowered lashes.

One of the unique things about Jaya was her subtlety. Where other women threw themselves at his money and position, she'd always seemed unimpressed. Not repelled or disgusted, but not moved, either. From things she'd said, he'd deduced that her cousin's husband had supported her to a degree, but she supported herself now and sent money to her family in India. She'd started at the bottom in Makricosta's, changing bedding and scrubbing toilets. She knew what it was to make do on a limited income, but she'd never tried to flirt or use her body to lift her circumstances or gain financial favors.

When it came to her womanly wiles, she didn't project any of her hidden depths of passion. Despite being pretty and keeping herself well-groomed, she made no effort to lure a man. Her sexuality was understated, not obvious at all.

He appreciated that about her, not because he was a man who thought women should hide their sexuality, but because he was a circumspect man all around. He admired anyone capable of controlling his or her basic, animal urges.

On the other hand, being one of the few people who knew firsthand her capacity for passion was an erotic secret that strained his control. Every time the word *marriage* whispered through his mind, the most masculine parts of him relived holding her. There'd been a couple of women since—he'd been convinced he'd never see her again and had almost been trying to inoculate himself against going after her. It hadn't worked and seeing her again was inducing the opposite: he kept imagining a lifetime of stroking smooth, warm skin, licking dark nipples that only grew more taut and firm against his tongue, pushing naked into hot, tight depths so wet and welcoming he'd nearly died on the first thrust.

"I, um, just wondered if your sister gave you the day off so you could watch her son," she finally said, not looking at him.

No outward acknowledgment of his leading comment.

He'd pretend that wasn't a sharp kick in the ego, even though they were long past pretending Bali hadn't happened. Hell, he was holding the proof.

"The cruise was supposed to be a family reunion of sorts," he explained. "Adara's idea. All the siblings were together at my mother's funeral, but it was hardly the time to catch up after not seeing Nic for twenty years. The cruise liner is a Makricosta hotel on a Vozaras ship so it would have been a working vacation, which is probably why Demitri was dragging his heels about showing up."

"He's quite the black sheep at times, isn't he?"

"And yet our father liked him. Which is why he gets away with what he does, I suppose. No one ever told him he couldn't."

"He didn't…I mean, your father never—?"

"Took a swing at him? No, I told you. Adara and I protected him. Kept him quiet when they were fighting, snuck food for him. Turned him into a spoiled brat, I suppose, but that's better than what we went through."

"You don't resent him?"

"Why would I? He was a kid. It wasn't his fault our father was a bastard."

"No," she agreed, eyes so liquid and dark he had to look away. "Only…"

Don't say it, he thought, giving all his attention to where Zephyr was now using his belly as a trampoline. Being able to see that a grown man ought to have more control over his actions than a little boy didn't make him empathetic. Being happy his brother hadn't been knocked around didn't make him paternal. It was common decency, that's all.

She came into his periphery, but only to stroke a soft hand over her son's head.

"He's having fun. Would it be an imposition to leave him with you while I do a bit more work, just while the other two are sleeping?"

An imposition? He was truly pathetic if that's how she thought he regarded holding a happy baby.

"It's fine," he said, disgusted with himself for giving off such an impression, but having a child was still a shock. And he was still so worried about damaging him he preferred to keep her close. If she wasn't hovering, how would he know he was doing everything right?

She must have read something in his tone. She glanced toward her laptop with indecision.

"Go ahead," he insisted, refusing to be frightened of a kid who couldn't even stand up on his own. "From what I've overheard, this place is still transitioning from good to excellent. You're doing a stellar job in pushing them gently, by the way. Obviously in your element. They're lucky to have you."

She checked and looked back at him. "Do you mean that?"

"Of course. I'm not surprised, either. Your knack with this kind of work was obvious to me the first time we met."

She cleared her throat. "Thank you. You're not just anyone. You know what it takes, what the pressures are. Your saying that means a lot." She gave a tiny sniff and wiped under one eye as she scooped up her laptop and moved into the bedroom.

Women. He'd like to see a male manager get all soupy from a pat on the back.

Of course, he was just as bad, still basking in her praise that he was giving his son some enjoyment. The boy had spring-loaded legs, seemingly incapable of tiring.

His son.

His chest walls gave an internal shudder as he faced a grinning countenance that seemed both foreign yet familiar. All the babies were crawling their way under his skin, but Zephyr was different. With the other two, it was easier to let himself develop some affection. There wasn't the same depth of responsibility. He imagined he'd be a fall-back for the rest of their lives, attached by bonds that nature cast like a spell for exactly this circumstance: to keep little ones alive if their primary caregiver was absent, but he wouldn't have to worry about Evie and Androu 24/7 the way he'd worry about Zephyr.

He took a moment to examine that nagging, anxious sensation. For all his concern that he'd crush this boy's confidence, the what-ifs about his future were worse. What if he was wet and this neighbor lady didn't notice? What if Quentin talked Jaya into taking the boy to some third-world country with exotic parasites and deadly spiders? What if something happened to Jaya?

The way Zephyr chewed a finger and thumb while staring deeply into his eyes—much the same disconcerting way his mother had, as if he trusted him implicitly—was a heart punch. It was as if the little guy was already relying on Theo to make sure all the what-ifs were mitigated. Who else would do it? Theo had a lot of faults, but shirking responsibility was not one of them.

His guts wobbled, like he'd taken a misstep on a high wire.

No, he didn't shirk responsibility. If Jaya had said *that* to him last night, rather than trying to prod him into admitting an emotional connection to the boy, she might have had him.

But who *would* look after Zephyr if something happened to Jaya? He'd seen what babies were like when Mama wasn't near. They were distressed. He wouldn't want Zephyr to go through that. Hell, *he* didn't want to go through missing Jaya again and he was a full-grown man.

Swearing under his breath, he tried to take back that thought, but it was acknowledged now. Was that why he was stressing out about Zephyr's future, he asked himself? Because the tyke was his best excuse to hang on to the mother?

No. He did not just see Zephyr as a means to an end. When he contemplated walking away from Jaya *or* Zephyr, everything in him went bleak and gray. His sense of responsibility toward the boy was quickly shifting beyond the desire to provide food and shelter. Quentin might be the better father figure, but Theo couldn't shake Jaya's comment that maybe he'd never developed any deep relationships because he didn't cultivate them.

It wasn't fair to Zephyr to not even *try,* was it?

Zephyr stopped bouncing and gave an exhausted sigh, like he'd finished chopping a cord of wood. Theo found himself grinning in amusement.

"Finally worn out?" He settled the boy against his chest where Zephyr let his head droop, fingers still in his mouth and eyelids heavy.

He wasn't a man who cuddled, preferring his own space unless he was busy with a woman between the sheets, but there was an addictive quality to a baby's snuggled warmth against his shoulder. It was a sense of all-powerfulness. Success at creating a moment of contentment for another human being. After a childhood of being found wanting, he wallowed in Zephyr's unconditional appreciation of having his simplest needs met.

It's just Mother Nature's plan, he tried to dismiss, but a very tiny voice—feminine and lilting with an Indian accent—whispered that maybe it was a father's nature to be happy when his child was happy.

Stunned, he swallowed a lump of emotion, hands cradling his son tenderly as the connection between them wound through him like a creeping vine, hooking into his vital organs in such a way there'd be damage to both of them if they were pulled apart.

Jaya's quiet voice grew louder, speaking to Evie as she appeared with the girl. Her eyes went soft when she saw him holding Zephyr so close, making Theo feel as though he was out on that high wire again, a brisk gale cutting up the canyon toward him.

He lowered his gaze. This was too personal a moment to have even Jaya witness.

"Trade?" he asked in a voice like sandpaper, reluctant to let the boy go, but he was so shaken by his flood of primal instinct to protect and nurture, he let her steal the sleepy baby and tried to distract himself by coaxing a smile from Evie with a promise of a swim later.

It was soon back to chaos, Androu waking shortly after Evie and both of them hungry. He was washing mashed banana out of Androu's hair, using the wet cloth to spike it into a Mohawk, wondering if he was getting the hang of this parenting thing after all, when a knock at the door interrupted them.

Jaya was in her room, answering emails while Zephyr napped in there with her. He sidled to the peephole and saw Nic, Rowan and Adara distorted by the fisheye lens.

Never one to appreciate unexpected visitors, he snapped open the door. "Why didn't you call?"

"Are they okay? Where are they?" The women rushed past him like fans into a rock concert, invading his space.

Nic entered at a more laconic pace, scanning the suite in the way of someone who made his living by sharp observations.

Theo suppressed a prickle of irritability. The place was littered in toys and dirty dishes. Much as he didn't really care about being judged over something like that, he also made it a habit to keep from providing opportunities to be judged.

"They were anxious so I chartered a helicopter," Nic said. "Gideon had to stay with the ship. Everyone is okay, but what a mess. I don't envy him. There's my girl." He broke into a wide smile as he caught Evie reaching from Rowan's arms into his.

"It's not that we didn't trust you, Theo. We just missed them so much," Rowan said, her light touch on his arm apologetic.

He gave a jerky shrug, subtly removing himself from her uninvited touch even though he didn't hate it. She was nice enough and being sincere. It was just he wasn't at his best, accosted by a lot right now with their unexpected visit and a distant, illogical disappointment he didn't want to examine. He didn't need her standing too close, sensing his tension, reading his vibe for him.

"It's fine, I understand," he said, and strangely, kind of did. His chest filled with pressure at the way his sister was smothering the life out of Androu. Her eyes were closed, her lashes wet. He had a new understanding of how precious their babies were to them and was suffused with a weird self-conscious pride that he'd been able to keep their offspring safe for them, whether they had really trusted him to do so or not.

"I knew he'd be fine. He knows you," Adara said, voice thick. "But Gideon threw you into the deep end with both of them. I'm glad you called Jaya—she's perfect—but what made you think of her? How did you know she was here? Where *is* she?"

Before Theo could get past the suffocation provoked by questions about Jaya, she said, "I'm here."

They all turned toward her voice.

"Sorry," she said with a flash of anxious eyes at Theo. "The commotion woke him and he needs a drink."

Zephyr looked sweaty and flushed, hair damp and pushed up in tufts around the face he buried in Jaya's neck to hide.

Theo moved to fetch the boy's cup, distancing himself from something he didn't want to face, then kicked himself just as quickly. This was exactly the kind of abandonment he would hate himself for inflicting on his son. Or Jaya, for that matter.

"I'm sorry we spoiled his nap," he heard Rowan say and glanced across to see her peeking at the boy over his mother's shoulder. "What's your name?"

"Baby Zepper," Evie provided from her happy perch on Nic's bent arm.

"Zephyr," Jaya corrected softly, smiling at Evie. "You've been my best little helper, haven't you? She's been very sweet with both of them."

"Zephyr," Rowan repeated. "That's lovely. Greek god of wind, right?"

Theo absorbed the meaning, wondering if it was a deliberate reference to his love of piloting, thinking, *I really don't deserve her,* as he crossed with Zephyr's sipping cup.

"Thanks," Jaya said with a flickering gaze of apprehension as he approached. She rubbed Zephyr's back to get his attention. "Want your cup, sweetie?"

Zephyr lifted his head and spied the cup, but rather than wait for Jaya to take it, he leaned out for Theo.

Theo was getting used to the boy's impulsive launches. He caught him in what was becoming a practiced scoop and hitched him up against his chest. The air in his lungs stopped moving as he held the cup for the boy, aware of how telling his actions were, how much like a father he must appear. How close a copy of Androu Zephyr was.

Zephyr's little hands settled over his big one while profound silence fell over the room like a dome.

Theo forced himself to lift his gaze and meet each pair of stunned eyes. They had to be reading guilt in him. It sprang from ignoring Jaya's attempts to contact him and thinking he could ignore someone as important as his son. He was ashamed of himself, not Zephyr.

Disgust with himself made him blurt, "He's mine," aware that it was the clumsiest possible way he could have

announced it, but he couldn't dance around it. Not when
Nic was drilling him a look that said, *You lucky bastard.*

His half brother blinked and the envy was gone, replaced
by a doting smile at Evie, but it was the reinforcement Theo
needed to keep inching across the hot coals cooking him
from the soles of his feet to his collar. Maybe he wasn't
doing this well, but he'd figured out what was right and
he'd do that much.

In his periphery, he saw Jaya lift an uncertain hand then
fold her arms defensively. *Don't,* he wanted to say. *Don't be
embarrassed for me. I don't care how stupid I look, only
that I not fail where it counts.*

Over Zephyr's loud gulps, Androu made a noise and
put out his hand.

"I told you before, sport," Theo said, trying to sound
normal while emotions log-jammed in his throat. "Yours
is the green one. It's on his tray," he told Adara, nodding
to the high chair where Androu had been sitting before
she arrived.

He hoped she'd move away and begin to defuse this
charged moment, but she didn't. Her gaze was fixed on
Zephyr's face.

The boy looked at her with his unblinking brown eyes.
Makricosta eyes.

"Theo." She spoke his name with myriad inflections.
Shock, awe, surprise, approval. Exasperated *dis*approval.

As he braced himself for whatever she would say, he
felt a feminine hand rest on his biceps. Jaya. If he'd had a
free hand, he would have wrapped it around her waist and
pulled her in close. He might be willing to face the scrutiny of his family without apology, but it wasn't easy. How
such a slight woman could be his shield against them, he
didn't understand, but he had an intense need to wield her
in just that way.

"He didn't know," Jaya said. The tips of her fingers dug into his tense arm. "Not until I told him yesterday."

Had it only been a day?

He drew in a breath, realizing he'd neglected to take in air for several seconds. Looking into Jaya's eyes, he let her know she didn't have to protect him *that* much. It was his own damned fault he hadn't known about his son.

It's okay, she seemed to reassure with a softening of her touch on his arm. *Our secret.* And therein lay her appeal. He feared every stumble, too used to being knocked down a second time for daring to err. She was a forgiving person, though. She was so softhearted, she'd help him to his feet after a face-plant. He wanted to kiss her for it.

Hell, he wanted to kiss her, period. He dragged himself free of their locked stare in time to hear Rowan ask Nic, "Will it be a full Indian wedding, do you think? I've always wanted to go to one."

Jaya's touch on his arm fell away.

Theo stiffened, struck anew by rejection.

"I'm making assumptions, aren't I?" Rowan said with a blush and a reach for her daughter. "Come on, Evie, let's find Androu's cup for him."

"I'll help," Nic said, taking Androu as he passed Adara. "Drink, champ?"

Jaya watched the Viking blond media mogul and his petite wife distance themselves toward the kitchen, leaving Adara staring at their ill at ease vignette.

Zephyr was comfortable enough, she supposed, taking a break from draining his cup to huff a breath and stare after his cousins, but she was hyper-conscious of Theo statue-stiff next to her.

"Will he come to me?" Adara asked, approaching with hands raised.

Her intense focus, the way she caught her breath as Zephyr went to her, the way she enfolded him and pressed

her smile into his hair, all made Jaya want to turn her crin-
kling forehead into Theo's chest.

Having Zephyr accepted by Theo's sister was beyond her
dreams. She wished she'd known it would go this well or
she might have tried harder to reach him. She might have
gone directly to Adara.

"I should have—" Jaya began.

"Don't." He caught her wrist. "*I* should have," he said,
as if he knew what she'd been about to say. His hand slid
to mesh with hers, palm to palm, fingers entwined.

It was such a startling gesture she could only cling to
him, at sea as to how to react. He'd surprised her by claiming Zephyr so openly when she'd been expecting to be
treated like a dirty little secret. Having him hold her hand
as if there was something between them besides a baby
was a kind of magic she knew she shouldn't believe in,
but she wanted to.

"I never thought I'd hold your baby," Adara said with a
misty smile. "I hoped Androu would rub off on you, but—
Wait a minute. How old is he?" She pulled back to study
the boy, eyes narrow as she lifted them to Theo's culpable
swallow.

"It was—" Jaya started to excuse, but Theo squeezed
her hand. Her entire being was warmed by his firm grip,
radiating heat up her arm and into her chest.

"I'm not going to offer excuses—or details. Fire me if
you have to," Theo said.

Adara gave him a look between stern and maddened.
"I'll assume that if you deserved to be fired, you'd say so.
Demitri is the one that needs reminders about employees
being off-limits. Besides, I can't be mad. We have a nephew.
Gideon will be over the moon." She smiled at Zephyr as
the boy reached for Jaya, letting him go.

Jaya had to pull her hand free of Theo's to take Zephyr
and secure him on her hip.

In the carefully emotionless way that Jaya was more familiar seeing in Adara she heard her ask Theo, "What *are* your plans?"

In the blink of one glance, a lot of teeming undercurrents were exchanged between brother and sister. It niggled at Jaya in a way she couldn't interpret. They seemed almost telepathic and it made her feel left out.

She imagined there were considerations with regards to the Makricosta fortune, though. Publicity to finesse and old-fashioned concern for family. Given Theo's dismay at learning he was a father, she expected him to request Zephyr's existence be kept quiet.

With an impactful look at Jaya, Theo became super tall, his posture and air very authoritative. She'd seen him take a hard line when it came to accounting rules, but had never seen him turn such an uncompromising look on her.

"I don't want to miss any more of Zephyr's life than I have," he said.

Oh. Jaya's heart fluttered, surprised by this evolution in his attitude. He'd been tentative yesterday, but she supposed that had been shock. This morning he'd seemed to accept he had a son, even if it had still been a perplexing addition to his life.

Now she could see acknowledgment had moved into something more implacable that was both heartening and threatening. It had never occurred to her that she might have to fight him for her child, but she saw something in his eyes that was resolute and possessive. Something that told her Zephyr had taken up residence inside him in a way she'd been dreaming of doing since Day One.

Why did that make her jealous? She ought to be happy.

"We haven't agreed on how we're moving forward," Theo continued. "But whether it's a big wedding or not— I'll be pushing for marriage."

CHAPTER NINE

THE WORDS CAME between them in an eclipse-like flash. For a second Jaya couldn't breathe, couldn't see.

No. She'd already told him no. Hadn't he heard her? But what she'd really been refusing was a marriage of convenience. If he loved her... Did he?

And how could he just announce it like that to his sister without consulting—without even *asking* her first?

"I haven't convinced Jaya yet," Theo said, taking the weight of his penetrating stare back to his sister.

Oh, sure, put it all on me, Jaya thought, working to keep a scowl off her face. Her instinct was to protest, but she didn't want to draw Adara into it. Given the look exchanged between Nic and Rowan as they returned from the kitchen, they'd heard Theo, adding to her feeling of being outnumbered.

No one needed to know her reasons for refusing to marry except maybe Theo and she'd share that only if and when it felt right.

"We haven't had much time to talk about anything except whose turn it is to change a bottom," Jaya murmured, stroking a hand over Androu's tousled hair as he toddled after Evie to their play area in the lounge.

"Understood," Nic said. "And we're incredibly grateful for your help. If you ever need anything, please let us know."

"I expect we'll be seeing a lot of each other regardless," Rowan said with a warm smile. "Evie's forever begging for Androu and seems equally rapt with Zephyr. I expect a few tears when we leave, to be honest. Brace yourself. She has a tender little heart."

It was true. After thirty minutes of letting the children have a last play together while the adults gathered up toys and clothes, they congregated at the door. Evie broke into pieces when she realized the other children wouldn't be coming with her to Greece.

"Peas, Papa," she begged through her tears.

"I'm sorry, but they have to live with their own mamas."

She wasn't trying to manipulate; she was genuinely heartbroken, weeping into his shoulder with loss.

Her suffering twisted Jaya's heart so badly she found herself promising to bring Zephyr for a visit.

After a tearful kiss and hug from the girl, she said goodbye and was emotionally wrung out as she and Theo moved into the quiet lounge.

"Did I just promise a two-year-old I'd fly to Greece to see her?" Jaya collapsed into a chair. "I can't afford that."

Theo gave her a dry, are-you-kidding look. "Nic has his own plane and so do I." He leaned back on the sofa, hands behind his head, gaze lifting from where Zephyr sat on the floor rattling the stuffing out of a toy bear. "I'll take you as soon as we work out a convenient time."

Her heart lifted while her stomach swooped. The word *honeymoon* blinked like a lighthouse flash in her mind, but she turned away from it. She stared at their baby rather than looking at Theo, nervous of the masculine energy he was projecting. He might appear relaxed, but they were alone now, the buffer of activity gone. The full force of his male magnetism was blasting into her, stronger than she remembered it.

"You're assuming a lot," she said, leaning forward to

remove a hard toy from behind Zephyr. "I'm not quitting my job. I'm not marrying you."

Silence, then, "I realize I threw that at you from left field."

"You did," she snapped. "That wasn't fair."

"I didn't mean to, but…" He sat forward, swearing as he rubbed his face. "Both Adara and Rowan had fertility issues. I could see Nic was thinking anyone who would turn away from the chance to be a father—"

"Are you seriously saying that the only reason you want to be in Zephyr's life is to avoid being judged by your family?" She *lived* that hell, but it was because she was determined to stay true to herself. For him to buckle to their expectations was a very dishonest start to his relationship with Zephyr, something she wouldn't tolerate no matter the consequences.

"No, it reinforced to me what a gift he is. Not everyone has the luxury of one night producing a baby. Yes, this has been hard for me to come to terms with." He waved a confounded hand at their son, but a subtle tenderness crept beneath his hard visage as he watched Zephyr discover his own toes and try to catch them in his waving hand. "I'm still not convinced I'm father material, but Nic figured it out. Maybe I've got a shot. And if there's one thing my childhood taught me, it's how to avoid making mistakes, especially big ones. Turning my back on my son would be a terrible one."

He was saying all the right things, but rather than creating a sense of relief in her, he was undermining her defenses. She needed resentment to keep her from tumbling back into the depths of her crazy crush on him. That sort of weakness would complicate things. She'd start thinking about what she wanted, rather than what she and Zephyr needed.

"We still don't have to marry," she mumbled.

"What would living together do to your relationship with your family?"

"You want to live together?" The words dissolved everything around her so nothing had substance. She was falling, unable to grasp anything that would ground her.

"Yesterday you pointed out that I don't stick around to develop relationships. It's true. If I want to know my son, I have to be near him. Physically." He frowned as he said it, like he wasn't sure, but would give it a try.

That's all she needed, to let him become a daily part of her life then have him quit on her. "I don't want to live with you," she insisted.

"Why not? You live with Quentin. I'll pay for everything."

Back to money. Was there a problem in his world that he wouldn't try to buy his way out of?

"I value my independence," she said.

"But you're not independent," he countered. "You have a son. You and I are connected through him and that makes us interdependent." He pointed between them, as if running lines of webbing that stitched them together. He didn't seem any happier about it than she was. "We have to compromise for his best interest. We'll have to do that for the rest of our lives. There's no getting around that."

Hurt that he was only trying to make a life with her because he thought it was the ethical thing to do, she rose to pace, winding up facing a window, arms folded.

"I grew up fighting tooth and nail for every decision I wanted to make for myself. I won't have the same fight with you. I won't give up and do as I'm told. You're making me feel like I have to live with you. That I have to marry you. I already live with a lot of have-to's as a result of my choosing to have Zephyr."

"You think I don't know how it feels to live under someone else's rules?" he countered. "You think I enjoy calculating interest rates and double-checking the inventory of hand towels? There's a difference between being subjugated and placing duty to family above self-interest. My father isn't around to disinherit me if I quit my job. I stay for Adara's sake, because I want her to succeed. Although we'll have to make adjustments to my duties if I'm going to spend any time with you and Zephyr."

He muffled a curse behind his hand, glowering while his gaze turned inward.

Her stomach did a flip flop, latching too tightly onto his *with you*. She shook it off, not wanting to be so easily drawn in by him. Turning, she considered the dual notes of frustration and sincerity in his voice.

"You hate your job?" she prompted.

He quirked the tight line of his lips before saying, "Don't tell Adara." He shrugged that off. "I don't really hate it, not anymore, but it's not what I would have chosen for myself. My father pushed me into it. He would have taken it out on Adara if I'd rebelled so I kept the peace and took an Econ degree. The work is more enjoyable now that she trusts my numbers and makes the kinds of decisions we always knew were the better ones. We actually see the profits we're looking for. I was constantly set up for failure while my father was alive. That was hell."

She came back to sit across from him. Linking her hands, she pressed her knuckles to her mouth. "I think I hate your father," she admitted in a muted voice. The man bore a lot of blame for Theo's inability to give her what she wanted from him.

"Join the club," he retorted, then expelled a tired breath. "But he's gone so do what I do. Forget him."

Releasing her inner lip from the bite of her teeth, she added, "He is gone, so don't turn me into something you think you have to do. You have a choice, too, Theo."

"I do," he agreed and hitched forward on the edge of the

sofa. "That's what I'm saying. I'm not acting from a sense of duty, although I feel a pretty strong one toward both of you. It's a different kind of 'have to.' The kind that means I wouldn't be able to live with myself if I didn't do what's right by the two of you."

Which framed her refusal to marry him as inexcusable selfishness.

"I can appreciate that you want to be part of Zephyr's life." She couldn't countenance anything less herself. "But live together? Like as roommates?"

"If that's what you prefer." He blinked once, keeping his expression neutral so she couldn't tell what he really thought of the arrangement.

"For how long? Until he's in school? Until he's grown? And what are you doing all this time? Bringing women home?"

"No," he dismissed flatly and cast a gaze toward the pool, one that was stark and seemed rather isolated and lonely.

Her heart shook. She willed it to still, not wanting to be affected. *Don't try to fix him.*

"Is there nothing on your side, Jaya? Of what we had before?" he asked quietly.

She caught her breath, plunged into the deep end, sinking and sinking, pressure gathering in her ears and pressing outward in her lungs. Her vision blurred because she forgot to blink.

"What did we have?" she asked in a thin voice, reminding herself that neither of them had been seeking a long term relationship that night. Her motives had been, if not emotionless, at least not as simple as his.

"More chemistry than I've ever felt for anyone else, before or since." His blunt words detonated a terrific blush in her, making her cover her hot cheeks and look anywhere but at him.

"I didn't mean to behave that way," she moaned, still embarrassed that once hadn't been enough. Twice had been decadent self-indulgence. The third time had been outright greed, stolen against the hands of the clock.

"I loved how you behaved," he said, voice low and taut with sweet memory.

Her heart tripped as he began speaking and stumbled into the dust as she realized it wasn't a declaration of deep feeling. She was still affected, still transported back to a night when touching a man had seemed the most natural, perfect thing in the world to do.

The glint of masculine interest in his eye sparked a depth of need in her she had worried she'd never feel again.

"Okay, then," he said in a satisfied growl, his fixed gaze weighted with lazy approval.

"Theo, don't!" She pushed the heels of her hands into her eyes. Her history with him, especially their night together, had stolen a lot of power from her darkest memories, but, "Don't make assumptions about me and sex. Please. Saying I'm attracted to you doesn't mean I want to have sex with you. It's not that simple for me. Ever."

"Hey, I'm not taking anything for granted," he admonished. "I realize sex could be a hindrance to our working out a good long-term solution. Much as I want to have an affair with you, if we burn out it would have consequences for Zephyr. I get that."

Did he? Because she hadn't got that far. All she could think was that she hadn't expected to have another shot at sharing Theo's bed and really didn't know how she felt about climbing into it again, especially long-term. Talk about assumptions. That would create a lot. All her conflicting yes-no signals were firing, making her cautious even as she found herself literally warming to the idea.

"But you have to admit, we're a good team, Jaya. That's all Adara and Gideon had going for them when they married. Maybe they had sexual attraction, I don't know. I would never ask," he said with a dismissing sweep of his hand and an expression of juvenile repugnance that would have been laughable if her thoughts weren't exploding like popcorn kernels in oil.

"You and I have as good a base as they had," he insisted. "Maybe a better one. We know each other a lot better than they did. An affair, living together… Those are too easy to walk away from. Marriage would force us to work out whatever differences came up. Zephyr needs that kind of stability and commitment. Doesn't he?"

Here was the clarity he'd told her he was capable of. He could see the right course of action even if he didn't know whether he could perform it. Even when he wasn't terribly keen to embrace it.

Still, she was half persuaded by his rationale. He was right and talking about it like they were negotiating a merger kept her from being swept away, allowing her to view the situation objectively.

That's what she told herself anyway, to counter the thick knot of disappointment sitting in her throat.

"Are you hesitating because of what I told you about my father? You're worried I'll resort to abuse?"

"No!" she blurted, heartfelt and sincere. Her waffling feelings were more about having her heart suffer from unrequited attraction than worrying about physical harm.

"If that's what's worrying you, admit it. I'll forget the whole thing. I totally understand." He stood and caught up Zephyr, repositioning him in the middle of the blanket, his movements hiding his face, but she thought she caught a glint of profound hurt. Maybe something else. A sort of hopeless defeat.

"Theo, I don't think you could hurt me or Zephyr even if you wanted to. If we needed a snakebite carved out of us, you probably couldn't do it."

His glance flickered toward her in acknowledgment, colored with ironic humor, but he moved to stand looking through the glass at the pool. He pushed his hands into his pockets, shoulders slumped.

"You've been so willing to listen to everything I've told you I let myself believe it didn't matter, but of course it matters. Of course you have to take time to consider what it means and decide whether you can trust me."

She was going to have to tell him. She could see his back tensed against the same kind of betrayal and injury he'd already suffered. She couldn't leave him thinking something as far out of his control as his childhood abuse would cause her to fear him.

Still, her abdomen tightened as if clenching to accept a blow.

"Theo, it's not you, it's me."

He barked out a laugh and sent an askance look over his shoulder. "Okay."

Not in front of Zephyr, she thought, but their son had tipped onto his side and was contentedly chewing a finger and pedaling his feet. And wasn't he the manifestation of the goodness that had come out of her bad experience? If she hadn't been assaulted, she would have stayed in India and married under her uncle's dictate. Instead, she'd left and wound up meeting Theo and he had changed her life profoundly, giving her this gift.

"I trust you, Theo. I wouldn't have slept with you in Bali if I didn't."

"That's different. One night is not a lifetime. A pair of lost souls finding comfort in physical pleasure is not marriage. It takes a lot more faith in a person to share every aspect of your life with him. I understand."

"No, that's not—" She sighed. "That's not what Bali was for me. Not all it was."

He came around a half step, body still in profile, his grave expression watchful. "What do you mean?"

She took a shaky breath. "The reason I left India…" She pinched her lip, trying to stay focused. "I should back up to explain. I've told you Saranya and I grew up very close? When I was six, my father had an accident on the tractor and was forced to sign our land over to my uncle. We moved in with them. Our mothers are twins. It's a big house, not a bad arrangement except that my uncle is quite controlling. He has very traditional views where women are concerned."

She set the jungle gym over Zephyr so he could swat at the dangling toys.

"Saranya grew up dreaming of being in Bollywood films. Uncle was fit to be tied. He was arranging a marriage for her when Quentin's crew came into the next village. Saranya was convinced this was her break. In a way it was. They fell in love and she eloped with him."

"And you were left with her angry, thwarted father."

She nodded. "And her two brothers and my younger brother and sister. Uncle became more domineering than ever, dictating to my parents how we should behave. It was one of the reasons I was so resolved to get a job, to give my parents money so they wouldn't be so dependent on him. He objected to me working, saying I should marry, but there were other young people going into call centers, bringing money home. A friend recommended me for a position and it was good work. I improved my English, used their lines to speak with Saranya," she confessed with a sheepish grin. "Uncle had disowned her, but I missed her."

"Are you trying to tell me you're afraid I won't let you work?"

"There is that, but no, that's not where I'm going." Rising to try to escape the cloying sense of helplessness that still managed to smother her at times, she paced across the room then halted, arms wrapped around herself.

What would he think of her? Would he blame her as her family had?

"The problem with my job was… There was a man there. My supervisor. He was older, in his forties. I wasn't even twenty yet. He flirted with me, but it wasn't flirting."

"Sexual harassment," Theo concluded flatly, his voice low and chill.

"One night, before I went home, it was sexual assault." Her voice faded into a whisper, but she knew he heard her because the silence took on a thick, heavy quality.

She smoothed a hand over the glossy hardwood of a side table, accidentally lifting her eyes to the reflection in the mirror above it.

Theo was arrested, pale under his swarthy tan, lips tight and outlined with a white ring. When their gazes clashed in the pool of silver, he flinched his glance away.

She caught back a gasp of pain.

"I never should have pressured you that night," he said from between his teeth.

"You didn't. I wanted to," she assured him, swinging around to face him even though her whole body suffused with self-conscious heat. Memories burned through her, sweet and hot. Hands knotting together at her navel, she said in a strained voice, "You know I enjoyed it."

She was dying over here, embarrassed that she had to be so bald in her confession. It was incredibly hard to practically beg him to remember how uninhibited she'd been by the time she'd slipped naked from his bed and reluctantly dressed, but she had faced him proudly in the dawn light, enjoying his admiring gaze as he watched her dress.

"That night was the first time since it happened that I wanted to be with a man. To let anyone touch me," she confided.

"I was your employer."

"No, you weren't. And remember how shocked I was

that you were attracted to me? As an employee I never once felt threatened by you, especially sexually. I was as grateful for that as everything else. I mean, I started out in house-keeping because it was all women, even the supervisors. Moving to the front desk, night clerk, those were all huge risks that I took because I knew I had to move past what had happened to me if I wanted to advance, but I was able to do it because you had this quiet command of everything. I felt like no one would dare touch me because I could go to you. I didn't have any recourse the first time."

He frowned. "You didn't tell your family? What about the police?"

Thick painful tears welled in her eyes and she had to look away to hold on to her composure. "My uncle was ashamed that I went to the police. He called me a slut and my parents weren't in a position to argue in my defense. They wanted me to marry the man, but he was already married."

Theo swore and started toward her only to bring himself up short. "Jaya…" His tone was one of deep shock and struggle.

She wished he'd make this easy and take her in his strong arms, but at the same time she could only stare at the floor feeling the tears drop from her eyes. The assault had been a nightmare, but the time afterward had been the darkest, most bleak and isolated of her life.

Forcing herself to remember it was over and she was safe, she swiped at her wet cheeks and lifted her head, lashes matted and eyes still bleary. Swallowing back the lump in her throat, she managed to say, "Fortunately I had Saranya."

"She came for you?"

"Couriered her passport. My uncle had learned his lesson about leaving them where the children could find them. We're only a year apart and always looked remarkably

alike. People mistook us all the time. Quentin was filming in Malaysia so she sent me a ticket to Kuala Lumpur.
She'd just had Bina. They took me in and she went with me
for all the doctor checks... I look back and think it's such
a miracle I didn't get pregnant, given you and I managed
it in one go." She gave a weak smile.

"I can't believe you still send them money."

"For my mother's sake, and my sister's. And even though
Quentin is quite successful, I don't want to be a burden.
I lived too long on my uncle's good graces. Earning my
own keep is important to me so I applied at a few hotels, ones that overlooked my lack of paperwork. Having
good English was an asset. I picked up Quentin's German
and a local dialect. When he began filming in Bali, I got
on at Makricosta's. After, um, claiming to the Indian em-
bassy that I'd lost my passport and needed it replaced." She
cleared her throat. "I know that was wrong—"

"Hell, Jaya, I'm not judging you. Your uncle, yeah, but
not you." He swore again and ran a hand down his face.

Zephyr squawked at that point and she realized he was
probably hungry. It was a much-needed few minutes of
distraction that allowed her to collect herself. Her hands
shook as she moved around the kitchenette and she was
aware of Theo standing in one spot the whole time, staring out to the pool.

The sense of being flayed raw stayed with her, making her attempts to be natural and smile at her baby feel
forced. Her cheeks were stiff, her brow hooking and pulling. Everything in her wanted to move into Theo's reach
and hope he'd take her in his arms, so he might smooth
away all the jagged edges and reassure her that what she'd
told him hadn't changed his view of her.

He didn't even look her way, which choked her throat
with a helpless ache.

The buzz of her phone, which was on vibrate, jangled

her nerves. She thought, *Work,* and it was the most vile four-letter word right now.

Except it would also be a healthy retreat. It suddenly hit her that she *could* leave. Theo didn't need her here. The babies were gone.

Oh. An even more profoundly bereft emotion enveloped her, but she needed distance from him. While her emotions were twining and growing around his return to her life, she couldn't tell what he was thinking. That marriage idea of his certainly wasn't being thrown at her any longer.

Against the ominous plane of his back, she said, "I'll take Zephyr home after he finishes eating. A lot has piled up here. I need to get into my office downstairs."

Theo turned and the withdrawal in him was almost frightening. He was the aloof man she'd first met, not dismissive, but giving the impression he didn't see a woman at all. Just a fellow robot.

The shift crushed her with disappointment. No, something worse. She was devastated. It was like all the accord they'd developed had evaporated and she was a stranger to him. He would be polite, but really, he didn't want to know her ugly secrets. She'd told him too much and now she felt small and soiled.

"Why don't you leave him with me?" he said.

"Wh-what?"

"I'm not going anywhere. We'll be close by if he needs you. You and I still have to figure out how we're going to proceed. I've heard all you've said, I understand why you don't want to marry me, but I'm not flying out of here to forget this ever happened. At some point word will get out beyond my siblings that I have a child. He's every bit as vulnerable as Evie and Androu, security-wise. We have a lot to work out."

He spoke from across the canyon that was the lounge, his words seeming to echo around her, but they weren't quite as empty as she'd begun to fear. She stood on uncertain footing, but this connection he'd talked about, their interdependence, was real. It was a thin thread, delicate as a dew-covered string of spider silk, but she stayed very still, wanting it to stick and endure.

"Okay." She had to clear huskiness from her throat and now her smile at Zephyr was soft and easy and relieved. She felt like she could breathe again. *She would keep seeing Theo a little longer.*

"If you don't mind a late dinner, we could talk then," she offered as she wiped Zephyr's face and hands.

"Downstairs? That's fine. What time shall I make the reservation?"

She had meant room service, but, "I can book it. I'll text you." Feeling gauche and self-conscious, she walked Zephyr across to Theo's tense presence and escaped to gather her composure.

Theo closed his eyes as the door shut behind Jaya.

It wasn't fair to look to an infant for comfort, but he snuggled the boy close against him and pressed his unsteady lips against hair dark and silky smooth as his mother's.

The surge of emotions in him was almost too much to bear, certainly near impossible to contain while Jaya had been in the room. Lovely Jaya who wouldn't crush a spider, brutalized by a man she'd trusted. He hadn't had the courage to ask for details. They only mattered if she felt a need to get them off her chest. He certainly didn't want to hear them. As far as he was concerned, the fact it had happened at all was infuriating and heartbreaking enough, but to then not even be supported by her family…

It was unthinkable, blasting him to overflowing with a need to insist—demand—that she marry him and be forevermore under his protection. He wasn't superhuman, but he had resources the average person couldn't touch. The proverbial shields he could place around her were near bullet-proof and his blood raced with the need to affix them. Now.

But she didn't want to rely on him, didn't want to marry him.

If her assailant had reached into his chest and clawed out his heart he couldn't have stolen anything more vital to him than Jaya's trust. Theo had suggested they eat in the public dining room because he was convinced she wouldn't want to be alone with him, and she'd agreed. What did that say?

And here he'd been fantasizing—not taking for granted, only indulging himself—that the sexual attraction was still ripe and strong between them. That it could form the basis of a marriage that stood half a chance.

His fury at the injustice made him want to scream, but he had a child in his arms. A tiny boy who had somehow come to life after Jaya had suffered one of the worst types of betrayal.

He brought the boy up so they were eye to eye. Zephyr's wide grin caused a crack to zigzag across his heart. Not one of damage, but as if the shell that encased it was breaking open. Tender hunger for more of those smiles, more time with Jaya, leaked out.

Never one to believe the Christmas present he wanted would actually be under the tree, he still let a nascent thought form: Maybe if he was very careful with her, there would be hope.

CHAPTER TEN

WHEN JAYA WAS called to the front desk because Bina was asking for her there, her first instinct was to send her cousin home. Quentin had sent the girl with her sitter to check up on her, acting like an interfering, if somewhat endearing, overbearing male relative.

But Bina had a genuine connection to Zephyr that helped the girl cope with the loss she was still grieving. Jaya didn't have the heart to send her away without a visit with her cherished baby cousin. Plus, an uninterrupted conversation with Theo for the first time since she'd seen him again held a lot of appeal.

She texted him that Bina and her nanny were coming up to stay with Zephyr and she'd meet him at the bell desk to go for dinner. Then, in a minor fit of vanity, she visited one of the hotel's boutiques, using her employee discount to buy a new dress and shoes.

Studying herself in the mirror of the staff washroom, she asked herself what she was trying to prove. Her hair was brushed, her makeup refreshed. The only pair of shoes she could find to go with this dress were much taller than she'd normally wear. They had bling. A line of sequins decorated the heel and a jazzy buckle drew attention to the toes Bina had painted a neon pink when they'd been having girls' night a week ago.

The dress was more feminine than sexy with its ruffled

layers of sheer red and orange and pink and fluttering split cut sleeves, but gave her a moment of sober second thought.

She refused to dress like a frump, though. Her confession this afternoon had been difficult. Part of her wanted to crawl into a cave now that her secret was revealed, but she knew better than to let her past cow her. She wouldn't deny the fact she was a woman. She wouldn't pretend to be ugly or asexual. That would only feed her shame and she had nothing to be ashamed of. Being pretty wasn't a crime. Wanting to please the eye of a man wasn't a broad invitation to be abused by all of them.

Still, it was an act of bravery to swipe a final layer of gloss onto her lips and take herself to the bell desk. The bellman was engaged and only Theo stood there.

He stared broodingly at the bobbing lights against the dark backdrop of water beyond the windows, his demeanor the quietly compelling man she'd so admired from afar in Bali. Pausing, she allowed herself a few seconds to take in his profile of statue stillness. He projected casual wealth with his gold watch and tailored shirt over crisp pants with their break in the cuff where they landed on his Italian loafers. Since he took these things for granted, he emanated power. And he was so *attractive* with his fit body and neat haircut and perfectly hewn, freshly shaved jaw.

She had always thought he had it all, had so much he was bored with the world, but she knew him so much better now. He held himself remote as a self-protective thing and that made her see him with new eyes. She realized he must be terribly lonely.

He glanced abstractly toward her, then started with a flash of surprised recognition. Maybe something else. She wasn't sure what she saw between his raking gaze from her lashes to her fancy shoes. He quickly masked his expression.

"No uniform," he commented.

No compliment, either.

"I didn't want to start any rumors if the Makricosta CFO was recognized having dinner with our general manager. I made reservations across the road."

He nodded without reaction and held the door for her as they walked across to *La Fumée Blanche,* The White Mist. She'd secretly wanted to try the dinner and dance restaurant forever, but it was a place for couples, not singles or a woman and her preadolescent niece.

They were shown through a dining room surrounding a small dance floor. On a dais, a trio played French jazz, filling the room with the Pink Panther sound of a brush against a cymbal. Their table had fresh roses, plush velvet chairs and a spectacular view of the Med.

It would have been perfect if she didn't feel like Theo was wearing his CFO hat and picturing her in her Makricosta blouse.

"Wine?" he asked.

"I thought you don't drink?"

"I thought you might."

"Sometimes." She flushed at how awkward this was. Maybe they needed Zephyr between them after all. "If it's a special occasion, but I don't need anything tonight."

This wasn't special, even though the candle glinted flecks of golden light off the silver and touched sparks in the crystal wine goblets. Even though a pianist tickled keys, accompanying a bassist who stroked sensual notes from her instrument.

Even though she was with the only man who'd ever melted her frigid libido and still managed to kindle heat in her when he seemed completely oblivious to her presence.

He ordered starters and painful silence ensued.

"Bina got to the room all right?" Of course she had or he wouldn't have left Zephyr. *Try harder, Jaya.*

"She looks like you," he said with a lift of his brows. "It

was startling. Made me think that's what our—your daughter could look like, if you had one. People must make that mistake often?"

"All the time." She swallowed, trying not to latch onto what she thought he'd meant to say. *Our.*

More silence. This dress, coming out, it was a huge mistake. He wasn't comfortable so she couldn't relax.

Theo eyed Jaya's tense posture. His own prickling tension was at maximum. She couldn't relax, probably because she felt threatened by his mood.

A pile of ferocious curses piled up in the back of his throat. He was so angry, he could barely think straight. Damn it, why did this exquisite woman keep winding up beyond his reach?

He wished he could take back his confession of his desire. He'd come on strong, had taken a lot of heart from her saying she was still attracted to him, but the rest... Hell, no, nothing between them was simple anymore. What had seemed like an obvious solution, marriage, was now a minefield.

And yet...

Bloody hell, he had to let it go. Maybe if he hadn't told her *before* she explained about her past that he was still hot for her. Maybe if he wasn't currently simmering with insane want, but wow, *that dress.*

Ah, hell, it wasn't the dress. He'd seen a thousand scraps of silk and sequins on a thousand beautiful women and this wasn't the most elaborate or provocative. It was exactly Jaya's style: pretty and feminine, accented with fine metallic strands, but rather sweet overall.

It wasn't the dress that smelled so good he felt drugged. He didn't want to run his hands over sheer fabric and frilly ruffles. He didn't want to taste stitching.

Her skin called out to him. Her lips.

He forced himself to look away and sip his ice water.

Cool his head. Somehow he had to kill off this attraction so he wasn't scaring or intimidating her.

"I shouldn't have told you," she said so softly he wasn't sure he heard her. When he glanced at her, her delectable mouth was pouted in misery. "It changes how you see me, doesn't it?"

"Yes," he allowed with brutal honesty, distantly aware that wasn't the right thing to say, but he struggled with emotions at the best of times and these were some of the worst he'd ever encountered.

Her deep brown eyes widened in a flinch of stark pain, gaze not lifting from the tabletop. Then she struggled to regain her composure, brow working not to wrinkle, mouth trembling until she caught her bottom lip with her teeth.

"For God's sake, Jaya. I don't think *less* of you. I hate myself. I shouldn't have taken advantage of you the way I did. You deserved better." His voice came out low and jagged, as if he'd smoked ten packs of cigarettes and was hardly breathing through the thickness clogging his lungs.

"Better than the first real pleasure I've known with a man? Better than Zephyr?" she challenged shakily.

He was rarely shocked speechless. When he pinned his lips, it was because he was prudent, not because he couldn't think of what to say, but her words blanked his mind. Bali had been a mistake, he kept telling himself, but she seemed to be lifting his actions out of reprehensible into something that was almost exalted. He didn't know how to process that.

"It's like your back, Theo. I'll always have scars, but they fade a little more each year. If you make enough good memories, they push the bad ones away."

He sat back, startled by her insight. He snorted. "I guess that's my problem," he admitted as realization dawned. "I've never made any good memories. Well, maybe one." He couldn't help the significance in the cut of his glance toward her. She was so beguiling. Their night together eclipsed every other memory he had.

Even in the low candlelight, he could tell that her brown skin darkened. Her flustered hands moved into her lap and she ducked her head.

"You know I wouldn't—" he began, catching himself from reaching for her. She was such a panacea for him. He wanted to eat her up. Drown in her. She was everything good that could ever be for him, but he couldn't be greedy about it. He had to hang on to his control.

Her reserve was more than natural modesty, he reminded himself. Her sexual inhibitions were well founded and he'd take a thousand beltings before he'd frighten her with his desire. If she had used him that one night, because she was having a brave moment, well, lucky him.

"I'm glad if our night is a good memory for you, but I don't expect it to happen again. If that's why you're reluctant to marry me, we can keep it platonic." He couldn't believe those words had left his mouth, but having even a small part of her in his life seemed like better than nothing.

Again her eyes widened like she was enduring a wave of agony. "Because now you know I'm soiled goods and don't want—"

"What? No!" His hand went onto her arm involuntarily. He had to hiss in a breath as he strove for control and lifted his touch away, but only managed to transfer it to the back of her chair. Leaning in close, he said, "If you think I'm not aching to make more first-class memories with you, then you are even more naïve than I've always feared. The appeal you have for me… It scares *me,* Jaya. You'd be terrified if you knew how intense my desire is."

He forced himself to retreat into his own space. A deep gulp of ice water did nothing to clear his head. The glossy window reflected his iron hard expression back to him as he braced himself for her to bolt. He should have kept all that to himself.

She sat in quiet contemplation, then confessed softly, "I don't know why you're the only man who makes me feel… well, *anything,* but you are. *That* scares me. I feel like I could be at your mercy, not because of your will. It would be lack of my own."

Excitement pierced him, the arrow so thickly coated in desire he had to close his eyes and concentrate on his breathing. Swearing under his breath, he opened his eyes and let her see the hunger in him, just for a second.

"You're killing me. You know that," he accused, voice buried in a chest.

Her lashes flickered and she quivered like one of those plucked strings that were trying to set a calm mood while he was a werewolf fighting to stay inside his human skin.

"I don't mean to," she whispered. "I just want to be honest."

A bleak laugh escaped him. "It would be a helluva better foundation for a marriage than my parents had."

She cocked her head. "They lied to each other?"

"My mother did, yeah," he said, distaste curling his lip. "She said Nic was my father's. When the truth came out, things turned ugly. The only way any of us coped was to pretend. We acted like we didn't remember Nic, like we didn't hate our mother, like we weren't scared of our father." He clenched his teeth, startled by the ugly truths that poured like fresh blood from a new wound. "Your honesty isn't comfortable for me. I'm not used to it, but… It's reassuring."

She offered a crooked smile.

His heart tipped on its edge, making him bold enough to add, "So whatever you're thinking about how I might be thinking of you differently, it's only that I'm trying to offer you reassurance as well. I won't force you into anything, Jaya. Not marriage, not my bed."

Her watchful gaze wasn't easy to bear. He felt like his entire future hung in the balance.

"I believe you," she murmured, leaning on her elbows. "And I don't feel coerced. I know that marriage is probably best for Zephyr, but a lifetime is a long time, Theo. I can't just leap in. I need to know what it would look like first."

"I have no idea," he admitted, tensing against the million ways he could fail her without even being aware of it. "What do you want it to look like?"

She sat back to consider that and her gaze snagged on the couple at the next table as they rose and moved onto the dance floor. Her face became younger, cast with the yearning of a woman who loved to move to music.

"Would you dance with me?" she queried.

"Of course." He stood and held out his hand while calling himself a shameless ass for seizing the excuse to touch her. Maybe it was even a small test to see if she would accept his hands on her. He could live within just about any limit, so long as he knew what it was. He was going crazy not knowing where his lines were with her.

"I meant, you know, are you the kind of man who would dance with his wife?"

"You weren't asking? Then I am. Will you dance with me, Jaya?" He picked up her hand, oddly pleased with the shy smile she hid with a dip of her chin.

He'd learned early that the guy who was willing to dance got laid. He was proficient at most of the ballroom moves, but she made him hyperaware of himself as he fit them together, especially because he was on guard against being too aggressive. He wasn't quite as smooth as he'd wish, but he wasn't standing on her painted toes, either.

She was awkward, her hesitation seeming more from surprise and unfamiliarity with formal dancing than apprehension. After settling her hand on his shoulder and her fingers into his palm, she took a step forward instead of back, then cringed in horror.

He grinned. "It's fine, just follow my lead."

She did and because she was naturally graceful and rhythmic, they moved well together—not unlike the way they'd meshed in Bali. It was her same quiet trust that made it possible, heating him to his core as he absorbed it, solidifying his need to take great care with her, stoking his need.

"Question answered?" he managed to say, trying to keep things light.

"You're sneaky," she accused. "Maybe you don't bully or pressure, but you're not above seduction, are you?"

He stopped dancing and drew in a deep breath, harking back to when he'd done everything he could to lure her by her own desire into his bed. "Jaya—"

"It's okay, Theo. I don't know what I'm doing when it comes to men." She nudged him back into leading. "I've never danced like this, never been on a real date. If you don't make advances nothing will happen because I don't know how. That's really why I'm scared to say I'll marry you. You're the first man who's asked."

Reservations paralyzed him, but when he used the excuse of an approaching pair of dancers to pull her close, his misgivings slipped from his mind. The contact of her abdomen hitting his hips detonated a subdued explosion that drained his thoughts.

Her lips parted as they held the pose for an extended few seconds, eyes locked.

She took a sudden step back, but didn't release his hand when he relaxed his hold on hers. Chewing her lip, she seemed to debate whether to continue their dance.

"I'm always like this around you," he admitted under his breath, throwing his ego into the wind. It might be the dumbest thing in the world to think this would reassure her, but if they had agreed on nothing else, they were being honest with each other. Maybe, just maybe, if she knew she could trust him, he could have her in his bed again some-day. "Every time I saw you in Bali, I was aroused. Just knowing I would see you would do this to me. I've only ever acted on it the once, Jaya, when you wanted me to."

They still weren't moving, only holding the half embrace while music and couples swirled around them. He searched for uneasiness in her, but her eyes were clouding with confusion and... Was it desire?

If he cupped her breast right now, he wondered, would he find her nipple pebbled and sensitive, aching for the pull of his mouth?

He swallowed, dying as he balanced on the knife's edge between hell and ecstasy.

"Would you kiss me, please?" she asked softly. "I've been wondering—"

He did, not debating, just grasping at permission to capture her parted lips with his. Deep in the back of his mind he reminded himself, *Easy. Go slow.*

It was agonizing to hold himself back. She was so exquisite, her mouth the pillowy satin welcome that tortured his dreams. By some feat of inhuman discipline, he kept his hand light when he clasped the side of her neck where she was warm and soft. He raked his mouth across hers in gentle ravishment, drinking in the clove and nutmeg taste of her.

Jaya liked these extra high heels. Her neck didn't hurt from tilting up to Theo's kiss. Her arms rose of their own accord to curl behind his neck. She opened to the tip of his tongue with a hitch of her breath and started to arch into him.

His hands hardened on her hips, pressing her into her shoes as he lifted his head.

"I was wondering, too." His voice sounded like it originated in the bottom of his chest and came out in a purr like a high performance engine. "We're still incredible together. Make sure you take that into consideration." He circled his thumbs on her hips.

She ducked her laugh into his collarbone, hand pressed to where his heart slammed in the tense cage of his ribs. *Oh, Theo.* She had missed him so much. In this second, all she could think was that she wanted to spend the rest of her life with him, feeling like this.

It reminded her of that fearful moment in Bali when she'd closed her eyes and grasped at her own future. There had been consequences to her actions that she hadn't foreseen. She ought to show a little more sense this time. Marriage was the oldest form of subjugation in history.

But she didn't believe it would be that way with him. Perhaps she was fooling herself, but she felt more like a mammal with the mate she was meant for. Whether she said yes today or years from now, no man was ever going to have this same effect on her. In her heart she was already tied to Theo. Hesitating to make it official seemed like fighting the inevitable.

On the other hand, was money and sex enough? Could Theo ever give her the things she really craved from a lifetime with a man?

"Our food has arrived," he said, nudging her back to their table.

Her pulse jittered from his touch as she sat down and tried to take in the scorched scallops atop crunchy potato cakes.

When they were alone she asked, "Where would we live?"

"With me," he deadpanned. "That's the point."

She laughed, but he only scowled as he chewed and swallowed.

"I need to talk to Adara about curtailing the worst of my travel. Whether you marry me or not, I have to be available to Zephyr, but I'll always have to do some globe-trotting. I don't particularly care for Paris as a base, but it's closer to India than New York. Could you stand it?"

"Could you?" she challenged, taking in the tight grip he had on his fork with a tilt of her equilibrium into caution. "I'm actually quite flexible. I've started over in new places several times. You live in your helicopter. You're used to doing what you like. Having a wife and child would turn your life upside down, Theo."

"I'm aware," he stated flatly, setting down his utensils to stroke restless hands up and down his thighs. "And I won't claim that I'd be easy to live with, especially in the beginning, but I keep coming back to what I can offer you in terms of security and protection. Marriage is the simplest way to accomplish that."

She ought to be flattered, she supposed. There was a type of caring in his bland statement, even if it was the kind one usually showed to, say, an expensive boat or maybe a herd of cattle. On some level he valued her, she deduced. That was nice, but it wasn't enough to sustain a marriage.

Their conversation drifted to what kind of placement she could have with Makricosta's, as his wife or not, and they didn't talk about marriage again until they'd returned to the suite.

First they had to release the matronly Madame Begnoche and Theo had to negotiate a peace treaty with Bina. She was very sad to learn that Theo wanted Zephyr living with him rather than coming to South America with her and Quentin.

"Pyaari beti," Jaya reminded gently, "You know I was going to stay in France and not come with you and your papa."

"I know, but, but…" Her voice threatened to crack into sobs.

Theo extracted a business card and wrote on it before he

handed it to Bina. "This is my personal mobile. Call any-
time you are missing Zephyr. We probably won't be able to
come to you that day, but we'll try to visit within the week.
Or, if your father agrees, I'll bring you to visit him. We'll
work it out, I promise."

"Thank you," she said in a heavy but mollified voice,
blinking her damp doe eyes.

When she held up her arms, Theo didn't get it. Jaya had
to touch his shoulder and nod. "She wants to hug you."

"Oh, um." Clearing his throat, he went down on one
knee so Bina could squeeze his neck with her spindly arms.
He patted her back awkwardly and deflated with a heavy
exhale after she left to meet Oscar and the limo, Theo's
treat.

"Thank you," Jaya said to him. "But you can't keep offering to fly me and my family around the world."

"Why not?"

Because I haven't agreed to marry you, she almost said,
but she suspected it didn't matter. He'd do it regardless.
"You're a soft touch when it comes to kids, aren't you?"

"I don't know what that means, but having Nic disappear
on us was a trauma I don't want to drop on my own son."

Oh, right. She swallowed, watching him run a fingertip
along his eyebrow. She wondered if he was looking for another argument to persuade her to marry him.

"Theo." She sat heavily in the middle of the sofa.

His head came up, expression patient.

Her heart grew achy and she had to look at her finger-
nails. "I don't want to string you along wondering what you
have to do to convince me to marry you. I'm not hesitating
because I'm afraid of going to bed with you."

She bit her lips, keeping her head down while stealing a
quick peek upward, noting that she had his attention, one
thousand percent. He was virility personified, all his mas-

culine features sharpened, his wide shoulders tense and defined beneath his crisp white shirt.

"Actually, I am a little nervous about that. I've had a baby since the last time and it's not like I've had a lot of practice..." She swallowed.

"We'll be amazing, Jaya. Just like last time." His voice reverberated deep in his chest.

If she hadn't been sitting, she would have fallen, he made her so weak. She grasped for the words she needed to say. "I'm not afraid you'd be violent or disrespectful, either. I know I could trust you about most things."

"But not all things." Tone cracked with a jag of disbelief, he recoiled in hurt.

She swallowed, knowing this would be difficult.

"You didn't call me back," she said in a small voice. "I know you said you wouldn't, but..." She tried to shrug off how foolish she felt, how bare this fantasy of hers left her. "I thought I was different. I thought you liked me."

His face transformed in slow degrees, falling from intense focus on her to inward comprehension, into lost hope and finally, self-hatred.

"I don't expect you to love me," she rushed to say, even though it tore open something inside her. "But I always wanted to marry for love." Such a girlish dream, so romantic and silly. That's the message she'd always received, but she still wanted it. "I need something between us that's not just practicality and hormones. Those things aren't a real bond. They're not something you fight for. But if you had any feelings for me at all..."

He did his thing where he froze. Not shrinking. He didn't cringe, but he braced himself. Like he refused to show how vulnerable he felt, while at the same time expected great pain. "I don't understand why you'd want me to."

Careful, she urged herself. He wasn't being arrogant or callous. He probably, genuinely didn't understand. She heard the barest inflection on *me* in his statement and knew this was more about his low opinion of himself than lack of regard for her.

Licking her lips, choosing her words with care, she said, "Everyone wants to be liked. Don't you?"

He shook his head. "It doesn't matter to me either way." Because he'd been reviled by someone who was supposed to love him. The abraded edges of her heart frayed and stung.

"What about your sister? Surely it matters to you that she loves you?"

His shoulder jerked, almost like he was deflecting a blow. "I'm sure she values my loyalty. I take satisfaction in knowing she can count on me."

He only took what pride he gave himself, would never ask for a smidgen more even from a woman he'd take a bullet to protect. How utterly abandoned he must have felt to mold himself into someone so inaccessible.

"Well, I want to be liked," Jaya said with one hand cupped in the palm of the other, trying to project calm control when emotion tore at her throat. "I'd like whatever attraction you feel toward me to be for more than whatever parts of me fit into lingerie. Because I think you're a very good-looking man, but when I say I'm attracted to you, I mean that I *like* you, Theo." *Love,* a voice inside her contradicted, but it was such a huge admission to be in love that she pressed it back into her subconscious, not quite ready to be that vulnerable.

Still, as she lifted her gaze, she was absolutely defenseless, like he must be able to read that her feelings were so much stronger than she was admitting, but she didn't want to scare him, only let him see she was sincere.

"Jesus, Jaya," he whispered in a ragged breath, looking away.

His image swam before her brimming eyes, but she

thought she'd seen a flinch of great anguish, like her words had touched a very raw part of him. He rubbed his hand across his jaw.

"For God's sake, why?" he expelled with disbelief.

Oh, you poor, poor man. She rose and went to him, unable to sit so far from him when he was hurting so much. Cupping his head, she forced his tortured expression to face hers.

"Why do I like you? You're a good man, Theo. When I told you about my assault, you didn't ask what I was wearing or whether I did something to encourage it. You never once lost patience with those babies even though they kept us up half the night. You protected your little brother when you were barely old enough to—"

"Shh, don't." He pulled her into his chest, crushing her so tight she could barely draw breath. His heart pounded against her breast and she felt his swallow where his damp throat was pressed to her temple. His breaths moved harshly in his nostrils as he tried to regain control, holding her against the rise and fall of his shaken breaths.

She let herself soften into him, hoping her signal of acceptance would penetrate.

His own arms loosened a fraction and she wound her arms around his chest. Their embrace became mutual. Tight and close, man and woman. He cupped the back of her head and rubbed his chin on her hair.

"People hate to see me coming," he said after a long time. "I criticize how they're doing things, ask for paperwork they can't find, make them account for items they think are insignificant. You always smiled at me, no matter what I asked for. I was never an imposition to you. That's so rare for me."

He combed his fingers through her hair while she closed her eyes against a sharp sting, feeling dampness gather on her lashes and keeping them hidden in his shirt, certain he'd stop holding her if he knew how moved she was.

"Do I *like* you?" he continued. "I don't have friends. I don't know how that works. I wish I could say I loved you, that I could give you everything you want from a man. Knowing you want love tells me I don't deserve you."

She hitched in a breath of protest, but he was continuing, arms tightening a fraction to keep her in place.

"But I'm not selfless enough to give you up. I want you in my life. Not just because my mouth waters when I think of you naked. Hell, you can feel how I'm reacting now, but there are a lot of beautiful women out there. There's only one you. You *are* special, Jaya."

She hugged him hard, biting her lips because they were quivering. "Thank you for saying that."

"But it's not enough, is it?" He slid heavy hands to her shoulders and eased her back a step. "You do deserve better."

Here was the crossroads again. She couldn't know if marrying him was the right choice unless she made it and looked back on having lived with it, but she couldn't hurt him by rejecting him. All she could do was remember how perfect they had been once and believe that, with time, they could surpass it.

Without breathing, courage gathered into a tight knot in her middle, she picked up his hand to cradle it against her cheek. "You're going to have to trust me when I say that I would be honored and privileged to be your wife," she quavered.

He searched her gaze, a small frown pulling his brows. "Are you saying—"

She nodded, unable to help smiling when he was so plainly taken by surprise. "I would like to marry you, Theo."

The flash of male triumph that streaked into his fierce

visage might have frightened her if there wasn't a helping of relief beneath it, endearingly softening his ruthless expression. In the next instant, he shuttered himself so thoroughly, she wondered if she had seen any reaction at all.

"Thank you. We'll get a ring in the morning."

And the CFO was back, armed with his tasks. Nevertheless, she'd seen behind the curtain and knew there was something there, even if it wasn't very clearly defined.

"I don't need a ring," she dismissed, and reluctantly let her hands drop. She didn't know how to bring herself out from intense emotional intimacy to distance with the swiftness that he did. A chill made her cross her arms and self-protect.

"I want to do this properly," he insisted, then grimaced. "I suppose that means we should wait until our wedding night. How long does it take to plan a wedding?"

"Wait for what? Oh." She ducked her head to hide that she was blushing, partly because she was dense enough not to have got his meaning right away, but also because she was disappointed. "We don't have to," she murmured.

"I want you to be sure." He pushed his hands into his pockets, but she could see he was still aroused. He was trying not to touch her, she realized, and glittering delight bounced through her at her effect on him.

"I am sure." She lifted her face so he could see she wasn't teasing, but she didn't know how to flirt or invite. Arousal was still too new.

"Sure about all of it," he clarified with a rueful look. "Given our track record, I'd knock you up by midnight. As you said, this is your first proposal. I won't trap you."

A small smile touch her lips at the prospect of him forcing a shotgun wedding, but another thought occurred and it was a big one. "Do you want more children?"

His expression blanked in surprise. "I haven't given it any thought. Hell, last week I didn't want any. Today...I don't know. Being a single child sounds lonely for Zephyr, doesn't it? I mean, Demitri is a complete pain in the ass, but I can't imagine not having him around."

"It's open for discussion, then?" she confirmed. This was a deal-breaker for her.

"Yes," he said firmly. "But let's give ourselves a chance to get to know one another again first." His gaze feathered over her cheek and lit on her mouth.

He knew how to say things that both flattered and intrigued. Despite his sweetly suggestive remark, however, a very somber mood came over him.

Her smile faded. "What's wrong?"

"Not one thing." He cupped her face and kissed her with startling tenderness. "You're very lovely, Jaya. How long until I can call you my wife?"

"I don't know." Her heart turned over and already she wondered if she'd done the right thing. "A few months?"

He grimaced.

"Unless you want a small wedding," she rushed to say. "That could be arranged in a week or two."

"I want to do this right." His hands fell to her shoulders and he looked over her head, his expression weighted by heavy thoughts. His hands massaged, but distractedly. Like he'd slipped miles away from her. "You'll want your family to come."

"My parents, yes, but it doesn't have to be a big deal. I've never dreamed of being the center of a society wedding. I can't imagine you have, either." She nudged his stomach playfully.

"More like suffered nightmares." His mouth twisted with aversion. "But we have business associates in New York and relatives in Greece who should be invited."

"Big weddings are expensive."

"Do *not* worry about the cost." He stepped away to state

decisively, "We should be able to make a strong statement in six weeks."

"A statement?" she repeated.

"As opposed to a splash."

"Okay." She tried to read his inscrutable expression.

"You should get some sleep. I'll listen for Zephyr," he said.

"You're staying up to work?" The way he shut her out was not the way she thought an engagement should start.

"I need to think. I'm used to having more time with my own thoughts than I've had in the last few days."

"Oh. Of course." She tried not to take that as a slight. *She* hadn't initiated this chain of events. If only he'd kiss her again, so the fragile bond between them would grow another layer, rather than fade. But he didn't.

"Good night," she said, confidence dwindling as she went to her room.

CHAPTER ELEVEN

As SOMEONE WHOSE life had changed overnight before, Jaya had learned to prefer a gradual, thoughtful approach to making shifts in her world. After her abrupt departure from India, she'd had months of notice before her move to Bali. Once settled, she'd dug in, comfortable in her role there. France had been a culture shock, but she'd had family to cushion the blow.

Nothing could have prepared her, probably not even time, for being pulled into the Makricostas' world. First she'd had to quit her job, which had been a tough decision even though Adara emailed with three job offers "to consider when the time is right." Then there was the travel, flitting up to London for two nights because Theo had a meeting and a thing.

"What kind of thing?" she'd asked when he'd requested she accompany him.

"A presentation. We paid to refurbish a historical building. One of the royals will be there so I've been elected to represent."

One of the royals. Like this was normal.

Which meant an upgrade to her wardrobe. No longer did she own a few nice outfits. Every time she turned around, Theo was bringing in a designer or a stylist or squiring her into a shop where the *prêt-à-porters* didn't even have price tags.

"I thought women enjoyed shopping," he said at one point.

"But the cost! I'm not even working."

He quirked a brow at her. "Do you have any idea how much money I make? How well I invest it? I never spend any."

Except on his fleet of airplanes and helicopters. He did some flitting of his own in those, disappearing to South America and Japan for a couple of days without her. She couldn't complain. She put off her separation from Bina as long as she could and needed the time to pack up her life, plan a wedding and look for a suitable home in New York.

The city was incredible. They spent a week there and she looked forward to living there permanently. However, the bit where Theo ensconced her in the family suite at the Makricosta Grand and visited his apartment without her bothered her immensely. It was too small for them, even in the interim, she agreed. She also understood he was a private man who liked his own space. Plus, as he pointed out oh-so-reasonably, here at the hotel she had help on tap—boy, did she have help. She used to be the one who jumped when a Makricosta rang. It was bizarre to be on the receiving end of that level of service from people a lot further up the corporate food chain than she'd ever been.

Then, just when her insecurities began to get the best of her and she convinced herself he'd be the most hands-off, distant husband, that this whole thing was a terrible mistake, he reassured her. After practically ignoring her all day in front of the real estate agent, he drew her into his arms as they closed the door of the hotel suite and kissed her breathless, saying when they came up for air, "I've been wanting to do that all day. You look amazing." She happened to be wearing one of her own modest navy skirts with a canary lace top over a lemon-colored cami. Nothing flashy or fantastic.

Then, when they'd decided on a penthouse apartment a few blocks from Adara and Gideon's, with a view of the park and a rooftop patio and pool, she'd watched him close the deal with an emotionless handshake. When the agent left them alone, an ominous silence descended, worrying her.

She rocked Zephyr on her hip. "Are you sure? You don't look pleased."

"You said you loved it." He snapped his head around.

"I do! You're the one who went into lockdown when I said I thought this was the one and could we have one more look."

He didn't like it when she called him on his standoffishness. She was learning his tells and noted the tick in his brow and the muscle that clenched in his jaw. But being blunt was the only way to get him to open up enough for her to understand him and not feel closed out.

"I didn't mean to." He kept one hand fisted in his pocket, his mouth tense and outlined in white.

The look he flashed at her was both impatient with himself and…not distrustful, but like he wasn't sure of her. With a cross noise, he shrugged. He kept a proud bearing, but it was like he was headed to the gallows, he was so stiff and withdrawn as he pulled his hand from his pocket.

"You know I'm the furthest thing from a romantic," he said gruffly. "But I thought if we decided this would be home, it would be a good time to give you this, as a sort of… Hell, I don't know." He showed her the sparkle he held. "An official start?"

She gasped. "You picked up the ring?" They'd chosen the stones two weeks ago, but she hadn't expected to see the finished setting until right before the wedding.

"I figured if you said yes to the apartment, you were probably going through with the wedding so…"

He was nervous!

Too awed to laugh, she rushed forward to kiss him. Zephyr got in the way, of course, little fists grabbing at Theo and catching a chest hair so he winced and pulled away long enough to take him. Then he pulled her back into him like a pirate grabbing a wench, angling her over his arm as he kissed her like he really meant it. Like he wanted to devour her because he desired her so much.

Jaya straightened her ring on her finger now, the memory of their kiss embedded into the piece as irrevocably as the oval cut sapphire. The goldsmith had created a setting that looked as if he'd cut a blond band open then twisted it, setting the rare purple stone between the scrolled ends. He'd finished the tails with ever shrinking pink diamonds. The result a piece with such femininity, it made the extravagance subtle and elegant.

Much like the stunning mini-villa behind her, she thought ruefully, lifting her gaze to the view of the Parthenon lit yellow-gold by the fading sun. They'd decided on Athens for the wedding. It was a less grueling flight for her family and worked for his.

It was like a fairy tale, but she'd had another run of doubts as recently as last night. They'd had dinner with Adara and Gideon. Nic and Rowan had their own apartment in the city, but had joined them in the family suite. The babies had reunited into a loud, happy flock that Theo had stood apart from while the others dove in with quick hands to retrieve a dropped toy or change a bottom. Gideon, as Adara had predicted, took to Zephyr like he'd made him, rolling on the floor with all the children, far more relaxed than she'd ever expected the cool, stern Director of the Board for the Makricosta empire to be.

Theo, on the other hand, wasn't as forward with his affection, waiting for the little ones to come to him, saying something about them probably not remembering him.

After a night of agonizing whether he shared her dream

for a loving family, she'd woken to find Theo on his back on the lounge floor, Zephyr lifted like a superhero above him, both of them laughing as Theo lowered him to make growling noises against his little belly. It was exactly the game Gideon had played with all the children the night before.

She'd pretended she needed her phone to hide her moved tears.

He just needs someone to show him how to love, she reasoned. She was that person. Somehow she'd overcome her mistrust and was falling for him. It was only fair to believe he had the capacity to love her back, given time and enough trust between them.

A door opened and closed in the suite behind her.

Her ruminations fell away and she smiled with anticipation, expecting him to come to her. Sometimes he checked on Zephyr first, if he was napping, which he was. Then they'd neck until they were breathless and oh, why weren't they married yet? She was growing impatient to feel his skin, his hands, *him.*

Swallowing the rush of feeling, she blinked the smeared colors of the Parthenon from her eyes and turned with a beaming smile.

And saw Theo making out with a woman against the wall, just inside the entry doors of the penthouse.

No.

Squinching the wetness from her eyes, she swiped her forearm over them as she stumbled on bare feet across the marble tiles of the rooftop garden, around the end of the pool and up to the point where the air-conditioning of the interior blended with the heat of the outdoors.

Maybe that was her own body causing the hot and cold baffling through her as she stared with disbelief at a familiar back. His shoulders flexed beneath his white shirt as he guided a woman's leg to his hip then slid his hand under the edge of her polka dot skirt. Sharp pink talons poked through his brown hair as they kissed.

A million thoughts whirled like tornado debris in her mind. He had said he was going for a haircut. That wasn't the shirt he was wearing this morning. Where did he think she was that he would bring some floozy back to where they were staying?

Nothing in the world could have prepared her for this. Except a senior chambermaid had taught her what to do in exactly this situation on her first day of work ten years ago.

"Housekeeping!" Jaya blurted in a shrill voice.

With a squeal, the woman's platform sandal clapped to the floor.

He barely lifted his head. "Come back another time." He chased another kiss.

It was Theo's voice, but the way he ignored her wasn't Theo.

"Demitri?" she hazarded.

His head came up again and he sent a laconic glance over his shoulder. "Jaya?"

"You're married?" the woman gasped.

"Hell, no. My brother's fiancée. Jaya, we're going to need some privacy. Can you...?" He gave her a "shove-off" motion.

"Of course." She grasped for her wits and searched for her purse. "I've been waiting for the baby to wake so I could go shopping, but if you'll listen for him—"

Demitri released his partner and reached for the door-knob, blocking Jaya's exit as he pressed his mate through it. "Wait for me at the elevator," he told her as he kissed her pout and gave her a pat on the behind before closing her out.

Jaya returned her purse to the side table and folded her arms, waiting for his next move with her brows in her hair-line.

He turned to her with an amused smile. "Well played."

Now she saw him properly, she could see the resemblance was strong, but not identical. He was obviously younger and not quite as handsome as Theo. *Too* devilish.

"I thought leaving babies with bachelor uncles was how your family does things."

He snorted. "I remembered you as shy and quiet. Made me wonder where Theo found the…"

His pause prompted her to fill in one of the thousand slang words men used to describe the source of their fertility and courage. She held her breath, waiting to hear which vulgar term he would pick.

"…temerity," he provided with a wicked tilt of his grin, "to date you."

He was a brat, through and through. She'd known it from her few interactions with him and now that Theo had explained about their family she even understood why. Demitri got away with his cheeky, outrageous behavior because no one stopped him.

"Speaking of dates, is that yours for the wedding? Because your family is staying in another suite. I'm expecting mine here shortly."

He shrugged off the information. "No, I don't even know her name. I picked her up in the bar." He was utterly without shame or consideration for others.

Genuinely curious about that, she cocked her head. "Why do you like to take people so off guard? Does it give you a sense of power to introduce chaos?"

He barely blinked, but narrowed his eyes in reassessment. "Here I thought I was behaving. The last time Theo was engaged, I picked up his bride."

When she caught a shocked breath, he smiled.

"He never mentioned that?"

She could have kicked him in his temerities, she was so infuriated by his smug air at having disarmed her. How

could he do something so awful as seduce his brother's intended? And be proud of it?

Why hadn't Theo told her?

"He knows you're not my type," was the best retort she
could manage.

The door lock hummed then opened.

Theo paused to take in Demitri slouched beside the door
and Jaya standing across the other side of the lounge, arms
crossed in dismay.

"Jaya was just reminding me I'm not her type," Demitri
said flippantly. "Good thing I've been preapproved down
the hall."

Theo stopped Demitri's exit with two straight fingers
poked into his chest.

Jaya found herself holding her breath, never having seen
him angry, not like that. Instant and icy cold, completely
ready to be aggressive and deadly. His mood was doubly
volatile because he didn't lash out, only asked with deadly
flatness, "Did he make a move on you?" He didn't take his
eyes off his brother.

"N-no," she managed, arms aching where she had them
wrapped around herself.

"Don't," Theo said to Demitri. "Ever. I have my limits.
You've just found one."

Jaya's insides trembled, all of her shaken by Theo's possessive, protective words. She wanted to be reassured it
proved he cared for her, but she was still reeling from the
news that he'd been engaged once before and hadn't told
her. Had he loved that other woman? Was that the real reason he couldn't love her?

The thought was as bad as those poisoned few seconds
when she'd thought it was him in the clinch against the wall.

Demitri calmly moved Theo's hand aside, like he was
opening a gate. He walked out without a word.

Theo watched him for a split second, the muscle in his

jaw pulsing, before he stepped in and closed the door. "I'll assume it was garden variety obnoxiousness on his part that has you looking so peeved?"

"Actually it was learning you were engaged before. Were you going to tell me?"

CHAPTER TWELVE

THEO SAW THE hurt Jaya made no effort to disguise and suppressed a flinch of guilt. At the same time, his heart pounded like a pile driver. He and Demitri had their moments, but he'd never been as close to getting physical with his little brother as a few seconds ago. Violence was wrong, but if Demitri had touched Jaya, had scared her...

Such a rush of complex emotions strangled him, his instinct was to turn around and walk out, find somewhere private to pull himself together and come back when he felt in control again.

Maybe if Jaya had been angry and accusing he could have walked away from her. Instead she had that vulnerable look about her, the one that wrenched his heart. Like she was exposing her throat and it was up to him to prove he wouldn't rip it out.

"Zeph sleeping?" he asked.

"He went down twenty minutes ago."

His wingman wouldn't provide a distraction then.

He rubbed his face, trying to push his expression back into stoic when he was still unsettled by what he'd walked into. Amazing how he'd become addicted to entering cheerful disarray where a woman and baby greeted him with smiles, maybe some homey smells, and he had to pick a path across scattered toys, but always found a reward of physical affection at the end.

"Theo?" she prompted.

He squeezed the back of his neck. This was why he'd kept to superficial relationships for so long. One-night lovers asked surface questions with easy answers.

Still, the more time he spent with Jaya and Zeph, the more he craved. He liked hearing her sing in Punjabi to their son, liked the homemade food she cooked, liked the way she drew attention when they were out, pulling it off him as people took in her exotic beauty. She'd always been pretty, but with the professional styling taking her appearance up a notch, he had himself a knockout of a fiancée and couldn't wait to have her legally tied to him as his wife.

He was surprisingly impatient to lock in that life and now realized what had subconsciously been driving him.

But to admit it all to her? *Hell.*

"It's humiliating," he said, tossing his key card on a side table and moving into the suite a few steps, then halting in frustration. He could feel her rebuff from here. An invisible wall sat between them, dense as lead and heavy enough to compress his chest.

"When?" she asked in a strained voice. "Since Bali? Because I never heard anything about you getting married while I was working there. I'm sure I would have."

"It was years before that," he dismissed

That detail seemed to relieve a fraction of her distress, but she still stared at him, willing him to provide more details.

"My father arranged it," he forced himself to say.

"Arranged. But you were so disparaging when you thought I was quitting to go to France for an arranged marriage."

"That's why." Everything in him ached for distance and privacy, but a different, unfamiliar compulsion kept him frozen here, longing to close the gap between them. He was learning the only way was to pick his path through the minefield of his past. He hated it, but for her, he did it.

"Did you love her?" The tentative edge in her voice told him how hard that was for her to ask.

"No," he assured with a disgusted exhale. "She was a socialite, a party girl, the daughter of a well-respected New York businessman who was down on his luck. They wanted the connection to our family, my father wanted an heir…"

"You said you never wanted to be a father!"

"I didn't," he said, recalling such heavy dread it had stuck with him until he'd learned how it really was to have his own child. "But I didn't have a choice."

"Men always have a choice," she said with resentment. "They're never as helpless as women in these situations. She was probably under more pressure to go through with it than you were."

"No, I don't believe that." He never went back over those memories, they made him feel too pathetic, but she forced him to with her accusation. "You're right that I could have walked away from my inheritance," he allowed, "but I couldn't do that to Adara. Not after what happened to us once Nic was gone."

No one would ever know how close he'd come despite that. He'd forgotten how his sister had been the tipping point for him. He'd been scared for her. If he hadn't been there to protect her, no one would have been. His unhappiness with a marriage to a woman he didn't care about had seemed like nothing against Adara's safety.

Somehow, remembering his motive loosed the old shame off him. Yes, he'd been browbeaten and yes, it had been his choice to allow it. But he'd had a good reason.

"Demitri said he slept with her," Jaya said.

"He did." He felt nothing making that admission because the act had become the mortar he used to thicken and heighten the walls he used to protect himself. From then on, he'd held everyone even more firmly at a distance, even his siblings. Why in hell would anyone want to be close to him? He was second best to his outgoing, funny younger brother. Everyone preferred Demitri, given the choice.

Except Jaya. Maybe the seeds of his deep admiration had been born in seeing her deflection of men who came onto her, especially the ones who took for granted they could impress with a grin and a flash of money. She had smiles for everyone, but she reserved her warmest for grandfathers with arthritis or little boys who got off the elevator on the wrong floor.

"Why would he do that? Just to prove he could or...?" She shook her head in bafflement. "To hurt you?"

He drew in a breath that burned. "It wasn't just once for bragging rights. They had an affair. I don't know who started it and God knows I won't make excuses for him, but he was nineteen to her twenty-three. She happily drove to Manhattan and paraded herself through the lobby so all our staff could see them carrying on."

And his father had berated him, like it was his fault when he'd been half a state away finishing exams. *Such* impossible expectations. He swore if Zephyr never aspired to anything more ambitious than flipping burgers in a fast food shack, he'd make sure the boy knew he was proud of him.

"What did she say when you broke it off?"

Here came the degradation, but it was losing its potency as they talked of this. For too many years, he'd let this make him feel weak. He been strong. Enduring. "I didn't."

"Didn't break it off? But...Why not?"

The easy answer was, "I didn't have to. Adara convinced our father the publicity was too damaging to go through with it. By then Gideon was on the scene. Her engagement let me off the hook."

"You would have gone through with it?" She sounded appalled.

He was equally galled with himself, which is why he never revisited this ugly time, but he'd been a different man then. One who merely survived, not one who cared about thriving or his own happiness or anyone else beyond the one person who had always been there for him. Looking back, he barely recognized himself.

The turning point had been Bali, he saw now, and not because of Adara's call—even though that had been a catalyst. No, he'd begun thawing toward his siblings after that, but he couldn't have managed it if he hadn't had that night with Jaya. She'd begun the melt in him with her kind acceptance of his weakness that night. He only recognized now that it was her influence because he'd changed so much since he'd seen her again.

Shaking himself out of the stunning realization, he tried to answer.

"All of my options were terrible. If I'd broken it off, my father would have done anything to hurt me, including going after my mother and Adara." He'd make a different choice today. He was stronger. Because he had someone else in his corner.

Didn't he? She was still struggling to understand why he'd kept this from her.

"But not Demitri," she said. "I can see why you're so loyal to Adara. She's always had your back, but I don't know how you tolerate your brother. Or is that your normal interaction with him? Are you two always hostile?" She nodded toward the door.

"No, we get along. The past is water under the bridge." He forced himself to open hands that had clenched into fists as he recalled his anger when he'd come in to find Demitri with Jaya, her expression cross and distressed. "I wanted him to know there will never be any forgiveness where you're concerned." He leveled a stern glance at her.

"You'll tell me if he crosses any lines. I'm serious about this being a red one."

"Because he did it once before." She looked to her linked fingers.

"Because you have entrusted me to keep you safe. I'd die before I'd let you feel threatened by him or anyone." He'd take on anyone for her, he realized. Not because he approved of violence, but because she was that precious to him.

"Theo." Her head came up in alarm. "Don't talk about dying."

"Hey," he deflected with a snort. "I hope it doesn't come to anything drastic like that, but I bring so little to this relationship, Jaya." The tiny flame in him that he barely acknowledged would never be enough for her. "At least let me give you this much."

"That's not true." Tension distended her neck as she took his remark like a knife to the throat. Could she blame him for not bringing his heart to their marriage though, when his own had been so chronically kicked around? "You bring yourself. Stop thinking that's not enough."

The silence was so profound she couldn't look up. Then, even from across the room, she heard his swallow.

"Is it?" he asked in a ragged voice. "Because you brought Zeph and he's pretty damned incredible."

"He is, isn't he?" she said shamelessly. "But he's half yours so—" She took a few faltering steps toward him, then hesitated, not sure if he was ready to close the distance. The things he'd shared had been hard for him. She'd had to pull the details like teeth and there wasn't any anesthetic for things like this.

He met her halfway, his strong hands reaching out to take hers in a gentle grip. Her own clenched convulsively, grasping for something more than his steady strength, even though she knew she should be satisfied with that. It should be enough.

Pressing her trembling lips into a line, she searched his face.

He didn't like it and looked away, obviously not comfortable with her need for reassurance. She dipped her head, suffering another wave of doubt that he'd ever open his heart to her.

"I'm sorry," he said gruffly. "I should have told you myself, not left it so you'd find out like that. It was like what happened last night, when Gideon told Androu not to touch the light socket and that just made him more aware of them. I didn't want to put the idea into your head."

"That I could have an affair with Demitri? He floated that balloon years ago and I stabbed it with a pen."

Theo snorted, thumbs stroking over her knuckles. "I don't know why he has to behave like such an ass."

"You and Adara hold your lives under tight control. If he turns things upside down he gains the upper hand."

"Now how did you see that and I never have?" He leaned back to absorb that.

"You've spent so many years putting up shields, you can't always see past them."

He blinked in surprise, seeming disconcerted. "But you can."

"Sometimes," she said warily. "Does that bother you?"

He drew a deep breath. "It's not comfortable." His hands tightened on hers and he looked into her eyes, even though he winced as he did it, like it was a kind of torture to let her see inside him. "But…" He swallowed, then, "I trust you, Jaya. I know you're not going to use anything I tell you to hurt me."

His grip crushed her hands, but she didn't think he was aware of it. She squeezed back, feeling they stood on a precipice that, if they took this leap of faith, they could land in new, rich, broad territory.

"I would never want to hurt you. Not ever," she promised, then held her breath.

Bringing her hand to his mouth, he ran the knuckle of her ring finger along his lips. His breath clouded warmly against her skin as he spoke, making her wrist tingle.

"I think half the reason I still speak to Demitri after what he did is gratitude. Ultimately he got me out of a situation I didn't want."

"Really?" This didn't seem the deep confidence she half expected. "Do you think he did it on purpose?" she asked, wondering if that was digging too deep.

"Hell, no. He'd never show that kind of forethought, but he created the excuse and I was glad. Swear to me you'll never reveal that to him."

A giggle escaped her, part relief, part joy that he was confiding in her a little. "Cross my heart and hope to die."

He took a deep breath and looked down on her with something like pride and…affection? His expression had softened into amusement and tenderness. It almost looked like happiness and made her warm all the way to the soles of her feet. He was solemn as he cradled her face and caressed her cheek with the pad of his thumb.

"I can't wait to marry you."

"Really?" She wanted to smile, but she was dissolving under his look and couldn't seem to hold any part of herself steady. "Because I thought it was you at first, when Demitri came in. He made out with that woman right there in front of me and I thought for a horrible second it was you and we were finished. I was devastated," she admitted.

His mellow smile faded. "I'll kill him."

Her turn to set a hand against his smooth cheek, freshly shaved and smelling of something tangy and fresh. "But then I realized it couldn't be you because you'd never do that to me. I never expected I'd be able to trust a man this much, Theo. I wish I could tell you what a gift you've given me with that." She slid her other hand up his chest and around his neck so her breasts pressed into the hardness of his chest and her damp lips touched his ultra-smooth jaw.

He gathered her in, crushing her close in tight arms and releasing a shuddering breath against her ear.

They sought each other's mouths, colliding with practiced alignment, parted lips meeting and sealing, plunging her into a dark jungle of sultry heat and velvet sensations. Combing her fingers up the back of his head, she reveled in the short, freshly cut strands, the new haircut, exactly as he'd promised. The thought made her want to smile but he was kissing her too intently.

He rasped his tongue down her neck, one hand palming her breast, making intense sensations race into her loins. She clenched to contain the deliciousness there.

This was moving fast and a distant part of her wondered if she should be worried about that, but desire flowed through her veins in rivers of lava, making her burn for him.

"God, Jaya," he groaned, stilling her rocking hips against the hard ridge of his erection. "The next two days are going to kill me."

"Oh, Theo, I don't want to wait anymo—*oh!*"

He scooped her up, his strength like a conqueror's as he bounced her into a high clasp against his chest, his arousal evident in the flush on his cheekbones and the sheen on his feral half grin. "If you're not going to stop me, then I won't."

She slid her hand from his shoulder to his ear, pulling herself close enough to kiss where his pulse pounded like a hammer in his throat.

As he started down the hall, two sounds halted him: Zephyr's cry and a knock on the penthouse door.

He swore and she softly wailed, "Nooooo," as he let her feet slide to the floor.

"That's your family, isn't it?" His gruff voice was rueful. "Better now than in five minutes when we would have been naked. I'll get Zeph. I need to pull myself together."

Snickering, she kissed his chin and started to walk away. He yanked her back for another deep swift kiss that included a taste of France. Dazzled, she bounced off the wall on her way to greet her guests.

Despite his sexual frustration, which was more acute than he'd ever thought he could bear, Theo was riding a natural high. Jaya still wanted to marry him.

He hadn't consciously been aware of that niggling concern. She always responded so sweetly to him and even though they had their differences, they always seemed to work through them. Still, a voice inside him had kept harping that he wasn't enough.

She thought he was a gift, though, because she could trust him. He swelled with pride knowing how hard-won that kind of reliance was for her. The determination to protect her ran through him on a current of reverence and resolve. In a few days he would pledge to uphold her faith in him and he'd do it with every fiber of his being.

Speaking of gifts...

Lifting his freshly diapered son to eye level, he took a moment to absorb the awe of fatherhood. While the magnitude of responsibility still scared him, and he wasn't yet a hundred percent confident he'd be everything Zephyr needed, he was learning. For most of his life, he'd been driven by the need to be perfect so he wouldn't catch hell. Now, he yearned to do well so he could be a better father than he'd had.

"That sets the bar pretty low, doesn't it?" he murmured

to his son before he kissed the boy's forehead and carried him out to the main lounge.

Heated voices speaking Punjabi fell into a wall of blistering silence when he appeared. He'd picked up a few words from Jaya and was working on a speech for the wedding, but he wasn't good enough with the language to follow any of what had been said even if he'd properly heard it.

He was the last man to judge a family for dysfunction, but Jaya had seemed to be making progress with them. Her tone had been growing lighter of heart when she'd spoken of them while travel and wedding plans had fallen into place. He had been counting on her finding some emotional fulfillment through her relationship with her mother and sister to compensate for his own lack. It was important to him that he not cheat her of love, that he give her every chance for it since he couldn't provide it himself.

This wasn't love, though. This was a tight army of angry young men backing up a grizzled bear with a thick gray beard. Two older women sat on the sofa, one in green, the other in blue. They bookended a young woman in yellow and a dazed older man. Their clothing seemed extracolorful against the white leather of the furnishings, their expressions taxed. The women seemed to be trying to make themselves smaller while the young men puffed up their chests under crossed arms.

Jaya stood apart from all of them, her anxiety palpable. The way she dropped her gaze after an initial tense glance at him seemed almost apologetic.

Theo mentally swore. He might have been swimming naked through these sorts of shark-infested undercurrents all his life, but he'd never grown comfortable in them.

"Welcome," he managed in Punjabi, then zeroed in on the woman beside the frail, confused looking man who must be Jaya's father.

"Jaya has been eager to see you all." He hoped that

wasn't overstepping. He hated it when people tried to talk for him. Forcing himself to move forward even though his joints felt rusted, he added, "This young man has been waiting to meet his *Naniji,* which is…Gurditta?"

He guessed correctly at the woman in the green sari.

Jaya's mother gasped and stopped dabbing a tissue into her eye, dropping it away so she could pull Zephyr into her lap. Her tears turned to joy as she gathered up the wiggling boy like a bundle of laundry that wanted to drop socks.

Whatever dark cloud had been hovering broke into beams of sunlight for a second as Jaya drank in the sight of her mother holding her son. Then she glanced at the bearded man with a mix of defiance, resentment and— Theo's heart took it like a stiletto—a remnant of shame.

Before he realized what he was doing, he had moved to her side and set a firm arm across her back. Belatedly, he wondered if his hand on her hip might be a familiarity that would repel someone with traditional views, but he needed her to know she wasn't alone. They needed to know if they insulted her, they insulted him, and he was not a naïve girl working in a call center.

"Thank you for coming," he said, falling back on manners because it was one of his few fail-safe strategies in a passive-aggressive confrontation like this. "I imagine you're tired from the flight. My sister has planned a reception for the families to meet this evening, but you have a few hours to rest."

Jaya's uncle, because that's who the hard-ass old grouch had to be, said something in Punjabi.

Theo looked to her. She had said they all spoke at least a little English and that her father would be the toughest to communicate with because of his injury.

With a level stare that looked through the line of young men, she said, "They object."

"To sleeping here? Because we're not married? I'm staying in another suite," he assured them. "My family owns the hotel. We have other rooms."

A snort from one of the men almost overrode what Jaya said, her voice quiet and uneven. "It's the marriage they don't support."

A quick blast of Punjabi came at her from her uncle.

She said something back, speaking firmly, but Theo could feel the tension in her was so acute she threatened to shatter.

"You're too rich, man," one of the young men blurted. "Look at my father. We can't pay a dowry that would keep you living like this." He waved at the opulence of the Makricosta Olympus suite. "Jaya should have known better than to agree. Are you that angry with our uncle you'd ruin him?" he demanded of her.

Jaya started to respond, but Theo gently squeezed her into silence, his fury nearly blinding him. It took everything he had to remain calm and civilized. He hated confrontation, but he'd been serious about fighting to the death for her.

"Dowries are illegal. I brought you here because Jaya wished to have her family at our wedding. If you leave, that will hurt her. I can't allow that." He held first her brother's gaze, then her uncle's.

Into the silence, her father said, "Jaya?" He patted Zephyr's leg and smiled.

Jaya drew a sharp breath and said, "Yes, he's mine." She drew Theo forward and crouched to the floor so it would be easier for her father to see her. She spoke slowly in Punjabi to him, something about their wedding and then she introduced Theo as her groom, straightening to stand beside him with pride.

Theo drew her close while the old man studied them. He felt on trial as he used the Punjabi he was still learning to ask her parents for their blessing.

She tilted her smile up to him, her pride in him almost too much to withstand.

When her father nodded, Jaya dissolved into happy tears, first kissing her father then wrapping her arms around Theo so tightly he could barely breathe.

He looked over her head at her brother, still twitching at all the animosity hovering in the room, but bearing it, for her. "I intend to take care of your parents. Leave if you wish, but if you'd like to hear the arrangements you should stay. Now, Jaya." He coaxed her to show her damp face. "Would you please introduce me to the rest of your family?"

As the days of celebration raged, Jaya agonized over whether it was too much for Theo. They hadn't gone with a full-out Indian wedding, but there was enough to be overwhelming.

That's why it surprised her he spent an hour with her male relatives without telling her. Then she was even more annoyed when her brother told her it had been about his arrangements for their parents.

"Every time Uncle raised an objection, Theo said, 'I thought of that, but…' Uncle underestimated him. We all underestimated you." He eyed her like he couldn't imagine how his disreputable sister had landed such a catch.

She quizzed Theo later on when he'd turned into a chauvinist and why he'd kept her from a meeting that impacted her.

"Two reasons," he said without apology. "First, I wanted your uncle to know that he can't manipulate you with guilt or fear any longer. You won't be padding his life with your earnings because I will provide your parents with their own home and income and a care aid for your father. If your uncle finds himself suffering financially, and needs to ask you for help, that will be at your discretion. You have the power now, not him."

"Oh." She was too overwhelmed by the sense of shackles falling off her body to know what else to say. "And the other reason?"

"I'm so angry with the way he treated you, I don't want you in the same room with him."

She didn't cross paths with her uncle much. All of them were so busy with the nearly two hundred guests that swelled the hotel to capacity. Cousins from both sides took over the two lower floors, work associates of the Makricostas' flew in from all four corners, and friends of Jaya's arrived wide-eyed with awe from Bali and Marseilles. Quentin and Bina were the last to arrive and Theo arranged for them to stay with his family, knowing there might be awkwardness with Jaya's.

It was a heart wrenching moment when Jaya's aunt, Saranya's mother, greeted Bina with open arms. Jaya grew tearful during the reception, recalling the way the little girl had broken down in her grandmother's arms, both of them united in grief. Bina had missed out on so much living in Saranya's exile, but her family connections were being restored now. Saranya would have been so happy.

"Jaya," she heard near her ear just before a broad hand settled on her waist and Theo's wide shoulders loomed to block out the Grand Ballroom. "Are you okay?"

She nodded and smiled through her tears. "Just wishing Saranya could be here to see how happy you've made me. You've given me back my family, Theo. They're healing rifts that have broken us apart for years. Thank you."

"I wanted that for you." His smile was so tender, she barely felt the knife of knowing he deliberately surrounded her with love from other sources so she wouldn't miss his.

"But you didn't expect all this, did you?" she said, sheepish at how she'd taken him at his word and put together a wedding that married their two cultures as well as themselves.

He glanced around the room draped in red silk curtains. Gold beads dangled in strings from the ceiling like sunlight caught in raindrops. Children were trying out the bride and groom's thronelike chairs under the floral covered *mandap.* Brilliant saris competed with designer gowns as people danced and stole exotic treats from the circulating waiters.

"This is definitely more socializing than I can typically swallow, but I'm not sorry. Everything is very beautiful." His gaze came back to her, his admiration evident in his slow, studied perusal. "Especially you. I don't know why I never pictured you like this, so exotic. You're breathtaking." His gaze paused on the pendant of her *maang tikka* dangling off the line of pearls in the part in her hair.

"You must feel like you've married a stranger." She lifted a hand to check her red-and-gold headscarf hadn't slipped. His gaze followed the sound of her abundant gold bangles clattering against the red and faux ivory ones anchored on her wrist. She felt like a pack mule, she wore so much heavy, ornate jewelry.

He looked striking himself, not wearing a turban or *pyjama,* but he was carrying a sword over his white morning coat.

"Thank you for including Adara and Rowan in the henna party. When they heard it was supposed to be only for the bride's family, they were devastated."

"They're my friends. Of course I would invite them." In truth, they were quickly becoming as close as sisters to her. "Did they tell you I could barely make it through having my feet painted?" All the women had bonded with laughter when it turned out Jaya's feet were so ticklish, she'd had to keep stopping the artist and making her work on others until she could withstand another few minutes of torture.

"They said my initials are hidden somewhere in the design. I can't wait to look for them." His smoky voice poured a wash of electric tingles over her.

She ducked her head, embarrassed by how badly she was anticipating being alone with him. Naked. It had been almost two years and so much had changed, her body, her feelings for him. They ran so deep now. If the henna artist was right about the color representing how intense her feelings for her husband were, her tattoos should last years.

He caressed the sensitive skin beneath her ear and along her nape, leaning in to ask, "When can we leave?"

A punch of unfettered desire clenched her middle. Her shoulder burned under the weight of his hand resting there. When he grazed his lips against her cheek her throat locked, she was so overcome by hunger.

"You're killing me," he said in a loaded voice. "Tell me. An hour? How much longer?"

She couldn't speak, could only lift her face so he could see how helpless she was to the feelings he incited in her. A muted ringing filled her ears and she realized it was her, trembling amid all this fine gold.

His tormented expression hardened into fierce excitement. *"Now."*

If he had swung her into his arms, she wouldn't have felt more swept away. He turned them toward the room and she wished they could disappear without speaking to anyone. This passion between them was nothing she felt shame over, but it was too personal and concentrated to endure a gauntlet of teasing over it.

Before they could move, Demitri lurched in front of them, unkempt, wearing a smear of lipstick on his cheek. "Hey, I'm ready to claim my dance with the bride."

"Too late," Theo said with only a hint of smugness. He waved away whatever Demitri tried to say. "Redeem yourself by making our excuses. We're leaving."

She thought Demitri might have tried to say something, but Theo stole her out a side exit. From there they broke into a run like schoolchildren and were both laughing and breathless when they tumbled into the elevator.

"We should at least say goodbye to Zephyr," she protested as Theo crowded her into a corner, his grin so boyish and lighthearted she grew dizzy.

"If there's any male getting more attention from women than my brother this week, it's our son. He won't miss us."

Curling his fists against the walls of the elevator, caging her in, he inhaled deeply without actually touching her, then growled in frustration when the elevator stopped, jarring them both into a small stagger.

"I know I'll appreciate the privacy once we get to Rosedale, but right now it's too damned far away." He pushed back and held the doors for her.

The wind had come up and whipped around them as they crossed to the helicopter. A uniformed pilot touched his cap as he helped Jaya up the stairs.

"You're not driving?" she asked Theo.

He gave her a look as he settled beside her in the passenger cabin. "We call it piloting," he drawled, accepting a glass of champagne from the flight attendant that he passed to Jaya, but declined for himself. He picked up her free hand and set a playful bite on the knuckle of her ring finger. "I knew I'd only be thinking of you at this point. Not the right headspace for getting us anywhere alive. This is Nic's crew. They make the trip all the time. Plus, all the pre-flights are done."

She saw the advantage to that as they lifted off the second her seat belt clicked into place. The attendant moved to the copilot's seat and lowered the lights. Minutes later they were high enough and far enough away that the city and sky blended into a blanket of pinprick lights. The moon sat fat and smiling a bluish glow.

Theo touched her chin, bringing her around from staring into the silver-laced waves and captured her mouth with the velvet heat of his. She opened to his pressure, tongue seeking the dampness of his, their union growing deep and wet between one startled breath and the next. Her hand sought the back of his head, urging him to kiss her harder as waves of delicious heat rolled down to the center of her, flooding sensations between her thighs, making her ache.

They were in another world, a bubble of white noise and shadow, straining against their belts as they twisted to be closer. She brushed at the lapel of his jacket, burrowing to his vest and seeking a way past it only to be thwarted by the silk of his shirt.

He groaned and skimmed his hand from her knee up her thigh, over her waist and cupped her breast, thumb circling over silk to tease her nipple. She wriggled in her seat, the erotic sensations building in her loins so intense she gasped and pulled away.

"Please stop."

"Damn, I'm sorry." He sat back, his face stark with self-recrimination as he closed his hands into fists on his arm-rests. "I misread you."

"No, you didn't." She threw her arm across him, face tilted against his shoulder so her whispered words could reach his ear over the din of the helicopter blades. "I'm afraid I'm going to…I can't. Not here, like this, with people right there who might know."

Theo's hands opened to clench into the ends of his arm-rests. She could feel the strain and flex in his biceps and across his chest as he nearly rent the crash-proof seats apart. His head tilted back and the sound he made was animalistic, somewhere between fury and helplessness.

When she started to pull back in alarm, he trapped her hand against his chest where his heart slammed. They sat like that until the bird landed on the lawn of a dark estate. An English mansion waited with stately patience, seeming out of place on this Greek island, but who cared? It was

Nic and Rowan's home, a gift of privacy for their wedding night, but Jaya barely saw any of it as Theo whisked her up the steps, past a housekeeper who said something about calling if they needed anything and practically booted her out the door.

"Are you cross? You seem angry," Jaya said, backing away from him in the dimly lit lounge.

"Because I almost lost it up there along with you? Hell, no, I'm going insane." He dragged at his clothes, shedding sword and bowtie and shoes as he stalked her. "Are you afraid of me right now?"

"What? No, not really, but—oh!" She came up against the bottom stair, surprised he'd steered her this way. "You seem really, um… What if the housekeeper comes back and finds your clothes all over the house like this?"

"She won't come back uninvited." His vest hit the floor. "Keep going." He jerked his chin at the upper floor, urging her to back up the stairs.

"You're kind of being, um…" She didn't know what the word was, but he was making her nervous. Not genuinely afraid, but she knew what a small animal felt like when stalked by a cat.

"Aggressive?" he prompted. "Impatient? I'm trusting you, my lovely bride. Keep going. One of these bedrooms is made up for us."

"Trusting me? To what?" She hurried down the hall ahead of him, sending anxious glances over her shoulder as he followed at an implacable pace. "What do you mean? Oh! It's so nice of them to do this…"

She entered an expansive bedroom where the scent of the sea wafted in through open balcony doors with the sensual push of each wave reaching for shore. Tea lights floated in glass globes of colored water, bringing a magical glow to the white sheets and sheer curtains around the canopied bed. An array of treats awaited on a side table beneath silver covers, but she didn't lift the lids, too aware of the half-naked man, his hands lowering his fly as he stepped through the door and left it half-open.

The low light burnished his muscled chest and flat stomach, accentuating his abs. She found herself shaking too much with excitement to be able to remove so much as her grandmother's heavy ring from her forefinger.

Theo moved toward her like he was a missile finding its target. His chest filled her vision and his aggressive masculine scent filled her nostrils, making her dizzy. Without thinking, she impulsively smoothed the narrow line of hair that arrowed down the center of his torso to his navel and lower to the exposed skin behind his loosened fly.

"I, um, don't know what you mean about trusting me," she said.

He sucked in a breath that pulled all his stomach muscles taut. He cupped the side of her face and made her look at him.

"I'm trusting you to tell me if I'm coming on too strong. Have you reached your limit? You're shaking."

"No! I want to touch you and be naked and feel you all over me but look at me! I can't get out of any of this on my own and—"

He kissed her, hard and fierce, the thrust of his tongue forceful, but so welcome, so good. She sucked on him, wanting to eat him alive. They'd been kissing and fondling and teasing for weeks. Her dreams had been full of how he felt thrusting inside her. She couldn't wait any longer. Modesty didn't enter into it. Instinct took over.

With a grunt of hunger he backed toward the bed and sat, pulling her to straddle his legs, gathering her sari and underskirt as he pulled her into his lap. She knelt with her knees parted to hug his hips. The position put her eye to eye with him, mouth to mouth. They never stopped kissing and she couldn't stop soaking in the feel of his skin with her splayed hands. Tiny noises escaped her, like an abandoned kitten then more of a purr when his hot hands slid up to cup the globes of her buttocks. She wriggled in his hold, loving the intimacy of it, wanting him to know how much pleasure his touch gave her.

Her whole body was filling with heat and excitement, blossoming like a flower coated in dew and sunlight.

With a ragged moan, he snapped her underpants, surprising her into gasping and lifting in surprise. He tugged them away and threw them to the floor then freed himself. She reached for the thrusting flesh he revealed, circling him with tentative fingers, reacquainting with the warm satin over hot steel.

The world contracted to this small circle of light where one man and one woman consummated their marriage, harsh breaths mingling as she helped him roll on a condom.

Wordlessly he guided her to lift and be open for him. She let her eyes drift closed as he guided his straining head to rub and tease. Soft gasps of anticipation escaped her and she dug her nails into his shoulders.

When she started to take him in, he gathered her swollen, aching breasts in two hard hands and bit through her sari at her nipples, making her cry out and arch, desperate for penetration. As she let her weight sink down, as her wet, ready sheath swallowed him, he dropped his head back and snarled at the ceiling.

Smiling, she scraped her nails across his chest and worked herself to find the tightest fit against him, heart expanding with joy at each pulse of his hard muscle inside her. He dug his hands through silk to snug her tighter and tighter still, causing delicate explosions as the right place was touched again and again.

They kissed, deep, sumptuous kisses, rocking themselves into ownership of each other's body. Soon their movements exaggerated, pulling away and coming together with more force. She had never ridden a horse, but she rode her husband, using her thigh muscles to rise and fall on exquisite impalement, feeling the strain in him as he balanced on the edge of the mattress, sweaty and strong beneath her, holding himself steady to let her set their pace. His breaths rang with strain and his chest and shoulder muscles bunched with tension. When her stamina began to fail, his hands grasped her hips and kept her rhythm steady so they approached the crisis together.

"Theo! I'm—" Her world was coming apart at the seams.

"Me, too. Now, Jaya. Let me feel you—ah, yes. Like that. Ah, yes, yes!"

She imploded then expanded like a supernova, his pulsing completion within her shooting her into a realm where they were one experience, one person. One.

Draped naked on her stomach across the bed, she lay acquiescent as her husband kissed and stroked his way around the henna on her feet and lower legs. Every few minutes he ran a playful fingertip down the sole of her foot or nuzzled too softly at her ankle—he almost got a reflexive kick in the eye for that one—but he was enjoying himself so she tried to withstand the tickling.

"Here," he finally said, kissing hotly inside her calf.

"Are you sure?" She sat up, scooping the edge of the sheet for a shred of modesty, then studied the scrolled *T.M.* "Should I have it tattooed there permanently?"

"Would you?" he asked. He was so sexy with his rakish stubble and relaxed grin, propped on an elbow and completely at ease in his nudity. He took her breath.

"If you'd like. Unless you have a different favorite spot?" The flirting came naturally after hours of physical contact that bordered on debauchery. They couldn't seem to get enough of each other, whether they were in the bed, against the shower wall, or on the sideboard. Morning was firmly coming alive outside. Birds sang and the air had gone from crisp to soft. The helicopter would be returning them to Athens by late afternoon, but they were very much still on their one-night honeymoon.

Lazy brown eyes perused her from hairline to toenails. "It's all my favorite."

"I never thought I'd be like this," she admitted. "Naked and comfortable with a man. I thought I'd have hang-ups forever. Thank you for making this so good for me." She tilted forward to touch her mouth to his.

"I'm not being too demanding? You would tell me if you're tender, wouldn't you? I look back on our night in Bali and it was incredible, but damn, I was stiff the next day. You should have told me to back off."

"Why didn't you put on the brakes?"

"Because I didn't want that night to end."

She smiled, feeling secretive and womanly and desired. "Neither did I."

"I've never had second chances before." He smoothed her hair behind her ear. The somber gratitude reflected in his eyes warmed her heart. "Don't let me screw this up. Tell me what I need to do to make this work, okay?"

Love me, she thought, feeling a pinch in her heart, but it wasn't something either of them could control. It would happen or not. Still, when he took his time caressing and kissing her, when their bodies writhed together in sensual perfection, she felt loved.

Seeking that, she eased onto her back, pulling him with her. "I'm the inexperienced one," she reminded. "You're supposed to be the one who knows how to make this work."

He flashed a grin, brief and endearingly playful. "If this is all I have to do, our marriage will be a cake walk."

CHAPTER THIRTEEN

FOR A MAN who had never wanted a wife and children, Theo was surprised how quickly he settled into marital bliss. Not that any of it was easy, but it wasn't hard in the way he knew life could be hard. It was little blips of leasing his New York apartment—it was too good an investment to sell outright—being away from Jaya and Zephyr because of a crisis in Sydney and managing child-care until the *au pair* arrived since Jaya was already getting her feet wet in her new job.

The flip side of these minor wrinkles was a smart, warm, stunning woman on his arm and in his life.

He wasn't a man who'd ever needed to bring the prettiest woman to the dance. Nevertheless, he'd had a roster of style conscious women who hadn't minded an evening out on short notice. He'd given them a shopping spree and they'd relieved him of the burden of conversation for a few hours.

Jaya elevated what he used to think of as endurance events to a new, very bearable level, bringing personality without getting too personal. Her people management skills made her the perfect hostess when they were forced to entertain. As a result, he found himself in the remarkable position of enjoying this evening's dinner.

Now that they were settled, she'd taken a job with the family business, choosing an upgrade project that would allow her to work closely with him. While some considered that a recipe for disaster, he had more faith. They tended to work like two halves of a whole and today had been no different, despite being a grueling one over all. However, they'd put their team in place and were kicking off the project with a dinner for spouses. It was also a soft opening for the revamped dining room in their centerpiece New York hotel.

"There will be times when we're asking your husband or wife to work late, so we wanted to let you know up front that we appreciate the sacrifice," Jaya was saying, her graceful fingers resting lightly on the edge of the white tablecloth. If she was nervous speaking to the long table of nearly thirty people, her boss included, she didn't betray it.

"We won't always be eating like this. I'm sure there will be sandwiches at midnight more often than not, but today was a very productive meeting and if we can keep up that momentum, we'll be enjoying another celebration like this at the end of a very successful project." With a teasing smile that impacted like a heart punch, she added to Theo, "Provided we're on budget, of course."

"You will be." Maybe he was biased, even a bit dazzled. He certainly wouldn't let her fail, but he had every confidence she'd pull this off beautifully.

"They're so in love," the wife of their IT specialist said, then pressed fingertips to her lips as everyone turned to look at her. "I'm sorry! I didn't mean to say that so loud."

She was mortified and everyone else seemed amused, but Theo felt as though he'd been stripped naked in front of all of them. Was that what this was? Love?

His sense of vulnerability, of having his deepest desire revealed, was so threatening he couldn't look at Jaya. It would only reinforce how much she meant to him, allowing others to wield his feelings for her as a weapon. He cut an instinctive glance to the place he'd always been able to count on for cover when he was at his least guarded.

Adara was already watching him and smoothly drew everyone's attention to her end of the table. "We're very excited about this pairing. Even if they weren't married, I would have wanted Jaya to head this project, but having them so closely connected should help you all get the answers you need so you can keep moving forward."

Gideon made some remark about the newlyweds curtailing their honeymooning to review software code, but Theo didn't absorb it. The luminescent curtain that surrounded them in this private dining area was supposed to give a waterfall effect, but he was drowning under the rapids at the moment. The pressure in his chest suffocated him while he tried to discern which way was up. Pressure in his ears made the room's music sound muted while the clink of crystal tableware was like shattering glass.

He was falling apart internally while he had to maintain an unaffected front, exactly as he always had.

Jaya was pretty sure she'd never be able to eat here again. She couldn't eat now, when an amuse-bouche arrived in the form of a tiny fried noodle nest with a grape tomato egg and a herb leaf feather floating in a spoonful of consume. She wanted to run away and hide from the terrible lie that she was allowing to prevail.

Her husband *didn't* love her. She wished he did. Every morning she woke next to him hoping today would be the day he'd find the words. In six weeks of marriage, no matter how happy they seemed on the surface, he had yet to speak of his feelings.

But she had to sit here and smile at a table of mostly strangers, reminding herself that her life was actually very fulfilling. Theo did care for her in his way. He had overturned his life for her and their child, provided for them in a way that was ridiculously extravagant and always made time for them.

Then there was the sex. As a couple, they might not be

given to public displays of affection, but behind closed doors they were the clichéd newlyweds who couldn't keep their hands off each other. They started most of their days locked in orgasm and fell asleep sweaty and tangled together.

So what did it matter if people assumed they were in love and it was only true on one side? She was still happy, wasn't she?

Don't be impatient, Jaya. Don't ruin it.

That was a bitter imperative to swallow when she'd spent the beginning of her life telling herself, *Go after what you want. Don't settle.*

The evening turned into the longest of her life and only became more intolerable when they said good-night to their guests at the coat room. Theo held her wool wrap and asked near her ear, "You okay?"

This from the man who had become Robot Theo for the last two hours, tense and barely able to string two civil words together, leaving all the talking to her. If she'd found the love remark disconcerting, he'd found it insufferable.

"I'm fine," she mumbled as she clutched the edges of the wrap across her aching breastbone.

Across the room, Gideon lifted Adara's hair out from beneath the collar of her jacket. His gaze on her was tender as he cupped her face to give her a light kiss. Her smile when she drew back was radiant.

Jaya wanted to cry. She'd settled and could never back out now, even if she hadn't loved her husband so much she thought she'd die of it.

"Don't lie to me, Jaya," he said beside her with quiet ferocity. "Even if you think it might be easier for both of us."

She met his gaze, but it was painful to hold. He'd see how much regret filled her. Funny how she'd thought the worst thing in the world had been being a financial burden on her uncle. No, it was far worse to be an emotional burden. She didn't want Theo to know she loved him when he couldn't love her back. It would be more weight on his conscience than he deserved to carry. It wasn't his fault he couldn't love.

"Adara," he called, startling Jaya with his sharp tone.

His sister turned back from exiting with her husband.

"Is something wrong?" she asked as she approached, looking between the two of them. The weird thing was, it was like she already knew. Jaya had a feeling Adara was as aware of how tonight's gaffe had affected Theo as Jaya was.

A gut-wrenching sense of rejection filled her as she saw Theo's not loving her blink larger than the sign in Times Square. Everyone knew.

"Will you swing by our place on your way home and take Zephyr overnight? The sitter can't stay," Theo said. "I'll text her to let her know."

"What? No!" Jaya protested in shock. "Why—?"

"Of course," Gideon cut in smoothly. "Our pleasure."

"But we're going straight home," Jaya insisted. "Aren't we?"

"We'll use the family suite here tonight."

"Theo—" Jaya began.

"Please let us do this." Adara set a light touch on her arm. "Theo never asks me for anything." Leaning in to buss Jaya's cheek with her own, she whispered, "Please don't give up on him." With a tight smile of concern, she and Gideon hurried away.

Speechless, Jaya watched them depart. "This is crazy. Why did you do that?"

"Crazy? We both know we need to talk."

She hugged herself into her wrap, cold despite their staying inside. As he nudged her toward the elevators, she stumbled.

"I don't want to talk," she mumbled. This was her problem, not theirs. She had known what she was marrying.

Maybe he would come to love her eventually, but not if she forced it.

"There's a switch." He eyed her as he brought out his card and got them into the private elevator.

"What is?"

"You being the one who doesn't want to talk. Especially after you taught me it's the only way to fix things. Why are you trying to take that away from me now?"

"I'm not," she protested as they entered the family suite. "I just don't see any use this time."

"Why not?"

"Because I don't want to hear *again* that you don't love me and never will!" The outburst surprised even her. She pulled her wrap tighter around her throat, turning away to hide her hurt.

He drew a long, harsh breath then heavy silence descended.

She waited.

Nothing.

A choking little cry of protest escaped her. "And there you go again, withdrawing—"

"It's not easy for me, Jaya! I don't even know how to love, not properly. I still feel awkward kissing my son, like the more I want and need him in my life, the more likely he'll be snatched away."

"Not by me! I'm not trying to take away your heart either. Love isn't something to *dread*."

"I know that," he cut in. "But people knowing how I feel... When that woman said we were in love tonight, I lost a bit of sanity. I couldn't bear for them to know how much you mean to me. It makes me too vulnerable."

It wasn't the statement she was looking for, but it was close enough to make her turn and look at him. "Do you mean that?"

"The last thing I feel toward you is dread, Jaya. When I

walk through the door, I'm relieved, like some kind of un-identified pain has stopped. I'm so damned happy to see you, it's embarrassing. Is that love? You tell me. I've never felt like this toward anyone. It sure as hell isn't anything like what I feel toward my sister," he growled.

She pressed a hand to her diaphragm, reminding herself to keep breathing because she felt as though the wind had been knocked out of her. Somehow she found her voice. "Each time I see you, I'm filled with intense *joy,* like I'm finally home and safe again, no matter where we are."

Reaction seemed to spasm across his features. "When you say things like that, I almost don't want to believe it. It means too much and I trained myself not to care, not to want, but I crave those things you say, Jaya. They make me start to hope."

"For what?" A fragile bubble of optimism was building in her, but she was afraid to grasp it in case it burst.

He visibly struggled, feet shifting, glance cutting to the door before he hardened his stance and lifted his chin, no defenses anywhere on him as he revealed both somber vulnerability and an achingly tender warmth toward her.

"That you might come to love me one day."

Her own controls fell away, leaving her floating in a void, jaw slack, mind wiped clean by shock. A hot pressure flared in the back of her throat, urging her to speak, but all she could say was, "I'm such an idiot."

Before she could cover her face and absorb how appallingly stupid she'd been, she glimpsed how her words affected him. The tightening and closing, the dimming of his eyes.

"I thought if I told you how much I love you, it would scare you," she blurted, lurching forward a step. "I'd make you feel too much pressure. Like you were failing me because we're not equal, but I shouldn't have held back. I should have told you."

"That you love me," he clarified in a voice that rocked between disbelief and shaken anticipation. He came forward to grasp her arms. "That's what this is? This feeling like if we have a disagreement, I'll die of loneliness? That if I'm hurting I don't want anyone around except you, and if you're there I can bear anything, that's it? That's love?"

She nodded, blinking matted lashes. A tickle of wetness ran onto her cheek. "That's how it is for me. I want to tell you things I'd never admit to another soul."

He cupped her face in gentle fingers, his eyes blazing with heat and admiration and adoration. "Then Jaya, I have loved you for a very long time."

She couldn't breathe. Her heart had grown too big for her chest. Her mouth wouldn't form words because her lips were quivering.

He soothed them with the pressure of his own. The tender kiss deepened by degrees past sweet wonder into heat and passion and a deep need to express their love completely. They knew each other's signals and they were even more evocative now. He cupped her breast and held her heart. She pressed her lips to the pulse in his throat and only a very fine, translucent wall separated her from his lifeblood.

"Oh, Theo, I'm sorry—"

"Shh, I shouldn't have made you wait, either. I just didn't know…"

"I know. I love you." She kissed him again, unable to control the outpouring of emotion, passion, her need to connect.

He slowly drew back, but only to offer a smug smile. "I scored us a free night of babysitting."

"How could I not love you for that?" She was bursting with joy at how carefree he looked. Like he'd fully broken free of his shell and all of him was available to her.

He swooped to whisk her off her feet and into the cradle of his arms, making her gasp in surprise. As he started for the bedroom, she toed off her shoes so they clunked to the floor.

"Are we going to sleep at all tonight?" she teased.

"You say when, you know that." He set her onto the bed and followed her in one motion, his strength and power entwining with hers in the familiar way she'd come to love. "But I'll make it worth staying up if you do," he cajoled.

He did, fulfilling her completely when, hours later, they were trembling with sexual exhaustion. Still panting, damp skin adhered and bodies locked in ecstasy, he smoothed her hair from her cheek with a shaking hand and looked into her eyes. "I love you. I will love you forever. Thank you for being my wife."

* * * * *

A sneaky peek at next month…

MODERN™

POWER, PASSION AND IRRESISTIBLE TEMPTATION

My wish list for next month's titles…

In stores from 20th June 2014:

❏ Christakis's Rebellious Wife – Lynne Graham

❏ Carrying the Sheikh's Heir – Lynn Raye Harris

❏ Dante's Unexpected Legacy – Catherine George

❏ The Ultimate Playboy – Maya Blake

In stores from 4th July 2014:

❏ At No Man's Command – Melanie Milburne

❏ Bound by the Italian's Contract – Janette Kenny

❏ A Deal with Demakis – Tara Pammi

❏ Wrong Man, Right Kiss – Red Garnier

Available at WHSmith, Tesco, Asda, Eason, Amazon and Apple

Just can't wait?

Special Offers

Every month we put together collections and longer reads written by your favourite authors.

Here are some of next month's highlights—and don't miss our fabulous discount online!

On sale 20th June

On sale 4th July

On sale 4th July

Save 20%
on all Special Releases

Find out more at
www.millsandboon.co.uk/specialreleases

Visit us Online

0714/ST/MB477

MILLS & BOON® Book Club

Join the Mills & Boon Book Club

Want to read more **Modern**™ books?
We're offering you **2 more** absolutely **FREE!**

We'll also treat you to these fabulous extras:

- Exclusive offers and much more!
- FREE home delivery
- FREE books and gifts with our special rewards scheme

Get your free books now!

visit www.millsandboon.co.uk/bookclub
or call Customer Relations on 020 8288 2888